WHEN WORLDS AWAKEN

ALANA FAYE WILSON

When Worlds Awaken

ISBN (Paperback) - 978-1-7393578-3-2
ISBN (eBook) - 978-1-7393578-2-5

2024 First Edition

Cover design – Dissect Designs
Copyright © 2023

alanafayewilson@gmail.com

In a world driven by greed and vanity,
be the one who fights for the air we breathe.

PART ONE

Redwood

Chapter One

My heart hammered against my chest as I stared at the human face only a matter of metres in front of me. Were these people friend or foe? With their arrows pointing at us, I was both confused and petrified. I didn't think I could take any more surprises. We'd been betrayed by the Akquarians. Another member of our crew was dead. What else did we have to endure?

A rogue tear slid down my cheek at the thought of Cora being dragged away by the Igknamai. All the while, the young man—the human man—looked at me.

"Don't be concerned," he said, speaking our language in a smooth and coherent accent, one not dissimilar from our own. "We are not your enemy."

"If you're not our enemy," Rooke stood near the rock edge with both hands raised in surrender, "why are you pointing your arrows at us?"

The man lifted his hand and the hooded figures surrounding us lowered their weapons. "Are you in charge?" he asked Rooke. His tone did not contain the calm, regal quality the Akquarians possessed. It was blunt, resonating a sense of urgency.

"I am." Rooke lowered his hands, flicking his eyes over each stranger. "Who are you?"

"We are a Redwood scouting party. We live here, in the forest."

My sore eyes widened. Redwood. *Redwood.* So many times had I heard Havav and Dybgo drop that word into conversation. So many times I had come to the conclusion it was an area or object. Not once had I thought it could be the name of a people.

"We mustn't linger," he continued. "We're not safe here. Our horses are just down that ridge."

Horses? Rooke and I exchanged a look. I watched him swallow, the desperation in his expression looked painful. "Do you know where our ship is?"

The man looked back at him. "I understand you want answers, but for now, getting to safety takes priority. This whole area is encircled with Igknamai. No thanks to that wretched Akquarian-Hybrid."

"You think…you think he brought them here?"

"We watched the Igknamai swarm to him. I'm sure you can figure the rest out for yourselves." He gestured for us to follow the group away from the rock edge, deeper into the trees.

Exchanging another look with Rooke, I realised he was terrified. Perhaps it was the realisation he had trusted the Akquarians when they'd clearly tried to kill us. Hindsight was a wonderful thing.

Following Rooke and the hooded figures, I wiped the tears from my face. My hands were covered in blood—red Igknamai blood. The front of my T-shirt was soaked in it. It must've splattered on my face as well.

Nux, I felt numb. We were walking away from where Cora had been taken, where she'd died. It felt as though we were leaving her behind. But she was gone. She was dead. The thought clogged my throat, making it hard to breathe as I trudged along the dry, barren soil.

As we emerged over the other side of a small ridge, a group of horses appeared amongst the huge trees. A hooded figure was mounted on one. He glanced back at us as the scouting leader called to him.

"Guz, we need to move out quick. You take one of the ladies."

With a pristine agility, he jumped off the horse, landing gracefully on two feet. "Hey." He smiled as he approached me. His skin was dark and pitted, and his friendly brown eyes, along with a warm, sincere smile, created a wave of nostalgia that hit me hard. I felt myself frown at him. He reminded me of Sym. Nux, I missed Sym.

"Do you need a lift up?"

I looked up at the large horse beside us. There was no saddle, no stirrups either. Only a leather strap draped around the horse's head and neck acting as a bridle.

"Um…" I glanced back at him—Guz. His physique was hidden beneath his cloak, but he was tall with broad shoulders. "Yes, I think so."

After helping me onto the horse's back, he swiftly jumped on, seating himself behind me. The warmth of his body made me feel uncomfortable. The heat of the day and the slick sweat across my back didn't help either.

Reaching around me, he grabbed the reins, and we instantly started to move. I glanced about at the others. Zamya was seated in front of a slighter male, Kobe behind another. Oz was clinging to a small female. His towering form looked awkwardly out of place; his massive backpack still glued to his back. As I searched for Rooke, the scouting leader rode past effortlessly, meeting my gaze for the briefest of moments. His expression was flat, yet alert, surveying the area and situation in the same way Rooke always did.

Movement ahead caught my attention. Two scouts were filtering back information to the group. It appeared the path up ahead was clear, and the horses shifted into a gallop.

At the speed we were travelling, it brought back memories. I'd ridden horses abundantly as a child. My mum had been an accomplished horse rider and trainer, and I had enjoyed training with her students. But since her death, I hadn't been near a horse. I found their presence crushing.

I painstakingly closed my eyes, wondering what my mum would've said if she could see me now—riding horses on mythical Earth. I batted the thought away before the tears made another appearance.

Heading into dense forest, we must've covered at least ten miles within twenty minutes. The smell of bark and soil filled the air, and occasionally the trickle of flowing water rose above the sound of the horses' hooves and my panting breaths.

The trees were getting bigger. In fact, as the horses slowed to a canter, I realised the trees were enormous, larger than they'd been back near the ravine. The ancient bark was gnarled and twisted, forming patterns in shades of red and brown, stretching upwards for what felt like miles. Only small glimpses of the blue sky could be seen between the thick, swaying canopy.

In amongst the majestic giants, a palisade formed of spiked

wooden poles, positioned at deadly, defensive angles, appeared up ahead. The horses didn't slow as we approached, and as we neared the dangerous obstacle, my horse leapt into the air, clearing the spikes with proficiency. Eyes wide, I sucked in a long, anticipating breath. Our horse agilely landed on the opposite side of the fence and Guz chuckled behind me. "It's something you'll get used to," he said. The warmth in his voice was comforting, but it didn't ease my nerves. This place was beyond extraordinary. I'd thought the Akquarian way of living was strange, but this…I shook my head. I couldn't find the words.

The horses began to slow to a more leisurely pace. The spiked wall must've been some form of boundary to keep the Igknamai out, which meant we must be nearing the Redwoods' home. But all I could see were giant trees in all directions. No village. No town. No sign of civilisation. But when the horses pulled to a stop and the sound of voices carried over my head, my eyes shifted skywards. What met my gaze left me speechless.

The towering, gigantic trees were inhabited. Wooden huts and platforms were scattered up high among the branches, most within or around the tree trunks themselves. Each tree had at least three huts distributed at different heights up its trunk, most with wooden shutters and circular, pointed roofs. Wooden suspension bridges linked the trees and levels together, and nets lay taut underneath, the lowest being only ten metres from the ground.

Through the haze created by the sweltering heat, the vision went on and on until I could make out the side of a mountainous rockface far in the distance. A city in the giant, red barked trees. *The Redwoods*.

I glanced about. There were no access points up to the lowest raised platform immediately in front of us. The platform looked sturdy, running the full width between three enormous trees. Figures armed with bows and arrows paraded the expanse, all wearing brown, rustic red, or black clothing. Each one blended in with the natural colours of the tree bark.

It dawned on me; they'd opted for this location purely to remain protected from the Igknamai. Even if the beasts got past the palisade, they wouldn't be able to access the village. They couldn't climb.

Voices called down to us and movement to my right caught my eye. There was an opening at the bottom of one of the enormous trunks, where a large, wooden shelf was being lowered to the ground inside the tree.

Guz helped me down from the horse, my eyes still taking in my surroundings. The scouting leader marched past and Guz ushered me to follow him. As I approached the tree lift, a soft hand caught mine. I looked back and found Zamya. She looked petrified. Her brown eyes were glassy and on the brink of bursting. I squeezed her hand and together we stepped onto the wooden lift inside the tree.

Only the five of us, the scouting leader, and two other scouts stood together as the lift was hauled upwards. It was big enough to hold at least ten people. The wooden floor was slatted, the middle section worn from years of use.

Darkness enveloped us for several seconds as we travelled up the interior of the veined tree trunk. The lift jolted to a halt when it reached the garrison platform. A spiked, iron gate was pulled opened, and the scouting leader proceeded onto the walkway, asking us to follow.

An awaiting leather cladded man fell in step with him. Still with Zamya's hand cupped in mine, we kept pace with them, listening to their conversation.

"There appear to be signs of Igknamai on all sides."

"Considering the heat, they're everywhere," grumbled the scouting leader. "Are all our parties back?"

"We're only waiting on one hunting party to return."

"Jader?"

"Yes."

"Pull the bridges in and raise access points. Temporarily open one when Jader's team return. But keep a tight watch on all fronts. Especially the grazing fields and here. I wouldn't be surprised if Akquarians turn up on our doorstep."

"And if they do?"

The scouting leader glanced back at me before replying, "If they do, find me."

Nodding, the other man scurried away, and the scouting leader continued on, whipping his grey cloak off and placing it in a basket at the intersection of another tree.

It was the two heavy looking swords sheathed in a crisscross over his back that caught my eye. When he turned, gesturing us to step into another lift inside the second tree, I saw the assault of daggers lining the brown leather across his chest. I frowned at what his weaponry meant—he was a defender of his people. A people who were terrorised by the Igknamai, perhaps the Akquarians, too. He was a warrior. A *human* warrior.

Even though he was smaller than the standard Akquarian, he was tall. His arm muscles large and solid, his chest broad and strong, with a young face full of experience and the most piercing blue eyes I'd ever seen. He was what I'd imagined a Nux warrior to look like. A legendary God of salvation. I found it hard to take my eyes away from him.

The lift travelled upwards, passing step off points every half a minute or so. As we neared the top of the towering tree, it eventually stopped. Stepping out of the barked cocoon, we walked along a swinging suspension bridge. Zamya squeezed my hand tighter, hissing curses. We were at least eighty metres up with only a swinging bridge to keep us from plummeting to the ground. The nets below didn't look like they'd help if anyone fell from this height. I swallowed back the panic, resting my eyes on Rooke in front of me.

We marched along suspension bridge after suspension bridge. Each one connected to a platform encircling an individual tree. Waist height, wooden railings were the only barrier between us and the fall.

We passed several dwellings. Each hut was at the end of their own individual bridge. Washed clothes hung on ropes, swaying in the breeze. The clattering of pots and pans, and the smell of cooking wafted over us. Giggling children ran to hut windows and railings, their eyes wide and excitable. Adults turned their heads in our direction as we walked by. They didn't seem alarmed, just intrigued. Many were women, some showing swollen bellies or carrying young children. Both men and women consisted of a range of ages and colours. A diverse civilisation, similar to what would be found on Allura.

The scouting leader led us to a hut near the edge of the village, a fair distance away from any of the inhabited areas. The circular structure was made of horizontal and vertical wooden panels weaved in and out of each other. The roof was a combination of branches and thatch which overhung the building, more so at the front where a platform formed a covered balcony.

"Are any of you physically harmed?" the scouting leader asked, piercing the silence among us.

"I don't think so," Rooke said, glancing at each of us. In confirmation, we all mumbled or shook our heads.

I followed the others along the short bridge, trying not to avert my eyes to the ground. I quickly stepped onto the balcony and entered the hut. It was sparsely furnished with only three hammocks and a fur rug to fill it. The two opposing windows were glassless, and a crooked, wooden door stood on the far side.

"Hey, hey!" Rooke's agitated tone made me turn back to the entrance. The scouting leader and his two men were hauling the suspension bridge back. The sheer drop from the edge of the balcony was now even more terrifying. We were trapped.

"It won't be for long," the scouting leader said. "Only until the council are ready to see you."

"You've got to be kidding me!" Rooke's expression was full of anguish and confusion.

"It won't be for long," the scouting leader repeated. His eyes rested on me, glancing at my clothes. "You have access to a sanitary room. There should be running water. It's not drinkable."

We all watched him and his men walk away, desperate for clarity on what was happening.

"It damn well looks like we're prisoners again," Zamya's voice wavered.

Rooke stepped inside surveying the small room. "We're safe, at least."

"Safe?" Zamya chuckled awkwardly, a tear trickling down her cheek. "You said we were safe when we were with the Akquarians, and look where that landed us?"

"Please, Zam, don't start."

"Don't start? You trusted a bunch of sadistic bastards!"

"I know!" Rooke snapped. "I thought we could. I don't know what happened..."

"CORA'S DEAD!" Zamya was trembling. Anger and despair

seeping from every pore. "That's what happened, Rooke! That's what happened." She began to whimper, the tears streaming down her face. "Cora's dead."

Oz stepped forward and cocooned her petite body in his large arms. She sobbed uncontrollably into his chest, probing the reserve I was trying so hard to retain.

"I'm sorry," Rooke murmured, rubbing his face several times. "Nux, I'm so sorry."

I should've gone to him. I should've shown him my support, but I couldn't find the compassion within me. Instead, I ambled to the crooked door, pulled it open, and found a tiny room furnished with a moderately clean toilet and basin. Not the rock holes the Akquarians made us use, but a box seat with a removable toilet pan, and a metal basin with a single tap.

I closed the door, catching a glimpse of myself in the tarnished mirror hanging above the basin. Turning to stand in front of it, the feeling of disgust overwhelmed me at the sight of my reflection. Dark, dried blood stained the top half of my grey-blue T-shirt. My bruised neck and the top of my right arm were drenched in blood. My hands looked as though I was wearing red gloves. Splatters of red dominated the left side of my face, parting where my previously dried tears had cleared a path. I looked like the physical definition of savage desperation.

The realisation hit me then. I'd almost died…again. We had all nearly died. And Cora…Cora was really gone. I shook my head. How the hell was I going to live with myself, knowing I'd survived, and she hadn't? She was so young.

Images of Cora being dragged away filled my conscience, and after a few moments of haunting silence, every single part of me broke.

Chapter Two

A knock at the door jolted me from my stupor.

"Eden, are you okay?" It was Rooke. His voice was soft and concerned.

"Um…yeah, I'm fine." I didn't know how long I'd been in the sanitary room. I only knew I had sobbed into my hands, hoping nobody could hear me. Then, I'd ripped my clothes off and aggressively scrubbed the blood off my skin, before reverting to sobbing.

"Can I come in?"

I wiped the fresh tears away. "Um…yeah, okay."

The wooden door opened outwards and Rooke stepped into the tiny room, his body taking up most of the remaining space. He looked down at me as I sat on the edge of the toilet, dressed only in my knickers and sports bra. If he'd noticed, it didn't show. "You've been in here a while."

"There was a lot of blood to get off." I stared at my hands. They still didn't feel clean enough.

"We realised you lost all your possessions and no longer have any spare clothes to wear." I looked up at him. He was holding a pile of clothes in one hand. "You've got the same length leg as Kobe, so he's given you some combat pants. Zamya's given you a vest top and socks, and you can have my jacket." He offered me the pile.

"Thank you," I whispered, fighting the tears that were trying to resurface. I took the clothes, aware of Rooke's gaze on me. Peering up at him, I tried to read his expression. He looked sad, and so, so worn out.

He squatted down next to me and snatched my hand up in his. "Please don't judge me."

"For what?"

His Adam's apple bobbed nervously. "For Cora's death."

What?

I swivelled my legs towards him, cupped my hands on either side of his stubbled jaw, and made him look at me. The sorrow in his dark green eyes broke my heart. "Don't ever think her death was your fault."

"I gave the order to end her life," he whispered.

"I would've done the same. It was the lesser evil, Rooke. She would've been ripped apart like Sym. We couldn't save her, but you saved her from suffering."

He closed his eyes and a rogue tear fell. My heart broke all over again.

"It was hard enough leaving Sym's body outside the ship the night of the first attack."

"I know." I wiped his tear away with my thumb, placing my forehead against his. "You mustn't blame yourself, Rooke. For any of it. We are all in this together."

He shook his head and another tear trickled down his cheek. "I thought…I thought I'd lost you today."

My breath caught. The waver in his voice was heartrending. I didn't know what to say.

"I trusted the Akquarians. I trusted they'd help us."

"They were useful for a time. Why they decided to rid themselves of us, who knows, but maybe it's a blessing." I didn't have the heart to tell him Dybgo had pleaded with me to return to the fortress barely an hour before the attack. Had Dybgo known what Llexzus was plotting? Had it been Havav's plan all along? "We *are* safe for now. Whatever happens next, I will be here with you. We'll do this together."

He grabbed the back of my neck pulling me closer. The impulse to start crying was immense, but I needed to be the strong one for once. I needed to comfort him, take the pain that haunted *him* away.

A knock at the door made us both flinch.

"Boss?"

Wiping the tears from his face, Rooke stood up. He inhaled a huge lungful of air before he opened the door, discovering Oz's large form hovering just outside.

Oz glanced at my half naked body and frowned. "Um…uh, sorry to interrupt whatever you guys are doing, but I really need a piss. I'd do it outside, but I doubt the locals below would approve."

Rooke looked back at me, and I nodded.

"Sure, sorry," I said. "Give me a sec to get dressed and it's all yours."

"Cheers." Oz grimaced and backed away. I heard the door close and began to dress. After pulling Zamya's tight black vest top over my head, I realised Rooke was still standing in front of me, his hands in his pockets. He was frowning, watching my every move, albeit with distant eyes. I couldn't help thinking he wanted to tell me something.

I stood up and pulled Kobe's grey-blue combat pants up over my hips. "Do you often watch people dress?" There was a smile in my voice which seemed to pull him out of his trance.

He squeezed his eyes together, shaking his head. "No, I didn't mean to. I, um…I…never mind." He raked his fingers through his hair, turned, and left the room.

No Redwood returned to us that evening. Nobody brought us food.

The sounds from the village faded as the night drew in, allowing the chorus of nocturnal animals to fill the thick air. The warmth of the day hadn't fallen, and the light breeze had disappeared completely.

In the distance, fires burned on the flat, mountainous rock. From the sheer size of them, I imagined they were pyres, burning the dead; releasing their spirits to the elements. I had read about this tradition in ancient Alluran texts. Although our culture swayed towards burials, I could understand the appeal of being freed, to become one with the air. It brought on thoughts of Cora and how she wouldn't be laid to rest. Nux, the thought of her body mutilated and left to rot sent a repugnant, anguished avalanche of emotion through me, churning away at my stomach.

Kobe found a candle in the depths of his bag. Lighting it, he placed it in the middle of the floor, and we sat around it, hand in hand, paying our last respects to dear Cora. This mission was proving harder than any of us had expected. I only hoped we wouldn't lose anyone else.

I woke with a gasp, expecting to find Llexzus standing over me, tapping my leg to taunt me awake. To my relief, it was just a dream. The tapping was the rope of the hammock flapping in the breeze.

I shivered; suddenly aware I was cold. A fresh breeze filtered through the slatted wooden walls. The gloomy blue light signified it was just before dawn.

Stretching my muscles, I winced at an aching pain in my right upper arm, discovering three shallow scratches on my skin that I hadn't noticed yesterday. They were now scabbed over, but the skin appeared raised and tender. I sighed. Just another wound to add to my collection.

I rolled over and found the rest of the crew still asleep. Kobe and Zamya had taken the other two hammocks, while Oz and Rooke had opted for the fur rug on the floor. But Rooke was nowhere to be seen. Panic fizzled through my veins. Where was he? He'd seemed unstable yesterday. I prayed he hadn't done anything stupid.

Trying not to wake the others, I carefully climbed out of the swaying hammock. Pulling Rooke's jacket on, I walked to the open entrance of the hut. A fine mist encased the lower part of the forest and I could barely see any signs of the village below. The calls of the birds seemed to be the only noise, along with the occasional rustle of leaves. Above me, the sky was clear with a semblance of night still clinging on.

I strolled to the very edge of the platform. The mist below obscured the terrifying drop, making the hut seem higher than it already was.

"I hope you're not intending on jumping." Rooke's low rumble made me flinch. I looked to my left and found him sitting on the floor, huddled in a Solarfleet blanket, resting his head back against the curving hut wall.

"I doubt I'd land graciously enough, so no."

He gave a small smile before a long sigh escaped him. He looked exhausted.

"Did you sleep at all?"

He shrugged. "A couple of hours, I guess. You all snore like warthogs." He smirked and lifted his blanketed arm to me. Chuckling, I walked over to him, sat down, and snuggled into his side. He pulled the blanket around my shoulders and rested his head on top of mine.

"Have you seen anyone around?" I asked.

"Not up here. I don't think the two huts next door are lived in. Further down there's been some movement, but I can't really see with the mist."

"These people…they're human, right?"

"I think so. I must admit, at first, I thought they could be the Igknamai controllers. But it appears they despise those beasts as much as we do."

"I would say more so."

"Their defences are incomprehensible. Did you see that spiked palisade? Nux! How the hell did their horses jump that thing, carrying baggage and multiple riders, without spiking themselves on it?" Rooke shook his head. "Absolutely crazy."

"Desperate times call for desperate measures. They don't have a giant fortress like the Akquarians do."

"True." He sighed, reaching for my left hand resting on his knee. "I'm glad to be away from that place."

Rooke examined the courtship bracelet still hanging around my wrist. Twiddling his black token between his finger and thumb, his gaze shifted to something forlorn. The memory of the Sparzak ball suddenly flooded my own mind. Remembering Rooke's lips on mine, how well we fitted together, and…Rooke pushing me away. My heart clenched at the thought.

"I need to cut that horrid thing off," I said. "It constantly digs into my skin." I felt Rooke's gaze rest on my face, but my eyes remained on the golden bracelet. I couldn't look at him, he'd see the pain and regret in my eyes. "Now we're away from the Akquarians, they won't chastise me for removing it."

He reached into his trouser pocket and pulled out an army knife. Extending a small pair of clippers, he snipped at the bracelet. After his third attempt the thin band snapped apart. "There," he said. "No more ridiculous Akquarian rules."

As I rubbed the skin around my wrist, I watched Rooke swivel the broken piece of jewellery between his fingers. Again, his gaze became distant, contemplative.

"Eden?" His tone lowered an octave, somehow stringing out the last syllable of my name. "Do we…" I looked at him. "Is there, um." He met my gaze. He seemed nervous. "Um…do we need to talk about what…"

His eyes suddenly shifted skywards, and I watched them widen with an aspect of shocked excitement. He stood up with urgency, lunging for the wooden railing. Bemused, I followed his line of sight.

There, where the leaves grew sparce at the top of the canopy, was a tiny light, travelling swiftly across the slowly brightening sky. I rushed to Rooke's side. "Is that?" I couldn't breathe.

Rooke looked as though he was holding his breath. "It has to be. What else could it be?" He looked at me. "It must be The Orka."

"It's in a lower orbit. If the ship was unmanned, it would've taken months to drop. Troy must've brought the ship lower to try to communicate."

"He's alive." Rooke smiled. A wave of relief slammed through me as Rooke grabbed my shoulders. "Troy's alive!" He snapped his arms around my back, pulling me in close. I could hear his heart hammering inside his chest. His elation was undeniable, and I felt the same. However, when he went to tell the rest of the crew the good news, there was a thought outweighing the joyous discovery, causing my mind to flood with dread…

If we ever reinstated the communication link with The Orka, how the hell were we going to tell Troy about Cora?

Chapter Three

Glancing at my watch, it was 10:52 a.m. Earth time. Zamya was still asleep. She must've been exhausted from the trauma of the past couple of days. Lounging on the comfortable rug, Oz dozed, while Kobe laid in a hammock, reading. I had finally convinced Rooke to take a nap in my hammock. He was currently sound asleep. I remained on the balcony, observing the village, waiting to see if anyone came for us.

The mist had cleared, but it became apparent the area where our hut was located was deserted. Nobody came up here. The closest dwelling was a good hundred metres away, not counting the two empty huts to the left of ours.

When I eventually saw movement from a suspension bridge close by, I scrambled to my feet and waited. A man marched onto the opposite platform, glanced at me as I began to speak, but turned to take the bridge opposite. I was starving and wasn't in the mood to be ignored, so I began to shout, "Hey…hey you, wait! HEY, ARSEHOLE!"

The brown-haired man stopped and turned slowly. His eyebrows lifted when his gaze met mine. I recognised him. He was the scouting leader. It appeared he had bathed. His hair looked lighter now that it was clean. His jaw was shaven making him appear far younger. He still wore the same brown sleeveless, leather armour, but today he was wearing a short sleeved, hooded top underneath. No swords. Only a small assort of knives sat diagonally across his chest.

As he slowly sauntered towards me, I held his intense gaze. He stopped at the very edge of the platform opposite, unphased by the imminent drop before him. Even with the barrier of air between us,

I had the urge to step back. His presence wasn't necessarily frightening, but there was something about him, something overpowering.

"Firstly," he said with a far calmer demeanour than I expected, "I do not like being shouted at."

"You were blatantly going to ignore…"

"Secondly, my name isn't Arsehole."

Was that a joke? By the look on his face, it didn't appear to be. Perhaps I shouldn't have called him that, but still, he was starting to exasperate me. "Well, you haven't been so obliging as to offer me your name. You just shoved us in this air prison yesterday and buggered off."

"Did I hurt your feelings? How awful of me." His sarcasm quickly turned into aggressive scorn. "Don't underestimate the lengths me and my men went to saving your arses yesterday. Chivalry isn't something we have time to abide by here. Now, as you've stolen my attention. What do you want?"

Nux, he was a bastard. I felt myself frown, glancing at the toes of his black riding boots hanging over the vertical drop. He was brave, a risk taker. I had no doubt about that.

"You said we aren't your enemy, so why are you treating us like prisoners?"

"We're not. Your segregation is for your protection as well as ours."

I rolled my eyes. "Nux, haven't I heard that before."

"It's only until the council are ready to meet with you."

"And when will that be?"

"When they're ready!" The way he stared at me made my blood boil. He let loose an irritated sigh and went to leave.

"Wait!" To my surprise he turned back. "Could we have some food? Please."

He chuckled to himself, glancing at the canopy overhead. "Too used to being pampered by the Akquarians, yeah?"

"We haven't eaten for twenty-four hours. We're starving."

"I doubt you have any idea what starving means."

I stared at him. A sense of selfish remorse washed over me. He was right. I didn't know what his people endured on a daily basis. Maybe they didn't have a lot of food to spare. Maybe the Igknamai's presence reduced the amount of food they could harvest. I doubted they could grow vegetables or keep pigs and chickens in amongst these trees. But glancing at the glow of his sun kissed skin and the bulk of his arm muscles, it was hard to imagine he knew what starvation was either. Bastard! He was being difficult, obnoxiously so.

I glanced down at my dirty boots, ready to accept defeat. But to my surprise, his voice softened. "I'll see what I can do."

Meeting his gaze again, I noted the sincerity they held underneath his stern exterior. Nux, his eyes were a vibrant blue. Dazzling, in fact.

"My name's Truro, by the way."

Wow, that was unexpected. "Um, thank you, Truro. It would be most appreciated, as was the rescue conducted yesterday."

He gave a curt nod, but instead of leaving, he cocked his head and asked, "Are you going to oblige me with *your* name?"

I lifted my eyebrows in jest and shrugged. "If you deliver that food, maybe I will."

I could've sworn I saw a hint of a smile flicker in the corner of his tight mouth. Holding his gaze for another second, I turned on my heel and strolled inside the hut. Hiding behind the wall, I listened as his boots marched away. I hadn't realised I was holding my breath until that moment. A long, relieved sigh suddenly filled the silence. Nux, he made me feel uncomfortable.

"That went well." Rooke chuckled. I found him awake, lounging in my hammock, hands behind his head.

"Thanks for the help, guys."

"I think you did pretty well," mumbled Oz from the floor.

"I second that," Kobe muttered from behind his tablet.

"With a guy like that," Rooke said, "I think a woman's touch works best. Feminine ammunition. More likely to get results."

I tutted. "I'm not a weapon, Rooke."

"Aren't you?" he teased, then threw me a dashing smile. I shook my head and made my way to the sanitary room.

Truro kept his word. He returned just after noon with two other men. They hoisted the bridge up and snapped it into place. A woman, carrying a basket full of freshly baked bread, apples, and drinking water trailed behind. Oz groaned at the smell of the bread, and I watched him and Zamya grab at the food, offering their thanks to the young woman.

Even though my stomach ached from the hunger, I stood, watching, suddenly aware Truro was standing beside me. I looked up at him. He was a similar height to Rooke, maybe taller; around six-foot.

"Thank you," I said softly.

"Like I said, you aren't prisoners." He glanced at Rooke standing on the opposite side of the small room. He was sinking his teeth into an apple. "The council will be ready to see you in an hour. They've requested only two of you attend."

Rooke nodded, swallowing his mouthful. "That's fine. I'll be there. As will Eden." He gestured towards me.

"Eden?" I realised Truro was frowning down at me, a flash of shock freezing his expression. "That's your name?"

"It is. You seem to be bemused by it."

"Do I? I'm not."

I didn't believe him, especially when he grazed his top teeth over his lower lip, trying to suppress a smile from forming. Clearing his throat, he said, "Be ready in an hour. I will escort you both to the meeting myself."

Without making eye contact, he left.

Chapter Four

Travelling over the multitudes of suspension bridges into the depths of the village, Rooke and I trudged behind Truro. Urging myself not to look down, I kept my gaze fixed to the diagonally crossed swords sheathed across Truro's back. I wasn't sure how long it would take to get used to the vertigo. I could fly a spacecraft at speeds that could rip the human body apart and not feel an ounce of nausea, but this? This was something entirely different. Death was staring me in the face every time I glanced at the ground.

"Get out of the way, you little toads!" Truro's voice was aimed at the children running in front and alongside him. Some giggled behind us. "Didn't your parents tell you to stay out of the way."

"But Truro, you said I was your best warrior," said a small boy of about five, staring up at him in awe. "I thought you'd need some help."

"Not today, Fheo."

"Oh, but…"

"Maybe later." Truro ruffled the boy's hair with his hand, landing himself a smile, then a salute from the child and his friends. I couldn't help smiling.

We travelled down a tree lift, emerging halfway down. More intrigued faces peered at us from all directions. Some watched from huts, others from bridges and nearby platforms. There were so many people here.

Following Truro along a far sturdier, wider bridge, I considered the enormity of the tree we were approaching. Even though it wasn't the tallest, it was by far the thickest. At a minimum of twenty metres in diameter, it dwarfed the surrounding evergreens. The end of the bridge was met by a large opening in the tree's bark, warped and gnarled at the edges as if it had been there for centuries.

Inside, we emerged in a large circular room where the smell of dried wood hit my nose. The room resembled a small auditorium with an everlasting ceiling, stretching up until there was nothing but dark shadows. Rows of benches encased the chamber. Scribed marks were carved into the wall behind them. Dainty yellow lights hung in clusters about the room, illuminating the area. I was uncertain if they were candles or something else entirely. Did they have electricity here?

A circle of tree stumps filled the main floor space before us. They were positioned a metre apart, surrounding a large metal dish resting on the floor in the middle. The dish was segregated into four sections. From where I stood it appeared the sections were each filled with a different substance. One with water, another with soil. The third was filled with dead embers, and the last one was empty. I presumed this symbolised air.

The four elements of nature.

Several people ambled about, coming to take a seat on the tree stumps in the centre circle when they noticed our presence. A slim woman dressed in black leggings, tall boots, and a long, leather jacket clasped at the waist, approached us. She was unusual looking in a striking way. Her large eyes were wide, her nose sharp, her mouth small and pouty. Sandy-blonde hair bobbed perfectly around her face. She didn't look a day over twenty but seemed to carry an air of superiority.

"Welcome," she said in a smooth, genteel tone. "Please, take a seat." She gestured to the two seats immediately in front of us. Both Rooke and I complied, catching each other's eye as we sat down.

To my surprise, Truro hadn't taken his leave. He made his way to one of the stumps to our left, seating himself next to an older man with tanned, leathery skin. One of the man's legs looked disformed, and the skin on his hands appeared to be scarred and disfigured. His leather armour was brown and scratched, with a large sword sheathed behind him.

"I do apologise for the prolonged wait," said the blonde woman. "We needed Quinn to return from a maintenance run before meeting with you." She gestured towards a young man to our right. His light brown skin was splattered with mud and dust, as if he had just returned from a long ride. "I hope Truro hasn't been too stern with you." The woman raised her fair eyebrows at Truro before smiling and resting her gaze on Rooke.

I noticed Truro roll his eyes at her comment, strands of his hair falling forward as he rested his elbows on his knees. It seemed he had a lack of tolerance for a lot of people—not just me.

"Let me start with the introductions," the woman went on. "We are the members of the Redwood Council. Together, we run this village. This is Quinn," she indicated the man needing a wash, "he heads up engineering." Gesturing to the woman to his right. "Nya is our lead doctor. She looks after healthcare. Blake runs the scientific department." She motioned to a young, bald man sitting beside her. Turning to the other side of the room, she pointed to an older man with thick, greying hair. "Ferrol is in charge of the food and agricultural side of things. You've already met Truro. He heads up security and defence alongside Elgin here." Elgin being the man with the twisted leg. "And I am Valina. I deal with relations and general wellbeing."

Other than the two older men, who I assumed were in their mid-forties, the rest of the council appeared to be young. Really young. At a guess each one must've been under thirty, perhaps nearer twenty. Such a young age to hold such highly responsible positions.

Rooke inclined his head in welcome and introduced us both, and I did not miss the look Valina gave Blake. A look of wariness, or was it understanding? Either way, it worried me. Rooke must have noticed it too. "But I'm wondering if you already knew who we were," he said.

Valina stepped back, flapping her long coat behind her before seating herself gracefully on her chair-stump. "To be completely honest with you, yes, we did."

Rooke and I exchanged a look of confusion, prompting Valina to explain.

"A lookout saw your ship arrive across the ocean. It took our scouts a couple of days to find your landing site. By the time they reported back, and we'd returned to your location, you were already residing with the Akquarians."

So, the rider on the clifftop had been a Redwood, not an Akquarian like we first assumed. I suddenly felt Truro's eyes on me. Even in the dull light, they were a vivid blue.

"We did approach the Akquarians," Valina motioned with her hands, "but they refused to grant us access to meet with you."

"They did not tell us of your existence," Rooke said. "You can imagine our shock when we came face to face with your scouts yesterday."

The doctor, Nya, shook her head, her dark, braided hair ruffled against her red shirt. "The Akquarians are selfishly deceptive."

"From what I gathered during several meetings with them," Truro's voice was low and solemn, "they were clearly concerned you would rather rely on us instead of them." I stared at him, digesting his words. He'd visited the Akquarian fortress when we were there? The number of times Havav and Dybgo had conversed in front of us, in their native tongue, about Redwood, it had never occurred to me someone else was offering us sanctuary. "It's a natural instinct to feel safer with your own species, after all."

"So, you are human?" Rooke asked.

"We are," Valina confirmed with a charming smile. "As are you, we presume."

"Yes. But what we can't understand…we were led to believe all human life left Earth three millennia ago."

"They did. Every single one of them."

"All except for a few indigenous Amazonians who refused to," Blake, the head scientist, said scratching at his dark beard. "We are convinced they met their fate with the Igknamai one way or another."

"We still have detailed books and digital files documenting the events of the Mass Exodus." Valina emphasised her words with her hands. "We know exactly what happened."

"Please enlighten us," Rooke said. "Our facts of the event have morphed into stories and myths over generations."

Holding Rooke's gaze, Valina made a small humming sound as if she was excited by the prospect. I watched Truro shift in his seat, scanning the walls with a look of boredom. I got the impression he either found the subject disinteresting or held a strong irritation towards the speaker. Inwardly, I smirked.

"In the year 2138, over four hundred thousand interstellar ships had been constructed in space. Each one had docking facilities for eight spacecraft, and each of those spacecrafts held at least two thousand people. The individual spacecrafts were launched from different sites around the globe. Once these crafts docked with their interstellar ship, they became cities within themselves."

I'd read this in the ancient book I'd found in the Akquarian library. Their enormous, rotating, interstellar ships were complex, if not ingenious for the time. Floating cities in space.

"Thousands of spacecrafts were launched from several sites not far from here. Including the ship our ancestors had boarded, The Pacifica. Shortly after launch, The Pacifica collided with another ship. By the sounds of it, in a chaotic panic, there were far too many ships being launched at once. You can imagine the destruction. Both ships dropped out of the sky. The Pacifica plummeted to the ground, crashing into the mountainous rock found at the edge of this very village. Out of two thousand and two passengers on board, only three hundred and sixty-two survived. Their names are inscribed into these very walls."

I peered up at the bark encircling the room. The marks I'd previously passed off as patterns were in fact names, thousands of them.

"The name of every person born since has been added to this wall."

I looked back at Valina. A glow of pride resonated from her. "What happened to the other ship?" I asked.

Valina shook her head. "It's believed they crashed into the ocean. I wouldn't be surprised if more ships experienced a similar fate. From the journals and reports I've read, the Mass Exodus was a misguided operation, overwhelmed by too many fat rats and not those with the intelligence needed. We learnt a lot from their mistakes."

"So, your ancestors made their home here, among the trees?"

"Yes. These are the legendary ancient Redwoods, giant sequoias. If you are familiar with Earth's cartography, we are located on the border of California and Oregon in Northern America."

I wasn't, but a wave of raw grief shot through my chest. Cora had discovered something along those lines from information she found in the Akquarian library. I felt my posture sag, my eyes prickle with moisture. Dropping my gaze to the floor, I tried to disguise my anguish. Cora would've loved this place. She would've thrived on the information and knowledge found here. But she was gone…

"The Igknamai can't climb trees," I heard a male voice say, "and they don't eat tree bark either. As well as the redwood bark being fire resistant, it was an ideal location."

"And it's stood for nearly three thousand years," Valina chimed in.

"What's your population now?" Rooke asked.

"To be exact, nine thousand and seven."

"Still so few?"

Valina sighed. "Unfortunately, on a daily basis, we are faced with a relentless enemy. The village provides us with the majority of our needs, but we still have to venture outside the security of these trees."

"We don't lock our people up like the Akquarians do." I looked up and found Truro resting his gaze on me. To my surprise, his eyes had filled with a sense of compassion. "Our people know the risks, but they are free. We have no boundaries or rules of restriction."

"On average, how many lives are lost to the Igknamai?" Rooke asked.

"This month, we lost nine, and that's an exceptionally good month. Last month, that number was forty-two."

Glancing at me, Rooke cursed under his breath. Even though we were potentially safer here from the Akquarians and their schemes, the risk of the Igknamai was evidently higher.

Valina's voice became a sympathetic purr. I noticed the brightness in her face dull momentarily as she said, "May I offer our sincere condolences for the tragic loss of your crew member. We emphasise with your suffering. The pain of loss never gets any easier."

Nux, this woman knew how to charm people. The softness of her voice was like a fluffy comfort blanket, encasing my body in a soothing hug.

Clearing my throat, I asked, "We don't know much about the Igknamai. Were they the reason the humans left Earth? Again, the stories back home are extremely vague."

"Yes, they were the reason. Human civilisation could no longer survive alongside them."

"Where did they come from?"

The room fell silent, and I looked over to Truro—who shuffled awkwardly in his chair—then back to Valina. Eventually she spoke.

"Back in the twenty-first century, there was a major plastic pollution crisis. Nonbiodegradable objects littered seas, rivers, land sites. It interfered with wildlife and natural processes. It was becoming a global detriment. Scientists discovered a new bacterium found in these littered areas which broke down and consumed the plastic substance. It was called Ideonella sakaiensis. As you can imagine, back then, the world was driven by money. Instead of solving the plastic crisis by ceasing production and recycling adequately, which would've dented the global economy considerably, somebody decided to genetically modify the Ideonella sakaiensis, hoping they would consume and eradicate plastic waste more efficiently than they had been. After a decade of experimentation, the Plastimite was born. A tiny brown beetle, with the breeding ability of bacteria, and the consuming ability of a locust."

I already didn't like where this story was heading.

"Well, it worked. The Plastimites devoured the plastic content dumped around the world. Plastic farms were formed where nonrecyclable plastics were taken after use. There, the Plastimites could be left to work their magic. It was cheap, and the experiment ticked all the right boxes. For over seventy years it was all well and good. That was until plastic production was eventually reduced and plastic waste sites became few and far between. The scientists assumed with the lack of food, the Plastimites would simply die out. But they didn't. They evolved. Quickly.

"They began consuming general waste, which was deemed acceptable by society at the time. But their appetite soon changed to metallic fences and metal structural beams. With a naive stupidity, the people didn't pay attention until the creatures started to invade their homes, eating furniture, clothes, or anything specifically covered in plastic or composite. Shortly afterwards, they discovered plants, and eventually crops. And this was when the global panic began.

"The Plastimites appeared to be resilient to pesticides. Even poisons didn't falter their exploits. Explosives, too, had no permanent detrimental effect. They were similar to cockroaches in that respect. Difficult to destroy.

"With their newfound food, over the next half century, the Plastimites grew considerably in size and number. People were struggling to sustain food supply production. Panic buying and looting began. Some households were wiped out due to starvation. Then, the Plastimites began to turn their ravenous appetites to cultivated animals. The final straw was when children became their targets. People laid traps; food laced with explosives to blow the beasts up from the inside. This worked for a time, but from their reaction, the intelligence of the beasts became apparent. They learnt not to touch the bait. The intellect in their retaliation was the most harrowing. They strategically attacked nearby hospitals, churches, schools. A war had begun between mankind and an indestructible enemy. It was the most horrifying entry in human history."

"Like something from a horror movie," I whispered to myself, reciting Captain Lewisham's words from her captain's log.

Rooke glanced at me. "We have a myth that is similar to what you have told us." Turning back to Valina, he shook his head. "In a conventional, subconscious way, I think the Alluran people are reminded not to interfere with nature. We live alongside it, appreciate it, work with it, but never exploit it. Maybe the truth of what happened here on Earth is what has driven that ethic."

"Perhaps you are right." Valina smiled sweetly.

"Why do you call the Plastimites by a different name now?" I asked.

"When the Akquarians emerged from the shadows of the ocean, they called the Plastimites, Igknamai. I believe it means De…"

"Demon of Paradise."

"Yes, exactly. It must have stuck with our ancestors."

"Wait." I glanced at Rooke. "The Akquarians mentioned the Igknamai have leaders, um…controllers. Is that correct?"

Valina paused, her eyebrows pulling tightly together. "Unfortunately, they do. They were created after the Mass Exodus."

"Created?" both Rooke and I chimed together.

"Yes." Valina sighed, an aspect of shame filling her facial features. "A thousand years ago, a Redwood woman decided she no longer wanted to live like a savage. She'd read about how humans used to live vigorous, indulgent lives. She craved the same freedom and prosperity. She was a scientist, a rather clever one we believe. After running scientific tests on Igknamai carcases, she discovered she could mix our genetic code with theirs without complication. Her notes stated it was like they were drawn to one another. It's hard to believe, isn't it? I don't know the specifics behind the science. I'm sure Nya will explain it to you if you are interested."

"I'm positive Zamya, our own biologist, will be extremely interested in the facts," Rooke said.

"I'll be happy to show her," Nya said amiably.

"Anyway," Valina continued, flapping her hand, "the scientist proposed creating a human-Igknamai hybrid. She believed the creature would be able to communicate with both us and the beasts, creating a bridge of negotiation and the potential to achieve peace. Her project proposal was rejected by the council—rated absurd. But she continued in secret. Using her own eggs, she grew three foetuses in her lab. When they reached full gestation, she nurtured them as her own. It was said you could've mistaken them for humans. It was the reason why the villagers allowed them to stay.

"When they reached the age of five, she formed an encounter with the Igknamai, and to everyone's surprise, her plan worked. The children could communicate with the beasts, literally commanding them. With the children in control of the Igknamai movements, the villagers ventured down to the ground more often. Some even built homes on the soil. It became a turning point in the fight against them. That was until the three boys reached adulthood. They suddenly felt a resentment towards their duty and refused to cooperate. The final straw was when they ordered the Igknamai to attack the villagers, killing hundreds, including their mother. Some believed their minds had maddened with puberty. Others presumed the Igknamai themselves had corrupted them.

"Following the attack, the three Hybrids left, and the villagers' daily struggle with the Igknamai resumed. A couple of years later, several young women were snatched by the Igknamai. They weren't ripped apart or killed, but purposefully taken. The three Hybrids had given orders to the beasts to retrieve certain individuals and take them back to their lair, presumably to breed with them. It appears they were successful.

"To this day, women of childbearing age are snatched every so often, never to be seen again. You see, the Hybrids only seem to sire males. They use our women to continue their lineage, creating a more intelligent specimen generation after generation. The war with the Igknamai isn't just about savage beasts against humans anymore. Since the first Hybrids were created, the fight is now intelligent, power hungered sadists, with an army of beasts at their fingertips, against a struggling civilisation. You may look at us and think we are comfortable. We are not. Our numbers are barely sustainable. We are always a step behind the Hybrids. We are struggling."

Rooke and I stared at her, completely transfixed by the traumatising facts she'd laid before us. Humans had created the Igknamai. A human had created and birthed their controllers. If Llexzus was anything to go by, these Hybrids were immoral, twisted demons—a terrorising force to be reckoned with. They'd created a hell on Earth through bad decisions made millennia ago. And the Redwood people were still facing the consequences of their ancestors' greed and selfishness. How was that fair?

The whole room seemed to fall silent. The Redwoods watched us, waiting to see our reaction. Coming to the conclusion we were too shocked to speak, Valina's voice chirped, "Now. You have heard our story, let us hear yours." She smiled sweetly, but the sentiment did not reach her eyes.

"Um…" Rooke glanced at me, shifting in his seat, nervously. "From our ancient texts and history lessons, we were told only three thousand…" He looked at me for direction. I nodded. "…three thousand ships arrived at Allura, approximately eight hundred years after they left Earth. Not the hundreds of thousands of ships you suggested." He shrugged. "Um…what met our ancestors was a strange world full of disease and, later, famine. Over the first few centuries, half the population died." He frowned, contemplating the facts. "It still baffles me how our people survived."

"A race of survivors, no less."

Rooke nodded.

I rested my eyes on Blake as he asked, "What is it like…your planet?" He was bald with a long black beard, leaning forward with an expression of intrigue. Clearly a scientist wanting to learn more.

"Allura is a planet slightly larger than this one. It's a golden world consisting of mainly water. There are only three small continents. The southern continent is uninhabitable, but the two northern continents now form our five nations. The last time I checked, the total population is two hundred and twelve point four million people."

Blake's and Valina's eyes widened with looks of shock, awe, and envy. Even Truro frowned, his gaze resting on the bark floor. A part of me pitied them. If their ancestors' ship had not collided, they could've been among the Alluran people. They could've been living the life I underappreciated. I realised that now. My life had been comfortable. Yes, I'd lost my whole family through tragedy, but I hadn't lived in fear every day of my life like the Redwoods had. If I ever returned to Allura, I would endeavour to cherish every single part of that life. From the mundane to the exceptional. It was a life worth living.

Blake continued to ask questions. Thankfully Rooke answered them. My eyes had started to tingle with tears again. I felt overwhelmed. Nux, I wanted to go home.

"Have your people ever thought about returning to Earth?" Blake's question pulled me from my thoughts.

"No," Rooke replied. "We'd honestly forgotten where it was...I...I don't think they wanted to come back."

"Until now."

"Technically, we did not know this was Earth. We stumbled across it when we were tracing a distress signal from a missing ship. It appeared it had been manipulated across the depths of space by a probe-like entity." Rooke sat up taller, squaring his shoulders. "Would you know anything about that?"

Valina and Blake exchanged an uncomfortable look. I narrowed my eyes. Had it been them? Was it their desperate cry for help? If they had the ability to grow Hybrid foetuses here, surely they also had the ability to use space tech?

"It wasn't us," Valina's voice pierced the silence.

Rooke frowned at her. He was throwing her one of his hard, inquisitive looks—a look I hated being the recipient of. "Did you know our people had arrived? The ship before ours?"

"No. Not at first. We found them when it was too late."

"And you left their dead bodies there to rot?"

Valina raised her chin slightly; however, it didn't erase the glimpse of worry warping her pleasant expression. "We assumed someone would come looking for them. We wanted you to be aware of the severity of the situation. If we had buried their bodies, you may not have been prepared for the extent of the Igknamai's savageness."

"So, who sent the probe?"

"We…we wouldn't be surprised if it was the Hybrids."

"Why do you assume that?" Rooke's voice was clipped. I sensed he was fighting the urge to swear.

"They…" She exchanged another look with Blake. "A few decades ago, they stole our satellite communication module. The module spoke to several old satellites orbiting the Earth and a number of observation probes. Our predecessors used them to monitor space activity, and to send signals, messages to see if anyone was out there…listening. The Hybrids…well, we are unsure of what they are doing with it."

"Luring more prey in?" Rooke huffed.

"Possibly. We don't know for certain."

"Does that mean the Hybrids have our ship?"

"I wouldn't be surprised. But you won't find it. We have no idea where they reside. It's been a mystery to us and the Akquarians for a thousand years."

This time Rooke did curse.

"May I ask," Valina clasped her hands together tentatively, "why do you need the ship you landed in? You have another in orbit, yes? Why hasn't that one come down to retrieve you?"

I glanced at Rooke. He'd kept the Orka a secret from the Akquarians. Clearly, that wasn't an option with the Redwoods. Rooke slowly blinked, wetting his lips. "That ship is for subspace only. It cannot enter atmosphere."

Blake and Quinn nodded their heads in understanding, while Valina stared with a look of confusion. "The radio frequencies are permanently jammed at the moment," she said. "How are you communicating with your subspace ship?"

"We aren't." I could hear the strain in Rooke's voice. "It's the reason why we need our ship back. My engineer was planning on building a laser signal to form a direct communication link. We only have nine days left to contact our subspace ship before it returns home…without us."

The panic on Valina's face was too visible to miss. She glanced at Elgin. His expression matched her own. Then she looked towards Blake. "Can this be done in time?"

Blake frowned. "I'm not sure about a laser, but an infrared

or microwave signal could potentially work."

"They can use the radio terminal in Pasa," Quinn's tenor voice echoed around the room. "I'm sure we can find whatever resources they need."

It suddenly dawned on me how desperate these people were to help us. And the desperation didn't seem solely for our benefit. I felt my heart rate hasten; my senses heighten. I was hoping Rooke sensed it too.

"Very good," Valina said, turning back to us. "We'll help you build your communicator." She took a deep breath, still holding Rooke's gaze. "We do have something to ask in return, though."

I knew it!

"Go on." Rooke's sceptical voice rumbled.

"If you gain communication with your ship, we would like you to relay a message to your leaders. Asking for their help."

"What type of help?"

"To help us eradicate our enemy. For good."

Nux, I wasn't expecting that. But how could we deny them? It was painstakingly clear they were fighting a losing battle against the Igknamai. They were desperate for a moment of respite, desperate to live in a world without terror; a world like my own. But how could Solarfleet or the Alluran government help? Our guns were useless against the Igknamai. Valina had said explosives hadn't touched them in the past. What else could we bring to the battle?

I realised Rooke had remained silent. His eyes were scanning the thousands of names on the walls surrounding us. A frown of reluctance and grief crumpled the skin on his forehead.

"Rooke," I whispered. He instantly met my gaze. The shadows had returned to the depth of his eyes, the same ones I saw yesterday in his moments of guilt and despair. He was crumbling under the pressure. A pressure of an entire civilisation.

I looked back at Valina, suddenly aware I had seven pairs of eyes on me. They needed an answer. We wanted to get home and the only way I could guarantee their cooperation was to give them what they craved. Even in their desperation they hadn't been forceful. My intuition led me to believe these were good people. They deserved our help.

Swallowing back my emotive thoughts, I said, "If you help us create a communication link, we will ensure Solarfleet are informed of your situation. I am positive they will assist with your endeavour, one way or another."

Valina seemed to accept my announcement. Smiling widely, sincerity sang from her lips, "Thank you. You truly are a god send."

I looked back at Rooke. His glare spoke volumes. He wasn't happy.

Chapter Five

When we arrived back at our hut, we were met by a hubbub of activity in and around the two deserted huts adjacent to ours. Rooke, Oz, and Kobe were ushered into the middle hut, while Zamya and I were escorted to the one furthest along. It was the largest of the three, segregated into two rooms. We were led into the back room where two simple beds lay flush against the wall, one on each side. Medical apparatus was laid out on a small table against the far wall under an open window, and to the right, another door led to a small sanitary room.

At the end of the council meeting, Valina had advised a full medical check was to be conducted on all of the crew. It was to check for any abnormalities and diseases we may be carrying. The last thing they wanted was for us to walk about their village and infect everyone with an Alluran virus that could potentially be fatal to them. In return, Nya had offered to inoculate us against the Redwood's common viruses for the same reason. Following our experience with bluepox, none of us disagreed.

I sat on one of the beds, processing the information I had obtained at the meeting earlier. I couldn't get my head around it. How could our ancestors have been so stupid, even at the very start? A power driven, money-monopolised society. It just seemed absurd.

But what dominated my mind, as usual, was Rooke. He was mad at me, that much I was certain of. He'd hardly uttered a word to me since leaving the meeting. But I knew he'd have something to say when we were alone. What I couldn't understand was why he had frozen in the moment his directive was needed. Why hadn't he jumped at helping these people?

A sharp pain in my arm made me hiss and I looked down at the needle drawing blood from my vein. A young, red-haired woman muttered her apology, continuing with the procedure.

I glanced across the small room to where Zamya sat on the bed opposite. She was laughing with Nya. They'd hit it off straight away. Two female doctors from different challenging backgrounds—it seemed inevitable. It was good to see Zamya smile, though. I'd never seen her as distraught as she'd been yesterday. The loss of Cora had crushed us all. I still felt numb.

The red-haired woman placed several tubes of my blood into a wooden stand, then placed a glass cover over the top. I frowned as she typed into a small digital screen. "Do you have electricity here?" I asked. She looked back at me and nodded.

Fetching up the tray in her hands, she turned to Nya and said, "All done, doc."

"Take it back to the lab. The results need to be processed as high priority. I want them back within the hour." Nya's words prompted the woman to leave, and the room suddenly felt less claustrophobic.

Nya injected Zamya with another vaccine, continuing to talk to each other like long lost friends. I watched Nya's tall, slender figure move methodically as she tidied the area and washed her hands. Her skin was a warm brown, slightly darker than Zamya's. But what caught my attention were her eyes. They were a light green, which appeared almost surreal against her brown skin. It was a genetic combination we never saw among the Alluran people.

She smiled at me as she approached the bed. "I need to check a few vitals before I pump you full of vaccines."

It was a joke. I knew it was, but I didn't react. I felt numb, strange. She frowned in concern. "Are you always this pale?" She looked back at Zamya for confirmation.

Zamya peered at me. "She does look a little pastier than usual."

"I'm fine." I rubbed my eyes. "Tired, that's all."

Nya didn't seem convinced. She grabbed a small, metallic contraption from the table and placed it across my forehead. "You have a temperature." She touched the skin behind my ears and around my neck. "You're perspiring."

"It's warm today."

"And yet you're wearing a thick, fleeced jacket."

To be honest, I'd felt cold for most of the day up until a few minutes ago.

Nya touched my forehead with the back of her hand and her frown deepened. "I heard you were all ambushed by Igknamai yesterday. Did they get close enough to touch you?"

"Eden killed one." Zamya came closer. "It fell on top of her."

Nya's eyes widened. "Do you have any cuts from the encounter?"

I fell silent, staring into a void of memories from yesterday. The visions chilled me to the bone. I shuddered.

"Eden!" Zamya snapped me out of my daze. "Were you harmed yesterday?"

I frowned. "I…um…I have a scratch on my arm. I'm not…I'm not even sure if it was from the attack."

"Can you show me?" Nya watched me closely as I unzipped Rooke's jacket. Her eyes grew even wider when she noticed the bruise around my neck. "What in god's name happened there?"

"Akquarians." Zamya's tone was full of disdain. So much so, Nya glanced at her.

"Don't tell me, Tektrasc?"

"Yep. They left her in a closed corridor with one. Utter bastards."

"It didn't happen exactly like that, Zam."

"Do not defend them, Eden. Dybgo would've…"

"Dybgo?" Nya frowned. "The one who attacked you was Dybgo?"

"Yes." Zamya replied for me. "Do you know of him?"

"Yes." Nya's voice was clipped but she didn't say anything else on the subject.

My jacket was now laying across my lap, my right arm exposed. Nya touched the scratched area and I winced. I hadn't realised the pain was getting worse.

"It's infected," Nya said, moving to the table.

Zamya eyed the scratches. "Eden, you should've told me."

"It was a tiny scratch this morning. I didn't even notice it yesterday."

"Any Igknamai touch that breaks the skin slowly develops into something infectious." Nya placed a cloth soaked in a cool liquid over the wound. I hissed away the pain. "Sorry." She frowned at the yellowing colour on the cloth as she pulled it away. "The Igknamai teeth and claws are covered in a lethal bacterium. Wounds become infected. If untreated, they can be fatal. You'll need strong antibiotics and a few days' rest. I won't be able to vaccinate you until the infection has begun to clear."

"But she'll be alright?"

"We've caught it early and the area isn't very big, so yes, I believe so."

Zamya watched as Nya tentatively washed and dressed the wound. My mind kept wandering. Images of Igknamai swarming the ravine floor. Visions of Cora being dragged away screaming, begging us to save her. I felt as though I was dying a little more inside with each hour that passed.

The red-haired woman returned half an hour later, and after another spout of assessments, Zamya and I followed Nya into the front room of the hut, where Rooke, Kobe, and Oz stood waiting for us.

"I have good news," Nya addressed us all. "Your blood test results have deemed you all fit and healthy. I suggest you all stay strictly in this vicinity for a couple of days to let the vaccines take effect. You may feel a little unwell for the first twenty-four hours or so, but you should feel fine in no time."

Rooke nodded, glancing at Kobe. "As long as it's only two days isolation, we'll still have enough time to set up the comms link before Troy leaves for Allura."

"Valina asked me to tell you that these three lodges have been allocated as your permanent residence. There are two more beds through there," Nya pointed to the room Zamya and I had just emerged from, "as well as the three hammocks in the far lodge. The middle lodge will be set up as a living space, and we presume you'd like this room as an office or meeting space, commander?"

Rooke glanced about the room, at the simple desk I was perched on, and the two wooden chairs behind it. He pouted his lower lip and nodded his appreciation. "That would be great."

"Good. Well, rest up. I'll return in a few hours to check how you're all doing."

Nya and her entourage of helpers left. Through the open doorway, Zamya watched them go. "I want her to be my best friend," she pined.

Oz laughed, commenting on Zamya's neediness, and I glanced at Rooke. He was standing with his hands in his pockets, peering at me under his dark eyebrows. He cleared his throat and said, "Can you guys give me and Eden the room."

Silence enveloped us before I witnessed the three of them glance awkwardly at each other. They left through the doorway to the right, connecting this hut to the middle one via a short bridge.

Adjusting my seated position on the desk, I let my legs swing, clasping my hands on my lap. I knew what was due; Rooke's wrath. His silence sliced through me, and I peered up at him. Nux, he looked so angry. The nervous tension he was creating forced me to speak in a vain attempt to lighten the mood. "First meeting in your new office, yeah?"

Continuing to watch me for several more agonising seconds, he eventually spoke, "What the hell did you think you were doing?"

"If you mean at the meeting earlier, I was answering their question. The one you seemed to blatantly ignore."

"Where's your sense gone? You promised them something we cannot guarantee."

"I promised them we'd speak to Solarfleet about their situation, nothing more."

"You promised them we'd help!"

"Solarfleet *will* help. Even if it's to provide them sanctuary."

Baring his teeth, Rooke shook his head in disagreement.

"These are our people, Rooke. Solarfleet are fair and..."

"Solarfleet are not the Alluran government."

"I'm sure they'll..."

"You literally promised them the world!"

"What did you want me to say?" I was beginning to lose my reserve. "You froze. You went silent. They were expecting a response. If you didn't want me to answer for you, maybe you should've opened your mouth and said something yourself!"

He launched himself forward, slapping his hands on the desktop either side of me, his face mere inches from mine. The line of his jaw tensed, his eyes narrowed, staring directly into the depths of my soul. "If you had kept your trap shut, you would've realised I was choosing the right words to respond with. Words that wouldn't chain us to them. We don't know who they are, what they want..."

"They are desperate people with the same ancestors as us."

"They could be as deceptive as the Akquarians."

"Is this really your way to try and redeem your mistake in trusting the Akquarians? By ignoring everyone else?"

"Don't you dare!" His snarl didn't cover the fragility that flashed in his eyes. I'd hit a vulnerable nerve and I suddenly felt ashamed. Closing my eyes I whispered, "Nux, I'm sorry. That was uncalled for."

He straightened up, placing his hands in his pockets. "My main priority is getting the five of us off this planet before anything else tears us apart. I did not intend on entangling myself in another messy situation with a civilisation that is not my responsibility. I do not have the authority to suggest actions you announced earlier. *You*, most certainly, do not. And if we do get in contact with Troy, I have no idea how I'm going to broach the extent of your promises with Solarfleet."

I paused, the guilt beginning to drown me. Had I really done something wrong in offering our allegiance? Hadn't these people suffered long enough?

Concern filled me as I noticed Nya striding along the bridge back towards the open doorway behind Rooke. She tapped the wooden frame, alerting him, and stepped inside. "Sorry to interrupt. Eden, I forgot to leave your antibiotics." She handed me a small, glass pot full of beige tablets. "Take one four times a day for three days. I'll take some more bloods the day after tomorrow to check your progress. With any luck I'll be able to vaccinate you then."

I felt Rooke's confusion as I thanked Nya. She gave me an odd, uncomfortable smile, then left. I stared at the bottle in my hand, sensing the tension shift in the air. Rooke's boots appeared on the floor in front of me and I slowly lifted my head to meet his gaze. He was frowning, his eyes full of worry. "What are those for?"

"An infection."

"What? How, why? Is it serious?"

I sighed. "The Igknamai caught my arm yesterday. It's just a scratch."

"But it's infected." He raked his hand through his hair. "Shit, Eden. Can you please start looking out for yourself?" He cut me off before I could say anything. "You put yourself in danger yesterday, saving Cora's ass. And for what?" He was leaning on the desk again, peering with intensity into my eyes. "She died anyway. And now…now you're sitting here, telling me you have a mere scratch, when you're clearly struggling with the repercussions of yesterday's attack. It's infected, yes? I'm guessing in a similar way to what Oz had?" I shrugged. "No, Eden. Stop it! Start giving yourself a little more respect and realise your worth. Okay, you sometimes promise ridiculous things to people we barely know, but…" He cupped the side of my jaw with his hand. The intensity of his frown doubled. "I can't lose you."

I stared at him, at the words he'd declared, and my heart ached. Shamefully, I glanced at his mouth, at the lips that had fitted perfectly against mine just four evenings past. I craved that kiss, hoping he'd convince me he needed me as much as I did him. Hoping he'd tell me he didn't regret what had happened between us that night.

Shutting his lips away from view, I closed my eyes and a rebellious tear streaked down my cheek. His thumb gently brushed the wetness away, then the warmth of his lips pressed against my forehead. Nux, I wanted to scream. He had no idea why I was crying. No idea whatsoever.

Oz and Rooke swiftly claimed the two standard beds as their own, along with the larger hut. Kobe, Zamya, and I didn't argue. The hammocks were comfortable enough, especially now we were offered the luxury of pillows and blankets.

I'd slept most of the next two days, only moving to the middle hut when I needed food and drink. I usually found the others lounging about, playing card games across the table. Sometimes, I joined them. Food was brought daily by the villagers. All of whom were clothed in brown or red fabrics with leather garments covering vital areas of their torso and legs.

Nya had paid me several visits, dressing my wound and generally checking in on us all. The others had no adverse effects to their vaccines and Nya deemed them ready to enter the village the following morning. She'd taken bloods from me, promising to return with the results. When she did, Rooke emerged in the hut doorway, carrying a shadow of intensity with him.

"How is she?" he asked Nya.

Looking up at me, she replied to his question, "The infection has pretty much cleared. Your blood levels appear normal, your temperature is good. As long as you feel well enough, I can give you your inoculation doses now."

"I feel fine." And I did. The shivers had stopped early that morning, the pain in my right arm was subsiding, and even though a headache loomed, I assumed it was from lethargy more than anything else.

Nya nodded and I caught Rooke's unsettling gaze.

"Are you sure?" he asked me.

"Yes. Rooke, I'm fine."

"Does she not need more rest?" His words now aimed at Nya.

A glimpse of amusement danced in Nya's bright green eyes. "She'll have to stay here for another day or two. Technically, she will be resting. I won't send her out into the village until I'm fully happy with her stats."

Rooke seemed to accept Nya's advice and left her to her work.

The following day, a selfish envy loomed over me as I stood in the doorway of the middle hut, watching the rest of the crew stroll down the bridge to the platform opposite.

"Now, Eden, don't go sneaking out," Oz japed. "We know what you're like." He grinned back at me, and I rolled my eyes. "Don't miss us too much."

"I'm looking forward to some peace and quiet."

"So am I." Zamya shot Oz a scowl. "Where are you and Rooke going? I'll make sure to avoid it at all costs."

"Mem, mem, mem."

"Oh, grow up, Ozmun."

I chuckled to myself as Zamya followed Kobe from the hut, out of view. Oz waited on the platform for Rooke, who appeared next to me a moment later.

"Are you sure you're alright?" he asked tenderly.

I sighed, glancing up at his dark, concerned eyes. "Yes. Stop worrying."

"Hmm…Valina's going to show me and Oz around the village today, so if you need me…"

"Get out of here."

He smiled before leaning forward to kiss my temple. I watched him and Oz disappear along the walkways and through the trees, and a sense of loneliness washed over me. For the past six weeks,

I'd barely had any time to myself. There had always been someone with me, even if it had been Yuska.

I glanced about the hut, deciding to return to my hammock for an hour or so. Sleep seemed to evade me, so I chose to sit on the balcony. With a leg either side of a sturdy wooden post, I let my feet dangle over the edge, watching the village below. People came and went, trudging along the bridges with food, timber, fabrics. Some stopped to talk with others, while children ran carelessly around them. Older children ambled along with books in their hands as if they were heading to school. I spotted a number of cats gracefully negotiating the thin railings of the bridges, leaping onto platforms from above. No sign of any domestic dogs. Maybe they hadn't adapted to life in the trees.

Something crawled onto the back of my hand, and I flinched. It was some sort of small insect with a fat body and eight legs. Nothing like I'd ever seen before. The insects back home only had six legs, but then again, the humans only took bees and butterflies with them when they left Earth, along with a multitude of animal species. Many had not survived or bred successfully in space. Eight hundred years was a long time for them to endure unnatural conditions.

Standing up, I brushed the creature from my hand. From the balcony, I wandered down the interconnecting bridge to the middle hut, grabbing a handful of berries from the table. Ambling through the circular room, I found my feet aimlessly walking across the connecting bridge to Rooke's new office.

Entering, I glanced about. He'd moved his desk into the middle of the room, separating the main entrance from the curtained off section behind, where his and Oz's sleeping quarters were. And on top of the desk, sat Rooke's handheld computer, connected to a small, solar charging pack.

I frowned, wondering why he hadn't taken it with him, and why he'd left it out for anyone to see. I tapped on the screen to ascertain if it was switched off, but it lit up at my touch. Walking around the desk, I realised the screensaver, now illuminating the five-inch screen, was a picture from his pilot graduation. He was standing with his parents either side of him. His older brother towered next to their mum, and I was wedged in beside his dad. I remembered that day as if it was yesterday. Rooke had dragged me along to the ceremony even though it had been strictly a family affair, and his dad had forced me to participate in that very photo. Being only eighteen at the time, I looked awkward and uncomfortable, grimacing next to an attractive family beaming with pride.

Smiling with sentiment, I stroked the screen, reminiscing about that day; about how the Maddox family always made me feel welcome. The screensaver cleared when I removed my finger, and another screen appeared.

What? Rooke had left his computer unlocked? "What an idiot." But the photo illuminating the screen behind a multitude of work icons, made my heart stop along with my breathing.

The photo—it was a cute picture of Rooke and his girlfriend, Miranda. She was smiling at the camera. A bright and wide smile reflecting a loved-up sparkle in her eye, while Rooke kissed her cheek, eyes closed.

Miranda was stunning. I'd always been envious of her. With flawless, tanned skin, and silky black hair, she could've been a model. Rooke's usual type.

For some reason, I had forgotten about her. They must have been together nearly eighteen months now, but…I can't recall Rooke speaking of her since…well, since we left our previous mission on Juno. Were they still together?

Staring at the photo, my stomach quenched with jealousy, tightening at my gullet. They must be together. Why would he have this photo as his backscreen if they weren't? An urge to take a look at his messages overcame me, and I tapped the comms tab…

Nux, what am I doing?

Cursing myself, I closed the screen down, pushing the computer out of reach as if it was contagious.

He had a girlfriend. I knew he had a girlfriend. Why was I upset? He always *had* girlfriends.

I assumed she was the reason why he had stopped me from going any further at the Akquarian ball. Rooke had never cheated on anyone. Yes, I always japed he was a Casanova, but he was loyal. Never the womaniser. But why had he kissed me? It was him who had instigated it.

Maybe being so far from home, full of desperation and loneliness, he'd looked to the only person available—me.

The tiny bit of hope I had left, the tiniest speck that made me believe he felt something romantic towards me, started to diminish. I was such a fool.

I slumped against the wall and stared at his desk. Why had he kissed me? Why? I shook my head, preventing the anger and frustration from forming unwanted tears. Why did I do this to myself? Why did I hold onto this obscene idea of being with him, when he clearly did not think of me in the same way? I was his adopted sister, for Nux sake, nothing more.

I'd shown him what I wanted from him, and he'd rejected me.

He. Rejected. Me!

Rubbing my face, I walked to the door. There was only one thing left for me to do. And that was to accept Rooke was strictly a friend. I needed to push past this obsession. I needed to move on.

Chapter Six

"I'm glad you're allowed out today," Kobe said, as we walked through the village of trees and bridges. "I was struggling to get anything done yesterday. Zamya kept disappearing to talk with the doctor woman. Not sure why Rooke didn't offer to help, either."

I tutted, thinking about how late Rooke had returned the past two evenings. "I guess he's keeping positive relations up with the Redwood head of HR."

Kobe huffed. "You'd think he'd forgotten we only have a limited amount of time to get this finished."

"How far have you got?"

"Honestly, not far." Kobe huffed again. "I'm using their comms room. It's the original from when the ship crashed."

"You mean the original ship? That crashed thousands of years ago?"

"Yes." Kobe pointed towards the mountainous rockface on the north side of the village. The top edges were coated in honey-gold rays from the morning sun. "The ship is embedded under the surface. The tech is old, but I'm optimistic it will suffice."

We approached the edge of the trees. The mountainous rockface loomed in front of us, and I could see it was separated into two, with a steep, yet narrow canyon in between. Several long suspension bridges linked the forest to wooden walkways which laid flush against the rock, accessing a number of dark caverns within the stone. Ladders ran up the edge to the very top of the cliff, where I could see green foliage swaying in the gentle breeze.

I followed Kobe over one of the bouncing bridges to the left. The forest floor was still over ninety metres below. Taking a deep breath, I glanced upwards, trying to ignore my roiling stomach. At the far end of the bridge, the wooden walkway was just as disconcerting. Thin wooden railings were the only barrier from stepping too close to the edge. Thankfully, an opening in the rockface appeared and I followed Kobe inside.

I paused, taking in my new surroundings. The area was highly illuminated and my feet were on a solid, metallic floor. It felt surreal. This really was a spaceship integrated into the rock formation. Modifications had been made, but from where I stood, it looked as though this area was once a main airlock. The open, thick, sliding metal doors had the same hydraulic levers and locks Alluran ships had. An opening on the wall in front of us appeared to be the inner airlock. Those doors, too, were metallic.

A faded sign above the doorway read, Pacifica. Although the *c* had been graffitied to look like an *s*, and a thick line struck through the latter half, excluding the *a*. It now read, *Pasa.*

Kobe pointed to the white overhead lights. "They have a small amount of electricity here, fuelled by solar and wind energy. It's used to keep the Pasa powered. Some electricity is used to light up parts of the village when it can be spared."

I continued to look around as we walked further into the ship, noticing areas and rooms used as labs and medical rooms. "This is very impressive."

"Other than what they're able to grow organically, they culture their own food." Kobe pointed to a room through a murky piece of glass panelling. "They use vertical farming for certain plant-based foods." He pointed to another closed off room. "In there is where they make cultures for antibiotics and simple medication." He led me along a wide corridor, past an open room, where a group of adults appeared to be taking part in meditational yoga. I noticed Nya among them.

"Down there are some shower blocks."

"Showers?" I glanced down the corridor to the right, realising how desperately I wanted to feel clean again. "Actual showers?"

"Yes. They have a water recycler within the ship. The water pressure's not great but it's adequate."

"I'll come back this evening for one."

"You won't be allowed in after 1800 hours. They shut the airlock doors and pull the bridges in from the village a couple of hours before sundown. Even though we're up high here, there have apparently been times the Igknamai appear on the clifftop. I wanted to stay later yesterday, but they wouldn't let me."

"Wow, okay. Shower tomorrow then."

Past another intersection, down another long corridor, Kobe entered a code into a keypad on the wall to the right. A sliding door opened, and a small, dark room illuminated. Three rows of communication panels filled the space. Judging by the dimly lit screens and buttons, it was hard to know if they were functional.

"Do these work?" I asked, touching the edge of a tarnished consol.

"A lot of the touch screen functionalities are no longer active. Such a crazy fad. Give me a proper push button any day. But yes, it seems to be in reasonable working order, just old." Kobe walked over to the desk panels on the back wall. "I've been using this terminal. It's connected to a small satellite dish on the clifftop directly above. If I can create an amplifier, we'll be able to wire one of our comms units in, then use microwaves to communicate with The Orka directly."

"Can we control the direction the dish is placed?"

"Yes, using those control panels over there." He pointed to the far left.

"And are we able to track The Orka's movements when in range?"

"Yes. The science department has a rather hefty working telescope. Blake's given me access to it. I've rigged the live footage to this screen here, which I'm hoping to correlate to the dish controls. The Orka has already passed overhead dozens of times. Troy is purposely shifting the natural trajectory. He's flying overhead on every orbit, sometimes using the engines to hover in place for longer spates. I have no doubt he's trying to communicate with us through various channels. But he thinks we're still at the Akquarian fortress."

"Which is why he's having no success."

"Exactly."

"Well then. Let's get this functioning. Show me what you need me to do."

Working alongside Kobe, I realised several things: How much he hated small talk. How much of a perfectionist he deemed himself to be. And how brilliant an engineer he was. His mind was astonishing. A walking, talking scientific calculator.

I checked my watch. It was past three o'clock and I was starving. So much so, I was finding it hard to concentrate. "Kobe, I think I'm going to have to find some food. Do you want anything?"

Currently positioned inside one of the console panels, his voice sounded muffled. "No, I'm good."

I stood up and walked to the door, scratching at the scabs on my right arm. "I won't be long."

In the corridor, I glanced about, trying to find someone to point me in the direction of where to acquire food. Finding myself back where the yoga class had taken place earlier, I recognised the slight, brown skinned man walking towards me. He was the head engineer. Pretty sure his name was Quinn. He must've been a similar age to me, wearing a pair of overalls not dissimilar from our Solarfleet jumpsuits. He smiled. "Hi. How's everything going with the comms?"

"We're making progress. Kobe may have a few requests for electronic components, though."

"I'll pop in to see him on my way past."

"Before you do," I inwardly winced at how desperate my voice sounded. I felt almost sheepish, "is there anywhere I can get some food? Although, I haven't got any money."

"Money?" He laughed, exposing a flash of white teeth. "We don't have money here. Come on, this way. I'll show you."

He turned back the way he'd appeared from and gestured for me to follow. I fell in step with him as he veered to the right, down a brightly lit corridor.

"So, how are you finding the Pasa?" he asked.

"The ship? The ship is unbelievable, considering its age. How much of it still remains intact?" I glanced about, noticing old scorch marks on some of the wall panels.

"Only a fifth is in use. A large amount crumbled under the crash impact. To be honest, it's amazing anyone survived. But, then again, I could say the same about your ancestors."

"We all have astounding histories."

"Indeed, we do." He stopped and looked at me. "I hope you don't mind me asking, but do many people have the same eyes as yours, where you come from? They're so…unusual."

He was gazing at me, studying my starburst irises with wonderment. I felt myself blush. "Um, no. My strange eyes are just that. Strange. And don't worry, they get commented on all the time. I'm used to it."

"I see. Well then. Here we are." We were at the far end of the corridor, where a large circular doorway stood open, and the hubbub of voices carried over us. "This is the food hall. You can get most available foods from here."

My eyes widened as I walked forward, scanning the enormous, bright room. Rows of stalls laden with bread, fruit, vegetables, fish, and meats filled the area. Wooden tables and chairs filled the gaps to the left, next to a large, rectangular open doorway. This must've been the original loading bay. A decked area was outside, where more tables and chairs were placed with a scattering of people eating and drinking.

"Wow," I heard myself say. "Where does all this food come from?"

"Grown on the clifftop or in our plantation labs. The meat is caught by our hunters. Occasionally it's from our livestock. The fish is bought from the Akquarians. The bread is made here, as well as the cheeses and yoghurts."

"What's that amazing smell?" My lungs were filling with a hearty, herby delicacy. It smelt delicious.

"Ahh, that's food from Pepa's Kitchen. She makes dinners, ready to eat."

"Like a takeaway?"

"Yes. That's one way of putting it. Her breakfasts are my favourite. Come, let's see what's on the menu."

We walked through the crowd, my eyes perusing the foods on display. The cheese, especially, looked tempting. I hadn't eaten cheese for over six months.

When we reached the last row of stalls, an intense heat hit me. A metallic counter stood in front, separating the area behind from the main hall. A couple of older ladies stood at a workbench, whilst food bubbled away in pots on stoves behind them. The smell was even more divine from this distance.

"Pepa?" Quinn called. "What have you got prepared today?"

One of the women looked up at him and instantly smiled. Her

face was round and wrinkled, her hair a dark grey pulled back into a neat bun. Walking towards us, she wiped her hands on her stained apron. "Vegetable stew today." She placed her hands on either side of Quinn's face and squished his cheeks together. "Good to see you, Quinn boy." She eyed me and said, "Is this…?"

"This is Eden." Quinn looked at me. "She's one of the…"

"I know who she is. Let me look at you?" She gently placed her warm hands on my cheeks and inspected my face with her small hazel eyes. She smiled. "Beautiful. What a miracle you are."

I felt a little awkward, but there was no animosity in her words. In fact, she seemed overwhelmed and humbled by my presence. She hummed a smile and set her hands down onto the counter. "Would you both like some stew?"

"Not for me," Quinn said, "but Eden may."

"Yes, please…if that's okay."

"Of course." Pepa flapped her hand and walked over to the bubbling pots.

I turned to Quinn. "How do I pay for this?"

"You don't." He chuckled at my surprised expression. "Everyone in the village is entitled to the standard necessities. Food, water, clothes, a roof over their head, healthcare. In return, anyone over the age of sixteen works for twenty-five hours per week in a job deemed as essential. The rest of the time they're allowed to do as they please. Housework, swim, make jewellery."

"Take yoga classes?"

"Exactly. Those who work over the twenty-five standard hours are given additional credits, which they can use on more luxurious items, such as jewellery."

"I see. So…am I entitled?"

Quinn paused and frowned at me quizzically. "Of course you are. Probably more so. Your people are helping ours."

I tried to hold his gaze, but couldn't. A sense of guilt pounded through me, along with Rooke's solemn words. I had promised these people something we couldn't guarantee and now I was taking their food.

Pepa returned with a steaming bowl of stew and a crusty bread roll. My stomach growled ferociously. Trying to offer a genuine smile, I took it from her. "Thank you."

She pointed to the tables through the open doorway. "Go sit. There's a lovely breeze today. It's carrying the smell of the lemon lily down from the hilltop."

I thanked her again, then thanked Quinn, before walking through the huge, rectangular doorway to an empty table by the wooden railing outside. I didn't care about the drop to the forest floor next to me, I devoured the stew. It was the best thing I'd tasted in a long, long time.

Wiping my mouth, I leant back and looked at the village before me. From the decked area where I sat, a bridge stretched across to a large tree hut fifteen metres away. Clusters of villagers sat there, eating, talking, laughing. This felt so normal, so civilised.

I glanced along the treeline, spotting a couple of taller trees. Lookouts ambled about in huts at the very top. Yes, this did feel normal, but realistically, it was far from it. We had to help these people. To leave them here to their demise would be inhumane.

A couple of days later, Kobe confirmed the microwave communicator was ready. We only had to wait for The Orka to orbit directly above us. However, the ship was no longer orbiting overhead on every pass.

"Troy must be restoring fuel," Kobe mused, watching the data flash up on an old transmission screen.

"When's he mathematically due to pass overhead again?"

Kobe pouted his lips to one side. "Two days. We're cutting it fine."

I nodded. "We'll keep a close eye on it."

Leaving Kobe to connect the satellite data to his personal tablet, I took a shower. The water was tepid and poorly pressurised, but it was better than nothing. I felt clean.

With my towel slung over my shoulder and my wet hair pulled back in a scraggly knot, I walked back through the village. I'd only spoken to Rooke in passing over the past few days. His time was taken up with meetings with the council and daily scouting missions with Oz and some of the Redwood scouts. He was still trying to find the Parvos in the depths of Igknamai territory. I wasn't sure if he was brave or stupid.

A gaggle of children's voices caught my attention from behind.

Much to my dismay, the suspension bridge bobbed and swayed as they galloped past. As I grabbed onto the railing, I recognised one of them. He was the young boy from the other day, destined to be Truro's replacement when he grew up. He was holding a wooden sword, leading the charge, loudly.

I smiled watching them go by, only to hesitate when one of the older girls from the back of the group stopped mid-bridge. She was now staring back at me. Feeling a little disconcerted, I continued towards her, avoiding her gaze.

As I neared, she took a step forward, gazing up at me with large blue eyes. Her auburn hair was a mess of knots and tangles, attempting to resemble a braid. "Are you...are you the one they call Eden?" I noted the awe laced in her voice.

I felt awkward. "Um...yes. That's me."

"Wow." The sound fell out of her mouth in a whoosh of air. She continued to stare, but I went to move round her, only to be stopped by her words. "Is it true that you came from the sky?"

"Um..." I looked down at her again. "I come from a different world. You have to get to it by going that way." I pointed upwards.

She looked like she was going to burst. Her bright blue eyes were wider than an ocean. "Is it...is it true that you have slayed an Igknamai singlehandedly?"

Grimacing, I scratched my healing arm. "I guess, but..."

"And you scaled the ravine wall in less than a minute?"

"Uh? No, no."

"My brother said you did. He saw you. And he never lies." Her small, round face gazed up at me as if I was some sort of idol.

"Your brother?"

"Yes. He..."

"Saff, what are you doing?" Halting her confession, a male voice called from behind. I turned and found Truro's Nux warrior form marching towards us. His muscular arms glistened gold in the evening sunlight, his hair flapping over his eyes. I smirked and looked back at the girl. "Is he your brother?"

She nodded.

The eyes. I should've guessed from her eyes. They were the same vivid shade of blue.

"Saff, leave her alone!"

"I was only…"

"You were interrogating her." Truro stopped next to me, glaring at his little sister. She must've been only ten, maybe eleven.

"To be fair she wasn't." From the corner of my eye, I saw Saff grin up at me, while Truro's gaze shifted to my face.

"I wouldn't encourage her, if I were you," he said. "She will talk your ear off."

I smiled at Saff's protests, still holding Truro's gaze. Nux, when those blue eyes looked at me, they made my stomach flutter. Thankfully, he turned his attention back to his sister. "Mum wants you at home."

Saff groaned, rolling her eyes skywards. "I did my chores this morning."

"Stop with the excuses."

"But…"

"Go!"

She sulked off, turning after a few steps. "Tell Eden to join training."

Truro pointed in the direction she was supposed to be travelling, and together, we watched Saff round the platform at the far end.

"Training?" I asked.

Still watching Saff, Truro rubbed his lips together. "There's a group of us who train the village to fight. We hold training sessions every morning. Archery, swordsmanship, self-defence. Anyone who is interested can join." He shrugged. "You may not be…"

"I am."

He looked at me with inquisitive scepticism.

"I've nearly died at the hands of the Igknamai twice. I have no doubt training to fight them would be anything but beneficial."

A flash of surprise caught in his expression, then he nodded. "Training starts at seven. East clifftop."

I watched him march away, following the same path Saff had just taken. Every ounce of him oozed alpha warrior, even down to his rugged brown armour and worn boots—a symbol of his durability.

Catching me off guard, he stopped halfway across the bridge and spun on his heel.

"Not sure if you're aware," he called, "but we hold a new moon celebration every month. It's tonight. Most people meet at the midway point." He pointed towards the centre of the village. "You're all more than welcome to join us." Before I could answer, he was walking again.

Watching him go, it genuinely amazed me how his curt irritation always softened into generosity. I smiled down at my boots. Truro...Truro was interesting.

Chapter Seven

Laughter and chatter filled the air as I stood at the edge of a vast platform. The midway point was a large expanse of decking, reinforced and held up, mid-level, by six thickset trees. Another tree trunk filled the space in the middle, where an open hut encircled it forming a drinks bar. Another sign of our related ancestry and common interests.

The hour was eight and the sun had only just set. Strings of lights dangled from wooden poles, softly illuminating the area. A raised section on the far side seated an ensemble of musicians, comprising of two acoustic guitarists, a violinist, and a single bass drummer. Dancers filled the floor before them, the floor vibrating under their joyous steps.

No longer dressed in their daily leathers, villagers watched the dancer's frivolous movement, skirts and scarfs swinging as they moved. Others drank and sang, while a handful of children dashed in and out of the crowd causing a commotion.

It certainly was a celebration. Rooke had been aware of the festivities when I'd mentioned it to him not two hours ago. He'd told me Valina expressed the new moon party was to create a spark of light during the darkest night of each month. Although, the night sky wasn't truly dark here. A similar occurrence happened on Allura during such a time. Back home in Torla, there were two nights of each year where the sun didn't set at all. Contrarily, we celebrated those nights full of endless light.

Scanning the area before me, I couldn't see any of the crew. I caught a glimpse of Quinn speaking with a huddle of villagers. There was no sign of Truro, either. I swallowed back the nerves. Why had I come?

Valina stood at the bar, speaking with the bar tender. She was hard to miss; a vision of lilac, draped in a flattering chiffon dress. She looked the part, head of relations. Here to keep everyone happy. Rooke hadn't stopped talking about her earlier. She had certainly captivated him. I closed my eyes, swallowing the envy.

Stop it, Eden.

I flinched when I felt a hand rounding my waist. Looking up, Rooke was frowning down at me. He hadn't shaved since we'd left the Akquarian fortress. He was fashioning a short, yet thick, dark beard. It suited him.

"Everything okay?" he asked.

"Yes, sorry. You…you startled me."

He smiled softly. "Clearly." He moved closer and swiftly brushed his lips against my temple. "I haven't seen much of you over the past few days."

"You've been busy." I glanced over at Valina, who had spotted Rooke already. My tone must've sounded off because in the next instance, Rooke spun me toward him, bobbed down to my level, and peered into my eyes. "What's wrong?"

I shook my head, trying to push away the jealousy starting to resurface. He had a girlfriend back on Allura, and now gracious Valina was always monopolising his time. Nux, I promised myself not to think about this. "I think I may head back."

"Already?" Rooke's frown deepened. "I wanted to spend some time with you."

"I think someone else wants that pleasure." I inclined my head towards Valina, who was now floating towards us through the sea of dancers. She smiled when Rooke looked at her. His eyes met with mine again, a flash of apology within them.

"Good news about the communicator." Valina appeared, breaking the unexpected tension straining between Rooke and I. Her fingers snatched around Rooke's bicep, and I forced an unconvincing smile.

"Yes." I could barely look at her. I had no reason to dislike her, but I did. "If you, um, excuse me. I'm going to take my leave."

Valina made a disappointed mewing sound, while I clung to Rooke's gaze for a fleeting second. He genuinely looked gutted, but maybe I was reading too much into it. I brushed past him and left.

Absentmindedly, I ambled back to our lodgings. Even if I'd stayed at the party, it wouldn't have felt right celebrating. Cora had only been gone a week. The thought of her flooded my brain with feelings of remorse. We hadn't given her a proper funeral. We hadn't buried her. Where her body was, if any part of it still existed, nobody knew.

She was so young, so gentle, wonderfully excitable, and optimistic. She was everything I wasn't. It should've been me who died, not her. Why had it been her?

Crossing the bridge to my sleeping hut, I slowed, noticing a pair of legs dangling from the balcony in the darkening shadows of the trees. The sight disturbed a distant memory; one I consciously kept locked away. Pushing it back down, I rounded the edge, and found Zamya hugging one of the railing posts, legs either side. The glazed look she offered me confirmed she'd been drinking.

"You couldn't do it either, huh?" she said, taking a swig from a bulbous, clay bottle.

I slid down to the floor, straddling the post adjacent to hers. "Do what?"

"Enjoy the party."

I sighed, still swallowing down the bitter taste that visions of Zamya's hanging legs caused. "No."

We both gazed into the darkness. The twinkling of a few lights trickled up through the trees. A faint wisp of music came and went as a warm breeze blew, rustling the leaves above and below.

"I miss her."

"So do I," I whispered, biting back another wave of grief. "She was struggling. I shouldn't have let her leave the fortress. I knew she was struggling…"

"She was pregnant."

It took a moment for Zamya's words to sink in. My eyes slowly shifted to find her staring into her thoughts. *Pregnant? What?* Nux, was that why she'd been vomiting, why she'd been clutching her stomach?

"She wanted to tell you." Zamya's words were incredibly soft. The truth within them seemed too painful to pronounce. "But I told her not to."

"Why?"

"Because you'd tell Rooke."

I stared at her profile, the frown on my forehead causing my muscles to ache from the intensity of it. Was that the reason Cora and Zamya had bickered so much at the fortress? Because of their conflict of opinion to tell me about Cora's condition?

Zamya eventually met my gaze, producing a deep, shaky sigh. "I realise, now, I was wrong."

"No." I reached for her, only finding air and the wooden floor between us. I shook my head. "I would've. You were right. And he would've hit the roof."

"And the rest. That's why she was so desperate to speak to Troy."

"Does he not know?"

"No. Cora discovered her condition when we were residing with the Akquarians. It was the week after she thought she was due her monthly. Her temperature was up because of the pregnancy."

"Nux."

"Yuska knew."

Of course she did. How hadn't I picked up on it? Cora was glowing the morning after the ball.

"The plan was to keep it a secret." Zamya stared down at the bottle in her hands. She missed Cora, possibly more than I did. How long had she resorted to drowning her sorrows in a bottle of Redwood wine? I was ashamed that she hadn't felt confident enough to speak to me before. "We assumed we'd have the Parvos back relatively soon. I had no doubt you and Kobe would fix it. We'd be back on The Orka in no time. By the time Cora would've started showing, we'd be nearly home. And Rooke, well, he wouldn't have been able to do anything about it."

"But...what about the radiation, the risk to the baby?"

Zamya shrugged. "We are all descendants of babies born in space. There are ways of creating better protection. I would've helped her." She squeezed her eyes together, a distant flicker of light briefly illuminating her face, exposing how wet her cheeks were. "I wanted to help her."

I stared into the darkness beyond the railing. Every night since that awful day, I'd dreamt of Cora falling. The sound of her screams filled me with terror as I tried to get to her. Every night, I'd been too slow. Every night, I couldn't save her.

"It's funny," Zamya slurred, "have you ever wondered why the crew of The Orka were chosen for this mission?"

"What do you mean?"

"Well," she took another swig of wine, "we're all reasonably young with no commitments and responsibilities back on Allura. Oz is divorced, Kobe is a loner. You and I have no family. It's as if Solarfleet knew we'd never come home."

I hadn't thought of it like that before. None of us were married or had children. None of us had mentioned long term partners or reliant relatives. Sym had a large family of sisters, but they were all married, leading their own lives. We were all expendable, even Rooke. Even Rooke who... "Rooke has a girlfriend."

"Pfft." Zamya chuckled sarcastically. "Another one of his fleeting women."

"He's been with her a while..."

"He can't hold a relationship down. He's too..."

"Zam! Don't! He *is* human. He does have feelings."

"He's a dick!"

"Why do you loathe him so much?"

"It's *his* fault we're stuck in this shithole. He bypassed protocol..."

"Zam..."

"We shouldn't have landed as soon as we arrived."

"That was as much my fault..."

"No, it wasn't. And I'm sick of you sticking up for him!"

"He's my friend, Zam. As are you."

With a clumsy abruptness, Zamya stood up. I could barely see her through the darkness, but I could sense she was scowling at me; the way she did when she made her point. "So was Cora. And where is she now?"

"Zam." I heard her amble and bump her way inside the hut. I chose not to pursue her. She was drunk—the worst kind of upset. Hopefully she'd sleep it off.

But she was right. Solarfleet had chosen us not because of our capabilities, but because we did not matter. I had no family. The only family I had was here. And already two of those members had been killed. Were we ever going to get off this planet?

I'd promised the Redwood people we'd help them. What if we all died before Solarfleet arrived? If they arrived. Nux, what if they didn't come?

Grabbing the clay bottle Zamya had left on the wooden floor beside me, I took one swig, then another. I coughed, then cursed. Whatever this was, it was strong. Zamya was definitely going to sleep well tonight.

Me? I doubted it.

Chapter Eight

Zamya and Kobe were still sleeping when I woke. It was just after six. I hadn't slept well. As well as thoughts of Cora spiralling around my mind, I had heard Rooke return from the party at three that morning. I didn't want to know what had kept him from returning home any earlier.

Instead of staring at the slowly brightening, unfulfilling ceiling, I forced myself up. Pulling Rooke's fleeced jacket over the clothes I'd slept in, I left to find breakfast.

When I entered the food hall, Pepa gave me a heart-warming smile. I accepted her offer of cooked meats with bread, then headed to the showers. The water was cold, but it freshened my senses, shaking me free from my troubling thoughts about Cora and her secret. Leaving the Pasa, I found myself wandering along the walkway on the opposite side of the mountain gap, where I found cave openings in the rockface to a blacksmith and a clay pottery workshop.

I didn't discover what was in the third cavern further along. Voices from the clifftop above caught my attention instead, and I witnessed a young woman descending a dual width ladder. The ladder scoured the extent of the rockface from the very top to where I stood. When she reached the walkway, I could see her nose was bleeding, cupping her hand underneath in a poor attempt to stop the blood splattering on her leather clothes and onto the floor.

"Are you alright?" I asked as she strode past. She was young, about fifteen.

"Yes. This always happens at training. Nya will fix me."

I frowned, watching her stalk over the bridge to the Pasa

entrance. *Training?* I glanced up at the clifftop and, without a second thought, made for the ladder.

It was a long way up. The girl had descended so quickly, it hadn't appeared to be far. I was gasping for air by the time I reached the top.

Bending over to catch my breath, I scanned the area. A large expanse of green grass laid before me. Horses grazed on the far side where a line of trees edged the area. A handful of brown cattle and recently shaven sheep were in groups further to the right. The remnants of three burnt pyres littered the ground behind them.

Smaller trees dominated the area to the left. And that's where I saw movement. A group of people stood with bows in hand, shooting arrows towards targets I couldn't make out.

Cautiously, I walked towards the area, keeping enough distance to not draw attention. As I neared the back of the group, I could make out fifteen young girls, all dressed in different shades of leather, standing in a line, aiming arrows from large, billowing bows towards a mound of sacks placed roughly fifty metres in front of them. Bright patches of colour adorned the sacks in several places. The older girls were exceptionally good at hitting their mark. The younger ones, not so much.

I recognised Saff, Truro's sister, standing among the archers with her auburn hair tied in a messy braid. She was looking up at a tall man, continuously interrupting him while he attempted to instruct her.

She'll talk your ear off, Truro had told me. Clearly, she was not one for listening.

"You're late."

The gruff voice from behind made me jump. A short, sharp squeak launched from the back of my throat, and I turned to find Truro standing beside a tree. His arms were crossed over his chest, but his solid stance of authority was deceived by the way he was trying not to laugh. I touched my throat, my cheeks flushing with embarrassment. Had I really just squeaked at him?

"You scare easily," he said.

"You shouldn't sneak up on people."

"Sneaking? Do I look like I can sneak?"

My eyes trailed down his brown armour, over the three buckles clasping it together. I glanced at the thickset muscles of his bare arms, his slim waist, the toned, horse-riding thighs, which shaped the top of his brown leather trousers. Even his scruffy black boots oozed masculinity. I swallowed back the physical admiration for this man and shrugged. "I've seen bigger men."

He sniggered. "I bet you have."

To be fair, he wasn't a large beast of a man like Oz was. He was…rather perfect, actually.

"I mean, I wouldn't put it past you to be stealth like. You are a scout and all."

"And all," he scoffed, stepping forward. "So, were you going to join in? You seem to be hiding." His tone made me pause. It sounded playful, not irritated or curt in the way he usually addressed me.

"I, um…was interested to see what goes on at *training*."

"Well, you've missed the warmup. And the sword exercises."

"Is that how the other girl got a bloody nose?"

Truro chuckled. "Uh, no. Dawna gets nose bleeds when she gets excited. Doesn't bode well for her, really. In any life situation."

I laughed, instantly regretting it. "Poor girl."

"Come on." Truro walked past me. "I'll introduce you." He didn't look back.

Fighting the urge to follow, it took four of his strides before I gave in. There was something about him, a force that tugged at me. Nux, I'd found my idol—a true Nux warrior with the most stunning blue eyes.

He called to the man still speaking with Saff. "Jader, we have a new recruit."

The man turned in our direction, along with several of the girls. My cheeks warmed, aware all of them were staring. It was Saff who lifted the awkward tension. "Eden!" She shoved her bow at the trainer and ran towards us. I inwardly chuckled as the man rolled his eyes, sighing with exasperation.

"You made it." Saff stopped in front of me, peering up with admiration.

"I was only watching."

"But you will join us?"

"Um…"

"She'll be joining," Truro said. I snapped my eyes to him. He smirked. "I have no doubt about it." Again, he used that playful tone.

The trainer approached, still with Saff's bow in hand. Standing next to Truro, I discovered how tall he was. He was a full head taller than Truro, and Truro wasn't short. His shoulders were slimmer, but his arms were just as strong. I noticed three faint scars running across the light brown skin on his forearm—three scars similar to those on my own arm—branding him as an Igknamai survivor.

He shoved the bow back into Saff's hands. "No slacking. You have fifty rounds to complete before the end of the session."

Taking the bow back, Saff groaned, stomping back to her marker.

"Eden, this is Jader," Truro introduced him. "He's a trainer, here. He also heads up one of our hunting teams."

"I'm also his best friend." Jader elbowed Truro in the chest. "Hi, nice to finally meet you." He smiled at me, sincerity reaching up to a pair of dark brown eyes.

"Hi."

"So, this is *the* Eden?" Jader said.

"Yep," Truro replied. Both men ran their eyes over me. Uncomfortable wasn't remotely close to how I suddenly felt.

"*The Eden?*" I asked, glancing between them. "What is that supposed to mean?"

They exchanged an all knowing look. Truro shrugged, Jader chuckled awkwardly.

"Okay," I placed my hands on my hips, "you need to tell me what it is about my name that makes people either amused, excited, or concerned." I waited as they exchanged another one of those looks.

"Maybe you should tell her." Jader rubbed his hand over his shaven head.

"Maybe *you* should," Truro replied, eyeing me again. I was now standing with my arms folded across my chest, my expression expectant. "Just tell me."

Truro coughed nervously, shuffling on his feet. "It's nothing, really. There's an old prophecy we have. It suggests…ah…that, um…when Eden falls, here on Earth, another one will arrive to replace it. With your unexpected presence, we're…um, starting to wonder if it's true."

I stared at him, bemused and disturbed by his words. An unladylike snort projected from the back of my throat. I quickly cleared it and said, "If you think I have anything to do with that you are very much mistaken. And judging by what I've seen and heard about this place, the Garden of Eden was lost a long time ago."

"She has a point," Jader said, but Truro narrowed his eyes at me. Those stunning blue orbs penetrating my wavering cool exterior.

"I suppose it was just a coincidence you were the one who offered to help our people, and not your commander."

Yeah, about that… "Oh, come on," I groaned. "It's a massive coincidence my name is Eden. For all you know, it's a nickname and my given name is Trura."

A rumble of amusement emanated from Jader's chest. Pensively, Truro continued to stare, sending a bout of tiny shivers shooting through my stomach. Seriously, by the way he had me pinned, I would fear for my life if I was ever reprimanded by the head of security. His demeanour was full of hard scrutiny and unyielding authority.

He finally snapped out of it and said, "I always thought the prophecy was utter nonsense anyway. Come on," he walked towards the line of archers, "let's get you started."

Jader laughed, then gestured for me to follow. Within minutes, I was standing at the far end of the line, holding a large, wooden bow.

"Have you done this before," Jader asked, watching me like the ardent instructor he was.

"A couple of times. A while ago." I placed the feathered nock onto the string. "Back home, older children are taught archery so they can participate in the annual Nux Games. It's a bit of community fun." I raised the bow, pointing the arrow at the padded sacks metres away, then loosed it. It fell short by at least ten metres. "It appears I am out of practice."

Jader grinned and showed me improvements on my technique. After half an hour, I was feeling frustrated. I swore the target was much further away than when I'd practiced at the age of eleven. I tried again. The arrow launched but fell just short of the sack base. I huffed. My left wrist was aching, my right bicep was cramping. I was ashamed to call myself a descendant of the Nux warriors.

Picking up another arrow from the quiver on the floor beside me, I set up another shot.

"You need to raise your elbow."

Nux, he really was the definition of stealthy. I dropped the bow's tension and glanced at Truro. He was standing slightly behind me, holding a bow in his hand. Several feathered arrows poked over his shoulder where one of his swords usually sat.

"Does the target have to be so far away?" I asked.

"That's not far."

"It must be at least fifty metres."

"Sixty, in fact."

"It's too far to hit."

In an impulsive blur, Truro grabbed an arrow from his quiver, nocked and aimed it. I stared in wonderment as the arrow's feathers shuddered where the pink spot sat on my target. The sheer speed he achieved that in was phenomenal.

"Show off," I mumbled.

He looked at me, a glint of amused pride dancing in his eyes. Lowering his bow, he said, "The target is placed at that distance because, technically, that is a safe distance to shoot an Igknamai from. Any closer and you should run." He stepped towards me. His voice became softer, full of conviction. "I suppose, if an Igknamai got too close, you could stop running, meet it face on, and stab it between the eyes."

I looked at the sack of straw at the far end of the shooting range, and I was suddenly transported back to the ravine. The Igknamai had been so close that day—too close. And Truro's scouts had witnessed our struggle from the trees. The number of arrows I saw embedded in the Igknamai was evidence enough that they'd been alarmed.

I shifted my eyes back to Truro. There was a genuine look of respect on his face. It felt almost sorrowful.

"I didn't expect you to get up after that," he said.

"I have no idea what I was thinking at the time."

"It's called survivor's instinct. And you were right to listen to it." He squeezed his lips together and clapped me on the shoulder. "Keep trying. You'll get better."

By the end of the session, I was intermittently hitting the sack.

It was better than nothing. But I was adamant I'd come back another day to obliterate that sodding thing.

"We're all going to the lake," Saff said to me, as I placed my bow and quiver in a wooden crate at the edge of the shooting range. "Do you want to come?"

"Lake, you say?"

"Yes. There's a lake a mile from the village. We all use it to bathe."

I frowned. "So, you don't use the showers in the Pasa?"

"No." She scrunched her nose up in disgust. "Those things are horrid. If you prefer falling water to wash in, the lake has a waterfall."

"That does sound amazing."

"So, you'll come?"

I sighed. "Not today. I've got to stay close to the Pasa. But I will come another day, I promise."

Back at the crew house I found Zamya and Kobe sitting around the table. Glancing through the opening to the right, down the bridge to Rooke's office, I wondered if he was about, but the area looked empty.

"Ah, there you are," Zamya said. She was smiling. Far from the sobbing, angry mess she'd been last night. "These came for you."

I flicked my eyes to the table where a small pile of clothes sat upon it. Most of them looked as if they were made of leather. I frowned, stepping forward to examine them. "Where did they come from?"

"There's a lady who's visited Nya's clinic a couple of times over the past week. She works as a seamstress. I mentioned you didn't have many clothes. Today, she came over and bought us all some protective leathers to wear. She brought you a little extra."

I shuffled through the pile, finding simple shirts, a hooded top, vests, and leggings. There were even basic cotton knickers. And a lot of leather attire.

Kobe watched me as I held up a black leather jacket. It was panelled and thick, similar to what some of the girls wore at training. A hooded collar with several clasps running down the middle, and the accentuated waist flared out to mid-thigh.

Another leather garment was high necked, held together by four small buckles, with flapped shoulders. The base sat just below the waist. It was similar to Truro's armour, but far more elegant. The third piece was in the style of a leather vest, laced down the front with a thick black string. It fashioned a low neckline and thick straps. I presumed one of the shirts was meant to be worn underneath. That would be perfect for training on a hot day.

"These are great." I glanced at Zamya. "Thank you."

"Don't thank me. Thank Wilma."

"You'll have to introduce me to her." I glanced at Kobe who seemed unimpressed by it all. "Did you get any?"

"Yes. But you won't see me dead in leather."

"Tempting fate, are you?" Zamya quipped.

"Not at all. I don't intend on leaving the village unless Solarfleet arrives."

Zamya tutted and rolled her eyes.

"Any movement on Troy's position?" I asked Kobe.

He shook his head. "He's following natural orbit. I wouldn't be surprised if he's regenerating energy, ready to head home."

"He won't give up until the last minute. I know he won't."

Kobe didn't seem convinced.

"Don't give up hope, Kobe. It's all we have left."

Zamya snorted. "That, and an awful lot of leather."

The next morning, I woke and dressed in my long-sleeved leather armour. It fitted well—snug but breathable. The leather trousers were something I'd have to get used to, but I felt comfortable, protected.

I'd woken early with enough time to eat and make the training session. I snuck out the door while Kobe and Zamya slept, and, for once, I didn't glance into Rooke's office as I passed the access bridge. However, a deep, playful rumble made me stop and smile.

"Where are you going, young lady? Dressed like that?"

I looked over at Rooke. He was filling the doorway to his hut with his hubristic presence. I raised an eyebrow noticing his attire—black leather armour and trousers. It looked as though he had new boots, too. My eyes traced the shape of him, trying to bat away the undeniable attraction. Nux, he looked good, and he knew it.

He sauntered towards me along the bridge with a playful smirk on his face. "What do you think?" Lifting his arms, he came to a halt in front of me. "Can I pass as a true Redwood scout now?"

I scrunched my lips to one side, pretending to assess his appearance with scrutiny. "You don't have a sword or an archer's bow. And," I met his gaze as he stepped closer, "you may need to beef up a little more."

He chuckled at that.

"Other than your shocking horse-riding technique, I think you'll pass."

"Who says I'm bad at horse riding?"

"Oz." I laughed.

"He can talk. Anyway, my butt isn't quite so sore anymore. And I do have a sword. They don't let me bring it home...yet." His eyes sparkled down at me, and I hummed my hilarity.

Leaning back, Rooke refocused his attention on the leather around my hips. "Damn, you look good in leather." He straightened up again. "And there I was, thinking you'd be a lace kinda girl."

"I'm not wearing leather underwear, Rooke!"

He laughed. "Now you mention it, there was a time, not so long ago, you didn't wear underwear at all."

I froze for a split moment. Was he talking about the Akquarian ball? When I hadn't cared about my lack of underwear whilst I straddled him seductively? I felt the blush rise to my cheeks, noting the extra ounce of amusement dancing across his face.

Placing my hand over his mouth, I pushed him away. "You're an arsehole."

"I'm only telling the truth," he said, chuckling.

"Can you two stop with the coquettish behaviour!" Kobe stomped onto the platform, parting us as he scampered past. "Troy's changed trajectory. He's in range."

Rooke and I exchanged a tight look before following him. Kobe half walked, half ran along the bridges towards the Pasa.

"How long do we have until he's out of range?" I called to him.

He glanced at his tablet. "Twelve minutes."

I heard Rooke curse, and we picked up our speed.

Inside the Pasa, the comms room illuminated as we entered. I scurried to the comms output we had constructed, placing the headset and mic over my ear. Kobe brought the telescope data up on a screen in front of him, then flicked the satellite controls on.

Rooke hovered behind me as we waited for Kobe's command to start transmitting. He needed to align the satellite to follow The Orka's path precisely. Only then could we transmit the signal directly to the ship. But he looked as though he was struggling with the controls.

"It's not working," Kobe moaned, continuously typing into the control system.

"What's wrong?" Rooke walked over to him.

"It's moving too slowly. I can't get the satellite to catch up with The Orka."

"Keep trying."

I felt the tension in the air thicken as Kobe's typing filled the silence. He was sweating, the look of concentration etched with panic. He was desperate for this to work. We all were.

Abruptly, he slammed the desk space beside the keyboard. He shook his head. "He's gone. It's too slow. We were too late."

I slumped back in my chair. "We still have time."

"We have a day, Eden!" Kobe snapped. "He may not come back again."

"He changed The Orka's trajectory. He'll do it again."

"Eden's right." Rooke tapped Kobe on the shoulder. "We'll be ready next time."

Kobe huffed. "I hope so."

Rooke left twenty minutes later, leaving Kobe and I anxiously awaiting The Orka's return.

It did two hours later. After another failed attempt, I was starting to feel the pressure. That time, we had aligned the satellite perfectly, but there was a slim chance Troy would be listening for a microwave. There were so many forms of communication, he could be trying any of them in a desperate attempt to contact us.

We waited another few hours. It was now 5:10 in the evening. We'd be thrown out of the Pasa in the next hour or so. Waiting patiently, I twirled my thumbs around each other, trying not to think about what would happen if we didn't make contact.

"He's back," Kobe's voice penetrated the pool of silence. He shifted in his chair. "He's changed velocity."

"How so?"

"He's slowed."

"That'll make it easier." I adjusted the headset and poised my finger over the communication button. "Let's do this."

The monitor in front of me flickered to life again, and I watched the tiny green dot, representing The Orka, flash up on the screen.

"I've got a lock," Kobe announced. "Start transmitting."

Pressing the button down, I spoke into the mic, "Orka, this is groundcrew, do you copy? Troy, are you there?" I repeated the words over and over for several minutes, watching the ships position move across my screen. My stomach flopped as it drew closer to the edge. I was about to release the button, accepting defeat for the day, when a clear, recognisable voice came through my headset.

"Eden. Eden is that you?"

"Troy!" I almost cried. "Can you hear me?"

"Yes, loud and clear. Hold on."

The transmission went silent for a couple of agonising minutes after which Kobe announced, "He's changed velocity again."

Troy's voice rang in my ear. "I can only stay here for a few minutes. I'm burning through the fuel to remain in range. Where the hell are you? I've been out of my mind trying to get in contact. Why have you changed location?"

"A jamming signal stopped our radio communication. We went to repair the Parvos in the attempt to penetrate it, and we found the ship had disappeared. We made for the forest, hoping to find it. Instead, we found a human colony. They've given us sanctuary."

"Humans? So, you're safe?"

"I believe so. Although, they've asked us to help them. Rooke needs to send a message to Solarfleet."

"Solarfleet are on their way."

"They are?"

"Yes. I sent a message home as soon as you went missing. I received their reply a week or so ago. It turns out, as soon as Rooke reported back that we'd found Earth, they came after us. They're a month into the journey already."

I looked at Kobe. The relief filling his face matched my own. "That's good news. That's really good news."

"So, is everyone okay? How's Cora doing?"

I paused; my breathing faltered. Staring at the transmission screen, I couldn't find the right words. How was I going to tell him she was dead?

"Eden? Are you still there?"

"Yes…I'm here."

"Is everything okay?"

I took a deep breath, filling my body with a strange sense of courage. "Troy, there's something I need to tell you…"

Chapter Nine

The evening sun was hot as I ambled back to the crew house. A complete contrast to how I felt. Inside, I was frozen, ready to fracture into a million, tiny pieces. Every emotion left me feeling numb yet disturbingly raw. Troy hadn't taken the news about Cora well. He'd fallen silent, then started shouting, before cutting communication and reverting The Orka to normal orbital velocity. Nux, I wanted to be up there with him, to comfort him, to help him get past the grief. The pain of empathy mixed with my own suffering was too much to bear. Every vital organ hurt.

I entered the middle hut of our residence and found Oz looking menacing. Dressed in his new leathers, he was sitting at the table, sharpening a dagger.

"Is Rooke here?" I asked.

"Yeah, he's in his office." Oz watched me as I made my way to the side doorway. "Valina's in there with him." I didn't care. This couldn't wait.

I strode down the connecting bridge, announcing my arrival at the opposite end with the thud of my boots on the office floor. They both looked at me. Rooke frowned, whilst Valina just looked a little put out. She was perched on the corner of his desk, one leg crossed over the other. Rooke stood next to her browsing a large map on the worktop.

"How'd you get on?" Rooke asked, straightening up.

"We made contact."

The strain of emotion on my face must've alerted Rooke to the dire situation. "What happened?"

I glanced at Valina. She was perusing the map, but she held a certain look about her, indicating she was pretending not to listen.

"Can I speak with you alone?"

Rooke glanced back at Valina, who looked up at him and said, "Oh. Oh, don't mind me." She waved her hands suggesting we carry on as she slipped elegantly off the desk and waltzed to the front doorway. Leaning against the wall immediately outside, it was obvious she was still listening.

Rooke's concerned gaze met mine again, and I stepped closer, lowering my voice. "I told Troy about Cora. He didn't take the news well. I'm worried about him." I watched Rooke rake his hand through his hair, resting it at the base of his neck, his eyes fixed to the floor. "I think you should talk to him."

Glancing up at me, he nodded. "Of course. When is he back in range?"

"If he continues on his current trajectory, he'll pass over tomorrow around 1600 hours. It may change."

"I'll make it a priority."

"Excuse me," Valina said sweetly, stepping over the threshold, "I couldn't help overhear…"

Really? What a shocker.

"…We have a councillor here, to help with grief and loss. Maybe they could speak with him."

Rooke frowned. "Maybe that would help."

I huffed. "Rooke, he's just found out his girlfriend's dead. He doesn't need a stranger tapping into his emotions. He's alone on that huge ship. He needs a shoulder to cry on. You are his commander and you've always got on well. You *need* to talk to him."

"Maybe Rooke isn't comfortable with that type of connection."

Seriously? What made Valina think she knew Rooke better than I did? He'd consoled me through my brother's and mother's deaths. He was a great listener, an ardent adviser, and a loyal friend.

"I think you'll find he's pretty good at it." I tried to hide the growl in my voice. But obviously not enough; Rooke shot me a cold warning look.

"I'll talk to him," he said. "I'll stay in the village tomorrow, so I'll be close to the Pasa when he flies over."

I gave him an appreciated look. "I'll let Kobe know."

We stared at each other for a few seconds longer.

"Is there anything else?" he asked.

I felt my strength crumbling. Inside, I was a distraught mess. I needed him to hold me, but how was I supposed to admit that when Valina stood two metres away. I shook my head and left.

As I staggered back along the interconnecting bridge, I heard Valina say, "Do you always allow her to speak to you in that way?"

I didn't hear Rooke's response, but I felt a sudden urge to scream. Who did she think she was? How dare she not give Rooke and I five minutes alone to talk. She'd monopolised his time all day, every day. She was the new Havav, and I found her *irritating!*

My breathing became tight and aggravated. I stomped past Oz and headed back to the Pasa. My intention was to find Zamya. At least she'd humble me with some sympathy. But my feet didn't take me to the Pasa. At the edge of the village, I found I'd travelled over the opposing bridge—the one where the ladder to the east clifftop adorned the rockface. Without a second thought, I climbed the slatted steps.

At the top, the cattle and sheep were still grazing to the right. A larger number of horses stood majestically on the grassed area directly in front. I marched over to the trees to the left, to where I'd practiced archery yesterday. The area was empty, although I could hear the clash of swords nearby.

Glancing further to the left, a suspension bridge swung gently in the breeze. I hadn't noticed it before. It connected this side of the flat mountainous rock to the other side, where the Pasa sat embedded underneath. Two men were sparring among a cluster of small trees. An orchard lay behind them, and a vast area of cultivated crops swayed in the distance to the right. Two rustic looking wind turbines whirled in the distance, where a satellite dish sat in between the patchwork metallic towers, pointing into space.

I wandered back to the archery field, noticing a bow and several arrows strewn on the floor next to one of the many trees. Picking them up, I headed to a marker.

The anger and grief-stricken frustration gave me strength. I was firing the arrows with such determination, I hit the sack base every time. Cora filled my thoughts. Troy, too. My heart bled for them. I needed to cry, to scream! I despised feeling this useless. I couldn't help either of them.

Releasing the arrow with such an aggressive effort, I grunted.

The arrow still didn't land on the coloured spots, frustrating me further.

"You're still dropping your elbow."

Heart pounding, I twirled, finding Truro standing behind me. His arms and clothes were covered in red dust. Red specks sat in his hair, changing the colour entirely. Movement in the distance behind him caught my attention. Several scouts were making their way back to the clifftop ladder. They must've just returned from a scouting trip.

Truro glanced about. "Is someone with you?"

I shook my head.

"You shouldn't be here on your own." Surprisingly, his tone wasn't scorning. It was edged with a compassionate concern. Maybe I looked so damned agonised that he could read me like an open book. "Even though we're safe up here from the Igknamai, the Hybrids sometimes make an appearance. You must always come up with an armed buddy."

"I'm sorry." Shamefully, I looked away. "I didn't think. I just…I just needed some space…to clear my head."

Truro stepped closer. "I can understand that. I've seen enough loss to tell you're grieving."

I met his blue gaze. He looked so young, yet his empathy was forged from experience, from a lifetime of hardship and war.

"The girl who fell in the ravine," he asked gently, "were you close?"

"I'd only known her for seven months. But yes…she'd become like a little sister to me." I took in a huge breath, thinking of Cora's terrified face seconds before Oz ended her torment. "I couldn't save her." Pulling the arrow string back, I positioned the bow. The remorse boiling up inside of me needed release. I was determined to gut that sack at the other end of the field. I wanted to make it pay.

A gentle warmth touched my elbow, raising it slightly.

"You need to keep your elbow higher."

Nux, I hadn't heard or seen him move. He was the epitome of stealth.

He shifted behind me as I held my position. Touching my chin, he pushed it up a fraction. "Keep your face and eyes in line with the arrowhead." My breath hitched as his right arm rounded my waist.

His hand pushed on my stomach, grazing his palm from one side to the other. "Make these muscles taut, as if they are ready to snap." His other hand gently cupped my aiming fist and raised it an inch higher. "Add height to compensate for the distance." His breath was fluttering against my ear as he said, "Now release."

I did, and the arrow hit the sack in the middle of the pink spot. A smile graced my lips, and I looked back at him. "As easy as that, huh?"

He walked around me, cocking his head. "Add a little more practice and well, you have potential. Does this mean you'll be joining training?"

I dropped my gaze to my hands gripping the bow. "Is training every day?"

"Yes. Not everyone attends daily but one of the trainers will always be here to instruct."

"Maybe I will."

A low horn sounded in the distance drawing my attention away from Truro.

"I'm afraid you'll have to wrap it up for today. That's the five-minute warning before the bridges are drawn in for the night. And I have a council meeting to get to."

"Right. Sure." I quickly jogged the sixty metres to the sack and collected my arrows. On my return, Truro took them and placed them in his own quiver. We casually walked back to the cliff edge side by side.

"These council meetings," I questioned, "does Rooke attend every one of them?"

Truro glanced at me. "Yes. As we have formed a partnership, Valina suggested he should be informed of all developments on any front."

"Is she in charge? I mean, she seems to have the aura of the village oracle about her. She doesn't look old enough."

"Wow, she'd love that status." Truro chuckled. "No, she's not in charge. All seven council members are. But, Elgin and Blake do have to rein Valina back in on the odd occasion. But she's good at what she does. She keeps the peace. Whereas I like killing monsters." He paused pensively, before saying, "She's twenty-six. Not sure how old you have to be to be called an oracle, and frankly, she'll never be given that title. It would go to her head."

"Still, she's pretty young to be a leader."

He shrugged. "Not necessarily. People don't last long here. The average life expectancy is thirty-eight."

"Thirty-eight?" *Shit.*

"Don't tell me what the Alluran average is."

"A lot more than that."

"I said don't tell me." He shot me a defiant look, followed swiftly by a dashing smile. "Don't get me wrong, there are plenty of people here older than that. Elgin is forty-eight. Although, I believe the injury to his leg saved him from a younger fate. He was near death after a Hybrid attack disabled him. But the standard Redwood soldier won't see past their thirty-eighth birthday. Theoretically, I've already lived half my life."

I frowned. "How old are you?"

He raised his eyebrows and peered down at me. A moment of silence passed between us before he gazed ahead and said, "Twenty-three."

Whoa! He was younger than I thought. "That's...that's young."

"You and your commander can't be far from that."

"A bit older, but Rooke only leads a small crew. Not an entire army." I peered up at him as we came to a stop at the cliff edge. "Are you really only twenty-three?"

He smirked to himself. "Why, is it a problem?"

"No, I...you're just...so young."

The red dust in his hair and around his face shone in the evening sun, emphasizing the brightness of his eyes. He gazed at me, pinning me in place. Eventually he smirked. "I'm old enough." He turned and descended the ladder.

When I returned home, Rooke had already been summoned to the council meeting. Concern and intrigue consumed me. I got the impression from Truro that Valina wasn't the epitome of perfection she portrayed herself to be. It was clear she'd taken an instant liking to Rooke, and considering her reluctance to leave us alone this afternoon, I worried she may now have the upper hand with him. Either Valina had genuinely sunk her claws into him, or Rooke was passively in control of the situation.

Either way, he didn't return until after I'd fallen asleep.

Chapter Ten

"Okay, team meeting." Drenched in rainwater, Rooke strode in through the doorway of the middle hut. It was pouring outside. The air was edged with a chill, and being up so high, the whirling wind was a little disconcerting, if not terrifying.

The floor creaked as we all took a seat, squeezing around the small wooden table in the centre of the room.

"We've been here two weeks now," Rooke said, wiping the raindrops from his face with his hands, "and I realise we haven't had much time together to voice any concerns." He looked at Zamya. "Zam? Anything?"

"No concerns here."

"Really?"

"Yes." Zamya huffed. "I feel fairly content. We're not restricted or faced with animalistic sadists every day. I feel comfortable."

"Good." Rooke looked at me. "As we're going to be here for a few months, we each need to play our part in the society cycle and find a job. Oz and I will continue to scout for the Parvos…"

"Is that necessary?" Kobe asked, sharply. "Solarfleet are on their way. We have a reliable comms link to Troy. We don't need the ship."

Rooke stared at Kobe, unimpressed with his bitter tone. "If the Parvos is in the hands of the Hybrids, it would be best to remove it from their grasp. Who knows what they're using the tech for? Also, if we find it, it may give us an indication of where their lair is located."

They stared at each other for an uncomfortable moment. Kobe eventually looked away. To be honest, I agreed with Kobe. Rooke and Oz were putting themselves at unnecessary risk by going out every day. We'd already heard of seven people being killed by the Igknamai in the past week.

"The regulations state everyone needs to work twenty-five hours per week in an essential job. Zam, I assume you're happy to continue with Nya at the medical centre."

"Yep. No problem."

"Kobe, Quinn or Blake could do with your expertise. Just try not to treat the other workers like they're mentally impaired."

Kobe sighed his annoyance.

"Eden, I'm not sure what you'd like to do."

"Do you not want me coming out with you?"

Rooke paused, his eyes roaming my face. "I'd rather you stay here. Keep an eye on things from this angle."

I nodded. I didn't necessarily like it, but it was a valid point. "I'm sure I'll find something to do."

"Are we allowed to leave the village?" Zamya chirped.

"What for?" Rooke eyed her sceptically.

Zamya gave me a quick glance. "There's a lake. Everyone keeps mentioning it. It's where they all go to wash."

"And swim," I added.

Rooke looked at Zamya, then back to me. A frown was forming on his brow. "I'd rather you stay here, where it's safe."

"Are you kidding me?" Zamya gave Rooke one of her pointed scowls. "We might as well be back at the Akquarian fortress if those are your orders."

"You just said you're far happier here."

"Still. I've made some friends, and they frequent the lake. I'd like to join them occasionally. And a decent place to wash is more than desired."

"I second that," I said quietly.

"There are showers in the Pasa, and a stream to the east of the village."

"The showers are crap," Zamya interrupted, "and I don't particularly want to start undressing where the Redwoods collect their drinking water."

Rooke sighed, sitting back in his chair. The raindrops in his beard and hair glistened in the grey light. He looked soaked through. "I don't want anything to happen to either of you. The Igknamai are everywhere."

"Yet, you allow yourself and Oz to leave the safety of the village every day." Zamya folded her arms.

Rooke flicked his gaze to me. I was peering at him under my dark lashes, watching the tension grow. I could tell he was waging an internal battle of wills.

Pinching the bridge of his nose, he sighed. "Okay, okay. You may leave. BUT…only to go to the lake, and you must be armed. Or even better, armed and with someone who knows how to kill those beasts."

"You are very kind." Zamya smiled, sarcasm ringing through her tone.

"To be honest, I'm not happy about it."

"I appreciate your unhappiness makes me happy. If we ever get home, I will make a point of providing HR with a five-star rating in regard to your command."

Rooke huffed his irritation and glanced at me. I tried not to chuckle as I offered him a look of appreciation.

After training the following day, I made for Pepa's kitchen. She was elated when I asked if she needed any help. I figured working in food was an essential job.

I became a waitress, ushering the food orders to tables and tidying up once the patrons left. I enjoyed it. Everyone was friendly and it kept my mind occupied.

Over the next two weeks this became my daily routine: I'd get up early, attend training for two hours, shower, get dressed, and work at the food hall until mid-afternoon. Occasionally, I stayed later to help with the late afternoon rush. I'd then either speak with Troy over the comms, if he was in range, or head to the lake, weather permitting.

With our new routines in place, I still saw Zamya and Kobe often. Oz only seemed to be home in the evenings. And Rooke; well, I barely saw him. Even Oz made a comment about Valina's persistence to see him. I couldn't believe every evening was taken up by a council meeting, which created a recurring swell of jealousy to form in the pit of my stomach.

Zamya and I had ventured to the lake a few times together. The mile stretch of secluded, glistening turquoise water did not disappoint. Trees loomed on the steep clifftops encircling the site, shading areas from the intense sun. The water was surrounded by a sandy beach on three sides. The fourth was lined with large boulders at the base of the rockface, where a glorious waterfall poured down from a flowing river high above. The area was breath-taking.

Heavily guarded, the upper edges were patrolled by Redwood warriors. More stood guard where an opening in the rock formed an access point to the attraction.

When we first arrived, the only issue Zamya and I had, was the embarrassment of undressing in front of each other. After the third time, I no longer cared. Everyone was naked and there was enough space to avoid people if I wanted seclusion.

Following a large group of armed women and children home, Zamya and I returned from the lake late one afternoon. The garrison platform appeared up ahead and both Zamya and I froze at what we saw below it. Standing near the base of the tree lift, dressed in their dark, fish scaled armour, was a platoon of blonde, broad shouldered Akquarian warriors.

I pulled Zamya behind one of the huge tree trunks, shielding our presence from their view.

"What are they doing here?" Zamya hissed.

I peered around the bark, spotting Truro, armed to the teeth, standing with a stern look of dominance on his face. Valina came into view. She was walking towards us. Her hands gestured as she spoke, a charming smile spreading across her face. My breath caught when I noticed who she was talking with.

Dashing back behind the tree, I tried to calm myself. "Dybgo's here."

Zamya cursed, squeezing my hand. "What do they want?"

I grabbed my left wrist, where the golden bracelet had once sat irritating my skin. The past four weeks had been blissfully uneventful. I hadn't missed any part of the Akquarian's hospitality. I felt safe here. But a sudden doubt dawned upon me. What if we couldn't trust the Redwoods?

I peered around the rugged bark again. Still in conversation, Valina and Dybgo had stopped walking. *What I'd give to be a fly buzzing around them right now.*

Minutes dragged by, but eventually a band of Redwood warriors escorted the Akquarians away from the village. We didn't move from our hiding spot until we'd lost sight of them. Only then did I feel my pulse recover, my breathing stabilising. "I need to find Rooke."

"Good luck with that," Zamya mumbled.

Peering towards the tree lift, Valina and Truro were conversing by the opening. Neither one looked happy. *Sod it.* I didn't care if they knew I'd seen them with the Akquarians. I started marching towards them, ignoring Zamya's groan as she reluctantly followed.

As I approached, the two council members fell silent, and I got trapped in Truro's blue gaze. His look was stern, unreadable.

"Eden!" Valina flashed an awkward smile. "How are you today?"

Breaking my stare with Truro, I looked at her. She was slightly shorter than I was, and so damn immaculate in every sense, from her flawless pale skin to her spotless black clothes. Not a single blonde hair stood out of place. Nux, I loathed her. "I'm feeling a little pissed off this afternoon. So, I strongly advise you get out of my way."

The glare she threw me was as cold as snow on a frozen lake, but I held my own. It didn't take long for her to buckle. Raising her head an inch higher, she stepped aside, presenting me with an exaggerated, fake smile. As I passed her, I noted the spark of respect in Truro's eye. I could've sworn a hint of a smile began to form in the corner of his mouth.

After gaining entrance to the village, Zamya and I took the shortest route to our lodgings. Thankfully, Rooke was in his office, collating information from his tablet onto the large map spread out on his desk. He looked up when I entered and smiled. "Hey you."

"The Akquarians were here."

His amiable expression instantly shifted to one full of alarm. "When?"

"Just now. We saw them leaving. Looks like Valina and Truro were playing host."

"Doesn't mean they were here because of us."

A shaky sigh escaped me. I hadn't realised how tense I'd become.

Rooke stood up, rounding the desk, reaching for my hand. "The Akquarians washed their hands of us, remember. Why would they want us back?"

Panic surged through my veins. The thought of Dybgo sent tremors of dread through every inch of my body. I hadn't realised how much his demands and proposals scared the shit out of me. "I didn't tell you before." My voice was a shaky whisper as I met Rooke's gaze. "Dybgo tried to convince me to leave with him, just before the attack. Just before…" Blinking rapidly, I shook my head. "I should've known they were planning something."

"That wasn't your fault, Eden."

"What if that trap was set in the hope I'd return to the fortress while the rest of you were disposed of? What if you were right about them having a plan for me? Nux, I don't mean to sound so self-obsessed because I know this isn't just about me, but what if?" Rooke stepped closer. "I don't want to go back. I can't."

He wrapped his strong arms around me. I pushed my eyes against the crook of his neck, meeting the pulse of his heart. It was steady, calming. Taking a long, deep breath, my senses filled with his comforting scent.

"You're overthinking this." Rooke's voice was as soft as a purr. "The Redwoods wouldn't sell us out. They need us. I would never cooperate if they handed you over to those bastards. I'd never let them take you."

I tried to form a response, but nothing came. Sinking further into his embrace, I felt safe. He had been my idea of home for so many years. Nux, I'd promised myself not to think of him this way. He was a friend, nothing more. But who was I kidding? I wanted so much more from him. I needed him. He was my everything. I loved him beyond reason.

I skipped training the next morning.

At 1100 hours I went to work. As always Pepa greeted me with her warm hands cupping my face and a peck on both cheeks. She frowned. "You look tired, mi amor. Do you need a day off?"

"No. No. Working will do me good."

She gave me a compassionate smile and took my hand. "Nicoletta isn't working today. You can come help me in the kitchen." She led me round the back of the metal counter. It was hot this side. I was glad I chose to wear a thin maroon shirt and my leggings; I would've melted in my leathers.

I began chopping vegetables, listening to Pepa's flutters of song. When she appeared next to me with more vegetables, I was astounded at how efficient she was at cutting them.

"How do you do that so fast?" I asked.

"Experience." She held up one of her fingers. It was moderately shorter than it was supposed to be. "Unfortunately, like any task involving knives, if you make mistakes, you pay the consequences."

I grimaced. "Ouch."

She tittered, continuing with her speedy work.

After yesterday, I had a lot playing on my mind. Could I trust these people? The intuitive part of my brain screamed that I could. I trusted Pepa. She was like a warm-hearted grandmother who fed the whole village.

"Pepa? What do you know of the Akquarians?"

She whistled, rolling her eyes back. "They're a bunch of hoity, self-righteous misogynists, who think they rule over everything."

"So, they're not seen as allies?"

"Pffft. The amount of trouble we get from them. There have been an awful lot of wars between their kind and ours. Thankfully, not in my lifetime. But plenty in my parents' and grandparents' eras."

"Wars over what?"

"Land, boundaries. They don't allow us to fish in *their* ocean." She shook her head. "A long time ago our ancestors waged war on them over the number of women they took from us."

"Took?"

"Maybe that's the wrong word," Pepa mused. "They used to coerce and woo our young women when they walked to and from the village. They claim to believe in some spiritual nonsense about foreseeing a union between our two kinds. It's all a ruse to cover the fact they were drugging our women with their lies. They have a lack of females, themselves."

"Yes, I am aware of that."

"For a long time, they used our women for breeding. Almost as bad as those Hybrid monsters." She tutted, shaking her head in disgust. "After convincing a young woman to leave the village, sometimes offering her father traded goods in return, the Akquarian lover would take his chosen mate back to their fortress. The woman would return six months, sometimes a couple of years later, confirming they'd given birth but had to leave the babe with the

Akquarians. They were never the same afterwards, as if their spirit had been broken."

I thought back to the claiming bracelet and Dybgo's proposal. Is that what he sought from me? He'd tried to woo me by saying all the right things a woman wanted to hear, when it's likely all he wanted was to mate with me.

"Does it still happen?"

"No, thankfully. A treaty was put in place a couple of centuries ago. Apparently, it keeps both sides happy."

I frowned at that comment, wondering what deal had been put in place. "Do the Akquarians come to the village at all?"

"I see them occasionally. They only ever come here to meet with the high council. Not often. They don't like to venture this far into the forest for safety reasons. Although, it never stopped them when they wanted our women, did it?"

That didn't calm my concern. It may have been a coincidence, but if they only met with the council on the odd occasion, why had they been here yesterday? I needed to find out.

I didn't push Pepa anymore on the subject. I'd ask more questions tomorrow when there wasn't a sudden influx of customers.

The lunchtime rush passed in a blur of food orders. My hands were sore from the chopping, cooking, and washing up. And my feet were killing me. Wiping the sweat from my forehead with my sleeve, Pepa tapped me on the back and said, "Go take a break. You've worked hard."

Relief washed over me, and I smiled my thanks. After pouring myself a mug of fruit tea, I ambled through the busy food hall to the decking outside. Taking a seat at an empty table, I leant back and sighed, rotating my ankles to ease the ache from taking hold. Closing my eyes, I soaked up the gentle rays peeking through an ominous looking cloud.

"Hard day?"

The familiar male voice made me flinch, causing my knee to bump the table, nearly toppling my tea over. My eyes found the brown leather of his armour first, then the assault of daggers across his chest, before locking with his blue eyes. "In comparison to your days in general, I'm sure mine is rather trivial."

He gave me a soft smile and pointed to the clay dish he was holding in his hands. "Do you mind if I join you?"

I sat a little taller, trying to hide the uncertainty in my voice. "Sure. Why not?" Watching him take a seat opposite, he hesitated to start eating. I realised I was scowling at him. Checking myself, I quickly flicked my eyes to the trees and sipped on my tea.

"You weren't at training this morning," he said, beginning to cut into his food.

"I didn't fancy it today." I began to wonder why he was here. Pepa had mentioned most of the council members, other than Quinn, didn't tend to dine here, and I'd never seen Truro take lunch here before. Was he checking up on me?

I watched him tucking into his food in the same way Oz did; as if he was starved. But he did it in a far tidier fashion than Oz. Inwardly, I smiled. There was something strangely intimate about watching someone eat.

He realised my attention and paused. "You're making me nervous."

I laughed. "Me? Making you nervous? That's a turn of the cards."

"How? Do I scare you?"

My eyes traced the contours of his tanned face, the strong, stubbled jaw; over his armoured chest and muscular arms. No, he didn't scare me. He did, however, intrigue me. I swallowed back the thought. "No. But can you be honest with me?"

"Certainly." There was no hesitation.

"Have you been employed to watch me?"

His fork was hovering near his mouth. Dropping it back to the dish, he frowned. He genuinely looked shocked, perhaps offended. "No. Why'd you say that?"

I glanced through the huge open doorway, over to the kitchen counter beyond. Following my line of sight, he smiled to himself, and a dash of pink tinted the area around his cheekbones. "Did Pepa tell you I don't eat here often?"

"She did mention you rarely come to the food hall."

"And because of that, you think I'm spying on you?"

I shrugged. "You tell me." I was hoping it was my paranoia playing havoc with my initiative. Deep down, I wanted to trust him.

Sitting back, his eyes met mine. He tapped the end of the fork on the table, then shifted in his seat. "If you want to know the truth…yes, I came here today to see you. I missed you at training. Jader tells me you've improved considerably in all areas. I was disappointed not to witness it for myself. And, well, after yesterday, I got the impression you were a little…agitated. I wanted to check you were alright."

I wanted to smile at his sweet candour, but I forced myself not to. Instead, I flattened my tone, "Why were the Akquarians here yesterday?"

He swallowed a mouthful of food before replying, "Negotiations."

"About?"

"Many things." I drowned in the colour of his eyes as he searched my own. He knew I was concerned about their appearance. He'd known yesterday. "Your crew's custody was brought up. We quickly shut their claim down. They seemed upset that you were now residing with us."

"Are you being serious? They tried to kill us."

"Apparently, the attack was not premeditated by themselves."

I grumbled my disagreement.

"They claimed their wretched Hybrid set up the attack. As a game. To see how robust you all were. They seemed displeased with him."

What the hell? I stared at Truro in disbelief. I felt sick.

"That demonic bastard will be the downfall of the Akquarians. They're deluded to trust him."

"I was under the impression they could control him."

"Not at all. He simply pays homage to them for his own convenience. He's looked upon as a deity by the Akquarians. Whereas, if he decided to approach his kind, he would be seen as a lesser hybrid or an outcast."

"Why?"

"Because he's half Akquarian, not human."

"So, you're telling me, the Hybrids have never snatched an Akquarian female to breed with?"

"They've never had the opportunity to."

"Because they're locked away behind the walls of the fortress."

"Exactly. Essentially, keeping them prisoner to protect them."

Wow. I guess that makes sense.

"Anyway," Truro said, "Valina sent Dybgo away happy. I doubt he'll disturb us again anytime soon."

With a sense of relief, I dwelled on his comment. "Maybe I owe Valina an apology for my abrupt behaviour yesterday."

"Nah." He noticed my quizzical expression. "She needs a bit of competition."

"Competition?"

"Quinn and I joke that she looks at herself as the current saviour of our people. Basically, a mortal goddess. Well," he shrugged, "since your arrival, that's what everyone's been saying about you."

Wait! What?

"By no means should you bow down to her. It'll go to her head." He shovelled another scoop of food into his mouth, then pointed to the dish with his fork. "This is really good. Do you want a bite?"

I eyed the half-eaten potato-topped pie. It did look good. Balancing some on the end of his fork, Truro offered me a sample. I leant forward, taking the fork into my mouth. My eyes closed as the delicious taste burst onto my tongue. Savouring it, I slid my lips off the fork slowly. On opening my eyes, I found Truro watching me. Something like arousal twinkling in his gaze.

Like I said, there was something rather intimate about watching someone eat.

It was late when I headed home. The bridges were being hauled in and it was raining again. Arms laden with dinner, courtesy of Pepa, I entered our middle hut.

"That smells amazing," groaned Oz. His large form loomed over me as I placed the heavy clay dish on the table.

"I've got enough for everyone. Is Kobe about?"

"I'll go get him," Zamya said, disappearing out the front door to our sleeping hut.

"What about Rooke?"

"He's…um…he's…in there." I looked back at Oz and found him gesturing towards the closed side door, where the bridge leading to Rooke's office was accessed. There was something about Oz's stance that suggested he felt uncomfortable about mentioning it.

Eying him sceptically, I walked over to the door and hauled it open. The rain pelted my face and arms as I glanced along the bridge into the warmly lit hut opposite. The sound of a woman laughing caught my attention and Valina came into view. Completely oblivious to my presence, she gracefully walked over to Rooke's desk and perched on the edge. Only wearing a black vest top and a pair of black knickers, her hair looked a little ruffled, her cheeks flushed. She took a swig from the bottle she was clutching, before offering it to someone in the corner, nearest to the open doorway.

Rooke emerged, swaggering towards her. He was shirtless. His bare back a mass of lean muscles and smooth, honey coloured skin. Valina laughed, tipping her head back as he approached her. Pushing her buttocks back onto the desk with a firm grip around her hips, Rooke opened his mouth, allowing Valina to tip the contents of the bottle into it. In the next instant Valina was licking the rogue drops from his chin, then his lips, whilst her legs encircled his waist.

I suddenly felt violently sick. Every ounce of jealousy I had caged up deep inside was fighting its way to the surface. I could cope with the endless stream of girlfriends, but this...this was agony. I now knew how his lips tasted, how his body felt against mine. I'd concluded he'd stopped our moment of intimacy because of his loyalty to the current girlfriend. That obviously wasn't the case now that he was fraternising with Valina.

The raw, relentless thought made my chest tighten and my gut twist. I was nothing more than a drunken mistake to him. NOTHING!

I stepped back, allowing the door to shut the scene away from view. For a brief moment, I stared at the wooden panelled door, trying to ease my irregular breathing. Shifting my eyes to the floor, I turned back to the table. I knew Oz was watching me. He wasn't stupid. He knew my reaction wasn't from general surprise. But I couldn't hide the pain from my expression; couldn't keep the raging spite from resounding in my voice as I said, "I haven't got enough food for Valina. We'll have to eat without him."

Oz stood next to me, readying the clay bowls. "More for me then." He smiled, attempting to ease the awkwardness, but it eased nothing. He continued to glance at me as I distributed the stew. I remained silent, relieved to hide behind Zamya and Oz's bantering when she finally returned with Kobe.

After dinner, I went straight to bed.

Chapter Eleven

It was my day off work. Waking early, and without a word to anyone, I left for training. I fought the urge to look in Rooke's hut on my way past. Oz had slept in the middle hut all night. I didn't need to question why.

Up on the clifftop, an unexpected pang of delight fizzled through me when I saw Truro standing with Jader. His eyes instantly found me. "Glad to see you made the effort today," he called in jest. "Why don't you show me what I missed out on yesterday."

Jader had deemed me an adequate ground archer. I could now hit a specified coloured target on demand, even when moving. The next stage was to shoot an object from horseback. It was difficult, ridiculously so. There was no saddle to cling to, no stirrups to balance on. Training had become hard work, but it had become my sanctuary. And I was determined to succeed.

While Jader instructed the ground archers, Truro took me to the far side of the grazing field, where he placed reins on a brown mare; Io was her name.

All of the horses were large, far larger than the ones my mum had trained back home. They were heftier, more robust. I mounted Io, and as I attempted to find a comfortable seat upon her back, Truro handed me my bow. A mass of arrows sat snug in the quiver behind me.

"Where do you want me to aim?" I asked.

He pointed to a line of trees edging the cliff. Not where the village sat, but to the east, where a stream flowed a long way below. "Any of those trees will do."

I warmed the horse up, rounding the large field to gain speed and rhythm. Clenching my thighs against her back, I raised the bow, aiming its arrow for the treeline. I missed.

I wasn't successful for the full two hours of training.

Truro sensed my frustration as we walked back to the cliff edge. "It will come with practice. I'll stay with you a few times this week if you like, for additional training sessions. I bet you'll have it figured at by the end of the week."

I didn't hesitate to accept.

Over the next few days, I trained for an hour with Jader, then joined a sword sparring team, who were instructed by a young woman called Wrenn. I had practiced a few times with her. Jader already seemed impressed with my swordsmanship, albeit using a wooden substitute. I had no idea where I got the knack for sword fighting from. It wasn't something anyone did on modern day Allura.

Once the rest of the trainees left for the day, Truro would meet me on the far side of the field. Today was the fifth consecutive day we met.

After helping me up onto the same brown mare, Truro said, "You do realise Jader sees a potential hunter in you."

I looked down at him as he handed me my archer's bow. "He did mention something last week."

"Would you want to? Join a hunting team and go out every day?"

I'd already thought about it. Working in the kitchen kept me occupied but it wasn't rewarding. Hunting would give me the stimulation I sought, a sense of worth. There would be a significant risk with going out into Igknamai territory, but I'd been trained how to kill them effectively. "I think I would."

"Is Rooke aware of your ambition?" Truro was staring at me. His eyes wider than usual, anticipating my reply.

"No." I looked down at my hands wrapped up in the horse's reins. Rooke wouldn't approve, I knew that much. "And I want it to remain that way. He doesn't need to know."

"Very well. I won't say a word."

I peered at him. Strangely, his stern expression felt soothing. Deep down I knew I could trust him.

He smacked the horse's backside and she leapt into a full canter. Rounding the field, we passed Truro for the fourth time.

"Are you going to shoot an arrow at some point today?"

I ground my teeth together. I knew he was teasing, but I felt exasperated with my lack of ability to feel comfortable riding my horse bareback. I tightened my core, clenching my legs against the horse's bulbous body. Feeling a little disoriented, I aimed, held my breath, and fired.

A loud curse carried over me before I had the chance to lower my bow. Searching for Truro, I realised he'd moved position. Shit, I'd nearly hit him.

"What was that?" he barked, clearly unimpressed.

"Shit…I…you moved!"

"You should always be aware of your surroundings."

"I know!"

"What type of goddess are you if you start shooting down your own people?"

I pulled Io to a halt and glared at him. "I'm not a goddess, Truro!"

He chuckled, walking towards me. "You sure as hell look like one up there."

"No, I don't! I'm a total mess, and I really wish you would stop with the prophecy crap. I'm not a goddess. I'm not a god send, nor *the* Eden. I'm just me. And you sure as hell know how to put pressure on someone."

Holding my gaze, his eyes softened, the vivid blue shooting sparks of electricity through every waking nerve. He came to a stop beside the horse. "I'm sorry. I was only teasing."

Scrunching my lips to one side, I took a deep breath. Truro began to chuckle. "You did nearly kill me, though."

I huffed a smile. "Nux. I have no intention of killing you, I swear." And I meant it. For the past week, he was the only one providing me with a purpose to wake every morning. It was Truro who was paying me the attention I needed. With him around, I forgot the trauma of losing Cora, I forgot my troubles with Rooke, and that was a huge step forward for me.

"Try again." He slapped Io's hind and she reared, then accelerated away. I was determined to prove I could do this. I wanted that hunting job.

Realigning the horse, I scanned my target, keeping an eye on Truro's position. I tensed my leg muscles, rising out of my seat slightly, then aimed. With a sense of assurance, I released the arrow, watching it fly. But I felt the horse slip from beneath me, and the next thing I knew, I was looking up at the cloudless sky with an immense pain paralysing my back. I wheezed, trying to blink the stars out of my vision. *What the hell happened?*

A figure appeared above me, blotting out the sun, and I heard Truro's calm voice. "Are you alright?"

"Yeah," I wheezed. "I think so. Just…give me a minute."

"Your arrow hit the tree."

"Did it?" I tried to smile. "Amazing."

My sarcasm made him chuckle and he stepped away. "You need to strengthen your thigh muscles. The stronger they are, the easier it's for you to stay seated."

"I am trying."

"You know, there's a really enjoyable exercise you can partake in, that'll help with that."

I laid there in the dry grass, catching my breath. It took a few moments for the penny to drop. I pushed myself up onto my elbows and peered at him. "Are you being rude?"

A devilish grin softened the planes of his face. "If you think sex is rude, then, yeah. I guess I am."

I scoffed and he offered me his hand. Helping me to my feet, he said. "It's just a suggestion."

"And who, exactly, do you suggest I do that with?"

He just stared at me, now with the faintest hint of a smirk on his lips. My mind suddenly flashed to images of his body pressed up against mine…

Nux, what the hell?

Aware my cheeks were blushing, I tutted, and ambled after my horse. My back was killing me, but I was determined to hit my target without any more distractions.

The day became unbearably hot. By the time I'd finished my shift at Pepa's Kitchen, I was a sweaty mess. With every intention of heading to the lake to cool down, I went home to change into my leathers. Passing the hut's external bridge, I commended myself for not attempting to look into Rooke's office.

"Eden?" Rooke's rumble sent unwanted flurries of butterflies through my stomach, halting my steps. We'd hardly seen each other since the night Valina stayed. I'd made a conscious effort to keep it that way.

"Yeah?" I called out, keeping my feet solidly planted on the spot.

"Can you come here?"

A short, sharp sigh expelled from my lungs. Turning on my heel, I walked across the bridge, holding my nerve. I could see him leaning over the large map on his desk. Nux, he wasn't wearing a shirt. I took a deep breath attempting to retain my composure.

Glancing up as I entered, he straightened, propping himself up with rigid arms against the edge of the desk. I swallowed back the desire. His body was beautiful. Light, lean contours of muscle framed his abdomen and chest. His skin glistened with a shimmer of sweat, and the black tattoo on his left shoulder lured my eyes towards it, tempting them to trace the intricate pattern up his left bicep, across his collar bone. He'd cut his hair and shaved his beard, now fashioning only a day's growth. He looked like Rooke again. My Rooke.

"I haven't seen you for a while," he said.

"I've been keeping myself busy."

He gave me an awkward smile. "Thought I'd let you know, Solarfleet have replied to my latest message."

"What did they say?"

"They're being rather ambiguous with their answer. Although I've made the situation clear, they want to witness it for themselves before they commit to helping these people." He sighed. "I'm trying to keep the council oblivious to the debate."

I cursed inwardly. "Who have Solarfleet sent?"

"General Murai. I've worked under her command before. She's a fair leader."

"That's all we can ask for then, I guess." I prayed she'd make a rational decision when she arrived, one that morally helped the Redwoods without casting me into the flames of hell.

Sensing my worry, Rooke eyed me and rounded the desk. With a double take, I gaped at the sight of him. He looked like he was wearing shorts, but they appeared to be his Solarfleet combat pants. They'd been torn just below the knee, displaying a jagged, uneven line.

"What did you do?" My voice was full of amusement.

He glanced at his shorts. "Ah, I got hot."

"There are people in the village who make clothes."

"Yeah, I know." He laughed. "I know."

I watched him perch on the edge of the desk in front of me. The same place I saw Valina wrap her legs around him not six days past. The sudden pang of jealousy made me feel sick, and I realised Rooke was frowning at me.

"Do we need to talk?"

Taken aback by the comment, I returned the frown. "About what?"

"I don't know. I never see you anymore. You're always up and gone before I wake. I'm concerned you've been working all hours of the day because...well, it feels like...you're avoiding me."

How was it possible he knew me so well but was oblivious to my feelings for him? I glanced up at the pitched ceiling above us choosing my words. "I prefer to keep myself busy. Otherwise...my brain tends to go into a depressive overload. The loss of Cora and Sym play on my mind. The whole situation plays on my mind." It wasn't a lie, just not the whole truth.

He stared at me for a moment before nodding. "Make sure you do get some rest."

"Sure." Wiping my sweaty forehead with the back of my hand, I tried to change the subject. "I was just on my way to the lake." Refocusing my gaze on him, he was staring pensively at the floor between us. He was right, I'd been avoiding him and perhaps that was a selfish, petulant way to deal with everything. To be honest, I missed him. I missed my best friend. Perhaps he felt the same. "Do you want to come with me?" The words slipped out of my mouth without thought.

I realised I was staring at him, and he was staring back. The green of his eyes non-existent. They looked black as night. It reminded me of one of those moments; the ones where he'd implied something to make me blush and feel flustered. But this time it was my words, and they seemed to be having an effect on both of us.

"Um..." He looked back at his map on the desk. It was littered with tiny red crosses. "That sounds good." He looked up at me and swallowed. "I've got a couple of things to finish up. Why don't you go on ahead? I'll meet you there."

I couldn't tell if he was being genuine or making excuses. However, I suddenly realised what I'd implied. I'd basically asked him to get naked with me. I felt my cheeks burn at the thought. Nux, I needed to get out of here. "Sure...um...I'll see you there...maybe." I quickly turned, leaving him to watch my swift exit.

He was sitting in the same position when I walked past five minutes later.

Chapter Twelve

Exiting the tree lift onto the forest floor, I found a small group of women heading to the lake. One, I recognised from training. She waved at me. I returned the gesture, but kept to the back of the group, keeping pace, albeit lost in my thoughts. And I only had one thing on my mind—Rooke. I guess that had been the case for years. But never before had I felt so confused.

The thought of him sitting on his desk, half naked, with that look on his face consumed my every breath. I couldn't tell if he craved my company or if he recoiled from it. It was all very well him claiming I was avoiding him, but the truth was, if he wanted to spend time with me, wouldn't he seek me out; make time for me? I swear since our unexpected kiss he had changed. He'd been different, not quite so attentive or playful. I missed him. I missed his teasing, our laughter. We were never alone here. Maybe in inviting him to the lake we could reconnect.

The mile walk to the lake was sweltering. A sense of delight struck me when I passed the two guards stationed at the opening in the rocks. The twinkling turquoise water called to me as I passed through the towering boulders. I stopped and took in the tranquil view. Every time I came here, I was overwhelmed by the beauty. A little piece of paradise in a world full of terror.

The group of women veered off to the left, huddling together as they undressed. I walked further up the shore towards the waterfall at the far end. Lost in my thoughts, I removed my boots, trousers, and leather vest, then sat down on the sand, watching the gallons of water cascade down the rockface opposite. Dipping my toes into the cool water, I waited.

Alana Faye Wilson

A small part of me hoped Rooke wouldn't come. Swimming naked together could prove awkward. Another part of me felt excited at the prospect. This could be the moment I discovered exactly how he felt for me. Even if it concluded I was just his friend, I needed to know. I needed to move passed this infatuation with him.

From where I sat, the group of women appeared as multiple specks, the size of small insects ambling along the water's edge. I watched the younger women splash each other, their shrills of delight bouncing off the towering walls around me.

I had no concept of how much time passed, but I was still sitting on my own—still waiting. The late afternoon sun remained hot, the air stifling. The sweat on my skin felt too uncomfortable to resist the sparkling ripples any longer. Starting to accept Rooke wasn't coming, I stood up and removed the rest of my clothes.

Wading through the smooth, fresh water, it quickly rose to my waist. I sunk beneath the surface, my skin tingling against the coolness. As I swam to the middle, I flipped over, letting the water lift my body upwards. I stared up into the blue sky. A sky so different to what I'd grown up with; so vibrant, so blue. The colour reminded me of Truro's eyes. Those beautiful, stunning eyes. My lips twitched into a small smile.

Truro. He was my Nux warrior who'd won my admiration. A part of me was convinced I'd won his. I found myself hoping I had.

A loud splash from the area around the waterfall alerted me. It sounded as if a large object had dropped into the lake. I righted myself, treading the water to keep afloat. Glancing up at the towering mass of falling water, I couldn't see any precarious looking pieces of rock. Maybe something else had dropped. Maybe it was…shit! What if it was an Igknamai?

No, no. Calm down. The Igknamai hate water. If any were nearby, they wouldn't enter the lake itself.

Still, my paranoia started to accelerate into a sense of panic as my eyes swept every surface nearby. In the corner of my eye, a dark shadow loomed in the water beneath me, and I flinched, violently. Whatever it was, it wasn't Rooke. He couldn't swim like that. The water was deep. Only someone, or something native and accustomed to these waters could swim so fluently.

My panic lurched up another few degrees. What if it was a

Hybrid? And then my mind came crashing to a conclusion, sending a shiver of dread through me.

Dybgo. It was Dybgo. He'd come to claim me!

Fighting against the anxiety pounding through my veins, I began to swim back towards the shore. Something tugged on my leg. I screamed, causing myself to sink, taking in too many mouthfuls of water. As I struggled to find the surface, strong hands locked around my upper arms, pulling me upwards. Coughing and gasping for air, I vigorously flailed my hands around, punching hard, smooth skin. I couldn't let Dybgo take me. I would never go back with him…

"Eden. Stop! It's me!"

To the sound of a safe, familiar voice, I stilled. On opening my eyes, I found the colour of the sky looking at me. "Truro!" The relieved anger rasped from my throat. "You frightened the life out of me!

"God, I…" Still holding my shoulders, he peered at me as I caught my breath. "I forget you scare easily."

I coughed, blinking the water from my eyes. "You would've scared anyone with that tactic."

Still trying to calm my ragged breathing, he pulled me closer. The clash of his toned chest muscles against my bare breasts did anything but calm me. My groin was pressing against his hip, one strong arm was wrapped around my waist, holding me in place. The other arm sculled the water in time with his legs, keeping us afloat. I met his gaze. He didn't seem fazed by our contact.

"Who did you think I was?" he asked.

Letting him take my weight, I rested my hand on his shoulder feeling more and more ridiculous as I quietly said, "Dybgo."

"Ahh…Nya told me what he did to you." Nya had most certainly been given Zamya's exaggerated account of the story, but still, in whatever context Truro had been told, Dybgo had attacked me. I could feel the warmth of Truro's gaze on my face as I stared over his shoulder at the rippling water.

"Eden, he wouldn't dare come here."

I met his gaze again. The blue was so vibrant, full of assurance. "It was an irrational thought. I panicked."

"It is allowed, you know. To panic. It's a natural instinct." He shifted his hold on my waist, creating a slight distance so I could see the aspect of command on his face. "Now, what I want to know is, why are you here alone?"

"I'm not," I protested. "I came with…" Glancing back to where the group of women were at the opposite end of the lake, I paused. "What? Where did they go?"

"They left. We abandon the lake a few hours before nightfall, for obvious reasons. You're so far up the lake and close to the waterfall, they probably didn't see you."

I felt ashamed, embarrassed. This situation could've been a disaster waiting to happen. "Nux, I didn't realise. I've been so lost in my thoughts this afternoon." *No thanks to Rooke.*

"Lucky for you, I was riding past." A smile graced his lips, softening his strong features. "Why don't you finish up what you're doing and go get dressed. Gives me time to swim a couple of lengths. Then, I'll take you home."

Still frowning, I nodded, and he instantly released me, leaving my body craving the heat and comfort of his. As I treaded the water, Truro exerted himself forward through the sparkling ripples, exposing his buttocks for the briefest of moments. Nux, even his bum was toned…and tanned. I bit on my lip. Damn it, I needed to get a grip.

I swam to shore, and whilst watching Truro slice through the water with the same speed and agility as a professional athlete, I got dressed. The air was still hot, and because I was beyond the safety of the village, I was still required to wear my stifling leathers. I opted to lose the shirt. Tying up the string at the front of my leather vest, I noticed Truro exiting the water at the far end.

Quickly braiding my wet hair, I picked up my towel and shirt and walked towards him. The glow of golden skin confirmed he was still naked, so I slowed my steps, reluctant to arrive before he was fully dressed. But I couldn't deny it, I found the shape of him appealing, even from this distance. I suddenly felt overly conscious. How much of my body had he seen or felt while we were in the water together? A couple of hours ago the thought of being naked with Rooke had caused anxiety. With Truro, it had felt…surprisingly comfortable.

Truro was buckling up his leathers when I approached. He looked back at me, and my heart pounded for a couple of beats. With his hair wet and swept out of his eyes, I could see how handsome he was. A square face with a strong jaw, those sparkling eyes surrounded by thick eyebrows and dark lashes, a straight nose and perfectly defined lips, all encased in golden skin. I could stare at that face all day.

Picking up his swords and bow, he then straightened and paused, combing his eyes over the full length of my body. A wide grin lightened his face and I frowned.

"What is it?" I asked, glancing down at myself.

He pointed at my torso with his swords. "I've never seen that style worn like that before?"

I peered down at the front of my leather vest. Okay, without the shirt underneath it was low, exposing a little cleavage, but I was covered. He was still grinning when I looked up. He shrugged and said, "You look god damn sexy though."

Completely taken aback, heat instantly rose to my cheeks, forcing me to laugh. I watched him graze his top teeth over his lower lip and he cocked his head.

"Come on. Let's get you home."

Truro must've sent the guards back to the village. There weren't any waiting at the entrance when we passed through.

"Where's your horse?" I asked, scanning the deserted area. "Or are we walking?"

Truro raised his eyebrows at me. "I'm not going to tie him up and leave him as a treat for the Igknamai, am I?" Putting his finger and thumb in his mouth, he efficiently produced a high-pitched whistle. The sound echoed about the vast forest before us. Instantly, the stamp of hooves was heard in the distance, and within the next few seconds, a huge black horse majestically emerged through the trees, slowing as he approached.

Truro stepped forward with his arms sprayed wide. "Where've you been, huh? I didn't tell you to go off on a jolly." The horse nudged Truro's shoulder with its muzzle. Stroking the horse's neck, Truro spoke to his companion. "You need to be on your best behaviour, okay. We've been given the task of escorting a rather beautiful lady home. So, don't mess it up."

I was smiling when Truro looked back at me. There was a glimmer of something in his eyes I found alluring. He held out his hand and helped me up onto the huge horse.

"What's his name?" I asked, as Truro seated himself close behind me.

"Titan."

"The name of the pre-gods."

"No. I just like the name. Gods don't exist." He reached for the reins in front of me and the horse began to move. "If they did, they deserted this world a long time ago. Though we tend to curse to a generic god, my people don't believe in them. We worship Mother Earth."

"Ah. That explains the dish containing the four elements I saw in the council chamber."

"It does. Nature gives us everything we need. It also takes from us. It's all about balance. Although this world has been severely off balance for far too long."

I pondered his comment; Earth, the Garden of Eden, had fallen to the devil millennia ago. Had this really occurred because of the mistakes of a past civilization who failed to care for their world, or was it something bigger, something beyond our comprehension?

"Can I ask you a question?" I glanced back at him. His eyes were trained on the path before us. "How did you get the job as head of security?" A rumble trembled through his chest behind me. A sound I portrayed as amusement.

"Do you still have an issue with my age?"

"No." I chuckled. "I'm curious."

"Hmm. Well, Elgin saw potential in me when I was fourteen. He took me under his wing and trained me in everything he knows. His intentions were for me to become his replacement when the time came. But as fate would have it, it was Luna, the younger of the two security heads who died first."

"When did that happen?"

"Two years ago. Elgin said I was ready, so he put my name forward for the job. The vote came back in my favour. The rest is history."

"Did you want the job?"

"Yes. I'm good at what I do." There was a tense pause, in which I got the impression he was questioning his own answer. His voice shifted into one far gentler, more forlorn. "Occasionally, I wonder what it would be like to hold less responsibility."

I sympathised with his statement. He was only twenty-three. Even in a world full of terror, the younger generation still enjoyed themselves. I'd seen them laughing, joking, meeting up for lunch, going to the bar in the evening, dancing, and flirting. Truro was always working, always striving to protect his people. I doubted he had time for such frivolities.

"I can imagine the responsibility can be a hardship to bare." I leant back into him, resting my head in the groove between his shoulder and collar bone. Unexpectedly, his arm wrapped around my midriff, pulling me a fraction closer.

"I spend more time with my horse than anyone else."

I chuckled. "Well, he's a very lucky horse."

Truro leant to the side and patted the horse's shoulder. "He's a very good horse."

In response Titan snorted, then seemed to kick up some dirt, stamping his feet. My amusement to his reaction was short lived.

"What is it, boy?" Truro said, his eyes darting in all directions. "Something's amiss. Titan only gets like this when there's danger nearby."

My spine straightened, my eyes scanning the area. Adrenaline surged through my veins and Truro pushed Titan into a gallop. We began to travel faster across the dry forest floor. For a large horse laden with two riders, he was still swift and elegant.

I knew the route we were taking like the back of my hand. We weren't far from the palisade.

Stripping the breath from my lungs, Titan suddenly reared. I gripped the reins with all my strength as Truro attempted to calm the horse. When he lowered his front legs, we saw what had been destressing him.

Two Igknamai were stalking up ahead. Their yellow-brown scales were covered in red dust; globes of saliva dripped from their mouths as if they were ravenous. It was the first time I'd seen one in over a month—since the day Cora had been taken. The fear of their presence hadn't eased in the slightest. My heart pounded in my ears; my stomach felt as though it had dropped.

Truro's body tensed, forcing the horse on, and taking us off the main road up a small incline to the right. Air whipped at my hair and a bow appeared in front of my face.

"Now's your chance to prove to me you can really do this."

My eyes filled with horror. I looked back at Truro. He was being serious. Releasing a ragged breath, I took the bow, then the arrow he was offering me.

Titan was moving quickly. We'd passed the Igknamai roaring and snapping up at us on the road two metres below. Their snarls filled me with dread as they began to keep pace with us.

Nocking the arrow in place, I noticed the sharp tip was glistening with a purple tinge. Clenching my thighs together, keeping balance, I took aim, estimating the closer of the two Igknamai's path. Like a vice, Truro's hand clenched down on my waist. "I've got you," he said. "I won't let go." Holding onto his every word, I tightened my core and released the arrow.

It struck the side of the beast's throat, causing it to sag to one side before hitting the ground in a plume of red dust.

"Good shot." There was no excitement or panic resonating in Truro's voice whatsoever. Another purple tipped arrow appeared in front of me. "Now kill the other one."

I swiftly nocked the arrow and lined up the shot, but I hesitated. Our path was dipping and merging back with the main road. My hands and arms shook as Truro pulled Titan to a stop, blocking the full width of the path. What was he doing?

"Do it," he said.

I aimed, watching the angry Igknamai charging directly towards us. My breaths were short and far too ragged. "It's too close, Truro!"

"Do it!" It was an order; one I had to obey. The difference between life and death.

Taking one last breath, I closed my eyes, grimacing as I freed the arrow.

In the next moment, there was a crumbling of earth, followed by silence. I peered through my lashes at an immobile Igknamai lying flat on the ground, my arrow embedded in the middle of its four black eyes.

"Did you close your eyes?" Truro asked flatly.

I swallowed down the bile, aware my hands were shaking fiercely. I nodded.

Truro huffed a laugh before reaching for the bow I was still holding. "You did really well." He took it from me, slinging it over his shoulder. "Just, keep your eyes open in future."

Slumping back, I released another long, deep breath. Truro turned Titan and we galloped back to the village, leaving the two dead Igknamai on the road to rot.

Chapter Thirteen

Titan jumped the palisade, his speed unfaltering even as he landed. Truro tightened his hold around my waist and my hand instinctively found his. Our thumbs entwined with one another's, then his soft rumble was in my ear, "Are you okay?"

I nodded. The shock hadn't taken root, but in relation to everything that had happened, I was fine. I was alive. But a harrowing thought had already trembled through me. What would've happened if I had walked home alone; if Truro hadn't ridden past the lake when it was being abandoned?

"I'm sorry if I was a little brash with you," he said.

"Don't be." I looked back at him. "It was what I needed."

"It concerns me that the Igknamai are out so early. The heat is stifling. They rarely come out before dusk on days like these."

"Could it be the Hybrids forcing them out?"

"That's what I'm worried about. It was the same the day your crew got trapped in the ravine. Even though the Akquarian mut called them there, why had they been so close to start with? It's becoming a regular occurrence."

I pondered his comment, worried about the implications.

Titan slowed as we approached the garrison platform. Truro called up to the guards, warning them of potential Igknamai presence, then continued. I frowned. "Where are we going?"

"Up to the grazing fields."

My frown deepened. I'd never contemplated how the horses got up there. The fields and trees where I trained every morning had a sheer drop on every side. Truro chuckled at my confusion. "Rooke and Oz were just as baffled when I first showed them the route."

"Route?"

"You'll see."

We travelled down the east side of the village, where a shallow stream sparkled in the afternoon sun. There were a few people still fishing. All of whom greeted us as we rode past.

The mountainous rockface appeared to the left as the village disappeared behind us. One hundred metres along, Titan began to ascend a steep, treacherous looking ledge carved into the rockface. I held my breath the higher we climbed. How the horse was negotiating the angle of the terrain, I had no idea. The Redwood horses were larger and sturdier than those I was used to on Allura. They must have evolved to climb the mountains, to find safety from the terrors found on the forest floor. It was the only way their species could've survived the years.

A sigh of relief escaped me as we rounded the top verge, spying the grazing fields and archery trees on the far side. Titan had climbed over one hundred metres in less than fifteen minutes. These animals were underrated.

Truro eased Titan to a halt, where another thirty horses stood grazing in the shadows of the trees edging the field.

Jumping down, Truro reached up for me, the metal hilts of his swords glistening behind him. I swung my leg over and slid down, resting my hands on his broad shoulders. His fingers clasped my waist, lowering me slowly. Our eyes locked, and a spark of electricity tingled through my stomach. I couldn't deny the connection we had. And it was growing with every interaction.

Gently placing my boots on the ground, his voice was as soft as a whisper. "You're trembling."

Still lost in his eyes, I forced myself to breathe. I wasn't sure if I was shaking because of the Igknamai attack or because of the way he was looking at me. There was a fine line between fear and excitement, one I had trouble differentiating between these days.

I looked away. "It's just the adrenaline come down."

His hand fell from my waist as I turned and pulled my towel and shirt from where I'd been sitting. "As long as that's all it is."

I watched Truro remove Titan's reins and harness, throwing the leather straps across his shoulder next to his bow. Side by side, we began to walk through the long gold-tinted grass towards the ladder on the south side of the field. My mind felt scrambled. I had come within seconds of death, again. Nux, that Igknamai had been so close. It could've killed us both. "I hesitated, didn't I?"

I felt Truro's gaze on me. "No."

"I did…I did. The fear nearly got to me."

"Eden." The warmth of Truro's hand gripping mine pulled me to a stop. Staring back at him, he stepped forward, closing the gap between us. "You killed two Igknamai using only two arrows. That's impressive in my book. You're an amazing archer. I haven't seen an ability emerge so quickly in anyone I've trained before, and I've trained hundreds. You have a natural instinct, a survivor's instinct. Don't let the doubt of hesitation deter you. We all fall victim to fear. Even I do."

"What if I hadn't killed the second one?"

"I had my dagger ready, and Titan is responsive. But I didn't doubt you for one second."

I felt a flutter inside my chest. Truro was young, two years my junior, and yet he was the best teacher I'd ever had. He encouraged, he inspired. The admiration I felt for him went beyond measure. And to add to the array of esteem I held for him, he offered more…

"I will never let anything happen to you. You're important. Special."

My heart swelled for a moment, before it sank to a level of despondency. I realised what he was suggesting. I'd promised to help the council eradicate the terrors of their world. I'd promised to save the Redwood people from their relentless enemy. I wasn't important in an individual, personal way. They didn't see me as a person. I was a purpose, a ray of hope, a prophecy coming true. The thought troubled me in more ways than what Rooke had chastised me for.

With my head hung low, I continued to walk through the grass, aware I had left Truro behind with a bemused look on his face. His footsteps followed and I heard him say, "Did I say something wrong?"

I shook my head. "You know I hate it when you talk about my promise and your people's alleged prophecy."

"I'm not…"

"I'm truly honoured you're offering your time to train me and provide me with the additional protection, but I do not deserve nor expect any more than the standard obligation you give to the rest of the community."

"Eden…"

"I get it. I do." I turned to face him. "Your people's fate is held in my hands, not Rooke's, mine. It was my promise. That doesn't make *me* special."

"I'm not talking about any of that." I found myself trapped in his piercing blue gaze. His expression was ardent and solicitous, forcing me to listen. "Maybe some people do see you in a different light because of your promise to help us. You are respected here, all of your crew are. But that's not what I meant. You're…you're special…to…to me…in a way I can't…I can't…" He looked at the ground and his Adam's apple bobbed in an awkward attempt to stabilise himself. "God, I'm useless with words."

He peered up at me, and before I had the chance to analyse what he was saying, he closed the distance between us and placed his lips against mine.

I didn't flinch. My eyes stuttered shut, savouring his warm breath against my mouth. His lips moved gently over mine, sending my head into a spiralling whirlpool of bliss. And I realised; this was what I'd been craving from him. My connection with him was more than the admiration I'd already freely admitted. It was attraction, affection, respect of the highest calibre.

From the moment I'd first laid eyes on him—when he revealed his face from under his hood at the top of that deadly ravine—I'd felt a pull towards him. It was different to the pull I felt with Rooke. With Rooke, I was a moth drawn to a hot, pernicious flame. With Truro, it was a magnetic pull that sent an array of sparks racing through me. Like two magnets, we were compatible. We connected.

Ending the sweet, gentle kiss, he pulled away, leaving me fighting against the dizziness he'd doused upon my senses. His face was a blur as I tried to refocus. Peering down at me, he was so close, I could smell his earthy scent. A scent I hadn't associated with him until now, but it had always been there comforting me these past few weeks.

"I hope that clears up any miscommunication," he whispered.

A sound, crossed between a moan, a whimper, and a laugh escaped me. "Actions do speak louder than words." I smiled up at him and saw the corners of his eyes crease.

He leant in and kissed me again, this time pulling me closer with his free hand placed on the curve of my back. "Promise me you won't go to the lake alone."

"I wasn't alone…but I promise I won't wander off."

"You can always ask me…or Saff. Saff would jump at the opportunity of you joining her group."

I laughed, then agreed, and we continued towards the cliff edge. With a contented smile on my face, my hand swished over the tall grass, grazing Truro's palm every so often. His touches were feather like yet playful, and in those moments of tenderness, I realised my whole universe had shifted. Rooke no longer sat predominantly in the middle. He was still there, I loved him—I knew I'd always love him. But currently, Truro's unexpected light was out shining Rooke's and for the first time in years, my focus was being drawn away from him. It was Truro who I was moving towards, and I wanted to get closer.

We descended the dual ladder, playfully racing each other to the bottom. Even laden with two swords, daggers, a bow, quiver, and horse reins, Truro still beat me. He openly laughed as I met him at the bottom, throwing him a whimsical scold.

"Council meeting tonight?" I asked, as we brushed the rockface, walking along the wooden walkway to the bridge crossing into the village. The caves where the blacksmiths and pottery workshops had closed up for the night. It must've been far later than I'd presumed.

"Not tonight," Truro replied. "I've promised Jader I'll join him for a drink." He looked down at me. "I could always postpone."

Inwardly, I smiled. "You shouldn't. You don't get a lot of spare time to spend with your friends." Through the trees I spotted Rooke striding towards the opposite side of the bridge. My smile faltered as an ounce of resentment rose to the surface. "I should really be getting back to the others."

Truro followed my line of sight. He nodded and I could've sworn I saw a hint of disappointment flash across his face. We approached the bridge where a scout stood eagerly awaiting his attention. Truro paused in front of him and as I boarded the bridge, he said, "I'll see you tomorrow then?"

I turned, walking backwards with a smile on my face. "I'm sure you will."

The gleam of delight illuminating in his eyes was hard to miss. With a newfound confidence, I turned and strode towards the man I had originally wanted to spend the afternoon with. I surprised myself in thinking I was pleased he hadn't shown.

Rooke eyed me as I approached, then frowned towards Truro, who was now speaking with the scout. "Have you just returned? You didn't wait for me, did you?" Rooke's voice was tight, ringing with concern.

"I did. You told me to."

"I didn't mean for you to stay so late."

I stared at him, baffled by his words. "Rooke, you said you wanted to spend time with me. You said you'd meet me at the lake. What exactly did you expect me to do?"

A look of shame filled his eyes as his hands slipped into the pockets of his self-made shorts. "I know, I know. I got stuck in a lengthy, tactical debate with Blake and Kobe. I couldn't get away. Did Truro bring you home?" He was frowning at him again.

"Yes, thankfully." I refrained from telling him about the Igknamai attack. It would only cause him to reconsider the freedom he offered Zamya and I to leave the village. But the attack had shaken me. What would've happened if it had been Rooke and I travelling home together? Rooke had been taught how to defend himself against the Igknamai as I had; he went out into the forest every day. But he never carried a bow, only daggers and a sword. Would we have survived the attack?

I swallowed down the disconcerting thought and threaded my hand through his arm. "Come on, you lousy friend. You can escort me home."

Still keeping his hands in his pockets, he huffed a small smile. "I suppose it's the least I can do."

We headed home over the multitudes of platforms and bridges, and when we arrived, we found Zamya, Kobe, and Oz sitting around a laid table, waiting for us.

"Finally!" Oz said.

"She hadn't got lost then?" Zamya said, rolling her eyes.

"No," Rooke grumbled. "She seemed to be in good hands."

I took a seat beside Zamya, smiling to myself. *I sure was.*

"Can we eat now?" Oz pointed to the middle of the table.

Zamya sighed and removed the lid from a large bowl. "I cooked dinner for us all," she said.

"Better check it for poison," Kobe jibed, eventually smiling at Zamya's hiss.

Rooke laughed, sitting down beside me. "Thought we could all spend some time together this evening, as a crew. No one else. Just us."

"Here, here." Oz raised his clay cup, glancing between Rooke and I. We all joined him in toasting to *us*.

I wasn't sure if it was because of my newly found revelation, or if we were all feeling the contentment of residing here, but the five of us seemed jovial and relaxed that evening. We laughed for hours, ate, drank, and played cards. It seemed everything *had* shifted.

Hopefully in the right direction.

Chapter Fourteen

For the first time in weeks, I didn't dream of Cora's death. I hadn't envisaged her being dragged through the dusty ravine with a look of anguished terror on her face. Instead, I'd heard her laugh, saw her pretty smile, and listened to her talk enthusiastically about her work.

I woke realising the raw grief was starting to lift. Although thoughts of her still plagued me—thoughts of how much she would've loved it here among the Redwood people—I was starting to feel acceptance. Starting to let her memory settle peacefully.

As usual, I woke before Kobe and Zamya. Laying in my hammock, listening to their light, slumbered breaths and the quarry of bird song outside, I studied the imperfectly pitched ceiling. My thoughts fell to Truro, and I smiled, touching my fingers to my lips. He'd kissed me. My inspiring Nux warrior had kissed me. Nux, I had the overbearing urge to see him.

Within ten minutes I had washed, braided my hair, and dressed in my leathers, now hunting through the middle hut for some breakfast. I grabbed an apple from the side and headed for the open door, but the sound of scuffed footsteps behind me halted my swift exit.

Twirling, I found Rooke reaching for me. He grinned, snaking his arms around my waist. I frowned up at him as he purred, "Where are you going?"

His face was so close I could feel his breath warm against my cheeks. I pulled back. "Um…w…work." Lie, it was a lie, but I didn't want him finding out about my training, about my daily interactions with Truro. I wasn't sure why.

"You're always sneaking out early. You're always working."

"I wasn't working yesterday afternoon."

His eyebrows knitted together, and I saw something surface in his dark eyes resembling regret. "How can I make it up to you?"

"You don't need to, Rooke." I tried to turn from his hold, but his arms were like a vice, trapping me against the solid columns of his stomach.

"Take the morning off." His voice was a soft rumble, his eyes searching mine in a manner I'd never witnessed before. Any other morning, I may have submitted to his passive demand, but today…today I wanted to see Truro.

"I can't."

"Why not?"

"I need to go." His muscles loosened and I slid from his embrace.

"Eden."

"I'm sure I'll see you later." I began to walk across the short bridge, leaving him frowning in my wake.

"It's the new moon party tonight," he called.

"Is it?"

"Are you going?"

Stopping on the platform opposite, I looked back at him. He was leaning against the wooden door frame with a determined scowl on his face.

"Probably."

"You're not going to run out on me as soon as you get there again, are you?"

I frowned at him, questioning the reason behind his behaviour this morning. "I'm starting to get the impression you want me to be there."

"I do."

"Fine. I'll be there. You could just ask instead of speculating."

He chuckled. "Where's the fun in that?"

I groaned, finding him unusually tedious. "Have a good day, Rooke." I waved and didn't look back.

Rounding the top of the east clifftop, I walked towards the archery field and my heart deflated when my eyes couldn't find Truro. Jader caught my attention. Standing in the middle of a throng of young trainees, he was a full head and shoulders taller, towering between them. Noticing my presence, he pushed through the huddle. As he approached, his wide smile looked strained, his eyes tired.

"I was going to suggest concentrating on sparring today," he said, casting his eyes towards the grazing fields. I realised the field was unusually empty. No horses stood about on the grass. Even the sheep and cows were missing.

"Where are all the horses?"

"There was a Hybrid sighting up here last night. The horses tend to scarper for a while when they appear."

"Hybrids?" My mind jumped to Truro's concern yesterday. Had the Igknamai's premature presence been related to the Hybrid sighting? "Why do they come up here?"

Jader shrugged. "To spy on the village, who knows?"

"Do they ever enter the village?"

"Thankfully, no. They'd be killed on the spot. Coming up here is a risk. They are easier to kill than the Igknamai."

"I guess that's reassuring."

Jader didn't miss the sarcasm in my tone. "I was speaking to Truro last night. He told me what happened yesterday. He thinks you're ready. As do I."

"Ready?"

"To become a member of a hunting team. If you still want it, that is?"

"Yes. Definitely!"

He chuckled. "There are no vacancies at present, but they come up frequently. And you need some progression with your swordsmanship. Which means," he unsheathed a long, steel sword from a leather scabbard I hadn't realised he was holding, "you need to practice with this."

I silently gasped with delight as he handed me the sword. It was longer than I expected, but far lighter.

"It's about time you got used to using one of these."

"Feels different to a wooden one."

"It will for a while. The other trainees need to concentrate on practising their archery, so you can duel with Wrenn for the first hour alone. You can join us afterwards."

I glanced across the long swinging bridge to the sparring ring on the west clifftop. Surrounded by trees, I could make out Wrenn practising a sword dance. Her vibrant red braid swung about her

117

neck as she moved gracefully. I thanked Jader and walked over to her. Anxious excitement fizzled through me. I was finally being given the chance to become a true Redwood warrior, to finally have purpose.

Wrenn halted her movements as I approached. She smirked. "Hey, lady with the stunning eyes."

I gave her a playful look. "Hey, lady with the amazing sword skills."

Wrenn laughed, brightening her usual stoic expression. "So, Jader's finally given you a proper sword."

"Yep." I lifted it up for her to see, the morning sun twinkling over the plain silver blade.

"Well, let's get started."

Using the training she'd given me during the past month, I danced about her, mimicking how Wrenn moved her blade effortlessly through the air.

Wrenn was the same height as me, sturdier in the fact her arm and shoulder muscles had been forged from a lifetime of wielding a sword. Her eyes were the same amber colour as her hair and the scatter of freckles across the bridge of her nose. She wore rustic red leather armour, again matching her features. It was no wonder Jader and Truro occasionally referred to her as Red Wrenn. At a guess, she was a similar age to me, but in a similar way to Truro, she seemed far older—hardened by a lifetime of strife.

After half an hour of practicing, my arms were burning, my breathing ragged, and I was sweating more than a hog on a spit. Wrenn offered me a canister of water. "You're better than I thought," she said, wiping her freckled face with the back of her hand.

"This sword technique, does it really suffice against the Igknamai?"

Swallowing a mouthful of water, she shook her head. "Swords can easily get embedded in the Igknamai's hard shell, which basically means you've lost your sword. Arrows and daggers are better against them. We use the sword against the Hybrids. We don't encounter them often, but we like to be prepared."

"How violent are the Hybrids?"

"Imagine a group of barbarians mixed with a pack of hellhounds and you've pretty much got it. There is a legend about a highly organised, elite division of Hybrids, dressed head to toe in devilish armour. Thankfully, it's a myth. Probably passed down over the years to scare us. Even so, the ones we do know of, tend to wield large, ragged sided swords, aimed to cause severe damage and painful deaths. That's why we have to be swift and concise when killing them. We have to be fearless."

I stared at her, contemplating her words. "I thought the Igknamai were bad enough."

"Starting to have second thoughts?" she teased with a smile.

"Not a chance."

"Good. Let's get back to it."

We practiced for another half an hour, dancing around each other, timing our steps to perfection, only stopping when a small group of trainees arrived at the sparring ring. The adrenaline buzzing through me was exhilarating. I enjoyed this more than the archery.

After thanking Wrenn, I left her to instruct the new group. Crossing the bridge back to the archery field, I glanced towards the fields. There were still no horses.

Standing at the far end, I joined the long line of archers. Picking up a bow and arrow from the floor, I took my aim, hesitating when I heard a whisper, "Psssst, Eden."

I looked down the line of archers behind me, resting my eyes on Saff. She was smiling widely, her blue eyes dancing with excitement. "Heard you killed half a dozen Igknamai yesterday," she said, her voice soft, attempting not to alert Jader standing at the opposite end of the line.

I rolled my eyes. "Did Truro tell you that?"

"Of course. He doesn't stop talking about you when he's at mums. Do you like my hair?" She swished her long auburn ponytail towards me. It wasn't styled in the usual braid she always wore. It looked as though she'd brushed her usual knotted locks, too.

"Looks nice."

"I couldn't get it quite as perfect as yours but that's the style I was going for."

I stared at her, a blush touching my cheeks. Was she styling herself on me? Did I really have celebrity status here? I didn't have the heart to tell her I'd started braiding mine. It was easier to manage now it had grown so long.

"I've got some black leathers ordered too," she continued. "That way, we can be a duo when we go to the lake togeth…"

"Saffron!" Jader's voice boomed over her head, and her face distorted. "Stop talking and get back to aiming. If you could shoot as well as you gossip, you'd be as good as your brother!"

I felt a pounding of guilt as he marched over to her, listening to him chastise her for not paying attention. I rubbed my lips together and turned back to positioning my arrow, only to flinch at a shadow in my peripheral.

How he could be so ridiculously stealth-like astounded me, but Truro was barely a metre away, standing in front of a tree to my right. His muscular arms crossed over his chest, his legs astride in a dominant stance, his alluring eyes trailing the full length of my body. If his actions were purely to assess my archery foot formation, I wasn't certain, but it didn't stop my insides from sighing, then turning to mush. Nux, I liked his eyes on me, maybe a little too much.

Still holding my bow and arrow in position, I raised my eyebrows when his eyes finally met mine. As usual, his direct, striking blue gaze sent a bout of sparks through my body. It didn't help that the smirk on his face suggested his assessment was not professional, causing another wave of desire to stir within me.

Holding his gaze, I rebelliously released my arrow without a care of where it hit. Breaking eye contact, Truro glanced in the direction of the target at the far end of the course. His face was a picture of stern authority when he looked back at me, slowly raising his eyebrows in question. "Just because you hit an Igknamai with your eyes shut yesterday, doesn't mean your eyes aren't required when using a bow."

I smirked. "You distracted me."

"You shouldn't allow yourself to be so easily distracted."

"Then, you shouldn't sneak up on me."

"I've told you before, I don't sneak." He sauntered towards me, those eyes still piercing every sane part of my mind. My breath hitched when he stopped at my side, the warmth of his breath fluttering against my ear. "Use your eyes in future, Goddess. Do it again, and I'll have to reprimand you."

"And how will you do that?" I found myself trying to keep a

straight face.

"You really don't want to know."

"Oh, I think I do." If I knew how to flutter my eyelids, I would've done it in that moment. A devious, flirtatious streak was rearing its head; one I hadn't realised I was capable of.

Truro gave me an unreadable look, and I suddenly felt concerned I'd overstepped the mark. Eventually, I saw the flicker of a smile. He moved closer, his voice a soft rumble, "Are you flirting with me?"

I grinned, dropping my eyes to the floor, before hardening my expression and meeting his gaze again. I gave my head a quick shake. "I'd never be so obstinate."

He snorted, grazing his fingers against mine as he went to move along the line. But he back tracked and whispered, "Save a dance for me later." I noted the devilish smirk just before he walked away.

My heart was thumping so loudly in my chest, I was worried the others could hear it. The heat our interaction had ignited was causing havoc with my senses. The next three arrows I shot, I missed my target. I hoped he wasn't watching.

After work, I showered and scurried home. Zamya was cleaning the table in the middle hut when I arrived. I slowed. She was humming to herself. I didn't think I'd ever heard her hum before.

"Lovely tune," I said as I walked through the open doorway.

"Don't flatter me. I'm atrocious. Oz tells me I sound like a drowning cat."

I laughed. "That's probably Oz's way of being complementary."

"Ha, you don't say." She continued to scrub at a stain on the wood.

"Um…" Nervously, I stepped closer. "Zam, I don't suppose you have something nice I could wear this evening?" I wasn't sure why I felt uneasy about asking her this, it was silly. But I sensed her clever eyes reading into my question.

Straightening her posture, she placed a hand on her hip and cocked her head. "Nice as in?"

"Not protective leathers. Or Solarfleet uniform. Something that makes me look…you know…nice."

"Uh ha." She smirked. "Maybe I do." Gesturing for me to follow her, we crossed the bridge to our sleeping hut.

Stepping between the hammocks, she leaned over one of the three wooden boxes we used to keep our possessions separate, then pulled out an item from within. I realised it was a garment made in a striking burnt orange colour. Zamya held it up against herself, revealing a dress with a respectful V-neck and thin spaghetti straps. Five large walnut-coloured buttons fastened it together at the front. "I made this for you," she said, handing it to me.

"What?" Shocked by her words, I took it. "You made this?"

Zamya nodded, proudly. "Wilma, the lady I told you about, she's been giving me sewing lessons. When I'm not at the medical clinic, I'm there. I really enjoy it. I find it therapeutic, and the other dressmakers are great fun."

I held the soft material up, admiring the stitchwork and the quality of the piece. "Wow, Zam. It's amazing. Thank you. Honestly, it's perfect."

"Perfect for what, exactly?"

My cheeks flushed. I knew she would be sceptically inquisitive.

Her face transformed into something a little cattish. "I like this." She pointed to me. "This you. You seem...sparkly. Happy. I can't recall ever seeing you like this. Whatever or whoever is doing this to you, don't let them go."

I couldn't help but smile.

Chapter Fifteen

"Whoa. Looking good ladies." Oz perched on a stool, watching Zamya and I walk across the expanse of decking towards him and Rooke. They sat at the midway point bar waiting for the new moon celebration to get into full swing. The hour was past eight thirty and the light was only just starting to fade. The array of fairy lights were beginning to sparkle overhead and the area was starting to fill up.

"I didn't realise there was a competition for best dressed this evening," Oz went on, eyeing Zamya in her short leather skirt and green shirt. "I would've thrown something a little sexier on myself."

"Oh, grow up, you oaf," Zamya chided, taking the seat to his left.

"Talk to me like that and I won't buy you a drink."

"I'm not stupid, Oz. I know the drinks are free."

"Not all of them, Zamya."

I smiled at their harmless bickering, taking a seat at the corner of the bar next to Rooke. He was watching the other two with an intrigued frown, nursing a pint of what looked like beer. "Those two are something else."

I watched Oz mimicking Zamya as she huffed her displeasure. "They act like a couple of siblings winding each other up."

"That's what people say about you and me."

"Aren't we the same?"

Rooke's pause made me look back at him. He chuckled awkwardly. "Yeah, I guess." There was something hidden in those words, something behind his tone that stalled me for a moment. But his voice quickly changed to a playful purr, "Loving the boots and dress look."

I glanced down at my outfit. The dress Zamya had made me fitted perfectly. So perfect, I questioned if she'd taken my measurements while I'd slept. The orange material fell to my calf, gaping slightly until it met the lowest button just above the knee, The V-neckline exposed only a small amount of cleavage, and the waistline hugged me, following the curve of my hip. I felt sophisticated, nice. The only issue I had encountered was I didn't have any shoes that matched the outfit, opting for my usual black lace up boots. I guess I was portraying the Alluran fashion of *grunge chick*.

"Thanks." Eyeing him, he was wearing a black T-shirt and —*Oh Nux*—his cut-up combat pants-shorts. I chuckled. "Are you still wearing those monstrosities?"

"Hey, I gave you a compliment!"

"Just, please give those to Zamya tomorrow. Believe me, she'll be able to fix them."

"She'll probably burn them." He laughed, taking a swig of his beer. "Glad you came tonight. I was beginning to think you'd bailed."

"Hey," I tilted my head and said, "I told you I'd be here."

"I know. I…I was going to ask," he said tentatively, looking down at his half-drunk pint. "There's something I'd like to discuss with you. Wondered if we could sneak off later." The nervous look on his face unleashed an erratic wave of anxiety, bounding its way around my nervous system, and I twitched.

"Is everything okay? Are Solarfleet throwing more objections?" I glanced around, hoping no one of importance was standing nearby.

"No, it's not that."

"I haven't spoken to Troy for a couple of days, is he okay?"

"Eden." For the first time that evening Rooke held my gaze. The darkness of his eyes melted into mine, sending bouts of warming nostalgia down my spine.

"It's not…there's nothing to worry about." He sighed. Again, I noticed the nerves. "I just want to talk to you, that's all."

Unable to shift the unnerved sensation, I offered him a meek, "Okay." But I couldn't help wondering if I was in trouble, or if an unprecedented problem had occurred.

Thankfully, the bartender appeared in front of me. I recognised him as one of the regulars from the food hall. "What can I get ya, young lady?" he asked.

I ran my eyes along the rustic shelves full of bottles behind him. I had no idea what any of them were. Most didn't even have labels. "Um, what do you recommend?"

"What type of beverage is your go to tipple?"

"Wine. Or brandy."

He nodded and started suggesting the different varieties. But my eyes clocked a tall necked bottle with a crystalised glass body on the top row. The peach-coloured liquid shone through the bulbous glass, and I instantly knew what it was. "Is that…" I pointed, cutting off the bar tender's knowledgeable speech.

"That's coral wine. Made by the Akquarians."

Why I felt excited by the prospect of drinking something made by the Akquarians, I wasn't sure, but I could vaguely recall how divine it tasted. "I'll have some of that please?"

"You have expensive taste. That'll cost you two credits per glass."

"She has enough credits," Rooke rumbled beside me.

"Do I?" I glanced at him for confirmation. I had no idea.

"Yes." He smirked. "Valina showed me the totals today. You work too hard."

"Says you." I turned back to the bartender. "I'll take a glass, please."

"Very good."

I watched him reach for the bottle, then fill a wide brimmed glass with the peach liquid, before checking a small computer for what I assumed was credit transfer. A physical shadow cast over me, and I glanced up finding Blake blocking the light, tapping Rooke on the shoulder. His buzzed hair and black beard seemed a stark contrast in the fading light. No longer wearing his standard drab overalls, he looked different; younger and less intimidating.

"Don't suppose I can have a word?" he asked Rooke in an undertone.

Rooke glanced at me momentarily, before accepting. They made their way to the opposite side of the bar where it was less crowded. I didn't watch them for long. The bartender returned with my drink. "Enjoy."

I thanked him and took a sip. The tantalising taste made my eyes close, humming my approval. I'd forgotten how delicious this wine was. I finished it in four, devouring gulps, asking the bartender for another one immediately. If Rooke had been correct, I probably had enough credits to buy the whole bottle.

With a fresh glassful in my hand, I glanced about the vicinity. The area had been organised in a different way to the last new moon celebration. The classical quartet weren't adorning the stage on the far side. In fact, the staged area was full of tables and chairs where friends, families, and couples sat and drank. Behind me was a smaller raised platform with strange, dark objects stood upon it. One looked similar to a classical piano, but there appeared to be buttons and dials poking out of the flush surface behind the keys.

Glancing over the increasing crowd, I recognised several of the older girls and boys from training. Saff stood in a younger mixed group. It was clear she was trying to act mature. She wore a pretty shift dress and her hair looked silky in the twilight. I smiled. My usual ponytail style suited her. Tonight, I had opted for a high bun, keeping the thickness of my hair away from my neck and back. It was too humid to bear otherwise.

Oz and Zamya's laughs brought my attention back to the bar. They were still bickering with each other, but their smiles confirmed their amusement.

On the far side of the bar, it looked as though Rooke and Blake's conversation had concluded. Blake scurried away, while Rooke started to wander back around the bar towards me, only to be intercepted halfway round by a blonde-haired woman. My heart sank to the pit of my stomach at the sight of Valina draped in a flowing dress of cornflower blue. She placed her hand on Rooke's chest, rose on tiptoes, and whispered something into his ear. Rooke leaned in, attentively listening, suddenly shifting his eyes to mine. I looked away. If anything, I didn't want to witness the extent of their relationship again. It didn't prevent the well of jealousy from reluctantly bubbling away inside.

Glancing back a moment later, I could see them walking towards one of the suspension bridges. I released a long, despondent sigh. *No chance of spending any time together this evening then.* I downed the rest of my wine.

The whole area suddenly fell dark, silence followed. I snapped my head in all directions, concerned something strange was afoot. But in the next moment, the objects on the small, raised platform behind me illuminated in fluorescent lines of colour. A soft beat began, steadily intensifying as if it was a countdown.

Electronic, musical sounds began to fill the air, projecting from several speakers distributed around the large space. People started to whoop and cheer, while others began to bob and clap to the beat.

After watching the strange spectacle for a few minutes, the area fully illuminated. Standing on the stage, a young man sang into a microphone, while two others played an electric piano and guitar behind him. The sounds moulded together, forming a fast paced, coherent song. The ease of excitement filled the air as more and more people started dancing, crowding the area.

Too engrossed in the scene erupting around me, I barely noticed someone nudge me on my shoulder. Zamya was standing next to me, pointing towards the crowd of dancers. Diverting my eyes back to the dance floor, they landed on a sight that made my heart flutter.

Truro was dancing at the edge of the crowd. Wearing a dark vest and a pair of non-leather trousers, he looked fresh and playful. His hair flopped over one eye and the cheeky grin on his face made my stomach fill with butterflies. Nux, he was gorgeous.

He pointed at me, beckoning me to join him. I shook my head, prompting him to pout just before he began miming the words. Something along the lines of taking an arrow to his heart and being brought back to life by a pair of beautiful lips. I chuckled, fixated by the way he moved so fluently to the music.

He beckoned me again. This time, I had no choice in the matter. Zamya forcefully pushed me off my stool and shoved me in his direction. Stumbling forward, I gaped at her over my shoulder, suddenly aware Truro's hands were pulling me into him.

"Hey," he said, swaying us to the music.

I met his beautiful eyes and the butterflies returned to my stomach. "Hey."

The next three minutes were filled with Truro dancing around me, twirling me under his arm, swaying his hips against mine in time with the music. I smiled and laughed as he sang to me, forgetting anyone else was there but us. The interaction was intoxicating. I hadn't felt this amount of joy in forever. He did something to me I couldn't retract from, making me crave his attention.

The song ended, swiftly moving into another. Continuing to sway us in a gentler motion, Truro held me close, gazing down at me with intent. "So," he grinned devilishly, "did you dress up for me?"

I almost choked, looking down at my dress. "This old thing?" I japed. "Nah. I found it in the bottom of my bag."

His smile grew. "I know that's a lie."

"Oh?"

"Your bag is at the bottom of a ravine."

"Oh." My smirk was coy, flirtatious. "I guess there's no way of denying that."

"You look beautiful," he said, pulling me closer. "You always look beautiful. I could drown in those stunning eyes of yours. It's like watching two stars bursting to life."

I smiled. "I thought you said you're rubbish with words?"

"I've had two beers."

"Ahh. The wonders of alcohol consumed confidence."

"It works."

"It certainly does in this case."

"Shall we get another drink then?"

Laughing, I took his hand. "Sure."

Casting fleeting glances at each other, we waltzed to the bar, only to be ambushed by a swarm of young boys and their wooden swords. The lights from the small stage brightened their faces in hues of green and blue. I recognised the boy standing in front with his sword drawn towards Truro.

"I summon you to a duel," he said. His posture was defiant.

Truro tutted. "Not now, Fheo. Can't you see I'm busy."

Fheo's sharp, young eyes brushed over me, seemingly unimpressed. "Not an excuse. You shall face me or face punishment."

Truro groaned. "Go away, you toad. And take your rabble with you."

"Twenty-two hundred hours. Greyson's bridge. Be there." Fheo jabbed Truro in the stomach with his wooden sword, shooting glares meant to intimidate.

"You should be in bed by then." Truro tussled the boy's hair, pushing past him with me in tow.

"Twenty-two hundred hours, general. That's an order!"

Truro ignored him, pulling us up to two free stools at the bar. I shuffled onto one, watching Fheo and his rabble of mini warrior's scurry away through the crowd. "What was that all about?"

"Ah," Truro groaned, taking his own seat. "The little brat is trying to get me to make the same mistake as I did last new moon."

"Which was?"

"He asked me to duel with him on one of the suspension bridges. His terms were, if I lost, I had to renounce my title as security general...I know, right. The audacity of the little toad. Well, Greyson's bridge has an adjoining platform which is renowned for having a lower than standard safety barrier. Humouring him, I waited as he'd requested. Only, him and his friends ambushed me, sending me over the barrier edge..."

I gasped, smacking my hand over my mouth.

"I was fine. I landed on the net below, but the little toad ordered his rabble to haul up the access ladder...then left. No one was around. Everyone was at the new moon celebrations or guarding the perimeter."

"So, what did you do?"

"I stayed there until sunrise, when one of my scouts found me...sleeping."

I tried to suppress the chuckle escaping from my lips. Truro sighed. "I haven't lived it down yet...little shit."

Throwing my head back, I outwardly laughed. The image of Truro stranded on one of the safety nets for hours because a six-year-old had outwitted him was more than amusing. "Wow, he certainly has courage. For some reason he reminds me of you."

"Why'd you say that?" Truro's voice suddenly sounded clipped, his expression hard.

I frowned, attempting to keep the smile on my face. "He's defiant, strong willed. He has your hard, unreadable stare down to a tee. I could see him becoming your apprentice."

Truro looked down and hummed a smile. "Maybe he will. But...if he continues those types of stunts, maybe he won't.

The little shit."

I laughed again, noticing the bartender placing a pint of beer on the bar in front of Truro.

"The usual for you, young sir."

"You good man." Truro picked it up and took a long sip.

"And for you," I looked back and found the bartender placing another glass of coral wine on the bar top, "another one of these?"

Eyes sparkling, I nodded, thanking him. He moved on to his next customer and I found Truro frowning at me.

"Akquarian coral wine?" He sounded bemused. "I got the impression you never wanted to endure anything from that place again."

I swirled the peach liquid around the glass, licking my lips. "This beautiful beverage got me through many tedious evenings of Havav's drivel. It's rather tasty."

"That it is. Highly addictive, even."

"That explains why I've missed it so much." I sipped it, sighing at the wonderful taste. "Other than the wine, the only thing I miss from my time with the Akquarians is being able to see the stars." I glanced upwards, only finding the shadows of the canopy overhead. Hints of the darkening sky peeked through the gaps, but I rarely saw any constellations, any proof that more existed outside of this bubble of soil and air.

"You like stargazing?"

"I guess. It makes me feel less…alone."

A forlorn expression rippled across Truro's face. His eyes shifted skywards before sliding off his chair and downing his drink. He reached for my hand and said, "Come with me, beautiful. Bring your drink."

A little taken aback, I nearly tripped as I slid off the stool. Truro pulled me through the crowd of dancers towards one of the suspension bridges. Struggling to keep pace with him, we travelled further into the village, interrupting several conversations as we passed people milling about, enjoying the party.

Trying to keep my drink from spilling, I giggled. "Can we slow down?"

Glancing over his shoulder, Truro laughed, then stopped, removing the glass from my hand. "Your wine's expensive. You should take better care of it," he japed, noticing I was holding my left hand up away from my dress. I had wine dripping through my fingers, down my forearm.

"Doesn't help that my escort seems to be rather impatient in removing me from the party."

"Escort?"

I laughed. "Is that all you took from that comment?"

"No, but…*escort*?" The air stilled as he stepped closer, staring me down with those dazzling eyes. "Is that all I am to you?" His tone was low, playful, seductive even.

"Well, no."

"No?" He smiled, his face mere inches from mine. I could feel his breath on my face, smell his earthy scent. Nux, everything about him was captivating.

"You're my trainer."

"A trainer you like to flirt with."

"Can you blame me? My trainer is rather dishy."

With my dry hand, I snatched my drink from his, taking a long, slow sip, keeping my eyes fixed on his. His devilish smirk widened to something cheekier. Tracing his fingers up the length of my drenched arm, I watched him pull that hand up to his face. He stared sensually into my eyes, and I gasped as he took one soaked finger into his mouth. With his eyes closed, he sucked the wine from the skin, hollowing out his cheeks. I almost choked, entranced by the pressure of his tongue and the intense heat of his mouth encasing my finger.

Reaching the tip of my nail, he said, "Mmm, tastes even better this way," before sliding another drenched finger into his mouth.

My breath hitched and a swell of desire rushed through my body. What was he doing to me? And, as if in answer to my question, he opened his eyes, meeting mine, and slid my finger slowly out through his warm, soft lips.

Frozen by his actions, I was pretty sure my mouth was agape, confirming the arousal he'd stirred within me. He stepped closer, his lips only a fraction from mine. "I can think of a few other places where it would taste good, too."

Glancing at his lips, I licked the dryness from mine. "Maybe we should've bought the whole bottle."

"That might've been a good idea." He leant down, brushing his lips against mine. But before I could taste those tempting lips, a young voice shouted behind me, "There he is!"

Truro straightened, cursing over my shoulder. Grabbing my hand, he pulled, hard. So much for the rest of my wine. It was all over the floor, leaving a trail behind us. I dropped the empty glass into a basket next to a dark hut, hoping it wasn't filled with anything important.

A war cry erupted behind us, and I couldn't help laughing. "Are we really being chased by a band of children who want to throw you off a bridge?"

"Yes," Truro grumbled, pulling me around another tree platform and over another bridge. We stopped behind a crevice in one of the trees and darkness enveloped us. The bark was gnarled and twisted creating a small pocket to hide behind.

Standing in front of me, I could make out the whites of Truro's eyes scanning the immediate area outside. His breaths were heavy but calm, and I found myself transfixed by the way his chest moved.

A few moments later we heard the boys roaring past. Truro's teeth flashed at me, tightening his hold on my hand. "We should be clear now."

He guided me out of our hiding place, turning in the opposite direction to where Fheo and his friends had disappeared.

Taking a tree lift to the top level of dwellings, we scurried over more bridges and platforms, passing another party taking place at a large bar on a tiered decking area. Acoustic music grew, then faded as we continued. We must've been nearing the edge of the village by now.

"Where are we going?" I asked.

"You'll see."

The last of the village lights twinkled behind, plunging us into darkness. The solid, unwavering wood beneath my feet indicated we were walking over a static bridge. A shadow of an enormous tree loomed at the far end and, as we neared, I could make out a cluster of small lights illuminating the bottom of a staircase.

We began to ascend the steps, curving continuously up and around a large redwood tree. As we passed another cluster of lights, I realised the stairs were carved into bark. This tree was huge, almost as big as the one the council chamber was encased in, but far taller.

Rounding the last step, the area opened out, revealing a large, decked balcony overlooking the entirety of the village. The sun had set but the sky was still a mid-blue, silhouetting the treeline. Lights from the village sparkled through gaps in the canopy below. The air smelt fresher up here, cooler.

I glanced around, taking in the furniture laid out on the decking. Solar lights dimly lit the area. A table and four comfortable-looking wicker chairs sat halfway between the balcony edge and the treehouse. Through a wide, open archway, looking into the interior of the enormous tree, I could make out a large bed, immaculately made with cream pillows and brown blankets. In the far corner, an armchair was positioned in between two smaller windows. Another armchair sat beside a log burner and metal flume to the left. An ornate rug and a low, wooden coffee table filled the space between.

"Wow," I rasped in awe. "Who lives here?"

"I do."

I glanced back at Truro. He was standing by the balcony railing, watching me intently.

"Alone?"

"Yes." A questioning smile graced his lips. "I *can* look after myself."

"I just assumed you lived with your mum and Saff."

He laughed. "No."

"This is…" I twirled slowly, visually embracing the beauty of his home. "This is stunning."

"Perks of the job. Tallest tree and highest dwelling in the village. Perfect to keep an eye on everything from up here. During the day, you can see the sea to the west, the grazing fields to the north, the stream to the east. Sometimes you can see the reflection of the river rolling down the mountains in the distance. And at night," he walked towards me, stopping halfway to look upwards, "you can see the stars."

I looked up and revelled in the sight that met me. Even in the semi-dark sky, I could see the multitude of burning light piercing through the darkness, stretching in every direction for eternity.

"It doesn't get overly dark here in the summer, but on a clear night during the autumn and winter months, I can lose myself staring up there."

Still gazing upwards, I felt Truro shift position, moving closer.

"What do you look for," he asked, "to make you feel less alone?"

"Home." My voice was a trembling whisper as I scoured the darkness for a sign of Allura's presence. "I have no idea what direction home is in, but I know it's there. Somewhere."

"Do you have someone waiting for you back home?"

I realised his words were a gentle interrogation. A way of establishing my relationship status, just as I had his. An ache inside my chest stifled my breath, and I struggled to breathe for a moment. "No. My family are gone. The few friends I have are getting married or having kids. My work always takes me away for long spates of time, I rarely saw them anyway. They probably don't even know I'm missing. The only person I call anything near to family these days is Rooke."

My eyes continued to scan the night sky, longing to touch it. "I've spent most part of the last four years working in space. I guess I find the darkness calming in a way. It's steady, familiar. Although recently…recently I stare out there and feel…I feel lost." I met Truro's gaze and my heart stuttered in my chest. Nux, I loved it when his hair fell over his eyes, when he looked at me like that through the segregated strands. He seemed to understand me. A guardian angel in a time of uncertainty. A haven in a relentless storm. "I don't feel lost when I'm with you."

I watched him process my words. He remained still, his face displaying that stoic hardness I could never read.

Torturously slow, he closed the gap between us. Stopping only inches from me, he reached forward, tracing his fingers along the three-slashed scar on my right arm. I could see his mind ticking over, his clever eyes assessing more than the healed wound on my arm.

When he glanced up, his eyes burned brightly. The vibrant blue clashing with the whirlpool of my supernova. He was searching for understanding, perhaps permission. But as my shallow breaths heightened in anticipation to what he was seeking from me, he closed the gap entirely, pressing his solid body against mine. Whispering against my lips, he said, "When I'm with you, I feel alive. More so than I have done in what feels like forever. My worry is that you're a beautiful dream, and you will disappear as soon as I wake. I don't ever want to wake."

I was no longer drowning in his eyes. His mouth was the only thing I could concentrate on. Those gorgeous, sculpted lips, glistening in the faint light. I smiled and said, "I'm sorry I called you an arsehole when we first spoke."

Inching forward, he whispered, "Are you kidding? That's when I fell for you." I heard his breath hitch before his lips took mine.

It wasn't the gentle, soft kiss we'd had on the clifftop. A sense of urgency had fallen upon us, an underlying hunger to get closer. And I couldn't get close enough.

With my arms wrapped around his neck, our tongues clashed, barely finding the time to breathe. His hand groped the back of my neck, the other clamped around my waist with possessive need. My skin tingled where our bodies connected. His hard muscles moulded against mine, casting sparks of lightning, sending us into a whirl of wanton desire.

He walked us over to the table. The rugged wood against my skin made me gasp as he sat me down on the edge, and in a blur of motion, Truro removed his vest, tossing it behind him. My gaze lowered. Nux, his body was insane. The gentle glow spilling from the solar lights, defined the muscles across his chest and stomach. Toned muscles fanned out from the ripple of his ribs. A prominent indentation surrounded his carved abs, dipping into the waistband of his trousers. He looked as though he'd been sculpted from marble, like the statue of a god.

Entranced by the raw beauty of him, I gently traced my fingers along the muscle definitions, aware my touch was affecting him. He moaned against my neck as his fingers began to unbutton the front of my dress. Pulling his head back and meeting my eye, he popped the last button free. My dress fell open, exposing my breasts and toned stomach, and I held my breath. Only my knickers were keeping the last part of my modesty hidden.

Truro's eyes soaked up the sight of my body. The hunger in his expression was undeniable. A ragged sigh escaped him and his mouth found my lips again, pushing me flush against the table. His lips began to travel down my naked body, pausing for a time over one of my breasts. My back arched at the sensation of his tongue swirling around my tight, sensitive nipple. The sound of my moans made him linger, pulling me near to the edge of insanity.

When, at last, he began to travel lower, planting kisses as he went, he tugged at my dark knickers. Nerves tingled through my stomach as he slid the fabric down my legs, removing them along with my boots. I laughed as I heard the soles thud against the floor. He, too, chuckled and began to place hot kisses to the side of my ankle.

Captivated by his touch, I writhed as he scaled the length of my leg, up my inner thigh. The sensation sent another bout of sparks through my core, imprisoning me by the heat.

Unexpectedly, he stood. The loss of his lips on my skin felt torturous. Standing over me, he'd become silent, and a sudden pang of self-consciousness flooded my mind. Other than the two straps of my dress sagging around my arms, I was completely exposed to him. He gazed down at my body, his face set in stone—stern, serious. But the sheer look of desire pouring from his eyes made me reach for him. Nux, I wanted him. I needed him.

With panting breaths, I wrapped my arms around his shoulders, and in a clash of teeth and tongues, I lost myself in him. Never before had I felt so impatient, so lustfully incapable of holding back.

Truro's warm fingers slowly slid each dress strap off. Groping the back of my thighs, he carried me into his home, placing me delicately on the soft bed. He removed the last of his clothing, and I watched him straighten again, scaling my eyes over his god-like body.

Never in a million years had I imagined I'd be lying stark naked in the bed of the abrupt, stern scouting leader, who I'd first encountered nearly six weeks ago. The man who intrigued me, who's blue eyes had stopped me in my tracks, subconsciously calling me. Those vibrant eyes were looking at me now as he climbed on top of me, staring into the depths of my soul.

"God, you're beautiful," he rasped, reclaiming my lips.

My body writhed against his, losing myself in the way he teased with his slow, mind-blowing kisses and his wandering fingers. A relieved gasp ripped through my lungs when he finally prodded my entrance, pushing his length slowly inside me.

It didn't take long for me to crash over the edge, crying his name as my body trembled beneath him with waves of ecstasy.

The quench of euphoria stilled my mind with contentment. And it wasn't until after Truro had flipped me over onto my stomach, after I heard his moans of pleasure in my ear, until we'd both flopped onto the mattress and began to fall into a sated slumber in each other's arms; I suddenly thought of Rooke. My heart stopped dead for a tenuous moment.

Why his presence filled my mind, I didn't know. But for some reason, I felt a swell of guilt. The thought gnarled away at me, leaving me fighting an unsettled, self-loathing sickness.

What was wrong with me? Rooke had Valina. I'd found Truro. Rooke's actions spoke volumes. Weren't my own actions a self-confessed declaration that I was finally moving on?

Weren't they?

Chapter Sixteen

The sound of soft footsteps had woken me, and my eyes opened to find the grey light of dawn. For my first few breaths, I wasn't sure where I was. The gentle smell of tree bark hit my nose and I could make out a figure hunching over in a chair in the corner of the large, circular room.

A small groan escaped as I propped myself up on an elbow, my dark hair falling around my shoulders.

Truro's head snapped up. "Hey," he said softly. "I didn't mean to wake you."

"What time is it?" I blinked away the sleep, discovering he was dressed in his brown leathers, tying the laces of his boots.

"Just after five."

I frowned. "Where are you going so early?"

"I've got a scouting trip." He stood, walked over to the bed, and perched on the edge in front of me. "The scouting teams have to take it in turns to go out first thing after new moon. Unfortunately, it's my team's turn. But you can stay. Go back to sleep. It's early." He swept a rogue strand of hair away from my eyes, tucking it behind my ear. "I was hoping you'd still be here when I got back."

A small, delighted smile graced my lips. Nux, he was adorable. "How long will you be gone?"

"A couple of days. Maybe longer." He searched my face, his eyes twinkling.

"Not sure I can stay in bed for that long."

He smiled, leaning forward, and brushed his lips against mine. "Stay as long as you like. I'll see you when I get back."

My eyes sparkled up at him, watching him walk over to the log burner and plucking his swords from the wall above. Sheathing them across his back, he paused and looked at me. It was obvious he wanted to say more. I felt the same. My heart was bursting.

"Please take care." I couldn't bear the thought of something happening to him.

He strode over and kissed me. It was soft, deep, filling my head with memories from last night and promises of the days to come. I felt dizzy when he stepped away. A sigh escaped him, sounding almost like a groan of reluctance. He wanted to stay, that was clear, but duty called. I knew that feeling.

Looking like the formidable, fearless warrior he portrayed to perfection, he told me to go back to sleep. Heading to the open archway, he swiftly left, taking a piece of my heart with him. I fell back into the comfortable blankets, registering how tired I was. With Truro on my mind, I drifted back to sleep.

The distant sounds of the village were the first thing I heard when I stirred. Opening my eyes, the sun had fully risen. How long had I slept for? I needed to get to work. Sitting up, clutching the blanket to my bare chest, I glanced about the room. I had no idea where my clothes were.

I scrambled out of bed, wrapping the blanket firmly around myself. Scouring the room, I couldn't find any clothing, mine nor Truro's. Then I remembered; he'd undressed me outside. With an impish smile across my face, I scurried through the wide, open archway to the table outside. Taking in the view, I paused. In the daylight the scene was breath-taking. The hut was higher than the grazing field. I could see the horses and cattle grazing in the distance, and the long cluster of trees where the archery field was situated. I smirked. How many times had he been watching me from up here?

Far to the west, through a dip in the landscape, a haze of blue indicated the location of the ocean. The expanse of the village loomed below, stretching for miles. Hundreds of upper-level huts could be seen with their solar panels and rain buckets on the roofs. Lookout towers dotted about, positioned in the tallest of the trees. These were the only huts relatively close in height to where I stood.

Breathing in the fresh air, a strange moment of jubilation fell upon me; I could belong here, with these people. With Truro. I frowned, batting the ridiculous thought away. Allura was my home. But, who's to say I would ever see it again?

Forcing my eyes away from the stunning view, I noticed my orange dress sprawled across the wooden table. My boots laid haphazardly on the floor below. I scurried over, picking the boots up, then the pair of knickers hiding behind a table leg. Reaching for my dress, I halted at the sound of boots scuffing the floor from the direction of the stairs behind me. Smiling, I imagined Truro returning to surprise me. Had he pulled a few strings and postponed his scouting trip?

I turned towards him, ready to make a coquettish comment, but my heart jumped into my mouth—I couldn't breathe. Standing on the far side of the decking was Rooke. The dark expression on his face made my knees want to buckle. He was angry. *Really* angry.

Staring at each other for several torturous seconds, it was me who spoke first. "What…what are you doing here?"

"I could ask you the same." His eyes dipped to the blanket I was desperately holding up in the attempt to keep my body covered. "I've been up all night, waiting for you to come home."

"What? I didn't realise we had a curfew in place."

Not amused, he snapped, "I was worried!"

"About what? I'm not an idiot. I wasn't going to leave the safety of the village. Am I not allowed to stay *out*?"

"You could've told me where you were going?"

My confusion transformed into a sneer. "How could I? You left the party with Valina."

"You should've told someone. I came back and you were gone!"

"I'm an adult, Rooke!"

"AND I'M YOUR COMMANDER!"

Yeah, he was angry.

"Yes, you are," I said trying to keep my tone calm. "Not that any of us have seen much of you recently. Are you suggesting I need to send you a memo informing you of my movements and intentions? Do I have to wait to hear back for your approval?"

"Don't be like that."

My frown deepened. "I don't understand why we're having this conversation." I turned to pick up my clothes. Feeling beyond uncomfortable wrapped in nothing but a blanket, I needed to get dressed.

"Is he here?" Rooke's soft grumble made me pause. I looked over my shoulder. He'd moved closer, peering into the treehouse; Truro's home which oozed with luxury compared to the humble residence we currently held.

"No."

"Good." He marched over to me, pulling a chair out from under the table. "I think we need to talk, don't you?" The thought horrified me.

"Can I get dressed first?"

"No!" He pointed to the chair. "Sit!" His voice was stern, unyielding. It was obvious I had no choice in the matter.

Blowing out an irritated sigh, I reluctantly sat down, dropping my boots to the floor, and clenching the blanket tighter against my chest. I watched Rooke pull out the chair opposite, repositioning it closer to me so the table no longer stood between us, only the thick tension resonating from him.

Resting his elbows on his knees, he clasped his hands together, pensively tracing his lips with his forefingers. Peering at me from under his dark eyebrows, he made me feel as though I was on trial. I'd been at the brunt of his wrath many times before, but I'd never felt so shamefully guilty. Never felt as if I wanted the ground to open up and swallow me whole.

My eyes shifted to the wooden table next to us. It felt wrong sitting here with Rooke, when several hours ago I was partaking in some rather explicit activities with Truro, right there, on that very table.

Trying to stabilise my breathing, I glanced anywhere but at Rooke, refusing to speak first, as I usually did.

"What do you think you're doing?" His tone was quiet but full of pointed scorn.

Baffled, I stared back at him, defending myself against the way his eyes burned deep into mine. What did he think I was doing? "Living." The single word sounded more like a question than an answer.

"For Nux Sake, Eden. Answer the damn question! What do you think you're doing…with Truro?"

Shit, his temper was peaking. I hadn't seen him like this in years.

Wasn't the answer obvious? "I doubt you want details, so in context...I haven't done anything different to what you've been doing with Valina."

"And what exactly have I been doing with Valina?!"

Huffing, I tried not to laugh.

"Eden!"

"Do I really have to say it?"

"Yes. Enlighten me!"

For Nux sake! "Having sexual relations. Sleeping with each other. Fucking. However you want to word it!" If he was going to scorn me for sleeping with Truro, then I was going to give as good as I got.

Rooke gaped at me, the frown between his eyes shifted into a vision of utter shock. "You think..." He released an incredulous laugh. "You think I..."

"Don't insult me, Rooke. I do have eyes. I see the way she looks at you, the way she's always touching you, manipulating you. I've *seen* you together...oh, don't give me that look. I saw you the evening when you were half naked, drinking in your office, hands all over each other. You can't possibly tell me nothing happened that night. Oz slept on the floor of the middle hut, for Nux sake." The memory of feeling sick to my stomach overwhelmed me. I'd tried to put this all behind me; tried to move on, but here I was experiencing the putrid jealousy all over again.

"Valina didn't *stay*! I took her home just before midnight. She was drunk. I didn't touch her. And Oz slept in the middle hut because he said our hut stunk of alcohol."

I scoffed, not convinced. I'd seen her licking wine from his lips whilst wrapping her legs around him. That didn't look innocent to me.

"Do you know how hard it is," Rooke pushed his fingers through his short hair, "having to pander to her on a daily basis? It's exhausting."

"Then, why do you do it?"

"To keep her sweet. To soften the blow when Solarfleet arrive and deny her and her people what they seek."

"Oh, I guess that's my fault then?" I mumbled.

He snapped again, "And this isn't about me and Valina! You still haven't answered my question. What are you doing with Truro?"

I shook my head, dropping my gaze to the floor. "Is it really that hard for you to believe I like him?"

"A little." Rooke was still throwing me a look of disdain. Why was he being like this? "You haven't shown an interest in a guy for, what, two years, at least."

"So?"

"Just an observation." He leant back in the chair, sweeping his eyes over my indecent state, making me feel wretched. "Was this the first time, or is he the reason you've been sneaking off every morning?"

I stood up abruptly, grabbing my clothes and boots. "You have no right to ask me these questions. Commander or not!"

With those dark eyes, he silently watched me march past. I was barely over the threshold into the treehouse when he called, "Are you out of your mind?"

I froze, trying to perceive what he meant. Glancing over my shoulder, I found him standing, hands in his pockets. The frown on his face had shifted to one of concern, but his voice still held the scornful tone. "No offence to these people, but they live like savages. He could be carrying something. Some sexual disease that he could've passed onto you. Eating you away from the inside out."

I stared at the floor, aware my breaths had quickened, my eyes prickling with tears.

"What if you get pregnant? Have you thought about that?" I felt him move closer, the tension in the air rebuilding. "Have you forgotten pregnant women can't subspace travel? Unless you're happy to have the baby here, of course. Of which the child won't be able to subspace travel until they're at least twelve. I don't see you as a mother who abandons her child, so, are you intending on staying here for another thirteen years? Do you not want to go home?"

I looked across the room at the unmade bed, hiding the shame and regret of my irresponsibility. I suddenly felt disgusted with myself. I'd been so caught up in the way Truro made it easier for me to breathe, that I hadn't stopped to consider any of this.

"Have you lost your mind?" Rooke moved closer, pulling my attention back to his face. He then snorted towards the ceiling. "I've heard of people becoming deranged after spending too much time in space, but with you," he looked down his nose at me, "it appears the return to gravity has caused a spate of nymphomania. I mean, it wasn't that long ago you were trying to ride me." He chuckled coldly and I felt my stomach convulse, violently.

How dare he?

Even if the comment was meant to be a light-hearted joke, it was tasteless, scolding, a personal assault. It left me seething to the brink of retaliation. My heart was pounding with adrenaline, and for a split second, I lost all control of my body. I felt the sharp sting of pain resonating over the palm of my hand before I realised I'd slapped Rooke across his face.

I must've struck him hard. Rooke was standing with his head to the side, mouth agape, rotating his jaw. His cheek began to redden when he looked back at me. I held his gaze for another agonising second, emphasising the extent of my actions. I hated him in that moment. I hated him!

Turning on my heel, I headed to the bed, dropping my clothes down upon it, hoping Rooke would take it as a hint to leave. But instead, I heard the soft anguish in his voice.

"Why can't we talk about what happened that night?"

My stomach flopped, sending a wave of pain through my chest. "We did." I swallowed down the warble, replacing it with curt courage. "You concluded it only happened because we were drunk on Akquarian sex juice, remember. End of story!"

"Is that how you see it?"

"Yes!" *No. Nux, no!*

Silence filled the air. I fiddled with the straps of my dress, listening to my heartbeat pounding in my ears. I didn't want to talk about this. I'd tried to move on from what happened that night at the Akquarian ball. "Can you *please* leave, so I can get dressed. I need to get to work."

"You're not going to work!"

I flicked my head in his direction. Still standing behind me, his face as hard as stone, shielding any sign of emotion whatsoever.

"That's an order!" He turned and marched away, leaving me struggling to breathe. My heart ached. My body trembled. The pure disgust seeping through every one of his comments struck me with dejection. Hot tears stung the corner of my eyes, and I sucked in a lungful of air attempting to disengage them.

Don't cry, Eden. Don't cry. You've done nothing wrong.

But I had, hadn't I? I'd slept with Truro when I'd promised to spend the evening with Rooke. For once I'd put myself before him. Was that so wrong?

I don't know how long I stood there staring into my thoughts, but it was only when the blanket dropped to the ground, pooling around my feet, I realised my hand clasping it had gone numb from how tight I'd been clenching.

With shaky hands, I quickly dressed. After lacing up my boots, I stood, glancing about Truro's home, and my heart began to break. What had I done?

Batting the tears away, I neatened the pillows and blankets on the bed, then walked outside and tucked the chairs in under the table. Taking one last glance at the stunning view, I sucked in a deep breath, heading for the stairs.

Much to my dismay, Rooke was waiting for me at the bottom. With his hands in his pockets, he was leaning against the huge tree trunk. I huffed my displeasure as I passed him, aware he followed behind.

Halfway along the sturdy bridge, I couldn't hold my tongue any longer. "I can find my way home, you know."

"Didn't want you to endure the walk of shame on your own."

I huffed again. More scolding, more sarcasm aimed to hurt me. My temper began to rise.

"Besides," he went on, "you're not going home. I want you to go and see Zam at the medical centre. She needs to check you over."

"Check me over? What the hell, Rooke?"

"Better to be safe than sorry. And if Truro has given you anything, we can catch it early. Including any unwanted accidents."

Was he being serious? Unwanted accidents? Is that how he saw pregnancy? My mind flicked to Cora and my blood grew cold. Zamya had been right. It was no wonder she'd told Cora to keep her condition to herself. Rooke wouldn't have allowed Cora to return home pregnant. I had an awful feeling he would've forced her to have an abortion before considering any other alternative. How could he be so callous?

I continued through the trees, down the tree lift, and across the main area of the village with Rooke still in tow. As I turned towards home, Rooke grabbed my arm, halting me. He pointed in the opposite direction. "The Pasa is that way."

I ripped my arm from his hold. "At what point in our relationship did you become my dad?"

"When I discovered you no longer look after yourself," he snarled back.

I swallowed back the resentment. "Why are you being like this?"

"You're clever enough to understand why."

I shook my head. "Can I at least go home and change first?" I gestured to my clothes. "Walk of shame and all?" I was crumbling beneath the surface. Failing to hold his hard stare, I was ready to accept defeat, but his voice suddenly softened.

"Fine. Be quick about it."

Utterly shocked by his behaviour, I continued on my original path, still aware he was following me like a prison guard. The anger was boiling away. My jaw felt tight, my body stressed. I'd never felt so wretched in my whole damn life.

Halfway home, and full to the brim with pent up resentment, I turned abruptly and glared at Rooke with a bitterness aimed to show my scorn. "How dare you?" He halted his steps, "How dare you just turn up like that? Truro could've been there. We could've been…" I wavered a breath trying not to think about the humiliation I would've felt if Rooke had walked in on us. "I would never do that to you. *Never!*"

I didn't care my words seemed to pain him, I marched home.

Leaving a safe distance between us, Rooke continued to stalk behind.

Chapter Seventeen

"He said what?" Zamya peered at me from across the medical room. Her pristine black eyebrows contorted into a frown of unequivocal disbelief. I knew her question was rhetorical. I'd already reiterated the order Rooke had demanded. And it *was* an order. A friend would never have marched me here, slammed the door button with aggressive annoyance, and left without a decent word to either of us.

As I sat on the solitary medical bed, so many unsettling emotions whirled about inside my head; stupidity, shame, humiliation. But the worst was the pure repugnance I felt towards Rooke, my dearest friend.

"He can't be serious." Zamya walked towards me, her frown deepening.

"You just saw him. He's being serious."

Zamya looked at the door, shaking her head. "I don't understand." She peered back at me. "There are no STDs here. I checked when we first arrived. I checked again when Oz started poking some of the native ladies…and Rooke is aware of it. He's the one who asked me to recheck."

Staring at her, I questioned if I'd heard her correctly. "So why…why is he…"

Her expression darkened, shaking her head again. "He's being a pompous dick, as usual."

What the hell? Why would he put me through that embarrassing spectacle if he knew? Why?

"And as for the pregnancy test, he can sod off. It's too early to test, anyway. Time will tell. Besides, I can give you a tonic to help with that. Although, if I were you, I'd go sleep with Truro several more times and purposely get pregnant, just to piss Rooke off."

I watched Zamya. She was clenching her jaw, staring at the exit, lost in thought. She couldn't believe Rooke's actions just as much as I could. But I suddenly couldn't dislodge the disturbing feeling that I was losing him.

Truro had become a shining light through a disconcerting, troubling time—a breath of fresh air. But I barely knew him. Regardless of what I'd been telling myself recently, Rooke was my world, and it was clear he felt a sense of aversion towards me and my actions. He'd sent me here to reprimand me, to remind me of who I was and where I came from. Recently, my actions had been brash, perhaps even foolish. And I was keeping more than my relationship with Truro from him. Maybe this was all my fault and I deserved it.

"Don't you dare feel guilty about what happened." I found Zamya throwing me a pitiful look. "I can tell what you're thinking. Don't you dare let him come between you and what you've found with Truro."

"I…I can't ruin the relationship I have with Rooke for a fling that will have to end in a few months."

"If Rooke can't see how much you need Truro right now, then he's not worth it!"

I held my head in my hands, fighting the tears.

"Eden, Rooke's an arsehole. You always ask me why I loathe him so much. Well, the truth is, I hate the way he treats you. I hate the way he uses you to do his bidding, uses you as a buffer between him and the rest of the crew. He gets you to do all the shitty jobs…like tell Troy that Cora died. That should've been him, not you. And you defend him like the loyal friend and servant you are. He keeps you on a tight leash while he dilly-dallies around, but never, ever, gives you what you want." She sighed, coming to sit next to me on the medical bed. "Just tell me one thing?" I could feel her eyes on me. "How long have you been in love with him?"

Closing my eyes, a single tear trickled down my cheek—the first one to escape all morning. "Nux. Is it really that obvious?"

"No," Zamya's voice was gentle, kind, non-reproachable. "I picked up on a few signs back at the Akquarian fortress. Oz, too, has recently started to wonder."

I cursed my frustration.

"He won't say anything. He's not that stupid."

I groaned, wiping my eyes. "I just…I hoped…I hoped Truro would distract me. Help me with the situation. Give me a reason to stop being so obsessed with Rooke."

"He still can."

"How? It's obvious Rooke disapproves of my relationship with Truro. I can't go against him."

"You can and you must!"

Like a reluctant toddler, I shook my head vigorously. My voice was barely audible when I said, "I can't lose Rooke, Zam. He's all I have."

Zamya's petite fingers gripped mine, squeezing them tenderly. "I do know how it feels…to have no one. No family." She sighed. "I don't speak of it. My…my whole family disowned me when I ran out on my arranged marriage."

I gaped at her, witnessing the flash of pain shimmer across her face. She squeezed my fingers again before returning hers to her lap, nervously fiddling with them. "I'd just graduated from med school. Being the grand old age of twenty-*three* and returning home without an intended husband, they set one up for me. Stupidly, I went along with it, wanting to please everyone. But on the eve of my wedding…I couldn't…I couldn't go through with it. So, I ran…I ran to Torla, and that's when I signed up to Solarfleet." With a forlorn smile she looked at me. "I haven't spoken to any of my family since, not even my sister. It's been four years. I'm dead to them."

"Nux, Zam."

"I know it was my decision, and, unlike you, I haven't lost my family through a series of traumatic events, but…I know how it feels…to feel alone."

"I'm so sorry. I didn't know."

"No one knows. Could you imagine what Oz would say if he found out?" She chuckled. "I wouldn't live it down."

I huffed a smile. "You have courage, Zam."

"As do you." She stood up and looked down at me. "Please don't bow down to him. You are your own person, and he needs to understand that. He has no right to control you."

I knew she was right, she always was. But the deep, grounding part of my conscience would not allow me to dent Rooke's opinion of me further. I would not sever the invisible bond holding Rooke and I together.

The more I thought about it, the stronger I concluded Rooke's reaction was justifiable. I'd been irresponsible, selfish. I was an Alluran, not a Redwood. I *wanted* to go home—with Rooke. He was my world. Even if our relationship remained platonic, he was the one who was always there for me, guiding me. I loved him.

But the thought of Truro shot razor blades through my heart. I had to do what's right, and that was to end whatever I had started with him. A swell of reluctance gripped me. Nux, I felt so torn.

I didn't attend training the next day, nor the next. I couldn't bring myself to face Saff or Jader. I was a fraud. I'd taken so much from these people, Truro included. And if Rooke was right, we wouldn't be helping them reform their lives when Solarfleet arrived. We'd wave our goodbyes and leave them to suffer, alone.

I still left the crew house early every morning, but instead of training, I'd help pick the strawberries and blackberries in the fields on the west clifftop, sometimes the nectarines from the orchards. None of the other pickers tried to converse with me, which suited me just fine. Those couple of hours in the morning sun became my moments of reflection.

Truro had said he'd be gone at least two days. It had been five and there was still no mention of his return. Even so, my body filled with dread at the thought of bumping into him. I couldn't face him yet. I had no idea what I'd say. If I was being honest, I didn't want to say the words. I longed to see him, to pick up where we'd left off. He'd become my friend, my saviour. But how could I go against Rooke?

It was the afternoon of the fifth day; I returned home from a long shift at Pepa's Kitchen, and the fear and anxiety of what needed to be done hit me like a ton of bricks. Standing eloquently on the table was a distinctive bottle of wine. With its bulbous, crystalised glass and peach-coloured liquid, I knew exactly what it was and who it was from.

Frozen to the spot, I stared at it from the doorway, trying to sieve through the suggestions in my mind of what to do.

"That came for you."

Panicked by the inanimate object, I hadn't noticed Oz in the corner of the room, lounging in one of the low chairs. He nodded towards the bottle. Another level of concern infiltrated my sense. If Oz was here, then chances were Rooke was here as well.

Taking a deep breath, I walked towards the table. A small brown piece of paper was tucked in beneath the bottle. I pulled it free, unfolding it cautiously.

Goddess,
You know where to find me if you need help drinking this.
~ T

Holding my breath, I reread the words several times. I began to feel lightheaded. "When did this arrive?" I asked Oz.

"About an hour ago."

"Does Rooke know?"

The uncomfortable look on Oz's face was confirmation enough.

Closing my eyes, I tried to find the courage to do the right thing. If Rooke hadn't known about this, I could've hidden the evidence. But he knew, which meant I needed to face the inevitable.

I grabbed the bottle and left the hut, marching across the village towards Truro's treehouse.

As I boarded the static bridge, where the carved staircase within the bark loomed at the far end, I paused, praying the slatted wood beneath me would give out and I'd plummet one hundred metres to the ground. I didn't want to do this. I had no intention of hurting Truro; the beautiful, strong, caring man I'd come to admire.

Nux, this was agonising. But all I could envision was Rooke's expression of disgust. I couldn't go against him anymore. It would break us.

Somehow, my feet began to move without command. My head was screaming for me to stop, to return home and tell Rooke to shove his expectations up his arse. But I continued to climb the curving stairs up to Truro.

At the top, I softened my footsteps as I crossed the decked

balcony. Truro's leathers had been washed. They were hanging on a short washing line segregating the two sides, hiding my presence from the opening into the tree. Taking one last deep, stabilising breath, I walked through the wet clothes, pausing on the threshold of Truro's home.

From the sight that met me, every word and sentence I had prepared to say to him disappeared from my mind.

On the far side of the room, reading from a ragged looking folder, he was perched on the edge of his armchair, dressed in a grey hoodie and a pair of black fabric shorts. He looked so fresh, so adorably handsome—so normal. I could've taken him in his current state, placed him in a Torlan village, and he would've fitted in.

He could come live with me. We could be together. I don't have to do this.

I flinched when his eyes discovered me frozen on his doorstep.

"Hey, beautiful."

No, No. Don't call me that!

His smile spread, lighting up the entirety of his face. Placing the folder on the window ledge beside him, he said, "I was hoping you'd come over." The way he looked genuinely thrilled to see me made my heart ache. I hated myself even more.

My inability to hide my emotions was evident. Still frozen on the spot, I watched his tanned face slowly distort into a frown.

"What is it?" He slowly rose out of his chair. I had to do this now, otherwise he would walk over, and I'd lose myself in those stunning eyes. He'd discard the tiny amount of willpower I had left.

Stepping forward, I placed the wine bottle on the piece of wood resembling a coffee table. "Thank you, but I...I can't accept this."

His frown deepened, flicking his eyes between me and the unopened bottle. "Eden? What's happened?"

"I just...I'm sorry." I couldn't disguise the warble in my voice. I needed to leave before I caved in. The confused look on his face was too agonising to endure.

Backtracking my steps, I made for the balcony, aware of his rushed movements following me.

"Eden. Wait!"

Passing under the washing line, I felt the invisible tug towards him just before his fingertips gently brushed against my wrist, sending a bout of electricity through me. Nux, I wanted to scream.

"Eden, please. What's brought this on?"

I turned, moisture lining my eyes, my heart pounding against my chest. I knew I should explain, but I couldn't think straight. Words and conflicting thoughts jumbled about my brain. I couldn't do this. The hurt and confusion in his eyes tore my soul to pieces. "I'm sorry, Truro. I can't…I can't see you anymore. I'm sorry."

He fell silent as I scurried away down the stairs. A part of me was grateful he didn't come after me. Another part of me was devastated.

My eyes began to leak uncontrollably. I loathed myself. I felt as though I'd ripped apart the last fragment of joy I had left in my miserable life. And in that moment, I despised Rooke. I hated him with every fibre of my being. He'd made me do this, made me feel guilty about something that should've made my heart sing, not ache in despair.

Usually in situations like this, it would've been Rooke who I ran to, who consoled me and told me what to do. But how could I run to him now? He was the one who was crushing my existence, making it hard to breathe. Truro had been Rooke's replacement, and I'd just severed our connection with a few nonexplanatory words. The feeling was raw, like a sharp knife digging deep, tearing me apart.

Drowning in my thoughts, I absentmindedly lost all sense of direction. I was still on the upper level of the village. I rarely came up here. Most people would've been at the markets or at work, and it felt eerily quiet.

Wiping my cheeks with shaky fingers, I glanced about the area, noticing one of the tall trees I'd spotted from Truro's balcony, moments before Rooke had arrived and shattered my heart five days ago. A small lookout hut sat at least twenty metres up. The wood looked damaged, scorched. It was clearly abandoned.

Walking towards the tree, I found the entrance to a roped ladder sectioned off by a heavy-duty chain displaying a rusted sign saying, *Persons not permitted.* Taking several turns about the platform, I was happy nobody was watching, so I rebelliously stepped over the chained barrier and climbed the ladder.

At the top, it was obvious the small hut had been burnt, damaging the structure. One section of the wall was completely missing. Its singed edges were black and brittle. Patches of the floor were cracked or broken. From the height of the tree, I assumed it had been struck by lightning, but the bark of the tree itself seemed untouched. Thinking back to what Blake had told us, redwood trees were fire resistant.

The wooden floor disconcertingly creaked beneath my boots as I shuffled around the trunk, avoiding the urge to glance towards Truro's treehouse. I sat on the floor, facing the large, jagged hole in the wall structure. From there, I could see the edge of the village merging into the expanse of the canopy, reaching towards the glistening sea on the horizon. The view was stunning. The same view I'd seen from Truro's beautiful home. The home that I had no doubt he would've shared with me.

I closed my eyes thinking of his tormenting expression of confusion and pain. Tears trickled down my face. "What have I done?"

I felt torn.

I felt lost again.

Chapter Eighteen

"Why are you still here?" Rooke's voice boomed through the doorway of the middle hut, his dark presence suffocating the room as he entered. The rest of us sat around the table eating breakfast, keeping our heads down.

It had been a week since I last saw Truro. I'd continued to avoid training sessions and, thankfully, Truro hadn't made any appearances at the food hall when I'd been working.

I tried to keep my melancholy demeanour at bay, but some days were harder than others. Days when my mind continuously ticked over, wallowing in thoughts of Sym and Cora, my family, Rooke, Truro; all clawing to create the question of, what if things had been different? What if?

Much to my relief, my monthly arrived. For some reason I cried when it did.

Most days I rose early, spending a couple of solitary hours picking fruit in the soft morning sun. Other mornings, like this one, I couldn't find the strength to get out of bed before eight.

"Why aren't you preparing the horses?" Rooke's angry snarl was aimed at Oz, who was sitting opposite me, trying not to grimace.

"We won't be going out today, boss."

Dressed in his black leathers, with his sword sheathed diagonally across his back, Rooke portrayed a dark, commanding warrior, ready to rage war. His boots stomped to a halt, peering down at Oz's large form. "And why is that?"

Oz braved a look at his commander. I noted his tone of hesitancy. "There are no horses or men available. We'll have to stay put today."

"Says who?"

"Says…Truro."

"Truro!"

"Yeah, boss. He said…"

"Yeah, I bet he did."

I felt Rooke's heated glance without removing my eyes from my plate. Thankfully, the sound of his boots stomping out of the room seemed to eliminate the tension building in the air.

"Well, he's in a delightful mood," Zamya groaned.

"He's always like that at the moment," Oz mumbled, picking at his breakfast.

I kept my head down, pretending not to listen, but when Kobe mentioned Rooke had received a couple of personal messages over the past few days from Allura, it piqued my interest. "It could've been bad news," Kobe concluded.

There was a short pause before I heard Oz say, "Maybe someone should speak to him. Check he's okay."

Another pause.

Looking up, I discovered three pairs of eyes on me. Flicking my cold gaze over each of them, I frowned. "Don't look at me. I'll only make things worse. He can't stand the sight of me."

"Don't you think," Kobe said with his usual blunt, nonchalant tone, "it's about time you and Rooke put whatever this tiff is behind you and make up. It'd be nice to resume some semblance of normality around here?"

I scowled at him, doubting he had any idea what the *tiff* between Rooke and I was. And I certainly wasn't going to bow down another notch to pander to the man who had already shattered my heart in more ways than one. "Why don't you grow some balls, Kobe. Then, maybe you could go talk to him yourself."

Pushing the chair back abruptly, I marched out the door, ignoring Zamya's soft plea. I couldn't tolerate Kobe's bluntness when I felt like this. The urge to climb the east cliff ladder and engage in a sword fight with Wrenn was beyond tempting. I had so much pent-up anger boiling away, it wouldn't be long before I blew my top. But instead, I plodded to the food hall, ready to assist with the morning's food orders. Another day of mundane work. The realisation that I had to endure this daily routine for another few months made my decisions so much harder to bear. I'd wanted that hunting job, and because of the pressure from Rooke, I'd given up my dream of that too.

I knew Pepa was watching me as I cleaned a table near the edge of the food hall. For days her kind, mothering eyes always landed on me when I was drowning in my thoughts, and today was no different. Because today I was lost in scenarios of what messages Rooke had received from Allura, and if his mood had worsened because of them. If they were personal messages, they weren't from Solarfleet pushing more concerning debate onto him. They had to be from family, or...Miranda, his girlfriend.

My heart slammed against my chest, a surge of heat rose up my neck. Maybe she'd ended it. It had been over eight months since we left Allura. Rooke had been adamant to get the job done when we first got here because he wanted to get home...probably back to her. His lack of following Solarfleet procedures had jeopardised the whole mission, and for what? For Miranda to end their relationship when he was stranded on an alien planet? It was a farfetched thought, but the more I tried to piece the situation together, the more intrigued I was to know what was in those damn messages.

"Have you started reading tea leaves?" Zamya's voice made me jump. Looking up from the hunched position I was in, I realised I had been locked in a pensive stare with the bottom of a teacup. I tried to laugh but it sounded more like a squawk.

"So, tell me," Zamya leant back against the table, crossing her arms across her chest, "do the tea leaves give you an insight into what mood our commander will be in later?"

From under my dark lashes, I peered at her. She flicked her large brown eyes at me, her lips pouting to one side. I knew that look. She was disappointed.

"I just saw Truro," she said glancing towards the market stalls, my eyes following hers in a poised panic. "He's really cute."

"Don't, Zam." The words came out sounding as feeble as they felt.

"Look, I get it," she said. "Why you choose Rooke over Truro. But for Nux sake, you can't choose this path and ignore him day after day. Rooke doesn't deserve you. And I was hoping you'd have changed your mind by now. But...I doubt anything could change it. You love Rooke...and even though it pains me to say it, Kobe's right. You need to get past this rift. *Talk to him*. Smooth out the craters that have dented the ground between you both. You need him. And I'm pretty sure he needs you."

I gaped at her, completely blown away by her opinion. "That was unexpected."

"Yeah, well…desperate times and all."

"Right." I sighed, leaning back against the table next to her, the dirty teacup still in my hand. "Why is it always me who needs to instigate a truce?"

"Because he's a dick."

I laughed. "I knew you'd say that."

"Well, he is. A stubborn one."

"I hope you're not talking about me." A deep male voice cut across us, and we both turned, finding Jader standing on the other side of the table.

"Um, excuse me!" Zamya snarled, standing. "Do you always eavesdrop on strangers' conversations?"

A hint of surprise flashed across Jader's face, his eyes running over Zamya's hostile scowl and her defiant stance. "My apologies." He held his palms up in surrender. "I'd like to speak with Eden, please."

Baffled, Zamya glanced at me.

"It's okay, Zam. This is Jader."

She turned fully towards me and mouthed, "Who?"

"I'm Jader." He stepped forward, offering Zamya his charming grin. "I'm Eden's trainer."

"Trainer?" She eyed me again, sceptically. "*Right.*" She took a few steps away but chose to loiter by the adjacent table. I didn't miss the look of puzzlement on her face.

Moving closer, Jader stared down at me, folding his muscular arms across his chest in an act of authority. "You haven't been at training for the past two weeks."

"Jader, I can't explain right now…"

"I don't want you to explain. I want you back at training."

I stared at him, prompting him to drop his stance and take a seat on the table next to me.

"Look. A hunter position in my own team has become available. I want you to have it. But I can't give it to you if you don't attend regular training."

My heart skipped with excitement, then worry. Again, I felt torn.

"I don't want to know what's happened between you and Truro, it's none of my business. But I do know he is away for the next two weeks. So there won't be any chances of bumping into him at training. And when he gets back, if things are still awkward, we can arrange alternative training routines."

"You're offering me a job?"

"Yes."

If he'd given me this news three weeks ago, I would've jumped at it. Now, I felt conflicted. I had no doubt Rooke wouldn't approve. So, if I accepted the offer, I'd have to lie to him, which given the circumstances, wasn't the best approach to rectify the issues between us. But on the other hand, even though I loved Pepa to bits, I was starting to resent the kitchen job. It had become tedious and mundane. It gave me too much time to think, and thinking made my brain hurt and my heart ache.

I glanced at Jader. He was eagerly awaiting my response. His dark, friendly eyes shifting between me and Zamya.

"When do I need to decide by?"

"Tomorrow morning."

"Alright." I swallowed back the moment of indecision. "I'll let you know by then."

He seemed to accept my response. Nodding his head, he rose to his feet, smiled at Zamya, before disappearing in between the food stalls. I watched him go, drowning in my own predicament.

In the corner of my eye, I noticed Zamya return. Placing her hands firmly on her hips, meeting my eye, she chirped, "What's *training*?"

I wandered back home early that afternoon. I needed rest. I knew I did, but my mind wouldn't switch off. Nux, I just wanted all the thoughts to stop!

Walking over the platform adjoining Rooke's office, I paused. Zamya's words swirled around my mind. Her opinion on the situation had turned on its head. But why? Was it purely to remove the tension within the crew, or did she really believe Rooke and I needed each other?

I glanced down the short bridge into the shaded hut. Was he there? I couldn't see him behind his desk. The thought of him sent bouts of anxiety racing round my body, but I couldn't leave the situation as it was. I needed to speak to him. I couldn't remember the last time we had a civil conversation.

I marched over the bridge, stomping my feet as way of announcement. His office was empty. The large map he always pooled over was spread over the desk, and on top of it—I held my breath, questioning my morality—his tablet lay at the edge, abandoned.

The temptation was too much to resist. I glanced about, checking Rooke wasn't there. After one final, satisfied look in his bedroom, I reached for the device and tapped the screen. The same photograph of me and his family at his graduation lit up. I swiped it away and the main page came into view. Shaking my head, it dumbfounded me why he was so lax with the security of his confidential documents. Solarfleet would sack him if they ever found out.

But then I paused. The picture of him kissing his girlfriend was gone, replaced with a cute photo of him and his mum. Had the message been from Miranda?

Scrolling down the screen, there were no messages highlighted on the main page. Selecting the comms tab, I discovered a library full of read video messages. My eyes scanned the list. I failed to find any from Miranda newer than five months old, so I scrolled back up. Sitting at the very top was a message from Noell Maddox, Rooke's brother. He'd received it three days ago. *That must be it, the message Kobe was talking about.*

Without hesitation, I tapped the play button…

The dark-haired, clean-shaven face of Rooke's older brother appeared. He looked pale, his expression drawn and forlorn. His voice; an unenthusiastic rumble filled with fatigue.

"Hey bro. I can't express how relieved we are to find out you're okay. We've been…we've all been out of our minds with worry." He pushed his fingers through his hair in the same way Rooke always did. He looked exhausted. *"Things aren't great here. After we learnt you'd gone missing, mum started having headaches. Bad headaches. The doc said they were probably brought on by stress. Well, as you can imagine, she's been pretty distraught. She thought…she was adamant you were dead. Couldn't get it out of her head that you were floating in space somewhere. And Eden…you know how much she loves Eden. We tried to console her. But…then a month ago, she had a seizure. Turns out she had a tumour on her brain. She's had it removed, but… but she didn't wake up. She's*

currently in a coma. I'm pretty sure the machines are keeping her from relapsing. Doc's not..." He shook his head before sucking in a stabilising breath. *"He's not sure she's going to come out of it. I just wish your news came sooner. We've told her you're alive, but who's to know if she's listening or..."*

"What are you doing?"

The sound of Rooke's voice filling the room made me jump so violently my neck muscles twitched and spasmed. Through glassy eyes, I looked over at him standing in the doorway.

"You should've told me," I said, as he marched towards me. The intimidation he expelled caused me to step back. For the first time, he scared me. His eyes were lifeless, his aura hostile. It was obvious he was struggling. The news about his mum was devastating.

Snatching the tablet from my grasp, he snarled, "Why are you going through my stuff?" I stared at him, watching him closedown the message and toss the tablet onto the desk. "Is it a regular thing? Do you spy on me often?"

I continued to stare, noticing the disdain in his mannerism, and something inside of me snapped. "If you're *that* bothered about me viewing your personal messages, maybe you shouldn't leave your tablet unlocked and unattended."

His face seemed to drain of colour. The dark gaze he'd jousted into me was now averted. I watched his Adams apple bob, realising how distraught he looked, and I suddenly felt ashamed.

"I didn't do it out of spite, Rooke. I understand you're under a lot of pressure, and your current mood is hard to miss. Don't look at me like that. It's obvious you're pissed with me, but *this* can't all be because of me."

He huffed, crumpling the map as he turned and perched on the edge of the desk.

"Kobe mentioned you'd received some news from home. I guess he knew."

"Nux, he's a sly bastard."

"Why didn't you tell me...about your mum? You know how much I adore her."

"What good would it have done? I knew you'd be upset. We can't do anything. It takes two weeks to send and receive messages. She could be dead for all I know."

"Rooke…"

"It's true! There's no point denying it…I just…Nux, I feel so *useless!* I should be there with her, with my family. But instead, I'm trapped here on this Nux forsaken planet with… with…"

With me.

He huffed again, pushing his fingers awkwardly through his hair. "I regret everything, Eden. I shouldn't have accepted this mission. I should've been more vigilant when we arrived. I shouldn't have let Sym and Cora die."

"You didn't let them die, Rooke." I reached forward, brushing his arm, but he retreated, almost disgusted by my touch.

"It's my fault!"

"You mustn't blame yourself…"

"I regret everything!" His gaze met mine and I saw the grief and despair spilling overboard. "Everything."

"Let me help you. Please. Let me help you through this."

Pinching the bridge of his nose, he shook his head. "Being around you at the moment is suffocating."

His words shocked me, sending a powerful blow to my heart. Why was he so angry at me? Had I really overstepped a line by sleeping with Truro, or was there more to his contempt?

"Eden, I don't want to feel like this. I never thought I was a control freak but…I…I can't cope with any of it anymore. I've never felt so…" Voices from outside caught his attention. A deep, infuriated groan resonated from his chest, and he stood up. "I can't deal with her right now. Get rid of her. *Get rid of her!*"

With confusion, I watched him disappear into his bedroom, tugging the curtain to conceal him from view. A tap at the hut entrance filled the silence, followed by a cheery, "Oh, hello." Valina stood on the threshold, immaculately dressed in her black leathers and knee-high boots. Her golden hair shone in the afternoon sun; not a single strand out of place. I stifled my own groan and walked around the desk towards her.

"Is Rooke about?" she asked sweetly, eyeing the curtain behind me.

"He's um…sleeping."

"This time of day?" Her quizzical look confirmed she didn't believe me, so I flattened my tone, "Look, Rooke's had some bad news from home. Family news. He needs some time to reflect on his own. He doesn't want to see anyone right now." *Especially you.*

"Oh, that's terrible." Valina looked genuinely devastated. "Of course. Um, okay, I'll postpone our meeting." She glanced at the curtain again. "Give him my regards. My thoughts are with him."

I nodded, almost disgusted by her sympathetic charm. Thankfully, she immediately left.

Turning to the curtain, I knocked on the wooden frame and entered. Rooke was sitting on the edge of his small bed, hunched over, staring at his feet, head in his hands.

"She's gone."

His only response was a single nod.

"Do you want me to stay?"

Without giving me the eye contact I desperately craved, he shook his head, dismissing me.

Standing there for another awkward moment, I processed the impact of his gesture. He didn't want me to stay. He didn't want me to console him like I always had, as he'd always done for me. I feared the foundations of our relationship were starting to crumble. And to worsen the impact, another crushing blow of rejection slammed into me when he asked me to leave. Those words finally fracturing the fragile pieces holding my heart together.

He didn't need me anymore. I felt broken.

Trying not to crumble in front of him, I turned and left without another word. In an absentminded stupor, my feet found purpose and I carried myself to the bottom of the east cliff ladder. Looking up at the steep rockface, I knew why I'd arrived here. I needed to find Jader. There was nothing stopping me now. I wasn't going to pass up the hunter job. It was mine.

Part Two

Nux Warrior

Chapter Nineteen

With my back flush against the bark of a tree, I slowly pulled the bow string, aiming the arrowhead at a huddle of rabbits thirty metres away in the middle of an open field. From the shadows of the forest edge, my movements were drowned out by the sound of rain pelting the soil and grass around me, concealing my presence perfectly.

I had learnt that most forest animals only ventured out during the height of the day, when it was stifling hot and humid, or, like today, hammering it down with rain. The Igknamai were never seen during rainstorms. And as raindrops dripped from the edge of my hood, across my forehead, and into my eyes, I could understand their logic.

I watched the rabbits hop about the field, pinpointing one who seemed to linger in one spot longer than the others. Releasing the arrow, the marked rabbit jumped a metre in the air before it plummeted to the ground, lifeless.

"That's six today, Eden. I think we're gonna have to make this a weekly competition." Wrenn crouched behind the adjacent tree. Only her freckled nose and pink lips could be seen underneath her dark hood. Her eyes were in shadow, her red hair concealed. The glint of her sword was the only thing that didn't seem to merge in with the colour of the tree bark beside her.

"She'll probably up her game if we do that," Jader japed from behind me.

I smiled to myself. "I'm having a good day. The bunnies seem sluggish."

Wrenn tutted. "Lies. All lies."

"Are you going to cover me while I go and pick up Fluffy or you going to sulk?"

"Sulk? Me? Never. I am, however, considering training without you. To up my own game if I'm gonna win this competition."

I shot her an amused look. "Wrenn, have you got my back?"

"I've always got your back." Wrenn grinned, adjusting her position, and I slunk forward, across the field, towards the dead rabbit. I scanned the tree line checking for movement while the rest of the rabbits scuttled away underground. Even with the torrential downpour, we never dropped our guard. We had to remain vigilant. It was what kept us alive.

My first couple of weeks of hunting had been nerve-wracking. Another new moon had come and gone, and I started to fit into my hunter skin. Nevertheless, venturing miles away from the village, we'd always stumble across hordes of spindly fingered footprints, mutilated dead animals, devastated fields of which would've been full of wildflowers, bees, and butterflies. It was disconcerting, especially when the number of Igknamai attacks reached my ears far too often. Twelve people had died in the past month. Most had been scouts, which left a harrowing thought in the back of my mind; concerned about Rooke and Oz's safety…and Truro's.

Rooke and I had hardly seen each other since he caught me snooping, and when we did, his mood was never inviting. I was desperate to ask him about his sweet mum, but I could never conjure up the confidence. He scared me, and the whole situation left me hurting. How had it come to this? For the past several years he had been the person standing behind me, supporting and encouraging me on my good days. And on my bad days, he was the one standing in front of me, guiding and protecting me. The fact he no longer stood anywhere near me made it feel as though a vital piece of my being was missing. I cried more times than I liked to admit, but I never let anyone witness it. My tears were for me and me alone.

Initially, the lack of Truro's presence had pushed thoughts of him to a secret corner of my mind. He always appeared in my head before I went to sleep, but it was only when Jader mentioned his return, that the remorse and rawness of the situation hit hard again.

Jader had explained Truro had been away at an outpost; a salvaging zone called Kala. It was an old derelict city, once used by the ancients. The Redwoods occupied several sites within it, extracting metal to use for weapons, electrical components, and

168

building reinforcements back at the village. Salvaging was easier than mining old quarries where the Igknamai could easily strike. The only issue was the city was eighty miles away, through Igknamai territory.

"Is it safe…the city?" I asked Jader, as our horses ambled along, side by side towards the village after a day of hunting. The prospect of it still intrigued me.

"Some higher areas are, but it's not as safe as the village."

"So, it's not a permanent stronghold?"

"No. It's the decaying remnants of how remarkable and ridiculous the ancients were. So unnatural, but highly resourceful. It's heavily guarded, but nobody freely offers to work there. That's why Truro recently visited, to oversee the turnaround of labour and guards. That's also why your hunting position came up. Your predecessor was called up to go hunt over there. Everyone gets called up occasionally. But it's necessary, to ensure the village has new building materials and weapons."

"How long do they work there?"

"Eight to twelve weeks. But only during the fairer months. The place is a death trap during winter, and that has nothing to do with the Igknamai. Snow and sharp metal do not mix well."

"You get snow here, even though it's so hot?"

"Yes. The temperature drops considerably in the winter."

"We get a lot of snow on Allura, especially in the rustic hills where I live. But the summers are a lot cooler there."

"You must miss home."

I pondered his comment for a moment. "These days home feels like a distorted dream."

"I sometimes forget you're not one of us." Jader smiled sentimentally. "You fit in so well."

I chuckled. "I'll take that as a compliment."

The thunder of hooves from behind alerted us. Glancing over our shoulders, we found a scouting platoon moving rapidly towards us, heading for the garrison platform only twenty metres up ahead. I froze when I saw who was leading them—Rooke, with Oz half a horse behind. Raindrops dripped down their faces, their leathers sparkling in the dull light. Mud splattered over the extent of their legs and lower part of their torso. I gulped at the sight of Rooke. The sheer scour of determination on his face made him appear powerful and intimidating. Nux, he looked every inch as much of a warrior as Truro did.

Thankfully, he was so focused on his destination, he didn't glance my way. Even with my hood covering my hair, I had no doubt he'd still recognise me. And what would happen then? Another reprimand? Another spout of verbal distaste towards my life choices?

Attempting to hide my face entirely, I looked down as he cantered past. The tail of riders followed, churning up the wet mud in their wake. From under my eyebrows, I watched the platoon of Redwood warriors filter past the garrison platform, but intrigue struck me when I noticed Rooke had stopped by the main tree lift. Oz remained on top of his horse next to him. From their exaggerated body language, they were having a heated discussion. It seemed Oz was pleading with Rooke, resulting in him jumping from his horse and grabbing Rooke's arm. Rooke shoved Oz's large form away, grimacing an assault of words back at him.

"Wonder what that's about?" Wrenn said, from her horse behind me.

As we drew closer, Rooke disappeared into the lift. I heard Oz swear profusely, and a weight of concern fell upon me. Their argument didn't appear to be trivial.

"Jader, I don't suppose you could take Io up to the grazing fields? I need to check this out."

"Sure. Want me to take your sword and bow too?"

I glanced at him. He was a good friend. He knew my occupation wasn't common knowledge within the crew. "Thanks." I handed my weapons over and jumped off my horse. As I approached, Oz was staring up at the platform, taking thunderous breaths in an attempt to calm himself.

He growled as I touched his arm. I could feel the aggravation radiating off his wet, tattooed skin. He turned, ready to snap, but his eyes softened when he saw me. "Eden!" His tone was one of desperation. He glanced about us. "Where did you come from?"

"Doesn't matter. Are you alright? What's going on?"

"Shit, Eden. Rooke…he's…he's gone mental. He won't listen to me…"

"What's happened?" I reached up to his shoulder, trying to calm him, but he winced. I'd never seen Oz like this. There was an onslaught of worry lining his brow, one he rarely showed. "Oz?"

"Rooke doesn't seem to trust the Redwoods anymore. Havav has told him things that have made him doubt them."

"Havav?" Was I hearing that correctly? "You've seen the Akquarians?"

"Yes." He swallowed hard. "You know how much Havav likes to talk in riddles. This time Rooke seems to believe every conflicting word. I'm worried what he's going to do. He won't calm down. The anger in him has grown over the past few days. He's on his way to see Valina. I'm worried what he's going to say to her."

I glanced up at the garrison. Rooke was marching across it towards the upper tree lift. I hadn't seen Oz or Rooke for what felt like at least a week. I assumed our daily routines hadn't coincided and our paths never crossed, much to my delight. I didn't realise it was because they'd been off site.

"Eden, you have to talk to him. Make him see sense. He'll listen to you."

"I highly doubt that."

"He *will* listen to you."

Whatever this was, it wasn't the normal ounce of anger Rooke was renowned for. He'd been on the brink of eruption for weeks. I met Oz's pleading blue gaze. "I'll give it my best shot."

Luckily, the tree lift accessing the forest floor was back at ground level. Leaving Oz standing in the red mud, I stepped inside, and it immediately started moving upwards through the inside of the huge tree. As I exited onto the garrison platform, Rooke was already riding the second lift towards the middle level. I knew where he was going; the high council chamber, to see Valina.

To save time, I climbed the rope ladder adjacent to the lift, practically running up the wooden slats. Racing towards the centre of the village, I caught sight of Rooke crossing the sturdy bridge to the enormous tree where the council chamber was held. Two warriors stood guard at the entrance. As I approached, I recognised one as the scout who escorted me here on the very first day. Guz, I think his name was.

Pushing my hood back, he recognised me and smiled. At first, I thought he was going to deny me entry into the council chamber, but after explaining I needed to speak with Rooke and Valina, he allowed me through.

The intense smell of dried wood hit my nose as I entered the huge, circular room. Blake sat on one of the stools to the left, scowling at the conversation that was heating up to the right. Standing, Rooke had his back to me, but from the look on Valina's face, I could tell his words were concerning, perhaps insulting.

"I assure you," Valina said with a little more bite than usual, "we do not owe anything to the Akquarians."

Rooke snarled back, "Not even after what was arranged?"

"Arranged? Nothing's been arranged?"

"Are you positive about that? Was it you who personally spoke with Havav?"

"Well, no." The look of defeat on Valina's face worried me. She looked to Blake who casually added, "All negotiations with the Akquarians were relayed back to the council. Havav is trying to confuse you."

"Is he?" The sarcasm in Rooke's anger-stricken voice rang true. "Who negotiated with him? Maybe that person is lying. Or are you all playing deceptive games?"

A short silence fell over the room while Rooke glared between Valina and Blake. Eventually Valina's voice hardened, "Get Truro. *Now!*"

A warrior, who I hadn't noticed standing in the shadows behind me, scarpered out the chamber at Valina's command. I looked back at Rooke, his eyes were now resting on me. The darkness pouring out of them was hard to miss, but for once in a long time, I didn't think his wrath was because of my presence.

Stepping forward I whispered, "What's going on?"

Rooke glanced about the near-empty auditorium, pushing his mud-soaked fingers through his sodden hair. "It appears we are not residing here by chance."

I noticed Valina shift awkwardly behind him. "What do you mean?"

"I am led to believe the Redwoods negotiated terms for our exchange of residence with the Akquarians. One in which they have not paid their dues."

"That is incorrect!" Valina snapped.

"How do you know?" Rooke snarled back at her. "You've already told me you weren't the one who negotiated."

"Rooke." I reached for his hand. To my relief, he didn't retract. I even felt a squeeze of companionship before he let my fingers fall. Pausing to savour the gesture, I kept my voice low. "If they negotiated, why were we led to the ravine? If the Redwoods wanted us alive, that wasn't a logical exchange point."

"Funny, though. The Akquarians didn't pursue us, did they? Perhaps it was all a ruse to make us feel indebted to these people."

I shook my head. His statement didn't feel right. Why would the Redwoods have made an exchange and not told us? Deep down I knew Rooke was wrong about this. But, either way, it made no difference. We were safer here.

Valina's voice echoed about the room. "The Akquarians rarely come this far into the forest."

Rooke huffed, shaking his head. "Eden saw them here a few weeks ago."

"Yes. But I assure you…"

"Just stop with the bullshit, Valina! I've had enough of it!"

Another spate of tense silence stifled the room. This time it was disturbed by Truro's gruff, authoritative voice. "What appears to be the problem?" I closed my eyes to the sound. For some reason his voice still sent an enthralling sensation through me.

"I'm glad you were close by." Valina raised her chin, eying him suspiciously. "Perhaps you can clear up this misassumption. You negotiated with the Akquarians when Rooke and his crew were residing there, yes?"

"Yes."

"Did you come to some kind of arrangement?"

"No. You know I didn't."

"Then why are the Akquarians specifying otherwise?"

Turning slightly, I could now see Truro's face. I had no doubt the frown forming on his brow was unfeigned. He glanced at Rooke—who I felt shift closer to me—then back to Valina. "Who's been to see the Akquarians?"

"I have!" Rooke growled.

Truro snapped his head in our direction again. "For what reason?"

"I sent them." Blake stood up, closing the gap between the two of them. "I came up with a plan to utilise them in helping us find the Hybrids lair." I could sense Blake's internal struggle not to shrink back as Truro's glare rained down on him.

"You sent him, and a platoon of *my* men, to see the Akquarians without my knowledge?" Truro glared at Valina. "Did you know about this? Did Elgin?"

"I did, and it was mentioned to Elgin."

"Mentioned? Why wasn't I informed?"

"We knew you'd oppose. And now is not the time to revisit that debate." Valina returned the glare, its emphasis holding Truro silent for a moment. There was far more going on here than met the eye.

"So," Truro stepped further into the room, placing his arms across his chest defensively. "What has Havav been saying?"

"We need to determine," Valina chimed, "what terms were agreed upon for the exchange of the Alluran crew?"

"None. You know this."

"Why?" Rooke asked. "Why didn't you agree on any?"

"Because no matter what I offered them, they would only agree to hand over five of you. I didn't think you'd appreciate any form of redemption if we left one of your crew behind with the Akquarians."

His words took a moment to sink in. But when they did, my heart began pounding violently against my chest, my breathing became ragged and unsettled. Rooke appeared directly beside me, brushing his fingertips over my palm. The look of concern on his face confirmed he knew the answer to his next question, as I did.

"Who did they intend on keeping back?"

I could feel Truro's eyes on me as his voice softened. "I believe it was Eden."

The only reason I didn't allow my legs to give out, was the look of understanding flittering across Rooke's face. It had me transfixed. What had he just realised? But before I could question him, he cursed, then marched out of the chamber. It took me a couple of seconds before I followed.

Outside, the rain had finally stopped pouring, but a fine drizzle commandeered the air. Thankfully, the bridges and platforms around the village had a brown, jagged tread built into the wood, which helped to reduce the fatal act of slipping. It also aided running.

I launched after Rooke, reaching him when he was three quarters of the way across the sturdy bridge. Repeatedly calling his name, he only paused when I grabbed his arm and screamed, "Stop!"

His eyes remained ahead, his breathing heavy, but I finally had his attention.

"Rooke, what have you just worked out?"

He looked down at me. I trembled at the sorrowful eyes that met mine, spilling with a sense of defeat. He was exhausted; tired of living this nightmare.

"Rooke, please. Talk to me."

"I don't trust anyone." He nodded back towards the council. "Not them. Not the Akquarians. Nobody. They can all go to hell." He went to move again, but I locked my hands around his wrists with all my might, forcing him to remain.

Peering up into his dark eyes, I pushed as much emphasis into my words as possible. "Havav is playing mind tricks with you…"

"Don't you think I know that? Shit, Eden, you have no idea!" A flicker of something like shame crossed his face, averting his gaze. "I am so done with this world."

"You can trust the Redwoods."

Grimacing, he shook his head. "No. No, we can't."

"Rooke…"

"Think about it!" Cutting me off, his eyes locked with mine again. "We are only here because the Redwoods need us. Do you really think they would've saved us from the Akquarians or the Igknamai otherwise?"

"Yes. Yes, I do. These are good people. They are *our* people."

Rooke huffed and pulled away from my hold. I could sense the fight in him fading. I wanted to hold him, comfort him, but the wall that had recently formed between us was preventing me from reaching out.

He took a few steps away, halting when I asked, "What are you going to do?"

To my dismay, I saw the aggression rise again; the anger that had recently encased every bone in his body, encouraged every word he spoke.

"I'm going to do nothing," he snarled through gritted teeth. "I have no obligation to help these people. As soon as Solarfleet get here, I am jumping on that transport, going back to The Orka, and flying her home. And I'm *hoping* you will come with me." His eyes shifted past my shoulder. "But then again," he glanced back with a hardened frown, and I saw the melancholy riding his gaze, "I'm not sure where your loyalties lie anymore."

Stunned by his words in more ways than one, I watched him march away. Glancing over my shoulder, I caught sight of Truro slowly walking towards me. I took a deep breath. It was clear Rooke was still enraged by the relationship I had with Truro, but I still couldn't fathom why. Did he know something about him? There was obviously a fracture of trust within the Redwood council. Perhaps Rooke knew what it was.

As Truro neared, I turned. The scowl on my face caused him to hesitate. Holding his hands up, he said, "I swear, Eden, no agreement was made."

"It's not me you need to convince."

"Then why are you looking at me as if you blame me for everything?"

Rubbing my brow with my forefinger and thumb, I sighed. "I don't. I just don't understand." My thoughts wandered to why Rooke was so adamant the Redwoods were untrustworthy. And then a pang of grief hit me when Cora came to the forefront of my mind. If Truro had taken the Akquarian's initial offer, perhaps she would still be alive. I couldn't help sliding into that pool of guilt. It should've been me who was left behind, not her. "Why didn't you take the offer?"

"I told you. We doubted Rooke would've cooperated if we left you behind."

"Cooperate," I mumbled. Rooke *was* right. The Redwoods had always craved our help. Even with the jamming signal in place, we never really needed them.

"Eden, I couldn't leave you behind."

"Because Rooke would not have cooperated, yes, you just said. Do you really think you have his cooperation now?"

"No. I doubt we ever fully had it. But we have yours."

"Mine? Nux, I'm not a leader."

"Well, you should be."

"Damn it, Truro. You should've left me there. You could've saved Cora!"

"And condemned you to a lifetime of being groomed for breeding? Do you think they would've ever let you leave? They are relentless with human women."

"I thought they didn't do that anymore?"

"They don't....not entirely."

"What does that mean?"

"Eden, not in a million years would I have left you with them. And not just because the others worried about Rooke's cooperation. I knew...I knew from the first moment I saw you. When you and Rooke stepped off your ship to assess the carnage the Igknamai had left on the beach. In the morning sun, you looked up at me and I felt it. The pull. The tug of hope I feel every time I see you. I knew...I knew that very day you'd be someone special to me. There was no way in hell I would've left you on your own with the Akquarians. Not over my dead body."

Lost in his words, I stared up at his intense, fervent expression. His blue orbs glistened with meaning, sending sparks of electricity pulsing over my skin.

It had been the second morning the Parvos had been grounded. That morning, I'd frozen when I saw a human on horseback, silhouetted against the brightening sun.

"The figure on the clifftop was you." Somehow, I had always known.

He nodded, the sincerity in his eyes threw waves of raw emotion crashing against my very being. "I couldn't believe it when I returned a few hours later with more men and horses, and you were gone. It wasn't long afterwards we discovered you were residing with the Akquarians. I tried to get you out...all of you. I tried. I came to the conclusion they didn't want to negotiate. They were finding my constant requests to meet with them a nuisance. The last time I spoke with Havav, he threatened to have you all killed. So, I left...empty handed, again. It was by sheer luck we discovered you in that ravine a few days later."

Dropping his gaze, I closed my heavy eyelids. I wanted to believe him, to trust him. Subconsciously, I always thought I could, but Rooke's words were chipping away at my once sound judgement. Could we trust these people?

"Is…is this all a ruse? An act, to make me soften to your cause? Did Valina and Blake make you say this?"

"What? No!"

"Please." Tears prickled the corner of my eyes. "I don't think I could take it if I ever found out you were lying to me." I peered up at him. He genuinely looked as though I'd just punched him in the gut.

"I'm not lying." He stepped forward, barely leaving two inches between us. "Eden, I could never. What I feel for you is real. You cannot deny the connection we have, the bond. I know you feel it too. The zap of intensity between us, the pull. Our souls speak to each other."

I felt so drawn to him, so completely intoxicated by his presence. How could I deny what he was saying?

"Truro…" With my dirty, mud splattered hands, I cupped his defiant face, aware my own frown was full of a desperation I could not shift. "Soul mates don't exist. This between us…" I swallowed down the hard truth that I agreed with him, trying to find a justifiable objection. All I could say was, "We are from different worlds."

"We are creatures of the same universe. Just because we were born on different planets does not mean we do not belong together." He leant in closer, gently touching the underside of my chin with his fingers. "I was meant to find you."

I believed in what he felt. Maybe I was a fool to do so, but I trusted him. He seemed to absorb all my troubles, take every ounce of pain away. I could allow those beautiful eyes to become my world, my ongoing sky…

Movement from the trees to my left ripped my attention away. From two levels up, the faintest glimpse of Rooke watching us forced the reality of the situation back into context.

I was an Alluran. My loyalty lay with my crew, with Rooke.

Nux, this was such a damn mess!

Dropping my hands from Truro's face, I took a step backwards, then another, and another, severing more than the physical connection adjoining us. I could feel my frown deepen and I knew my face spoke a thousand words. But the words I voiced left Truro in a frozen state of sorrow. "I can't."

As I turned and marched away, my heart breaking all over again,

I left him standing on the bridge in the fine, misty rain. Like the true hypocrite I'd become, I left him drowning in rejection.

Chapter Twenty

"Hey Troy," I tried to sound as enthusiastic as I could, "how are you doing up there?"

"Ah, you know. Pretty bored of my own company these days." Troy's crisp, monotone voice came through my earpiece as I sat alone in the comms room aboard the Pasa. I'd skipped training that morning. The Orka was in signal range, and I hadn't spoken to Troy for several days. He'd been the sole resident of The Orka for seventeen weeks now. That amount of solitude could cause the sanist person to go crazy. But then again…

"What I'd give to trade places with you right now."

He chuckled. He seemed far more jovial than he had been a few weeks ago. I didn't doubt it was a front to stop us worrying about him. Cora's death hit him hard. There was no possible way he was over the grief.

"How is it going down there?" he asked.

"You don't want to know."

"Ah…Zamya did tell me you and Rooke are going through a rough patch."

"You make it sound like we're a couple."

"Maybe you should be."

Sharp needles prickled their way up my spine, delaying my response. "Why would you say that?"

"Cos you're both kinda perfect for each other. I never told you before, but when I first started working with you, I was shocked to discover you weren't an item."

Staring at the blank screen in front of me, I shifted awkwardly in my chair. I'd worked with Troy for nearly two years. Who else had thought the same?

"First impressions can be deceiving," I mumbled. "We were friends. Currently, our commander despises me."

"I doubt that very much."

"I don't."

"Just talk to him, Eden."

"Easier said than done."

"Hmm. Did he tell you about the jamming signal?"

"Troy. He doesn't *talk* to *me*."

"Okay, okay, Nux. I can sense it's a sensitive subject."

I chuckled, "What, Rooke or the jamming signal?"

"I don't think you have a romantic interest with the jamming signal."

"What?" I groaned. "I'm going to frigging kill Zamya!"

A loud belly laugh erupted through my earpiece.

"I'm glad you find my lack of a love life amusing."

"Do you wanna talk about it? I have plenty of time."

"No, I want you to tell me about the jamming signal. Shit...stop laughing, Troy! MacIntosh, focus! Jamming signal!"

"Right, sorry sir, jamming signal. Well, the main point is, it's stopped."

I felt my eyebrows scrunch, my eyes narrow. "When?"

"Last week."

My mind began swirling with questions. "Why are we still using the microwave signal and not the standard radio?"

"Kobe deemed it a more reliable communication link. Also, it's far more secure. Less likely to have anyone listening in."

"Are we talking Hybrid or Redwood eavesdroppers?"

"Both."

It was clear the trust between Rooke and the Redwoods was slowly spiralling to a close. I still had no idea what Rooke's claim to distrust them was, but the whole situation was becoming more and more disconcerting. Solarfleet were still six weeks away. There was too much time lingering in between then and now to allow for something bad to happen, something that could disrupt our safety.

"There's more," Troy announced. A glimmer of concern wavered in his voice. "The interstellar signal has also stopped."

"You mean the one Rooke's been chasing?"

"Yep. It stopped around the same time. I never really got a true lock on its location. It seemed to jump about as if it was being intermittently transmitted from different sites…or, it could've been transmitted from some sort of mobile device."

My mind jumped back to the first day Rooke and I met with the council. Valina had told us the Hybrids had stolen their satellite module decades ago. But I'd never questioned what exactly it was, or how the Hybrids were able to steal it.

"Does Rooke have any idea where the Parvos is? I mean, I've seen his multitude of red dots on his paper map, but, you know, he doesn't talk to me anymore."

"We've pinned it down to an area with a fifteen-mile radius."

"Fifteen miles? Nux, that's…"

"Yeah, seven hundred and six square miles."

The figure left me dumbfounded. "Why is he bothering. It's too vast?"

"He needs a purpose, Eden. As I'm sure we all do."

If Rooke didn't endure the endless task of finding the Parvos, I wouldn't put it past him to start waging a war here within the village. The unchecked anger writhing inside him worried me. He was under an immense amount of pressure from Solarfleet and the Redwood council, perhaps all because of me and my promise to the latter. How would I ever repay that burden? Maybe I would never be able to do so.

Once Troy was out of range, I made my way to the main Pasa entrance. Standing outside on the wooden walkway, basking in the morning sun, were Jader and Zamya. Jader was smiling, leaning back against the walkway barrier, unfazed by the drop behind him, while Zamya threw her head back in laughter. Her smile spread across her attractive face, her dark eyes sparkling as the two of them conversed.

Were they…were they flirting? I smiled to myself as I neared.

"Hope I'm not interrupting anything," I said, throwing Zamya a teasing look. One that could've rivalled her own. I could've sworn the brown skin around her cheeks gave way to a flash of pink.

"Not at all," Jader said. "I was actually waiting for you,"

"Am I late?" Glancing down at my watch, it read 10:47. I had over ten minutes before I was scheduled to hunt. I went to playfully scold him, aware he was still talking to me, but his words didn't register. Still looking at my watch, I noticed the date. The Earth date was 29th July, which held no significance. The Alluran date, however, sent a cascade of emotions shredding their way through my chest, down into my gut. I felt paralysed.

15th December. That date was tattooed onto my heart—the anniversary of Jacob's death.

Ten years ago, I'd lost my dear brother. Ten, long, Alluran years! Memories came flooding back. Every year since his death, I had spent the anniversary with Rooke. Wherever we had been, whether it was at home, at the Solarfleet base, or on one of the many ships we had flown together, we always sought each other out and found the time to light a candle in Jacob's honour. Always drank to celebrate his life and recited our memories of him. Always held each other when the grief took hold again.

It pained me to think today would be different. Rooke couldn't stand the sight of me, let alone the closeness I would need. Apparently, he found my presence suffocating—whatever that was supposed to mean. Among his bouts of aggression, I doubted he even knew what day it was.

"Eden? I was only joking." Jader's voice pulled me out of my distressing thoughts.

"About what?" Refocusing my vision, I realised I was staring at him.

"About you being in trouble. You're not late. I came down here because I was at a loose end. Another trainer decided to take the lesson. Wrenn stayed to watch. Are you alright?"

"Yes. Sorry. I…" I glanced at my watch again. "Shall we go?"

Exchanging a baffled look with Zamya, Jader stood up, gesturing for me to lead the way. I hesitated, then said, "Actually, I need a word with Zam. Could you give us a minute?"

Smiling, Jader winked at Zamya and began to walk away. I gaped in his wake. *Did I just see that?*

"Are you sure you're okay?" Zamya asked, genuinely concerned.

Peering back at her, I pointed. "You…will you please stop discussing my personal predicaments with Troy. It's embarrassing."

"Oh, come on." Zamya placed her hands on her hips. "Troy is depressed and lonely. A little gossip helps boost his mental stability."

"Gossip? I don't appreciate you using my life situations as gossip."

"What are you worried about? That he'll tell Rooke?"

"Yes!"

"In that case, maybe you should tell him yourself?"

"Damn it, Zamya! I knew I shouldn't have admitted anything to you."

"Don't you think he has a right to know how you feel about him?"

"What, so he can throw something else in my face? No, thank you." I went to walk away.

"Eden." Zamya grabbed my hand, lowering her voice. "Don't you think it will help the situation?"

"No." My frown deepened as I looked back at her. "I personally think Rooke needs medical help. He's on the brink of a mental breakdown."

"I'm the medical professional here, and my prognosis is Rooke needs you."

I stared at her. Was she being serious? The empathy in her eyes outshone the scrutiny I usually saw there when discussing Rooke. I shook my head. "Please don't. Don't emotionally blackmail me into telling him. I've lived with this secret for years. It will only make things worse."

Shrugging her shoulders, she continued to give me that look.

"Zam, please. Promise me you won't tell him."

"I don't even like Rooke, so why would I?" A strange gleam twinkled in her eye. "Go on, Jader's waiting."

Eyeing her sceptically, I slowly turned on my heel. As I strode away, I heard her call, "Is he single?"

Frowning, I stopped and turned back to her. "You mean Jader?"

"Who else?" She rolled her eyes and a youthful expression danced across her face.

I smirked. "Yeah, I'm pretty sure he's single."

"Good to know. Asking for a friend."

"Yeah, whatever."

It was late when we returned from our hunt. The guards had to reinstate the bridges and reopen the Pasa for us. The sun had already set by the time we offloaded our catch with the overnight butchers working inside the ship.

Parting ways with Wrenn and Jader, I walked across the bridges towards home. Funny, after so many months here, it was actually starting to feel like home.

Hundreds of solar lights lit the bridge pathways, imitating the night sky. The illusion caused my train of thought to switch to my real home; to Jacob and Rooke. Even my mum jumped into my thoughts, and the way she sealed herself away following Jacob's death. Rooke had been the one at Jacob's side when he died. Rooke had loved Jacob. He'd lost a brother in the same way I had, and his empathy pathed his reaction to always being my support, my friend. But now…now I couldn't fight the pain of recognising I was losing him too. I didn't agree with what Zamya had said. Rooke didn't need me. I doubted he ever had. He had a family, he had friends.

Me? I had him and only him.

I had tried not to think about it all day, but wandering over the dark bridges and platforms, catching glimpses of families eating their evening meals in their glowing huts full of love and warmth, it hit me hard. I was losing my best friend; the best thing that had ever happened to me; the only semblance of family I had left.

I paused at a narrow bridge, allowing a couple to clear it. I barely acknowledged their words of thanks before striding over the bouncing span of slatted wood, towards a dark hut on the opposite platform. As I rounded the edge, the rumble of a familiar voice stopped me in my tracks.

"I went to find you today. Thought we should spend some time together given the date. For Jacob's sake." There was a pause, and I heard the sound of his steady footfalls moving closer. Then a dark figure emerged from the abandoned hut beside me.

"I asked for you at the food hall. They told me you haven't worked there for weeks. That you go hunting with Jader. You can imagine my confusion."

As my heart raced with uncertainty, Rooke took another step closer. I looked up at his barely visible face, and I noticed the distant solar lights twinkling in his eyes. To my surprise, there was no anger residing there, only softness and concern. His voice, too, took on a hint of tenderness. "Why didn't you tell me?"

"You never asked." My own voice was as soft as a whisper, trying to conceal the rising emotion. *He'd remembered. He hadn't forgotten the date.*

"I don't like the thought of you going out into the forest every day."

"Perhaps that's why I never told you."

"Really?" I noted the sarcasm. "I assumed it was because you're pissed with me?"

"Me? Pissed with you?" *What the…*

"Perfect way to get back at me. Taking away the only control I have left over your protection?"

"I didn't do it to spite you, Rooke."

"Why hunting? Why not engineering with Kobe? You're good at cooking. What was wrong with the food hall?"

"It was tedious work. I was going out of my mind with boredom."

"Working nine hours a day, seven days a week would do that. You burnt out. I told you to rest…"

"I wasn't there all day!" Grimacing at my spiteful tone, I lowered my voice, softening the edges. "I rarely started work before eleven."

Rooke leaned back against the door frame. His look of intrigue sent a wave of guilt through me. "Go on. I'm listening."

Swallowing back the hesitation, I said, "Every morning I…I'd go training. I learnt to fight. To hunt. I trained to become…this." Pointing towards myself, I realised I was still wearing all my weapons. I usually gave them to Jader to house overnight, refusing to return home in possession of them, in case Rooke saw. Well, he was well and truly aware of them now. He eyed the feathered arrows and the hilt of my sword peeping over my shoulders. His gaze followed the bow string across my chest, travelling down to the dagger sheathed at my hip.

"I needed a purpose, Rooke."

The corner of his mouth attempted a smile. "To become a Nux warrior?"

I hadn't thought of it like that, but I supposed I had.

"Hunting is dangerous."

"It's not so different to what you do?"

"I think you'll find it is." A hardness returned to his voice, one that troubled me. "I have eight warriors with me, plus Oz. I'm told, there's only three of you on your team."

"I can defend myself."

"Clearly." He stepped away, huffing his disapproval. "I'm surprised Truro allows it."

He gazed out towards the brighter part of the village. I could see his profile clearer now; the profile I'd be able to draw from memory. I doubted any amount of time could erase his handsome face from my conscience. The only difference these days was he rarely smiled.

"It was my choice and Truro respects that. He has no intention of restricting anyone's movements, especially when they show potential and ambition."

"And I do?" Rooke peered at me, eyebrows raised.

"I didn't say that."

"But obviously you don't think I respect you enough to be told."

"I didn't say that either!" An exasperated sound left my lungs, heightening my concern the conversation would lead to another argument. But Rooke sighed, lowering his voice, "I can't bear the thought of losing anyone left of my crew. Especially you…especially now. Why didn't you tell me about the job?"

"Would you have listened?" The shock lining his face was visible even in the darkness. "I didn't think you'd be interested. You don't seem to have time for me anymore."

"You're the one who's been sneaking out early every morning! I wouldn't be surprised if you were purposely avoiding me so I wouldn't find out!"

"Rooke, please. Please don't get angry." My pleading didn't seem to affect him. He didn't move, nor did the rising irritation in his eyes subside. I took in a shaky breath and stepped away, aiming to leave. But his next sentence, and the manner in which he spoke it, froze me to the core.

"What's happened to us? We used to be inseparable. We used to tell each other everything."

I peered back at him. The frown on his face was fervent, forlorn. The distance we'd created between each other was hurting him just as much as it was me. I could see that now.

"I never told you everything, Rooke. And you've certainly kept plenty from me recently."

"Like what?"

Glancing down at my hands, I realised I was shaking.

"Like *what?* I didn't tell you about my mum because I knew you'd be upset."

"I'm not talking about that."

"What else is there?!"

"Why you distrust the Redwoods. When the jamming signal stopped. Why you went to visit the Akquarians. The list goes on. I'm supposed to be your second, but you tell me nothing. You say I keep you in the dark, well, put yourself in my shoes for once. Everything seemed to change between us since…since…"

"Since you met Truro?"

"No!"

"Then when?!"

"Since the night you kissed me!" My voice wavered and the panic began to tingle up through my legs, higher and higher it climbed, swamping me with regret. Nux, what had I just said?

Maybe I was still overreacting about those five minutes of bliss I had found myself pondering too many times to count. But the situation had wound itself so tightly around me, it had become hard to think beyond it. The distance he had created, the reason why he pushed me away, the way he reacted to my intimacy with Truro; it all formed a dark cloud I'd become imprisoned in, submerged in a hurricane full of confusion and doubt. I felt battered and bruised, and it had all stemmed from that night.

My words seemed to silence Rooke. His posture, too, stiffened. Nux, I hated it when he just stared, leaving my words hanging in the air between us. And as always, I found the need to speak. "This has all escalated from that kiss. And I know it was just a kiss, but…oh, it doesn't matter."

I went to leave, but Rooke flinched from his frozen stupor, heaving himself in my direction. "Wait." He went to snatch up my hand, but paused, reconsidering, before taking a step back. Pain surged through my chest. He couldn't even bear to touch me. I wanted to laugh when he said, "You're clearly upset about what happened."

But the subject matter was becoming too close for comfort, and I was drowning in rejection and embarrassment. I turned away from him, silently gasping as I felt his hand gently touch my elbow. I looked down at our interaction, questioning everything.

"Talk to me," he whispered. "Please."

With an uncomfortable quandary beginning to mould itself around me, I couldn't avoid the power within his gaze. Those eyes, which usually soothed me, felt torturous. I focused on the darkness below us, trying to ease the tremble in my voice. "You have a girlfriend, Rooke. One I had forgotten about because you never speak of her. I can understand you're homesick, you miss her. But I never thought you'd use me in a way to relieve that longing. I'm your friend, not a…not a…."

With a shame dipped in slander, I chose not to finish the sentence. I glanced at my feet, noticing Rooke shift position. When I looked up again, he was standing in front of me, his shoulders hunched, hands in his pockets. There was a new tenderness in his gaze, one I couldn't read.

Overflowing with the reluctance to be here, the heat of humiliation swamped me. I couldn't take this anymore. "Nux, Rooke, say *something*!"

"Miranda and I are no longer together."

We stared at each other for what felt like an eternity, more than the understanding of his words passing between us. I felt a flurry of hope. My eyes had dried out by the time he finally blinked, releasing a deep, pent-up sigh.

"She, um…she ended it, about two months into the mission. I received a message from her. I thought you'd seen it on my tablet."

What? Was that the message I'd seen sitting on his home screen when I first found it unlocked, months ago?

"Apparently, she never signed up for a long-distance relationship. I got the impression it was an excuse to justify her moving on so quickly. Apparently, she's now shacked up with my neighbour."

Nux, I felt awful. "I'm sorry, Rooke."

"Don't be." He huffed a smile. "She was too high maintenance for me. It was a blessing in disguise." And it was another thing he hadn't told me about.

A new frown dominated his face as his eyes studied mine. I watched him straighten his shoulders, pushing the awkwardness of the conversation to a new level. "By the time the Akquarian ball had come about, I hadn't thought of Miranda for months. I…I shouldn't have kissed you; I know that…I was drunk on that blue shit. No excuse, but we were reminiscing about home and I…I lost myself for a moment. Well, several, actually. As did you." A small smile graced his lips for a brief moment, and I couldn't help wondering if he ever revisited that moment in his mind. If he had enjoyed what had passed between us.

He stepped closer, scanning the trees around us. His mannerism seemed unusual, awkwardly so. "I apologise if in kissing you, it caused confusion on my part. I never suspected you'd take my drunken actions with offence. And in my mind, our relationship hasn't changed because of it. But...I...I certainly didn't envisage my ex when I kissed you. I never intended to mistreat you."

"I never said you did. You're putting words in my mouth again."

"I'll put my tongue in your mouth again if you'd prefer."

Stunned by his comment, I flashed him a pointed glare, only to discover he was smirking. The tease in his eyes lightened his expression and I saw the Rooke I loved and desperately missed. My own smile spread across my lips, and he laughed. "Can you imagine what Jacob would say if he knew what we did?"

"Ha! He'd vomit."

"He'd kick my arse, that's what he'd do." Rooke's grin transferred into a solemn muse. "He was more protective of you than I am now."

To be honest, I had no memory of that part of mine and Jacob's relationship. I was fifteen when he died. He was my big brother who snuck out late at night, drank alcohol down by the lake, and played a lot of hockey. He poked fun at me more times than not. But I had admired him. He was fearless and outgoing. Everything I wanted to be.

Then it dawned on me. Maybe Rooke had stopped me from taking our kiss further because of Jacob. Because of the respect he held for his deceased best friend. Maybe I was being a selfish, petulant idiot in thinking Rooke's actions were pure rejection. For years we had been closer than just friends. The night of the Akquarian ball we *had* been reminiscing about home. We *had* been drinking crazy coloured, alien drinks. I had no right to blame him for stopping me. He had acted out of respect and maturity, not primal desire like I had.

Pulling myself from the depths of my thoughts, I found Rooke watching me. The troubled frown had returned to his face, and I fought the urge to reach up and iron those lines out with my fingertips. Nux, I loved this man, warts and all.

"I have a candle ready." Rooke's soft rumble pulled me back to why we were here, why he'd been waiting for me. "Will you help me light it? In Jacob's honour?"

He held his hand out and I stared at it, swallowing back the grief clumping up at the back of my throat. Without another thought I took it, allowing him to lead me into the dark hut.

As we crouched around the candle, watching the small flame dance in the gentle breeze, a sense of triumph settled over me, as if a barrier had been brought down between us. Not all of them, by no means. But it was progress, and I was now determined to fight harder, to pull them all down.

I wanted my Rooke back.

Chapter Twenty One

I could feel Rooke's eyes on me. It had been the same every morning since the night we'd talked. He'd watch me leave for work, whether in full view from the doorway or from a dark corner of his office, but I knew he was there. There was no doubt he opposed where I was going, and I assumed he had chosen to let me go. Well, that was until I reached the clifftop that morning and noticed Jader standing with two male warriors.

I approached, watching the trainee archers behind him taking instruction from another trainer.

"What's happening?" I asked. "Are we not training today?"

Jader scowled at me. "No. We're going out early."

I eyed the two warriors beside us. One I recognised. Broad shoulders, dark skin. It was Guz. I smiled in acknowledgement and looked back a Jader. "Care to explain?"

"Your commander has specified he does not want you out later than four. *And* we have to travel with protection." He gestured to Guz and the other warrior.

In despair, I squeezed my eyes together. What the hell was Rooke doing? Hunters weren't supposed to travel in large groups, it defeated the point. It had taken Rooke less than a week to intervene and take back a semblance of control over me. I wanted to throttle him.

"He's also said he doesn't want the group size smaller than six, so I've asked Dawna to come along."

"Dawna?" I frowned. She was the young woman who had an alarming amount of nose bleeds. She must've only been fifteen. "Is she ready?"

"More so than any other trainee and I don't have any other qualified hunters spare. I'm not going to sacrifice the safety of another hunting team to ease his paranoia."

"Nux, I'm sorry, Jader. This is my fault."

"It is what it is. It was inevitable he'd find out."

"Can you see why I didn't want to tell him?"

Jader hummed his understanding and stalked towards the horses. I'd never seen him looking so mad.

Once Wrenn and Dawna arrived, the six of us headed east towards the mountains. Why, I wasn't sure. We usually headed south or west. I wondered if Rooke had suggested that as well, to ensure we were less likely to encounter Igknamai.

After a few hours, Dawna was proving her skill set. She'd killed two squirrels while riding her horse at a canter. She smiled back at Wrenn and I, moments after striking the second one.

"Keep this up," Wrenn called, "and you'll have to join us in our weekly competition."

I tutted, eyeing Jader and Guz up ahead. They'd both stilled their horses, and Jader was holding his hand out to silence us. Instantly, my senses heightened, and I shushed Wrenn and Dawna. Yohan, the second warrior, appeared next to me, his hand travelling to the hilt of his sword.

Time seemed to pause as we all remained silently still, staring through the small white barked trees surrounding us. The impulse of adrenaline flooded my legs, readying me for fight or flight. I felt Io, my horse, trembling beneath me.

There was slightly more undergrowth here. The Igknamai didn't tend to venture up the mountain. I assumed the incline deterred them, but some areas were fairly flat, like this one. It wouldn't surprise me if they stalked prey up here, using the low foliage as cover.

The sound of rustling and a muffled snort had us turning frantically. My heart was pounding in my ears. I couldn't see anything other than swaying green leaves. A flash of movement in front of Dawna had Yohan pushing his horse forward, his sword hissing from its scabbard. Hideous squealing and the tip tap of non-delicate footsteps had my head snapping to the ground in front of Yohan. A dark, solid animal, the size of an average Alluran pig, was running through our group with the dead squirrel, Dawna had just killed, in its mouth.

"Hey!" Dawna shouted, urging her horse to pursue. Wrenn glanced back at me with a devilish grin on her face. I knew what she was thinking; the competition was on. With Yohan following close behind, we surged after Dawna, in hot pursuit of the squirrel thief. Jader smirked, shaking his head as we shot past him.

I realised the animal was a boar. It wasn't an ancient animal we had on Allura, but I'd heard Jader and Wrenn talk about them many times. Apparently, they were a culinary delicacy, especially when smoked. There was no way we were going to let the little thief out of our sights.

We followed the squealing beast for a couple of miles. It was Wrenn who passed Dawna and caught up to the scarpering animal. A harrowing series of squeals echoed around the forest once her arrows hit its bulky body, immobilising the beast. Wrenn jumped down from her horse. Standing over the whimpering animal, she took her dagger and sliced its throat, thankfully silencing the horrifying noise.

Panting, Wrenn sat back on her legs, her eyes closed.

"Don't tell me," Dawna said, slowing her horse, "Wrenn's one boar beats my two squirrels." I glanced across at her. She was smiling from ear to ear, a dribble of blood trailing from her nose. She touched her philtrum and rolled her eyes.

"You could dispute it, but I wouldn't." I laughed. "Wrenn is evil when she gets overly competitive."

"I heard that." Wrenn glanced over her shoulder at us but seemed to double take the view to her right. I watched her eyes grow in what looked like shock mixed with awe. She slowly stood, mesmerised by the sight.

As if she was in a trance, she walked forward. I tried to glimpse what had captivated her, but the trees were too thick. Jumping down from Io, I jogged over to her. "Wrenn, what's…"

My eyes widened. The colour that hit my irises felt surreal, unnatural. Never in my wildest dreams had I seen such beauty.

Through a gap in the trees, was an enormous clearing full of vibrant lilac flowers—an ongoing sea of purple. The expanse stretched for miles, rolling down the hillside to the left. It only stopped when it met rockfaces or towering trees in the distance. To me, an Alluran, who had grown up surrounded by a golden, yellow, and orange countryside, this was an incredible sight. But I couldn't understand Wrenn's astonishment. I peered at her. She took a long, deep breath and smiled. It was a smile full of joy, and sadness.

"Wrenn?"

An explicit string of curses erupted from behind us. Jader appeared, his gaze as wide and wistful as Wrenn's. "How is this possible?" he said breathlessly.

"I…I don't know." Wrenn whispered back.

I looked between them both, baffled. "Can someone please explain what's going on?"

Jader bent down to examine one of the purple flowers. "You know the purple tinted poison we put on our arrow heads to use against the Igknamai? Well, this is the flower we extract it from."

Stepping closer, I realised I'd seen one before, in the ravine, prior to Cora's death. Both she and Zamya had been fascinated by it. A bulbous body with a multitude of tiny purple petals, protected by a hoard of barbed spikes.

"This flower wasn't around when the ancients were here. It was only discovered a few hundred years ago. The poison is deadly to the Igknamai and the Igknamai alone. Don't get me wrong, humans aren't immune to it. It's not quite as detrimental to us, though. If we inhale it, we get a bad headache. If it enters our bloodstream, we are taken with a nasty fever for a few days, but it passes. But it kills the Igknamai almost instantaneously. That's why we call it Mother's Promise. As if Mother Earth is trying to help us rid this land of those monsters."

"And The Mother has definitely spoken today," Wrenn mumbled.

"Indeed. These flowers are rare. We only ever come across them in small clusters, not fields. Never fields."

I glanced across the vast expanse of purple. What this meant was overwhelming. The direction of this war could drastically change in the Redwood's favour, with or without Solarfleet's help.

"We could build some kind of weapon," Wrenn mused, following the same train of thought.

A spate of pensive silence fell upon us, until Guz and the others came up behind, all stunned by the sight.

"Let's call it a day." Jader turned back to the horses. "We should get this news back to the council."

There was a poised excitement within the team as we rode down the mountain path to a familiar part of the forest. We headed towards the palisade on the east side of the village. Slowing the horses to a casual trot, a band of scouts on horseback trotted past. I heard Jader call out up front, "You're going out late." He stopped his horse, forcing the rest of us to follow.

"A group of children have gone missing." Truro, atop of Titan, came into view, stopping next to Jader. "We're heading out to see if we can find them. Don't suppose you've seen anyone?"

Jader shook his head. "No, nothing. How long have they been missing?"

"A few hours. I'm sure they'll show up. It's Fheo and his rabble."

"Why doesn't that surprise me?"

Truro grumbled, then glanced at the rest of us, resting his gaze on the boar tied to the rear of Wrenn's horse. "Woah, where'd you find that?

"In the mountain pass."

"Make sure you save some for me." A cheeky grin spread across his face.

"You'll have to wait in line like everyone else, I'm afraid," Wrenn japed back.

"Talking of rarities," Jader said, "we made an intriguing discovery today. I'll tell you about it when you're back at the village."

A quick frown crossed Truro's brow before his stoic expression returned. "I'll find you when I return." He instantly pushed Titan forward, flicking a glance at me for the briefest of moments as he went by.

I glanced over my shoulder as our party continued on, watching him eloquently canter away. Every part of Truro called to me. He was a true protector, a leader, an amazing friend. But why did I feel so guilty for thinking it? Perhaps he was everything Rooke was renowned for too. I just didn't appreciate Rooke's protection right now. He made me angry more times than not. Whereas the thought of Truro made me sad—a sadness full of regret.

A bone chilling scream ripped through the forest air. All six of us stopped rigid as a clash of shouting and another calamity of cries echoed around us. It was hard to distinguish where the voices were coming from.

Eyes wide, we remained silent, listening, waiting. The forest seemed to fall silent alongside us. The only thing I could see was the uneven forest floor shadowed by red-barked trees. The scene stretched for an eternity. We were still at least two miles from the palisade.

A female scream shattered the quiet. It seemed louder, closer.

Jader and Yohan launched into a gallop, drawing swords and arrows. Without hesitation, I jeered Io after them. If these were villagers needing our help, I would be brave enough to encounter whatever it was they were facing.

Driving Io upwards, I rounded a steep ridge, gasping at the sight that met me on the other side. My heart, too, juddered against my ribcage in horror. In the same way Cora had been, two Igknamai were dragging an adolescent across the forest floor. Her legs were locked in their jaws as she fought to right her body. Her arms were covered in blood, and the hilt of a dagger was clasped in her hand. She was desperately trying to reach for the spot between the Igknamai's eyes, desperately fighting for her life.

Cries of terror pulled my eyes further to the left, to where another large Igknamai was pacing at the bottom of a thinner tree. It jumped, snapping its teeth upwards, and I realised there were children in that tree, holding on for dear life.

Wrenn and Dawna appeared next to me on the ridge. Wrenn didn't pause to think. She steered her horse towards the children. Jader and Yohan were already surging towards the two other Igknamai dragging the trapped girl. Calculating the tasks at hand, I accelerated down the hill after Wrenn.

Arrows flew from Wrenn's bow as she approached the Igknamai stalking the base of the tree. The arrow tips punctured the top of its legs, causing it to hiss with irritation. The beast turned in our direction. Hopping excitably on its spindly limbs, it roared, spitting saliva over itself. Nux, these creatures were disgusting. There was a hint of their stench in the air, adding to their vulgarity.

Wrenn didn't slow as she hurtled down the hill towards the

monster. Raising her hand, she sneered as it ran towards her. And in the next moment, the beast was skidding in the red dust, eyes glazed, body motionless. In that moment, I appreciated how skilled a warrior Wrenn was. Her dagger stuck out from between the Igknamai's eyes.

My body was raging with adrenaline when I stopped my horse at the base of the tree next to Wrenn. She was reaching upwards, coercing the children down. There must have been at least eight of them hidden within the branches.

Dawna arrived, placing her horse next to mine. I looked over at Jader. One Igknamai was wounded, hissing, and thrashing its body on the floor. Jader was carrying the wounded girl towards his horse. Her head was limp, her bloodied limbs were lifeless. Behind them, Guz was now vigilantly encircling the other Igknamai with Yohan.

"Eden!"

I glanced up the tree and flinched when I saw Saff peering down at me. Her face was damp with tears, reddening her delicate cheeks. The blue of her eyes was a vivid contrast in comparison, but it was the look of terror on her face that alarmed me.

I reached up to her and she climbed lower, jumping the last metre into my arms. Throwing her arms around me, she whimpered something inaudible, then pulled back and said, "There were Hybrids."

"How many?"

"At least two."

Wrenn cursed beside me and shouted the information over to Jader. We all glanced about, scouring the landscape for movement.

Tapping Saff's back, I said, "Come on, we need to make space for a couple more."

She manoeuvred her body around mine while I reached up for a boy, one I recognised as part of *Fheo's rabble*. After climbing behind Saff, another smaller boy fell into my arms. I placed him in front of me. He was so petite. He must have only been about four. It terrified me how dangerous this situation was for someone so tiny, so young and inexperienced. Why were they out here alone?

"Get them back to the village," Jader called to us as more roaring was heard from the depths of the forest. "Don't stop!"

With our horses laden with three children each, Wrenn, Dawna, and I encouraged our horses up another incline. The little boy in front of me squeezed my thumb and fingers so tight, they began to go numb. He was terrified. They all were.

A putrid smell hit my nose, and in a blur of brownish yellow, something jumped out in front of Io. Thankfully, she leapt out of its way and kept running. But the sounds of snarling and snapping, followed by more screams of terror, had me whipping my head in all directions.

Dawna's horse was now on its side, lifeless. A lump of flesh had been ripped from its throat, blood pooling on the soil around it. Dawna was struggling to free a child trapped under the horse. He was wailing and writhing. I had no doubt the boy's legs and pelvis must be broken. The other two boys were running away from the scene, but what troubled me was I couldn't see the Igknamai who had caused the incident. Where the hell was it?

Turning, I saw Wrenn's horse up ahead. It was being chased by two smaller Igknamai. With her passengers clinging to her body, Wrenn was struggling to aim her bow backwards towards the beasts behind. A part of me knew she'd be alright. Dawna was the one who needed my help.

Io sped towards the slain horse. I had no idea what to do. There wasn't enough room for all of us on Io. Maybe hiding in the trees was an option, then wait for Jader and the others to find us. Nux, I hoped they were okay.

Suddenly, Io squealed, rearing almost vertically, nearly succeeding in throwing me off. Clenching my thighs and teeth in unison, I remained seated, but I felt Saff's grip around my waist loosen, followed by a duo of desperate cries. Before I had the chance to do anything, Io bolted.

Trying to regain control, I glanced over my shoulder. I could feel my frown burning into my forehead as I witnessed Saff and Fheo's friend scrambling to their feet. Dawna was a few metres away from them, still trying to free the young boy. Her bow and quiver lay on the floor behind her.

With panic surging through my veins, I pulled on Io's reins, hard. She reared again, then skittishly danced on the spot, flicking up dirt in the same manner Titan did when a threat was nearby. I tried to coerce her back down the hill towards the children, but she refused to move.

"Come on, Io," I growled. The little boy sitting atop her hunches peered back at me. I needed to get him home. I needed to get Saff and the other boy home! "Damn!" Io wasn't budging.

A flash of movement caught my eye, and I snapped my gaze back to Saff and the others. My breath seized inside my lungs as I witnessed a huge Igknamai, as large as a fully grown stag, pounce towards Dawna. My voice was a bellow of warning, but it was too late. The beast flipped her over, grabbed her legs, and began to haul her away, all the while Dawna's screams piercing the air.

I jumped down from Io and looked up at the small boy. "Take Io home. She knows the way. Get help!"

The boy's eyes began to water but he didn't sob. With an enormous amount of courage, he nodded and took the reins. I smacked Io's rear, and she lurched forward, heading towards the village.

Reaching for my bow and quiver, I ran down the shallow incline. Saff was sobbing into her hands, while Fheo's friend stood frozen in shock. The other boy, trapped under Dawna's dead horse, was now unconscious. I bent down, touching the boy's neck with my fingers. There was no heartbeat. He was gone.

"Saff, get off the forest floor. Now!"

I didn't wait to check if they followed my orders, I ran after Dawna, pursuing the huge Igknamai. It hadn't gotten far; Dawna was making the task difficult. She was stabbing it in the face, but to no effect. Instead, she was irritating it. The beast dropped her for a second and roared in her face. She fell to the ground, whimpering, before it snatched up her legs in its jaws again.

Poised and stable, I heard my intake of breath as I drew an arrow—one with a purple tinted arrowhead—and aimed it in the same way I'd been practicing for months. Releasing the bow string, the arrow flew, hitting the Igknamai exactly where I wanted it to. Its eyes widened but it continued to haul Dawna through the dusty earth.

I cursed, setting up another shot. This time the arrow hit one of its four eyes. The beast jerked, causing Dawna to scream again, but it began to sag, easing its lock around Dawna's legs.

Bloodied and laboured by her injuries, Dawna struggled to her feet as the Igknamai slumped to the floor. Clasping a hand over her mouth, she hobbled towards me, shaking fiercely. I ran towards her, turning suddenly, when Saff's words of warning hit me. "Eden! Hybrids! *Hybrids*!"

Something solid slammed into me, and the next thing I knew, I was lying face down in the dirt. Heavy hands grabbed my shoulders, hauling me to my feet. I could barely breathe, I felt winded.

One rough hand encircled my neck and my fingers instantly shot up, clawing at it. Raising me higher, I was now standing on the tips of my boots. A pair of hauntingly black eyes, held within a dark, human face, met mine. His scraggly, long hair was black, full of dirt and red dust.

He smirked at me. It was a cruel, taunting smile, reminding me of Llexzus. However, he was not as pristinely dressed as Llexzus, nor as strikingly broad. In fact, this Hybrid seemed to be wearing rags.

He was strong, though. I could see his bulging arm muscles through rips in his sleeves as he held me steadily with one hand. My lungs were crying for air, my panic surging.

Hybrid. This was a Hybrid. Evil, demonic, unnatural.

"This one smells different." His voice was a growl, coarse and jeering. Who was he talking to?

"She could be one of those sky humans Manta's been talking about. We'll be rewarded well if we return with one of them." Nux, there was another one. His voice was coming from the direction of Dawna. Where was she? Had she escaped?

"Take the other one." My captor sneered at me again, this time licking his ridiculously long, sharp canines. "The more the merrier."

It was then I heard Dawna's murmur. She sounded barely conscious. I tried to call to her, but the Hybrid's fingers around my neck were too tight, reminding me of Dybgo's crushing grip. I was going to pass out soon. I needed to do something to save myself, to save Dawna.

Using his hand around my neck as leverage, I jumped and forcefully kicked him in the stomach, then the groin. With a grunt, he dropped his grip, but before I could react, his fist collided with my stomach, sending me staggering down to the floor.

Clutching my stomach with one hand and holding my neck with the other, I wheezed, trying to crawl away. I heard his growl a moment before my head was yanked backwards. He was tugging at

201

my braid, pulling me to my feet. The sting of pain at my scalp caused tears to form in the corners of my eyes.

My back crashed against his solid body and my fingers fumbled for my dagger on my hip. Still pulling my hair back and down, I was forced to stare skywards. From behind, he loomed over me, meeting my petrified gaze with his dark, taunting smirk. He was tall. Far taller than the average human male. I had no chance of winning a fight against him.

"You're a frisky one," he grumbled, abruptly turning me round to meet him face on. His hand returned to my throat, squeezing harder this time. Gritting my teeth together, I thrust my dagger forward, but he was quick, unnaturally so. He grabbed my wrist, forcing me to drop the blade. "What were you going to do with that, pussy cat? Scratch my eyes out? Why don't you give up and pass out like the other one did? It'll make this a lot easier."

Nux, had the other Hybrid taken Dawna? I couldn't see her in my peripheral vision anymore.

Uncertain if it was my slowly faltering vision or not, but I thought I saw the Hybrid flinch. Trailing my gaze over his dark, torn shirt across his shoulders, I discovered an arrow protruding out of the skin. Red blood gushed from the wound as he grabbed the wooden spike, pulling it free. I flicked my eyes in all directions, trying to figure out where the arrow had come from. Then a flash of black leather and auburn hair caught my attention, and I swore I saw Saff with a bow in her hand.

I instantly panicked. Why wasn't she up a tree, out of reach? I had to keep her safe. Straining to catch another glimpse, I saw a body lying in the soil. His leathers were slashed across his chest, the ground red with fresh blood. It was Fheo's friend. The Hybrid must've killed him before attacking me. That was how Saff knew they were coming.

Another arrow grazed the side of the Hybrid's neck, and he roared his disapproval. His temper was more animalistic than human; predatory, impulsive. With a force raged by anger, he threw me backwards, sending another bout of pain quaking through my body.

Trying to breathe through the intensity of the pain, I stumbled to my feet. The Hybrid was stalking towards Saff, a jagged sword now in his hands. It was huge, like an elongated saw encrusted in rust.

Saff was standing twenty metres away with a scatter of arrows laid at her feet, aiming Dawna's bow at the monstrous man. I could see her trembling, her bow swaying almost uncontrollably. She shot another arrow, missing her target. A sheer look of panic engulfed her expression at the realisation the Hybrid was getting closer. Too close.

Reaching for the sword sheathed across my back, I began to sprint in their direction. I had no idea where my bow was. I'd dropped it when the Hybrid first collided with me. My sword technique wasn't as refined as my bow, but I couldn't let him kill Saff. She was my friend. She was Truro's baby sister. I had to try.

The hiss of steel, followed by a blur of black surrounded by churned up earth, was the last thing I was aware of before the Hybrid's severed head dropped to the floor. I skidded to a halt, glancing at the rolling head and slumping body, then back at Saff. Her look of shock matching my own.

The unmistakable sound of a horse snorting had me glancing behind. With blood splattered across his face and over his brown leather armour, Truro jumped down from Titan. He looked furious. "I thought you knew better?" He was glaring at Saff. "Why the hell are you this far from the village, on the wrong side of the fence?"

Saff began to cry, dropping the bow to her feet. I reached for Truro, brushing his arm as he marched past. "Truro, she saved me."

He turned to look at me, tenderly touching my cheek, then my neck. Stepping closer, his frown deepened. "Are you hurt?"

"I'm fine, but one of the Hybrids took Dawna. And there are other children scattered about."

"I'll find them. You two get home."

"My horse…"

"Your horse is there." He pointed over my shoulder. I turned. Io was cantering through the trees towards us with the tiny boy sitting on top of her. Sending him a tenuous smile, he looked at Truro with reverence. Had he gone to find Truro instead of heading home as I instructed? *Nux, these kids!*

Truro tenderly embraced Saff before helping her up onto Io. Offering me a hand, he paused, reaching for one of his swords. Stepping away, his eyes and ears had become alert, listening, scanning. He cursed under his breath, and I followed his line of sight.

Through the tree line, was a young boy holding a child sized sword. Using both hands, he was pointing it at a snarling Igknamai. The beast was at least four times his size, saliva dripping from its mouth. The boy jeered at it while standing protectively over the immobile body of another boy. I realised they were the two boys who had run away after Dawna's horse was slain.

I heard Truro's breath stutter beside me. He looked terrified, more so than I'd ever seen him before. "Fheo," he whispered to himself. He looked at me with pleading eyes. "Get home. Now!" In the next moment he was running.

I jumped onto Io, watching Truro slow as he vigilantly neared Fheo and the enormous Igknamai. As I rode away, a pounding of guilt thundered down on me. I should've stayed and helped. What if something happened to him?

Saff tightened her grip around my waist reminding me of the task at hand. I had to get her and the little boy home.

Passing a pair of smaller Igknamai who laid dead on the path, Io jumped the palisade. All three of us had been hauntingly quiet. We'd left the dead body of the boy killed by the Hybrid behind, as well as the one trapped under the horse. I felt too horrified to cry. I don't think the reality of what happened had sunk in yet.

A resented sense of relief struck me when we arrived underneath the garrison platform. We were home, but how many weren't coming back? I'd heard so many times about Igknamai attacks. I'd seen the funeral pyres burning on the clifftop, but I'd never known who had died, never witnessed the massacre with my own eyes.

After helping Saff down from Io, the tiny boy leapt into my arms, tightly locking his around my neck, and burying his head into my shoulder. Holding him like that was painful. My neck felt bruised, my stomach tender. But I continued to hold him until we reached his home.

The boy leapt from my arms when a young woman appeared in the doorway of a small hut. She paused for a split moment before opening her arms to him, the look of sheer elation on her face. He ran straight into her embrace and began to sob. Wrapping her arms tightly around his small body, the woman looked up at me, and through tear filled eyes, she mouthed, "Thank you."

Hand in hand, I walked Saff home. She was silent, reflective. I was trying to hold myself together for her. I wanted to ask her why the group had ventured out, but chastising her wasn't going to bring her friends back.

As we approached a cluster of huts surrounding a large platform, an older woman scurried across one of the bridges. I instantly knew who she was with her blue eyes and auburn hair.

"Oh my word, Saffron! Where have you been? You've had me so…" Her words muffled against Saff's hair as she reached for her, hugging her close.

"I'm sorry, mum." Saff's tears were streaming down her face. "I won't do it again. I promise. I swear. I won't…"

Watching their interaction made my heart ache. I missed my mum. Even as a grown woman, I sill missed her.

They remained in each other's embrace, mumbling soft words to one another, and I tried to silently slip away. I didn't get far. Saff's mum's frantic cry had me turning back.

Truro was walking towards them with Fheo's small body cradled in his arms. The boy's head and limbs were limp, the skin around his mouth and ears blue. Truro's face said it all. Fheo was dead. Truro's mini nemesis was gone. My heart broke for him, for all of them.

My own tears started to fall as I watched Saff's mum run to Truro, hysterically touching Fheo's face in the hope he was still breathing. Saff sobbed as she followed them into one of the huts. More female cries came from within. I assumed Fheo's mother.

I couldn't take it anymore. Everything felt agonisingly out of control. Scurrying away, I headed for the burnt-out treehouse. I needed to be alone.

But I stopped walking, staring down at the village below. No, I didn't need solitude. I needed the one person who resented me. I needed Rooke.

Chapter Twenty-Two

My whole perspective felt tilted. I couldn't think. The overwhelming emotions of remorse and unfounded guilt darkened my vision, intensifying the pain in my head. The well of grief overflowed, consuming me, drowning me. I wanted to scream but I couldn't breathe.

I heard laughter as I boarded the bridge to Rooke's office. His voice sounded relaxed and jovial as he spoke; a sound I hadn't heard in what felt like an age. He broke out into another bout of laughter, and I suddenly felt angry.

Ignorant. He was blissfully ignorant, and he wanted to remain that way. Well, I wasn't going to let him anymore.

"If I were you, I'd keep your laughter a little quieter." My tone was cold, unforgiving. Both Rooke and Oz instantly fell silent, eyeing the bruised and dirty warrior standing on the threshold.

Rooke shot to his feet, rounding the desk to get closer to me. "What the hell happened?" Worry monopolised his features, but he paused when he caught the glare I was throwing him.

"You have to help these people." A tear slid down my cheek, shattering my portrayal of a confident, fierce warrior; one who was trying to convince her commander to see the morality of his recent decisions.

"What happened to you?" He stepped forward, reaching for me but I pushed him away.

"Tell me you will help them!" More tears fell and I met his dark green gaze. It was spilling with concern and affection. "Four young children are dead. Children, murdered! Two teenage girls were snatched. One was taken, the other probably dead from her injuries. Will you really leave the rest of them to face these monsters alone?

Leave them to pay for the sins of our ancestors? Not just theirs. Ours!"

"Eden, it's not that…"

"Is this not enough proof that we need to help?"

"Listen…"

"Please tell me you'll help them! Tell Solarfleet to help them…"

"Eden."

"PLEASE!" My vision fogged with tears. I felt myself crumbling, succumbing to the need to weep. My legs began to buckle and I started to slide down the hut wall. Warm hands snatched me up before I hit the floor. Colliding with a solid chest, the smell of citrus hit my senses.

Rooke allowed me to sob into his chest. Encased in his arms, I remembered what it felt like to be his friend, when I relied on him regardless of any indifferences, when we relied on each other unconditionally.

Pulling me to arm's length, Rooke bobbed down to my eye level. I could feel his eyes searching my face, resting on the soreness around my neck.

"Look at me," he said gently. "Look at me." I met his gaze, and his thumbs wiped the wetness from both my cheeks. "You have a heart of gold, you always have. Me? Not so much. What I said before, I was angry…"

"These are good people, Rooke."

He rested his forehead against mine, tracing his thumb over my cheek bone. "I will help them," he whispered. His thumb now tracing the line of my lips. "I will. I'll help them…for you."

A sombre yet contented moment passed between us. We remained silent, foreheads touching. Watching my hands clutch at his black T-shirt, I contemplated the words he'd spoken, conscious his thumbs were still stroking my cheeks, my lips.

His palms lowered to my neck and I winced. Pulling back, Rooke began tugging on the small, upright collar of my leathers. "How'd this happen?"

I swallowed, grimacing at the soreness growing there. My voice was a reluctant whisper when I replied, "Hybrid."

Eyes widening, Rooke sucked in a breath, and I sensed the pause, the tension building. I prepared for his backlash of protective authority, but to my utter surprise, it never came. Instead, his fingers began to unfasten the top two buckles of my leathers, pulling the neckline open to view the bruise developing underneath. He gently touched the tender area, the frown on his face filling with unspoken concern.

Closing my eyes, I savoured the warmth of his touch, the feel of his fingers against my skin. It had been weeks, months, since we'd touched one another as a natural gesture. Too long since we had any semblance of the relationship we'd built. Now, he was touching me with such tenderness, my heart was aching with want. A tear trickled down my cheek at the thought. I was expecting him to wipe it away. I wasn't expecting to feel his lips against my neck, softly kissing the bruised skin—a delicate, warm caress full of affection.

I couldn't disguise the sharp inhale of breath, nor dissuade my body from sinking back against the wall behind me. Opening my eyes, he pulled away, holding my gaze, moving to the opposite side. My breath wavered again as his lips touched the skin there, and I suppressed the sob from forming in the back of my throat. I felt vulnerable under his touch, powerless, but I didn't want him to stop.

He pulled back again replacing his lips with his warm hands. Those dark eyes had become unreadable, the complete opposite to mine. Mine were spilling with desire. I wanted to kiss him. And I had the oddest feeling that's what he was going to do.

"Rooke, are you home? Oh, oh!" Valina's voice ripped the essence of sensuality heightening between us. "Am I intruding?"

Rooke noticed how I squeezed my eyes together in despair, and his hands dropped from my neck.

"No," I said, replying to Valina's question, at the same time Rooke ground out the word, "Yes."

We all fell silent for an awkward few seconds before Valina stepped fully inside the hut. "An urgent council meeting has been called." She cleared her throat, fully aware she was thickening the tension filling the room. "I thought we could go over together."

Remaining silent, Rooke continued to stare at me. The intensity behind those eyes was far too heavy, and I found myself pushing away from the wall.

"I need to go shower, anyway." I began to walk to the hut's side opening, but he grabbed my hand coercing me to look back. I didn't. I continued walking, letting his fingers slip through mine. It was in that moment, I realised Oz was no longer in the room. He had left. We'd been alone.

The thought gave me pause as I walked over the interconnecting bridge. Was Rooke really going to kiss me?

I turned, looking back through the open doorway to Rooke's office. Valina's voice filtered through the opening, but Rooke wasn't taking any notice of her. His eyes were still on me, as if he was anticipating something.

Dropping my gaze, I did the only thing I was confident enough to do. I walked away.

Chapter Twenty—Three

The pyres burnt bright on the clifftop that night.

The Redwoods didn't seem to hold funerals. With the number of deaths they endured, they'd be inundated with them. Whether it be by natural causes or by the monsters of this world, the pyres were lit every evening after someone had passed.

The families gathered to pay their last respects, viewing the pyres from their homes or platforms, just as I was. I'd hid myself away in the burnt and abandoned lookout hut, towering above the highest level. Everything seemed hauntingly quiet up here. Only the distant roar of the pyres travelled to my ears, a sound I found deafening sitting alone in the darkness.

I couldn't remove the boys' faces from my mind, and what I could've done differently to save them. The loss of anyone was hard to bear, but the loss of multiple children? How must their parents be feeling? The death of a child must be soul destroying. No parent was meant to bury their child, it was an unwritten law of nature.

It was no wonder my mum hadn't coped with Jacob's death.

My mind cast back to Truro holding Fheo in his arms. I knew Truro well enough to know he was blaming himself for his death. I wondered if he was up on that very clifftop absorbing the heat of the flames, scolding himself physically as well as mentally. A part of me longed to be there with him.

The first thing I felt when I woke, was the soreness around my neck. Gently touching the area, I discovered it wasn't anywhere near as painful as when Dybgo had attempted to strangle me. But then again, I got the impression Dybgo had wanted me dead. The Hybrid, however, simply wanted me to pass out so he could kidnap me. Which one was the more disturbing, I couldn't decipher.

After washing and dressing, I left for training, well aware Rooke was watching me from his desk. I forced myself not to think about yesterday, about his actions. They only confused me to the point of frustration.

I caught up with Wrenn as she crossed the bridge towards the east cliff ladder. As soon as she heard me, she turned. Her expression was full of sadness. Throwing her arms around me, she squeezed my shoulders. "I tried to find you last night. To see if you were alright."

I squeezed her back. "I'm fine."

Pulling away, she eyed me sceptically. "I came back for you. After dropping the three kids off. I went back and...I must've missed you. I saw Dawna's horse and..." Her gaze drifted to the trees around us. "I found Truro nursing over Fheo. He died in his arms."

The thought ripped my heart to shreds. What had happened after I'd left him yesterday? "Is...do you know if Truro is okay?"

"He tends to deal with these things in his own way. I'm sure he'll be fine." She linked her arm through mine, turning to walk along the rockface walkway towards the ladder. "Let's see if we can find more boar to hunt."

I tried to smile but I couldn't stop thinking about Truro. About Fheo and... "What will happen to Dawna?"

Wrenn's sigh held a heaviness that unsettled me. "No one knows. Nobody has ever come back. I assume they will use her to procreate." She shook her head, the disgust on her face hardening her freckled features.

"Is that what the Hybrids come for? Young women?"

"The Hybrids only tend to appear when they want something. It's usually steel or...yes, women."

"This world is so barbaric."

I felt Wrenn's eyes studying my profile as my attention flicked ahead, to where Jader stood at the bottom of the cliff ladder. Similar to yesterday morning, he didn't seem his usual jovial self. His standard welcoming grin was replaced with a scowl.

"I wouldn't bother," he said, pointing to the clifftop.

"What is it this time?" I watched his chest heave in and out, huffing his displeasure.

"I'm sorry, Eden. You've been taken off the team."

It was Wrenn who expressed her disapproval first. "You've got to be kidding. Eden's efforts yesterday were courageous…"

"It's not about that."

"Then why have I been taken off the team?"

"Orders from Truro."

"Truro?" *What the hell?* Was he taking a leaf out of Rooke's book for protective arseholes? "Why?"

Jader screwed his lips to one side and replied slowly, "I believe he was acting on demands voiced by your commander."

A string of profanities fell from my lips. This was what Rooke had wanted since he found out about my change in occupation. The harrowing events of yesterday had finally given him cause to pull rank. The bastard. The utter bastard! I was going to throttle him!

Riled with pent up frustration, I flounced back across the village, entering Rooke's office with a loud stomp of my boots. "How dare you?!"

Dressed in his dark leathers, Rooke sat on the corner of his desk, talking to Blake. Oz and two other Redwood warriors stood beside them, all browsing over the damn map on the desk before them. They all looked at me, all except Rooke.

"Good morning, Eden, my darling." There was the faintest hint of a smirk on Rooke's lips as he finally turned to me. "How are you today?"

Taken aback, I stared at him. Clearly unfazed, the others returned their focus to the map, not slightly alarmed by the disdain in my voice.

"Don't!" I snapped. "Don't call me that! And don't use that patronising tone with me!"

"You seem angry."

"You know why I'm angry! You *knew* I'd be angry! That's why you let me traipse across the entire breadth of the village so Jader could inform me of *your* decision! What makes you think you can dictate what I can and cannot do? This is my life, Rooke! Mine! My own!"

He continued to stare. An elevated manner of authority exuberated from him. He knew I'd be upset. He knew, yet he sat there without an ounce of remorse. For once it was me climbing the anger scales. He remained calm, unperturbed by my outburst. I wanted him to shout back. I wanted to have this out with him. "Why? Just tell me why?"

"Because," he slowly stood, his hands slipping into his trouser pockets, "you are my second. *And…*" Walking towards me he appeared to pick his words carefully. "It's about time I utilise you for my own benefit. I need your help."

"With what?"

He gestured to the map. "Finding the Hybrids' lair."

Unconvinced by his declaration, I scowled at him, then at the others hovering over the map behind him. "You've taken me off the hunting team so I can join you in your pointless escapades around the forest?"

"I don't think pointless is the right word."

"Neither do I," mumbled Blake from the desk. Taking a quick glance at him, I could've sworn he was smirking beneath his black beard. That didn't bode well with my temper.

"Look, Eden," Rooke stepped closer, lowering his voice, "if you have to leave the village every day, it will make me far happier if you are with me." He stopped barely a metre in front. With that gleam in his eyes, he looked devilish, like a rake ready to gobble me up. I hated how handsome he was, how he excited an abstruse part of me even when I was raging with contempt for him.

"And what if I don't want to?"

He flashed his teeth, his eyes sparkling with amusement. "I'm still your commanding officer, and I'm giving you two options. One, is to come out with me daily on my *escapades*. Or two, you remain in the village with strict instruction not to leave."

"What?"

"Those are my terms."

"Who are you, the new Havav?"

"Don't insult me."

"You insult me! You're taking my choices away."

"I'm protecting you."

"Protecting me." I wanted to laugh. "You…you are *impossible!*"

"And you are as stubborn as a mule." With a brazen look in his eyes, he peered down at me. I wanted to scream, but by the way his gaze soaked into my bones, bending my thoughts, I felt my stance soften, my frown and my temper ease. Without any conviction and as a half-hearted curse, I whispered, "I hate you."

His lips turned up into a smirk, and he winked. He knew he'd won.

Within the next half an hour, I was walking behind a line of scouts towards the garrison platform. My temper had calmed. I was beginning to understand Rooke's reasoning, although the manner in which he appointed it still ruffled my feathers.

"I received word from my brother yesterday." Rooke appeared beside me. His words piquing my interest. "My mum is awake. She's frail but improving."

"That's good news."

"It is." He smiled at me. "It really is." To be fair, Rooke did seem different today. Perhaps word of his mum's improvement had lightened his mood. Perhaps in forcing me to change my job, it too had lifted a worry weighing him down.

Travelling down the tree lift, we exited at ground level. A team of horses waited for us. I followed Rooke through the crowd of scouts and horses, noting the men and women who were joining us. It didn't surprise me to find Guz and Yohan were among them.

Voices ahead caught my attention. Rooke was talking to a young woman dressed in brown leather armour. The pretty brunette was smiling at him with a blush touching her cheeks. Inwardly, I groaned. This was what I didn't want. I couldn't cope with watching him flirt. That was another reason why I had preferred hunting; to be far away from him and his interactions.

"She's definitely back in good shape, so look after her," the brunette said to him, stroking the horse's neck they stood beside. She was still blushing.

"I will." Rooke threw her one of his dashing smiles. "Are you coming out with us today?"

"No, not today." The young woman flicked her eyes to me as I approached. "You have more than enough scouts this morning." There was a shyness in the way she kept dropping her gaze. She seemed modest, sweet.

"Hopefully tomorrow, then."

"Yes." She dashed behind the horse Oz was mounting, and

Rooke turned to me, smiling to himself. "I believe that's your horse." He pointed to the dark grey mare next to me. It was by no means Io.

"Am I not allowed to keep the horse I've bonded with?" There was too much bite in my tone for Rooke to ignore.

He eyed me sceptically. "I'll ask Ayelle to make sure you have your horse tomorrow."

"Is that her name?" I felt irritated again. Rounding the grey horse, I reached for the reins. I didn't realise Rooke had followed me until his hands appeared on the horse's bridle, making far less work than I did to adjust it.

"There," he said, looking down at me. I was still staring at the leather straps. "I'm told this horse is obedient and responsive. I'm sure you'll get along fine."

Grabbing onto the horse's shoulders, I nimbly hoisted myself up and took my seat. Blatantly avoiding eye contact, I turned my horse and fell in line behind the other riders. Within seconds Rooke's horse was beside mine, but to add salt to my jealous wounds, he glanced over his shoulder and called to the attentive brunette, "Have a good day."

It was the last straw, and I snapped. "She's a bit young for you."

Rooke flicked his head in my direction. "What has her age got to do with anything?"

The chuckle that escaped me was full of sarcasm.

"Eden, I'm not sleeping with her."

"I'm pleased to hear it." I glared at him. "Otherwise, I would've thrown the word hypocrite at you."

Eyebrows knitting together, he looked dumbfounded, which exasperated me further. It didn't help that everything this morning had put me in a foul mood, but I wanted to have this row with him. For making me feel like a piece of shit for seeking out a relationship with Truro, when Rooke was allowed to flirt and encourage. It was only his word that suggested he didn't take anything further.

"So, tell me. Why is it one rule for me and another for everyone else?"

He sighed, his nostrils flaring. "It's not."

"Really? Do you reprimand Oz every time he sticks his dick in someone?"

"Eden…"

"No, you don't. You turn a blind eye and let him do whatever or whoever he wants."

There was a tense pause, one I had recognised as the familiar aura that dwelled between us these days. It was thick and unsettling, full of uncertainty and unsaid words.

"You're clearly still upset with me regarding a certain personal situation."

"Wouldn't you be if I cock blocked you?"

Unable to look at me, his gaze remained ahead. "If you're looking for an apology, you'll be disappointed."

"I never expected an apology, especially from you. But an explanation would be nice."

"You know my reasoning."

"And why is that not a reason to reprimand Oz?"

I knew I was exasperating him. His loud huff was confirmation enough, the adjustment of his seat was another. "It's different."

"No. It's. Not!"

"Look, Oz has gone above and beyond his duty to keep us safe. To keep *you* safe."

"Above and beyond?" What the hell was he talking about? "Haven't we all sacrificed…"

"You wouldn't understand."

"And why is that?" I glanced at Rooke. His jaw was set, his knuckles white from gripping his horse's reins so tightly. He was starting to show annoyance. I was playing with fire, but I needed this. We'd avoided the subject for far too long. "You chastised me for keeping my training from you, yet here is proof of your reluctance to voice anything of importance to me. If I'm your second in command, shouldn't I be informed of such things?

"You don't need to know." The rasp in his voice indicated the soreness of the subject. What had he made Oz do, and why? I noted Oz riding up ahead, laughing with another male scout. I would never have guessed he had suffered any trauma, nor any sign of resentment towards Rooke or his position. The situation baffled me.

"Oz can do as he pleases," Rooke said, aware of my gaze. "The rest of us will abide by my rules."

"The rest of us?" Inwardly I chuckled. He didn't have to worry about Kobe, I was pretty sure the phlegmatic scientist was an

216

asexual man with the emotional ability of a pair of shoes. Zamya, on the other hand, would never follow Rooke's demands on this. She would go against him out of spite. "Does that include you?"

For the first time during our heated discussion, he found the courage to look at me. "Yes."

I wanted to laugh. "So, you're telling me you've remained celibate the whole time we've been on Earth?"

"Why does that shock you?" Shuffling in his seat again, he mumbled, "I prefer Alluran women."

He would say that. It was a good comeback. But the thought of him consorting with Valina, and the way he clearly flirted with Ayelle, boiled my blood.

"Maybe you should stop shooting your dashing smile at the locals then."

I didn't think my anger was fuelled by jealousy anymore. Now, it was resentment.

Chapter Twenty—Four

North. We always scouted north. I'd been following Rooke and his scouts for over a week and the task was monotonous. It was no wonder Rooke felt frustrated. We never discovered anything more than a scatter of Igknamai tracks, leading in various directions. It was pointless.

I had remained nonchalant, keeping my opinion to myself, purely to keep Rooke in a good mood. Thankfully, it had been working. He seemed his usual bantering self, far from the anger driven, infuriated man I'd encountered over the past couple of months.

Sitting at Rooke's desk, I ran a critical eye over his map. There were hundreds of small red crosses penned onto it. He'd told me these indicated where the scouted areas came up as negative finds. The few green and blue crosses intrigued me. These were areas of confirmed Igknamai attacks or Hybrid sightings. However, I felt certain he'd been looking in the wrong direction this whole time.

Footsteps and a tug of the curtain behind me announced Rooke's presence. Rising from the chair, I glanced his way. He was dressed in a dark pair of Alluran jeans, wearing a clean black T-shirt that hugged his upper arms and chest. Running his palm over his jawline, he walked over to his leather jacket hanging on the wall behind me. As he started to rummage around inside one of the pockets, I noticed he'd trimmed his stubble and neatly styled his dark hair. A knot formed in the pit of my stomach, twisting at the realisation of why he was looking so good. Tonight was the new moon celebration and, regardless of what had been announced last week, he was out to impress.

Trying to rid my face of the frown forming, I looked down at the map again. "Why do you always head out in the same direction?"

His hands paused, and I could sense him looking at me, then the map. "We had intel that north is the region the Hybrid lair is in."

"Why? How? Is it because of the signal you were tracking? Is this the monitoring area Troy helped you create?"

"At first, yes...but I now believe the signal isn't anything to do with the location."

"Because it jumps about?" I felt Rooke's eyes shift to me, and I turned to him.

"Did Troy tell you that?" Something in his mannerisms made me believe he was surprised Troy had.

"Yes. He also told me it had stopped."

"Well, it's started again." Choosing a different pocket, he resumed his blind search. "Its location is baffling. So, I've stopped chasing it and started using other methods."

Leaning over the map, I used my finger to trace where the Redwood village was. "Do you want my opinion?" There was a pause. I peered over my shoulder and found him watching me. Feeling undermined, I straightened. "Do you not?"

"No. Yes. I mean, yes. Give me your opinion." His Adam's apple bobbed, and the furrow between his eyes indicated his mind had briefly wandered. Something had distracted him. He stepped closer, gesturing towards the map. "Go ahead. Show me what you think."

"*Okay.* Well, during the attack last week, the Igknamai and Hybrids appeared on the east side of the village. When they were trying to leave, they were hauling the snatched girls southeast." I bent over the map, looking for the area the attack had taken place. Rooke appeared beside me, placing a balancing hand on the thick paper in front of us. I pushed his fingers slightly, finding the area I was looking for underneath. "We were here." I tapped the location, then traced my hand south-eastwards, noticing a large expanse of water surrounded by more dense forest. "Maybe we should look in this area. Head out twenty, maybe thirty miles."

In my peripheral I saw Rooke nod, scanning the area with intent.

"It's a good opinion," he said. I felt his eyes shift to my face and a smile brightened his. "This is why I need you."

"Have you only just realised that?" I smirked in jest.

"Why do you think I appointed you as my second two years ago? It wasn't because of your looks, you know."

I threw him a scolding look, watching him chuckle and return to his jacket. His perseverance made me frown. "What are you looking for?"

"Ah." He looked slightly embarrassed, then huffed before reluctantly explaining, "I can't find my little pot of hand cream. It's the last one I have."

An amused smile loosened the muscles in my face. "Hand cream?"

"Look, I'm an Alluran boy, now living in a brutally harsh world. I grip horse reins all day and I'm made to wield a sword. My hands get sore, okay." As he watched my smile spread, he rolled his eyes.

Reaching under the map, I pulled free a small glass pot. I'd seen it before I opened the map up earlier. "Here you go." I was still smiling as his warm hands brush over mine, taking the pot from me. He hesitated, letting his touch linger. Glancing up, I discovered he was studying my face.

"I've missed your smile," he said softly. "You don't smile enough these days."

"Well...I'm an Alluran girl, now living in a brutally harsh world full of terrorising woes. Sometimes I find it hard to smile."

He cupped my neck, stroking the faint remnant of the bruise residing there. Thankfully, the injury had been far less damaging than Dybgo's attempt, which in turn had given me a conjecture that the Akquarians were stronger than the Hybrids.

"Come on," I said. "It's getting dark. The party will have started by now."

Rooke stepped back, opening the tiny pot, and spreading the cream over his fingers and palms. As I folded the map up, I watched Rooke with a small smile on my face. These were the little things about him that I found so endearing.

Walking to the side opening, I glanced down the bridge to the middle hut, noticing Kobe sitting at the table. "Is Kobe not coming?"

"No. Not his type of thing." He placed the pot on the table. "Do you mind if we go to a different celebration site this evening? Oz said there's a far better one on the east side. It saves me having to avoid Valina all night."

"Sure. That sounds good to me."

Hand in hand we walked through the village, my long skirt rustling around my legs as I kept pace. The twinkling solar lights lit our way and the sound of distant music and laughter floated on the warm breeze. There was a soft smile dancing on Rooke's lips when he glanced down at me. He had seemed happier over the past week, remarkably so.

We approached a brightly lit area on the east side of the village. Recognising where we were, I found myself glancing towards the tall, thickset tree not a hundred metres from where we turned to access the party. I found myself wondering if Truro was there.

As we pushed through the swarm of partygoers, I suddenly realised why Rooke had wanted to come here. On the far side of the circular platform stood Oz with a few scouts I recognised...and Ayelle. Her eyes found Rooke as soon as he came into view. The smile that spread across both their faces was enchanting, full of delight, completely genuine.

Pausing on the threshold of bodies, I allowed his hand to fall from mine. I don't think he even noticed, his attention was fixed on Ayelle. She looked beautiful draped in a simple blue dress, with her thick brunette hair bouncing around her bare shoulders.

Watching their sweet interaction, I felt my forehead wrinkle. She made him laugh, a sound I didn't hear often enough these days. He looked so happy, and I felt happy for him. Perhaps she was why his mood had shifted, why he had climbed out of the darkness that had been consuming him. How could I possibly resent their relationship when he genuinely enjoyed her company? Would I be the hypocrite? He needed someone just as much as I did, and she was an amazing, young woman. I had spoken to her a few times over the past week, and she was sweet and timid, yet carried an air of modest confidence. She was perfect for him.

Yes, maybe I wanted it to be me who made him smile like that, but things had changed—unexpectedly changed.

I slunk backwards into the crowd, disappearing from their view. I didn't need to be here. Rooke did glance back, scouring the sea of faces, but he didn't seem concerned when he couldn't find me. He turned back to Ayelle, laughing again.

I didn't know what to do. *Should I stay or leave?*

Small hands groped my waist, and Zamya's voice was in my ear, making me instantly smile. "Where did you get this amazing skirt?" Her words were slurred and playful. I presumed she'd been drinking.

Laughing, I turned, not surprised to find Jader standing with his arm around her. Their height difference was ridiculous. He was nearly two heads taller, but they looked so cute together.

"Thanks for the skirt, Zam. It really is gorgeous." She'd made it for me just before last new moon, but I hadn't had the opportunity to wear it, until now. The material was a floating green fabric that reached my ankles. I'd worn it with a black vest top and a pair of sandals I'd borrowed from Wrenn.

"Think nothing of it." She glanced about. "Are you here on you own?"

I shrugged. "I came with Rooke and…"

"Rooke's here?" Zamya scrunched her nose up in disgust. She glanced up at Jader and huffed. "We can't stay if he's loitering about. If he sees me with Jader, he'll put two and two together and make me start wearing a chastity belt."

Both Jader and I laughed.

"I'm being serious," she said. "We should go somewhere else."

"If that's what you want, sweetheart." Jader kissed the top of her head, then glanced at me. "You gonna come?"

"I don't want to be a third wheel."

"Are you sure?" Zamya looked concerned. I had no doubt she could read me like a book.

I shoved her away. "Go. I'm going to get a drink and then probably head home."

Confirming my suspicion Zamya was drunk, she hugged me, planted a wet kiss on my cheek, and told me she loved me. Chuckling to myself, I waved to Jader as he was pulled through the throng of people, disappearing into the darkness beyond the party lights.

I sighed. Everyone else seemed happy. Nux, I needed a drink.

Finding an empty stool at the bar, I glanced over my shoulder, spotting Rooke and Ayelle. Oz was close by, balancing a stunning blonde on his knee. The conversation Rooke and I had last week flittered through my mind; *One rule for Oz, another for the rest of us.* What the hell had Rooke made him do? The thought troubled me.

The sound of the bar tender placing something on the bar top nearby was a welcomed distraction. I looked at the young woman, realising she was standing directly in front of me with a glass of coral wine in hand. The question on my face made her smile. She flicked her head over her right shoulder and said, "Compliments from Truro."

My eyes shifted past her to a hooded figure sitting at the far end of the bar. It was no wonder I hadn't seen him. Resting up against the bark of the tree, his brown hooded top blended in with the shadows. He raised his glass to me, and I noticed his hand was heavily bandaged. After attempting a smile as a signal of thanks, I sipped on the delectable beverage, closing my eyes to savour the taste. Nux, I needed this.

Failing to fight the urge to glance over my shoulder again, my stomach clenched at the sight of Rooke up on his feet, dancing. His eyes sparkled down at Ayelle as she smiled widely. I couldn't sit here and watch this. Despite my acceptance, it was torture. Downing the rest of my glass, I summoned the bar tender.

As she strolled over, I pointed to the coral wine bottle on the top shelf. "How much for the rest of the bottle?"

She eyed me, then the bottle. "I'd say twelve credits."

"Do I have enough?"

Without needing to take my name, she walked over to the machine behind her. After examining the details on the screen, she said, "Yeah, you have enough."

"I'll take it then."

She reached for the bottle, placing it in front of me with two clean glasses.

"Thanks." I stood, grabbing the bottle neck. "I won't need the glasses." I was walking away before she had time to reply.

A wave of loneliness washed over me as I headed to the burnt-out hut. It wasn't far and it was the only place I allowed myself to ponder. Yeah, it was a bad idea, especially in possession of a bottle full of addictive wine.

Climbing the ladder wasn't easy whilst holding it. And the long, layered skirt restricted my movements. Tripping slightly, I groaned a curse as I rounded the top. The familiar smell of singed wood filled my nostrils, and I suddenly realised I wasn't alone. Where the hut wall had been damaged and destroyed, a silhouetted figure sat on the very edge of the platform.

Stifling the disappointment in my voice, I began to retreat. "Sorry, I…I didn't realise…"

"Stay."

I froze, before a zap of static ignited my skin, warming my core. That voice, I knew too well, craved it too often. The disappointment fell away, and I turned to him. "How did you get here so quickly?" I asked, squinting through the darkness to visually confirm it was Truro. "You were just at the bar." I saw the flash of his smile.

"I obviously know a quicker route."

I huffed a laugh, walking over to the wooden wall next to the gap where he sat. I marvelled at how carefree he was; sitting on the very edge with his back propped up against a broken support beam. One leg dangled over the side while the other foot rested on the creaking, slatted floor, knee up.

Sitting down, I placed my back against the secure section of wall. "I didn't realise anyone comes up here."

"They don't." I heard the laugh in his voice when he said, "There's a sign keeping people out. Other than you, of course. You seem to use this place like a second home."

"How do you know I come here?"

"It's my job to know."

Not surprised in the slightest, I smiled down at my fingers grasping the open bottle. Taking a swig, I handed it to Truro. "Thanks for the drink."

"Looks like you needed more than one."

I heard the liquid rise and fall before he handed the bottle back. Noticing the glow of the bandage wrapped around his palm, I asked, "What happened to your hand?"

There was a short pause before he sighed. "An Igknamai caught it last week, the day of the attack." His voice had taken on a far more melancholic tone. I realised why.

"I'm so sorry about Fheo. I'm sorry about all of them. But I could tell Fheo was special to you."

"He was defiant until the end." Truro leant his head back and I saw the distant lights catching in his eyes. "Do you know what he said to me as I approached him standing off against that enormous

Igknamai? He said, 'Don't worry Uncle Truro, I've got this.'" A brief smile mixed with sadness and pride danced across his face. "Even his last breath was fighting talk. What I'd give for him to push me off a bridge this evening."

"He was your nephew?" I handed Truro the bottle again. He took a large swig, wiping his mouth with his sleeve. Staring at the bottle, he nodded. But then shook his head. "No," he said, the word barely audible. "He was mine…but I…I selfishly refused to be his father."

He watched me, gauging my reaction. A tear dripped down his cheek and the reality of what he'd confessed hit home. He'd lost his young son. Fheo had died in his arms.

I shuffled tentatively closer wanting to comfort him, but something in the way he poised himself made me hesitate. "You don't have to explain, Truro."

His eyes shifted to my face again and he handed back the bottle. "His mother was my dearest friend. She had been since I was six. She died minutes after delivering him." He forced a smile. "Fheo was a little toad from the start." There was a pause. Lines of historical anguish plagued his handsome face, and I could sense him reliving the drama. "I was seventeen. I'd just lost the woman I adored. I was still covered in her blood when…when they placed this babe in my arms, and I didn't…I didn't know what to do with him. I hated him. I hated him for killing her. It wasn't his fault, though…it was mine. I'd gotten her pregnant." Another tear dropped and he quickly wiped it away. "I couldn't find the courage or strength to be his father. I was devastated…and every time I looked at him…my heart broke. My brother and his wife took him in. Called him their own. Not many people knew any different…including Fheo."

I thought back to my comment from two new moons previous. I'd mentioned Fheo reminded me of Truro and Truro's expression had fallen. I now understood why.

"I was always Uncle Truro. But when my brother died a year ago, Fheo began to follow me around like a shadow. He looked up to me, wanted to be me, and I…I kept him at arm's length, never letting him get too close. Never letting myself get too attached. I promised myself I'd always protect him. But I couldn't even do that." He shook his head. "I couldn't save him from the monsters I'd been fighting my whole damn life."

"I'm so sorry." I grimaced at my words. They didn't express the extent of how much my heart pained for him. I knew from experience the word *sorry* wasn't what someone grieving needed to hear, but it was the only word people tended to offer. Reaching out, I touched his booted foot, hoping he was aware I was present, that I was here for him.

"I can't work it out," Truro muttered, "why they had all ventured out so far. Someone mentioned it had been a dare, but Saff won't talk to me about it. I think she feels responsible. She's been training every day this week, trying to perfect her aim. She told Jader she missed the Hybrid too many times and she would never let that happen again. Jader said he's never seen her so quiet and attentive."

"She saved me," I said, remembering the arrow jutting out of the Hybrid's arm while my vision started to fade. I touched my neck where the Hybrid's fingers had squeezed. "I would've been taken if she hadn't shot him." The troubling thoughts of what could've been my fate had stunted me enough times since the attack. Dying was one thing. Being taken, raped, and forced to bear hybrid children was another.

I felt Truro's eyes on me, but he remained silent. Reaching forward, he took the bottle from my hand and downed a large quantity. When he handed it back, I did the same. We repeated the exchange several times, continuing to sit in silence.

"I didn't intend to offload my dirty laundry onto you," he said. "Please forgive me."

I touched his foot again. "Don't apologise. I'm glad you can confide in me."

His tone of voice lightened slightly. "In return, maybe you could tell me something of a delicate nature. It might make me feel better."

I laughed. "Like what?"

"Oh, I don't know. Let's start with why you've been avoiding me?"

Oh...oh Nux.

Staring at the shadow of the tree trunk, I thought of Rooke. I thought of him dancing with Ayelle in her pretty blue dress while her timid smile captivated him.

"Did I hurt you?"

Shocked by his words, I looked at Truro. "No."

"Am I really that crap in bed, then?"

This time I laughed. "Not at all."

"So why did you run from me?" Pulling his leg up over the precarious edge, he moved closer. I could see the sharp outline of his face, the curve of his lips, the gleam in his eyes. I could smell his earthy scent mixed with a subtle vapour of coral wine.

"Tell me why." His breath fluttered across my cheek, and I felt myself uncontrollably drawn to him. Nux. I wasn't sure if it was the wine or just his intoxicating presence, but I was melting.

"Um," I couldn't hold his gaze anymore, "our intimacy, um...caused a stir with my crew."

His unexpected silence sliced through my decorum and when I found the courage to look at him, he was staring at me, eyebrows raised.

"You mean our intimacy caused a stir with your commander."

I huffed my irritation. "If you know, why are you asking?"

"Because I wasn't one hundred percent certain. Now I am. I always got the impression he was wary of me, but...I just don't understand why our relationship would cause a stir. Am I stepping on his toes?"

"What? No!" My heart jolted, thinking of last week, when Rooke had kissed my bruised neck and...I swore he wanted to kiss me. But...but he couldn't be jealous of Truro. He'd acted out of protection, to enforce protocol. He didn't *like* me in that way...did he?

No...no, he didn't! He was currently wooing Ayelle in full view of the locals, and for all he knew, me.

"So, let me get this straight. He told you not to engage with me anymore. At all?"

"Truro, I...I felt compelled not to engage with you. Otherwise, I'd continue to evoke what happened between us."

"And you don't think I do, regardless?" He moved back to his previous position, leaning up against the broken beam. Huffing, he looked down at the village. "I meant what I said that night. You make me feel alive. Since Fheo's mother died, I haven't felt that way with anyone, until you. I thought we...ah, I don't know. What does Rooke hold over you anyway?"

Squeezing my eyes together, I groaned. I wasn't sure anymore. But when I considered it, it always reverted to the beginning. "Rooke's helped me through rough times. He's not just my commander, he's been my friend for far longer. When my brother was eighteen, he suddenly collapsed and died whilst playing hockey. For years, Rooke had been Jacob's best friend. From the day Jacob died, Rooke became mine. As we grew older, he became my support, my security. I have no other family. He *is* my family." *He's my everything.*

I continued to stare into my thoughts as they churned up old memories, some happy, others sad.

"What happened to your parents?" Truro's voice was tentatively soft, his question startling me.

The reluctance to recall those memories was overbearing, but I reminded myself he'd just confided in me about Fheo. I felt I owed him something in return.

"My dad...he died when I was seven. He was a scientific engineer for Solarfleet. At the time, he was based on Gyprono. It's a moon that circles a neighbouring planet in the Alluran system. It's rich in iron and aluminium. He was helping to open a new mine, when one of the tunnels collapsed, trapping him inside. Days later they pulled eleven of them out. Every one of them had suffocated." I froze, recalling the day I'd been told. "I'd always been a daddy's girl. I remember the news confusing me. Being so young, I guess I was able to adjust, move on.

"I don't think my mum ever recovered from my dad's death, but somehow, she held herself together. But following the unexpected death of my brother, then in quick succession, my grandma died, and my mum seemed to cave in on herself. She became a shell of the woman I once knew. When I was eighteen, she...she had tried to stop me from leaving home to go to piloting school. She'd wanted me to stay with her...but I left...I selfishly went, aiming to come home every couple of weeks to see her. I thought she was doing okay, until...until...the day after my twentieth birthday. I went home and...and found her...I found her hanging from the wooden gazebo in the garden." My heart tremored at the horrific memory; one I had kept locked away for so long. Tears prickled at my eyes. "I don't think I'll ever forget the image of finding her like that. Cold and blue, lifeless. The...the coroner said she'd been there a couple of days. I'd been out celebrating my birthday the day before, and she'd been hanging there. Alone. She didn't even leave a letter to tell me why." My voice cracked and several tears trailed down my cheeks. "It's been nearly six years and I still, I still don't understand…why she did it.

"Rooke's helped me through the grief. Assisted with all the legalities I couldn't get my head around. I was suddenly plummeted into the big world with no family support. Rooke remained by my side, offering me so much more than he had to. I…I don't think I would've survived without him. I owe him so much." Nux, I missed him—missed what we once had. I couldn't deny it any longer, our relationship was slipping through my fingers.

"I didn't mean to make you cry."

Defogging my eyes, I focused my gaze on Truro—my handsome Nux warrior. I hadn't noticed him shift closer. It still astounded me how silently he could move. Now sitting inches in front of me, I felt the heat from his body, the pull to fall into his embrace.

With flustered hands I wiped the wetness away from my cheeks. "I always cry when I talk about mum. It doesn't get any easier." I shook my head, allowing more tears to flow. "My brother and dad's deaths were tragic, but…but my mums could've been prevented. I shouldn't have left her. I should've declined my college placement and stayed with her. I didn't realise the extent of her depression."

"Eden, even if you stayed, her actions may have been prolonged but not avoided. And where would that've left you? Motherless with no prospects." Truro cocked his head and briefly pouted his lips. "I guess it may have prevented you from ending up on this god forsaken world."

I tried to smile. "But then I would never have met you."

His eyes shifted to mine, holding me paralysed with a power I could not break from. My words seemed to have startled him. He leant forward, placing his fingers lightly under my chin. "It may not be an appropriate time," he mumbled wistfully, "but I really want to kiss you."

Drowning in those eyes, I felt my heartbeats quicken, and the goosebumps rousing my skin reignited my inner desire for this beautiful man.

"I really want you to kiss me," I said in response. And in the next moment, his soft lips were upon mine.

Chapter Twenty-Five

Heading southeast, we'd left the village two hours ago. Finally adjusting to a slower pace, my horse ambled along near the back of the scouting party. To be honest, I had no idea if we'd found anything intriguing. My mind was fully consumed with thoughts of last night; thoughts of Truro.

I'd lost myself in that soft kiss, melted into his embrace. After being forced to venture away from the edge of the hut by the sound of creaking and cracking floorboards under our combined weight, Truro had guided me over to the centre, where the floor was more stable. With my back pressed up against the tree trunk, he'd retaken my mouth and devoured me.

My skin tingled at the thought of his touch, the caress of his lips, the feel of him between my legs. We had made love up against that tree. The act had been passionate, raw, full of desire and eagerness. But there had been something else lingering between us, something stronger, combining us. I didn't believe in soul mates, but I was beginning to agree with what he'd said about there being something special between us. We knew what each other wanted without speaking a single word. We cared for each other regardless of rank or restricted rules. He was always capable of easing my pain, as I did his.

"You're quiet today."

I flinched, flicking my eyes to Rooke sitting atop his horse beside me. I hadn't noticed he'd dropped back from the front of the group.

Trying to rid my body of the aroused thoughts Truro had sparked, I adjusted my seat. "I'm tired. I didn't sleep well." It wasn't a lie.

"I don't suppose drinking the whole bottle of Akquarian wine helped." Rooke smirked, then noticed my surprise. "I saw the bottle lying on the floor under your hammock." Concern flooded my mind. When had he checked on me? "I'm not allowing you to take any of that wine back to Allura, you know. You're going to have to go cold turkey."

"I'm not addicted to it."

"No?" He raised his eyebrows, amusement dancing across his face.

"No." Attempting a smile, I registered how cheerful he seemed this morning. My mind jumped back to the party. "You seemed to be enjoying yourself last night."

"I did. No Valina. Good company. Where did you get to?"

Shit. "I was around. Ayelle seems a nice girl."

Rooke fell silent, gazing up ahead. "She is. She hooked up with Guz last night."

Struck with a wave of confusion, I watched Rooke's expression. It didn't change. "Are you okay with that?"

"Why wouldn't I be?"

"You...you seem to get on well."

"Not in that way. I told you before," he met my gaze, "I prefer Alluran women."

I swallowed back the guilt. The whole night I had believed he was charming Ayelle. Had he been looking for me when I was with Truro? I'd avoided him this morning, running to Zamya's medical room before breakfast, asking her for some contraceptive tonic. I'd gone against him again, overstepped the boundaries he'd built to protect us. What type of person did that make me?

A voice called Rooke from up ahead. The group had stopped moving. I followed Rooke to the front and found Oz and Guz standing over a mutilated animal, one I could not recognise.

"Igknamai have definitely been here," Guz said. "As well as this body, we've passed evidence of others, and there are several trails of blood in the soil, going back for miles."

Even though the temperature was dropping day by day, it hadn't rained for a couple of weeks. The blood trails could've been injuries from the recently snatched girls. My stomach twisted with the question of what had happened to Dawna, what *was* happening to her.

"We keep heading southeast," Rooke commanded. "Follow the blood trails as much as possible. See where they lead."

With a swift nod, Oz and Guz were back on their horses, leading the way with Rooke close behind. Although Io kept pace with them, my mind kept drifting, spiralling through images of Dawna, Cora, then my mum, pausing soundly on Truro and the events of last night…

"Stay with me tonight," Truro whispered against my lips.

"You know I can't."

"No, I don't, actually."

"We've spoken about this already." Pulling away from him, I slipped out of the tiny gap I was wedged in between Truro and the tree, forcing his hands to drop from my waist.

"I don't understand," he said. "If Rooke cares for you, if he's your friend, shouldn't he want to see you happy…I see the sadness in your eyes."

I had no explanation. I couldn't fathom that aspect of Rooke's rules out either.

A heaviness hung in the air between us as I watched Truro discretely adjust his trousers, then zip up his hooded top. He wasn't happy. I wanted to reach for him, to tell him I wanted to stay, but what could I do? I felt torn.

Truro's intense gaze landed on me, sending sparks of electricity down my spine. I melted at the way he looked at me, especially with that stern, doting expression.

"Every day that passes is another day closer to the one that takes you away. These fleeting moments, they're…they're not enough. I want to be with you, Eden. I want you. I want all of you. Can't you see…this world is cruel. It's barely tolerable. But in finding someone who brightens the darkest of my days, it's the difference between existing and living. You make me want to live."

All I could do was stare at him, trying to prevent the tears of frustration from forming.

Unsure of how to respond, I stepped closer. Rising on tip toes, I placed my lips upon his. I wanted to give him all of me…but how could I?

Stroking the scruff of his cheek, the only words I could say were, "Goodnight, Truro."

…Why couldn't I have met him at college, or at a random bar in Torlan City? Why did he have to be of a different world, literally? Was I really asking too much in wanting to love him?

I squeezed my eyes together, recalling his strong arms around me, the smell of his skin. The regret of walking away from him last night stung like a knife in my back, but what was I supposed to do when Rooke was being attentively watchful? If I hadn't returned home last night, Rooke would've sought me out, and then what?

"Lieutenant commander!"

With a jolt, I discovered several pairs of eyes on me, including Rooke's, whose scowl threw daggers. "Where are you today?" he barked, the cheerful look I noted earlier completely gone.

"I, um…" Swallowing back the awkwardness, I shook my head. "I'm sorry, I didn't hear what you said."

Eyeing me sceptically, Rooke pointed to a break in the trees where a river flowed through a lush, green field. "All the scouts confirm they've never seen this river before. Guz said no villager has ever mentioned it."

I glanced at Guz, then at the bright, rippling water behind him. "How is that possible?"

"We don't know, but I have an inkling we're moving in the right direction." Rooke jumped down from his horse and headed towards the water's edge.

After sliding down from Io, I caught up with him. "Doesn't it worry you that no one has seen this river before? How far from the village are we?"

Continuing to walk across the field, Rooke frowned at me. "You really haven't been paying attention, have you?"

"I told you, I'm tired."

"Where were you last night?"

To my utter horror, Rooke stopped and glared at me. Did he know? I don't think I was able to hide my panic as I stuttered a response, "I was…I was at…the bar for a while. Then…I went for a walk. I needed to clear my head."

"Didn't work very well, did it?" Thankfully, he carried on walking.

Nux, I was such a bad liar.

Stopping at the edge of the fast-flowing river, I glanced back at the others. To my relief all eight were following behind, horses in tow.

"These are Igknamai tracks," Rooke said, bending down, examining the grass and mud. "They stop here. They must cross the river."

"Igknamai don't like water. This river looks deep enough to drown in. I can't imagine them swimming across. The current would take them."

Standing, Rooke scoured the extent of the river stretching either side of us. "They must cross somewhere."

There was nothing but a few algae covered rocks jutting out of the middle, plus the odd fallen branch, which looked far too fragile to climb across.

"They may not, Rooke."

"They do. Where else would they go?"

He was rushing, being irrational, jumping to conclusions. I wanted him to take a breath and calm down. It was obvious the new discovery had pumped him full of adrenaline, and his impatient excitement worried me.

Guz's voice called from up the riverbank. "There are several boot marks here."

Rooke's interest piqued. Walking over to him, he asked. "Do you think they're Hybrid?"

Guz pondered, examining the floor with the tip of his dagger. "They're odd-looking tread marks…and inconsistent. Definitely not ours."

"Could they be Akquarian?" I asked.

Guz shrugged. "Akquarian footprints tend to be longer and slimmer."

Adrenalin, fuelled by anxiety, raced down my legs—Rooke being the main reason. His eyes were alert and calculative. I was petrified by what he may do.

He pointed into the water near the footprints. There was an inconstant line of rocks forming possible steppingstones. "They cross there."

Before I could react, he was jumping down the shallow bank to access the first steppingstone.

"Rooke, stop!" I knew he wouldn't listen, so I followed him in his ridiculous task to cross the river, trying not to slip on the slimy rock surfaces. "Rooke, you need to think this through." I groaned, nearly losing my footing.

The river wasn't overly wide, but the current was fast. Taking my time, I caught up with him on the opposite bank. "Rooke!" I grabbed the back of his leather jacket, pulling him to a stop. With a questionable frown, he looked back at me and said, "We're onto something."

"I'm not disputing that, but we need to stay vigilant, take things slowly."

"I'm not hanging back when we're so close to finding our ship."

"We could be miles off…and I thought you weren't looking for the ship anymore."

"Until Solarfleet get here, I will never stop looking for our ship." The old strain of anger flared in his eyes, and I felt my body shudder. He pulled away from me, marching towards the new section of forest. I watched him step over the threshold of trees, and to my utter horror, he physically disappeared.

I blinked several times, wondering if stress had caused trauma to my vision. But when I heard Oz and Guz mutter a string of curses from across the river, I knew what I was seeing, or not seeing, was real.

"Rooke." I began to panic. "ROOKE!"

I raced towards the spot he vanished from. Where the hell had he gone? "Rooke?" I paused, reaching a nervous hand forward. My eyes widened with a petrified intrigue when my fingers began to disappear from view, then my hand. I felt no pain, no tingling, only a visual spark of electrical light warped the area of skin around my wrist.

Something grabbed my missing hand and I screamed. Wrenching my arm back, Rooke reappeared holding it. I was too stunned to understand what was happening. "What the hell just…"

Rooke peered up at the invisible barrier before us. "Hologram," he replied in wonderment, brushing his fingers across the invisible boundary, creating ripples of sparkling light. "It's no wonder this river has never been seen before. I suspect it's been hidden for some time, behind this."

"Then…then why has it suddenly moved?"

Rooke ignored my question, turning to the stunned scouts standing rigid and confused on the other side of the river. "I need you all over here, now. Leave the horses."

"Wait. Wait!" I glanced at Rooke, then gestured to the scouts. "No! Ignore that command!"

Rooke's sharp eyes narrowed. "Excuse me?"

"I will not allow you to do this."

"This is my command. And I'm taking my platoon through the hologram."

"Rooke, you can't be serious! It could be suicide. You don't know what's on the other side of that screen. You could be triggering an alarm every time you penetrate it. There could be an army of Igknamai or Hybrids watching, waiting to attack. We don't know why the hologram's been put there."

"It's a chance I'm willing to take." He turned back to the river, coercing the scouts across. A couple began to navigate the steppingstones, while others hesitated; Oz being one of them. I caught his eye, silently pleading for his allegiance. With a subtle shake of his head, he told me his decision. Inwardly I groaned.

"Rooke." I caught his arm. "Please think rationally…"

"I'm not turning back now."

"Anything could be hidden back there. Listen…Kobe and I could rig up some kind of drone to fly through. We can map out the terrain and pinpoint any threats before we enter."

"And how long will that take?"

"A few days, a week. Two at most."

He shook his head, almost laughing. "I don't have two weeks."

"What's the rush?"

"I need to get my ship back!" He glared at me. "So, I can take *you* home."

"Be serious, Rooke! That's not going to happen until Solarfleet get here. Even if we find the ship, I doubt it'll be anywhere close to salvageable."

"Why are you disregarding this?"

"I'm not…"

"Just because you have the eyes of a fucking Nux leader, does not give you the divine right to undermine my leadership."

"Don't even joke, Rooke. You know how much I resent the dark fairytale associated with my eyes. And I'm not undermining you.

I'm trying to make you see sense!" I glanced at the Redwood warrior's crossing the treacherous rocks. A couple of the younger ones looked scared. "These soldiers aren't yours to command."

"I think you'll find they are," he snarled, turning his back on me.

"Well, I am challenging your decision! I do not agree to risking their lives for your benefit."

Rooke's head snapped in my direction. His eyebrows furrowed and the muscles in his jaw grew taut. Stepping closer, his face was so close, I could feel the anger radiating off him. In a quiet, intimidating voice, he said, "Don't you think I'll be putting my neck on the line for these people in the next month or so? That's what you want, isn't it? For me to die fighting for *them*."

I felt myself tremble at his words, the rage in his eyes freezing the breath inside my lungs. I didn't know this man anymore. Never had I seen him so crazed in anger, so impetuously driven.

"I never asked that of you," I whispered back. "I asked you to show some compassion. To…to agree to persuade Solarfleet to help them."

He chuckled, sarcastically. "You're a contradiction, Eden. Really, you are." Stepping away, he avoided my eyes entirely. I couldn't understand him. What had changed? We always used to reason with one another civilly.

"The scouts have never seen this river before," I continued, aware his temper was worsening, but I couldn't let this rest. "The land through there is unchartered…"

"Isn't that what we do for Solarfleet? Chart land?" He looked dumbfounded.

"That's different. You know it is. There isn't biological life on asteroids and moons, trying to kill us."

Rolling his eyes, Rooke growled, "You're being dramatic."

"These aren't your men, Rooke!"

"No, they're Truro's!" His voice hit a new peak in intensity and volume. I felt everyone's attention turn to us. "Is this what this is all about? Truro? Has he asked you to do this? Knock me down a peg or two?"

"What? No!"

His chuckle whipped at my conscience before a cold zap charged the air between us. "Why are you undermining me?"

"For Nux sake, Rooke, I'm not!"

"You don't think I'm fit to lead you anymore."

"Stop putting words in my mouth!"

"Do you know, I wouldn't be trapped on this shithole planet if it wasn't for you. I would be piloting luxury space liners to Harma Moon Hotel if I hadn't felt compelled to watch over you. I've spent the past ten years protecting you. Ten years holding true to a dying man's wish. Yes, that's right. Jacob *begged* me to look after you. They were his last words to me before he closed his eyes and welcomed death. I loved your brother, and for him I've held true to those words. And for what? For you to turn your back on me when I need you the most."

"I haven't!" My own exasperation was rising to a level of utter despair. Why was he telling me this now? Was it the truth, or was it a pointed quip to injure me in the hope I would back down?

"You've been acting differently," he growled.

"You complained that I didn't pull you up on your reckless ideas when we first arrived. That's what I'm doing now!"

"I'm not talking about that. I'm talking about your behaviour. At the Redwood village. You sneak about. It's as if you want to become one of them. Is that what you're doing? Impressing Truro?"

"This has *nothing* to do with Truro!"

"You're an idiot for thinking I don't know what you two get up to."

"Rooke…"

"You've changed! Truro' s changed you, reformed you into his shining huntress."

"That's not true!"

"Does he tell you what to say and do while you're sucking his cock?"

"Rooke, stop!"

He chuckled. "You're not even denying it. You're not the Eden I used to know. You resent me."

"No…no, you're wrong."

"Am I? Because you sure as hell have a funny way of showing it! Maybe I have wasted all my time and effort on you."

"Rooke, just stop!"

"Does it hurt?" His snarl was full of venom. "Does it? To learn the truth about why I've stuck around. Funny how truths and secrets can hurt like fucking hell!"

I tried not to whimper. "You say I've changed, but have you taken a moment to look at yourself? I don't know you anymore!"

"And who's damn fault is that?!" His glare was as violent as his tone, aimed to burn and impair and scold. All I could think about was how my life was a lie. I always assumed it had been Rooke's choice to take over from Jacob's role as big brother. Never in my darkest dreams had I thought Jacob had shackled Rooke to the responsibility. It had been a dying wish, an emotionally blackmailed burden...Nux, I couldn't breathe.

"Don't start with the tears, Eden, we have a job to do. And my orders still stand." Rooke marched away towards Guz and two scouts standing in front of the hologram. All the fight inside of me had seeped out of the fractured hole in my heart. It lay at my feet, defeated.

Forcing myself through a huddle of scouts hovering at the water's edge, I began to navigate the steppingstones to the other side. I wasn't going to witness Rooke getting himself and the others killed. I'd tried to make him see sense, but his arrogance was intangible.

Oz offered me his hand when I reached the opposite side. Taking it, he pulled me up the bank. I couldn't look at him, I felt ashamed, humiliated.

Touching my shoulder, Oz said softly, "Don't leave him now."

"Did you hear what he just said?"

"Yes, but...he's under a lot of pressure..."

"No, Oz." Finally meeting his gaze, I noticed the concern grounded within his blue eyes. "I can't do this anymore. I've tried...I've tried to be what he needs, but it doesn't help. I can't fix him." The truth hit me like a bolt of lightning striking the centre of my heart. I quickly wiped away a tear trickling down my cheek. "I can't work with him anymore. I quit." I went to walk to Io, but Oz caught my hand.

"Where are you going?"

"Back to the village."

"You can't go alone. The guidelines..."

"I know what the sodding guidelines are."

"I'll come with you."

Rooke's voice carried over to us. "Oz, get your giant arse over here. If Eden is too much of a coward to join us, she can stay with the horses."

I watched Oz's mind tick over. He called back, "On my way, boss." Grabbing my arm again, he whispered, "Make sure you get back to the village in one piece and I'll do the same for him."

It was a hopeful promise, but I nodded my understanding.

Before I rode away, I looked across the river and witnessed the platoon of scouts disappearing into thin air.

Chapter Twenty-Six

Io must've sensed my anxiety. She took flight, effortlessly navigating the forest floor. We'd been travelling at a speed between a gallop and a canter for nearly an hour now. Not wanting to exhaust her, I slowed her to a walk near a small lake and stopped her at the edge.

As she drank, my eyes scoured the area. I felt vulnerable, foolishly so. The more distance I placed between Rooke and I, the worse it became. I shouldn't have left the platoon.

Rubbing my eyes with my sweaty palms, I tried to defog my mind. Rooke's words echoed about, his look of disdain imprinted into the back of my eyelids. Nux, he hated me.

Shaking my head, I jumped down from Io. I bent down next to her, scooping up a palmful of clear water and throwing it over my overheated face. Sitting back on my heels, I thought about Rook's promise to my brother. Had it always been the case that he'd shown up for me purely because of his conscience? Was I a mere pain in his arse; a burden; a chore he couldn't rid himself of? I'd always assumed he held me in high regard. In a way, I thought he loved me. Nux, I was such an idiot.

The snap of a twig caught my attention. Io stomped her hooves beside me, snorting her displeasure. With fierce eyes, I flicked them over every surface, every dark crevice and shadow, attentively listening.

Slowly rising to my feet, I reached for Io's reins, readying myself to mount her. She stomped and scuffed again, whining and snorting. Movement caught my eye. I snapped my head towards the treeline, only to feel a jolt of the reins ripping free from my grasp. I silently yelped in despair as I saw Io's rear end speeding away.

I didn't move. The sensation of being watched simultaneously ignited and paralysed my body. Roving my gaze to the trees behind, I slowly spun, only to freeze once more. This time, at the sight of a pale, dark-haired man on the far side of the lake. No…it wasn't a man; it was a Hybrid. He was watching me with a dark, offensive stare as he knelt at the water's edge. Dressed in dark leather armour— fish scaled armour—the realisation slammed into me. It wasn't just a Hybrid, it was the Akquarian's Hybrid, Llexzus.

Backing away, panic surged through my veins. If he was here, that could mean….

Snapping my eyes vigorously at the trees, I felt sick. Adrenaline finally sparked in my legs and I bolted in the same direction Io left, praying I'd find her not far off.

Without looking back, I ran. I ran as hard and as fast as my legs would take me. If there was one thing I wasn't going to allow to happen today, it was to be taken by the Akquarians.

My sprint lasted a mere few minutes. After frantically jogging for several more, I collapsed behind a tree, catching my breath. Io was nowhere to be seen.

Great! I was horseless, lost in the depths of a humongous forest, possibly being stalked by Akquarians. I should've stayed with Rooke. Being alone out here could prove more suicidal than taking a platoon of heavily armed warriors through a hologram. What the hell was I thinking?

I needed to get home. It was just after one in the afternoon. I could find my way home before dusk. How long it would take, I didn't know. But one thing was for certain; I needed eyes in the back of my head.

I'd been walking for hours. My back hurt from the tensed muscles in my shoulders and neck. Every sound had me on high alert, the slightest movement caused me to panic. I'd heard voices in the distance several miles back, but without knowing for certain if they were Redwoods, Akquarians, or even Hybrids, I didn't pursue them.

Maintaining a good speed, I headed northwest. Thankfully, the day was cool with the canopy cooling the forest floor even further, and the flask of water at my hip was still half full.

Trudging over the monotonous terrain, it wasn't hard to slip back into my thoughts. Thoughts of Rooke from over the years and his affection I thought he'd given freely.

As I recalled the last round of words he spat at me, I felt the agony tightening around my fragile heart. I had no doubt he meant every word. I knew I'd overstepped his line of command with my intimacy with Truro, but I was starting to wonder if Rooke had used that as an excuse to lash out at me. It was as if he'd been holding back his resentment for years. And the pressures of being stranded in a strange, terrifying world had tipped him emotionally overboard. I knew he was stressed. It wasn't my intention to conflict his leadership decisions. Oz had clearly learnt to keep his mouth shut on such matters. Unfortunately, I dived headfirst, meeting the full brunt of Rooke's wrath, well aware he'd take it personally. Maybe I deserved it. Maybe I had overstepped the mark. Perhaps I had taken too much from him over the years. But had I not given as much in return?

I'd seen our relationship fragmenting for months. Nevertheless, the truth within his raged outburst hurt like hell, worsening as the hours passed.

My attention pulled away from my thoughts, spotting a huddle of fur up ahead. Two small deer laid motionless, blood darkening the red soil around them. My body froze, my mind went into overdrive. Were there Igknamai nearby? I frantically searched the area for signs. The only sound was the leaves rustling from above and the odd squark of a bird in the distance.

This section of the forest was unusually open. Tall trees grew lower on the left than the right, and I realised I could see the sea from where I stood, glistening on the horizon. I must've walked too far west. Shit, I was more lost than I thought, and the dead deer up ahead sent cold shivers down my spine. I was a sitting duck. How had I lost my concentration so easily? Rooke was playing havoc with my emotions, with my sound instincts. I'd never felt so disorientated in my whole, entire life.

Damn it! And here I was again, thinking about him instead of concentrating on the danger surrounding me.

I scurried up the steep incline to my right, attempting to gain a vantage point. Squatting low, I listened and waited, sweeping my eyes in every direction. Everything seemed hauntingly quiet.

Clutching my dagger, I tried to calm my breathing. Remaining low, I scampered away into a denser part of the forest. Gripping the bow string across my body, my heart hammered fast inside my chest. With paranoia tightening its grasp, I glimpsed over my shoulder, scouring the forest floor, checking for movement. My breath hitched at the faintest rustle, forcing me to pull an arrow free from the quiver. I stopped walking, making sure it was nothing but the breeze, but…

I began to run. I couldn't waste time doubting myself.

My legs accelerated down the hill, jumping over broken branches and tree roots. The trees seemed to be getting larger, and I prayed I was heading in the right direction. But a wave of despair took over. I had no idea where I was! I was completely lost!

Large boulders jutted out of the ground, unnerving me even more. I'd never seen them before, and anything could be looming behind, waiting. But I continued to run. I was running for my life; a life I wasn't sure how to live without Rooke. He'd been my rock, my salvation.

My eyes began to fog with tears, and to my utter horror a swift, dark shadow moved in my peripheral. Reaching for my dagger I staggered just before I came face on with a horse's chest.

As the black horse reared, my feet stumbled and I tripped, landing on my knees, only inches from where the horse's hooves came crashing down into the dirt. Its rider immediately jumped down. Their black booted feet came into view, and as I peered up at their face, a sob of sheer relief ripped through me.

"Eden?" Truro loomed over me. "Are you alright?"

I stood, throwing my arms around his shoulders, pushing my eyes into the crook of his neck. I welcomed the smell and taste of his sweat. I don't think I would've cared if he was covered in horse dung; the relief he was here overpowered everything.

"Hey." He cupped the back of my head, wrapping his other arm affectionally around my back. "What are you doing out here on your own?"

"I got lost," I mumbled against his neck.

"Lost?" I sensed he suppressed a disapproving groan before pulling away. "Why are you alone?"

Avoiding his eyes, I shook my head. "Please, don't ask. Not

now."

"Okay…come on, I'll take you home."

Truro helped me up onto Titan, mounting himself behind me. He directed the stallion further down the hill, away from the boulders.

Titan moved swiftly. He cleared the palisade a few miles northeast, immediately falling into a comfortable walk. With reassurance I was now safe, I allowed my muscles to relax, but my mind went into overdrive. I felt so foolish. What would've happened if Truro hadn't found me?

We remained silent as we bypassed the garrison platform, heading for the small stream and the steep rock path on the east side of the village.

Rounding the top of the rockface, the luscious green grazing field appeared. A cluster of horses grazed to one side. Io was among them. *The little cow!*

Titan stopped and Truro jumped down, offering me a hand. I avoided his heated gaze as he lowered me to the ground. When he didn't release his hold on my hips, I peered up at him, meeting those vibrant eyes. Concern and intrigue swam in them, along with a hint of scepticism.

"What happened?" he asked.

I didn't want to cause any drama. I wanted to hide away, to forget it all.

"Eden!" The demand in his voice heightened and I found myself trapped in his authoritative gaze. "You left with Rooke's team this morning. Tell me what happened. If you don't, I will find out for myself!"

The thought of Truro confronting Rooke hit a new level of despair. It seemed Rooke despised Truro more so than his obligation to me. Who knew what he'd say or do.

"I left my post," I blurted in panic.

"Why?" He was pinning me against Titan's side. His firm hold indicated he wasn't going to let me walk away, and with Titan as a solid force against my back, I couldn't move.

Holding my nerve, I told Truro about the hologram. "Rooke didn't take lightly to my objections. We argued and I…I rode away, alone. Halfway home, Io bolted." I didn't tell him about Rooke's personal assault. As well as not wanting to talk about it, I feared it would cause further issue.

With drawn eyebrows, Truro remained silent. It was clear he was still sceptical.

"My actions were reckless," I offered, "and my pride prevented me from following him. I was angry. I still am angry. Nux, I don't even know if they're okay. What if something has happened to them."

"I'll make some enquiries. I'll find out." His tone had softened, but the look in his eyes hadn't. "Regardless of what happened, you should never be in the forest alone."

Finally releasing his hold, Truro began to unbuckle Titan's bridle. His movements were abrupt, proving he was perturbed. Leaving him to work, I walked over to Io.

"Call yourself my loyal steed," I mumbled to her. "You're a rotten scaredy-cat." She snorted and I gave her a rub behind the ears. "I'm glad you got home in one piece. I'm sorry for putting you in that position."

As if in response, she whined, shaking her mane. Giving her one last neck rub, I headed for the cliff edge. The golden hour sun was hitting the ranging canopies, shining a golden hue for miles around. It was beautiful, reminding me of Allura, of the Torlan forests that surrounded my cottage. I missed home. I missed the simplicity of my life there. But Rooke was a part of that life.

Sensing Truro's presence behind me, I turned and looked up at the god-like warrior. The hilt of his two swords glistened behind his shoulders in the magical light. His hair shone a reddish brown, and those intense blue eyes were dazzling.

He lowered his face to mine and whispered, "That sadness has returned to your eyes. Tell me what I can do to help?"

I shook my head. "Is there…is there anywhere else I can stay? I need some space from Rooke."

"You can stay with me." The unspoken questions reappeared on his face.

I was unsure if it was wise to accept his offer, but I needed a break from Rooke's needs, his spying, his aggression. He wasn't the man I loved anymore. And I had, I'd loved him with every ounce of my being. But it wasn't enough. It had never been enough.

***

Truro settled me in at his treehouse, leaving swiftly to speak to the garrison about Rooke and his platoon's return. The treehouse had a shower room, hidden away through a door to the left of the main room. The water pressure was far better than the showers in the Pasa. The temperature was cool, but it snapped me out of my stupor; woke me up.

Stepping out of the shower, I heard voices. I quickly dried myself and pulled on one of Truro's warm jumpers. Walking back into the main room, I stopped when I heard Guz's voice. I couldn't see him, nor Truro. They were outside on the decking near the steps. It was getting dark.

"The Hybrid lair must be somewhere in that location. Isn't that the area a few people have gone missing from?"

"Yes, if I'm correct in where you're suggesting. Did you see anything?"

"No. We didn't get far. The landmines convinced Rooke to turn back."

"How many were injured?"

"Three. I wouldn't be surprised if Yohan loses his leg."

My eyes widened, placing a hand over my mouth to stifle the gasp.

Truro cursed. "Everyone made it back, though?"

"Yes…well, no."

"No?"

"Eden tried to persuade Rooke to reconsider passing through the hologram. Her reasoning was sound and, to be honest, I agreed with her. Rooke didn't react well to her debate. In fact, he shot her down in the most humiliating fashion."

"I'm sure she can stand her ground against him."

"She tried, but failed. Rooke said some nasty stuff…personal stuff that I could see was affecting her emotionally. He was relentless and so, so spiteful. He kept on and on at her until she lost any momentum to argue back. After which she couldn't look anyone in the eye. She retreated across the river. Oz tried to stop her from leaving. I think he wanted to return with her, but Rooke was having none of it. She must have headed home. But the thing is…I checked before I came here. Her horse returned riderless. No one's seen Eden."

There was a short silence, followed by a flurry of hushed words. Whatever was said prompted Guz to leave. I was still frozen on the spot when Truro entered the treehouse. Noticing my presence, he paused.

"Will Yohan be okay?" I asked feeling shaken.

"We won't know until tomorrow. He's inside the Pasa being treated." Truro rubbed the back of his neck, his eyebrows drawn. He looked up at me and said, "I knew you hadn't told me the whole truth. You never would've left them." He stared at me expecting a response. The only thing that occurred was the swell of tears forming in my eyes.

Tentatively, he stepped forward. "Are you alright?"

I shook my head, burying my face into my palms. In the next moment, I was encased by Truro's strong arms, pulling me against his chest. He kissed the top of my head. The action made me cry harder. Two months ago, I'd chosen Rooke over Truro. I didn't deserve Truro's affection; I didn't deserve him.

"What did he say to you?"

I shook my head again. I didn't want to relive Rooke's words. They'd already gouged out a crater in my heart.

"After what you told me last night," Truro said against my hair, "I'm sure he didn't mean anything by it."

Pulling my head back, I mumbled through the tears, "He hates me. He's never wanted to care for me. I was an errand that became an ongoing inconvenience. He only stayed around to serve his conscience. He never wanted to be my friend. He hates me. He hates everything about me." I was sobbing. I couldn't stop.

Truro walked me over to his armchair and I slumped into it. Kneeling in front of me, he pulled my hands away from my sodden face, but I couldn't find the strength to look up.

"Without him," my breath stuttered a few times, "I have nothing left back home. Every part of my Alluran life includes him. I've become so reliant on him. Not in a million years had I imagined…"

"Eden." Truro cupped the side of my face, gently coercing me to look at him. "I'm sure you can work things out."

"Not this time. He meant every word."

"In that case, if needs be, you can walk away. You are strong. You will find a new life without him."

An ache in the pit of my stomach intensified. How could this be happening? I assumed Rooke would be in my life forever.

"There is another option." Truro's hand scaled down my arm, squeezing my fingers when he reached them. "And I'm not saying this for my own gain. You...you could stay here. On Earth." My eyes suddenly found his. He was being serious. "Before you say anything, hear me out. If you truly have nothing left to return to on Allura, stay with us. I know this world is hell compared to yours, but hopefully that will change soon. You cannot deny how well you fit in here. People love you, and I'm not talking about the sodding prophecy. I'm talking about everyone who's gotten to know you. Pepa loves you. Saff adores you. Jader and Wrenn love you...I love you. If you stay, you'd make family here. I have no doubt about that."

My heart swelled with a humbled warmth, and a new type of tear threatened to surface. These people were beyond amazing. They lived their lives each day filled with terror and despair, yet they still found light and happiness. They appreciated one another, helped each other. Allurans were so complacent with their comfortable lives, they moaned about trivial things, conflicted with their neighbours over the most pathetic issues. Perhaps I *would* find peace here.

"Thank you," I whispered. "You have no idea how grateful I am to you for saying that."

He leant forward and kissed my lips. "If I had it my way, you'd never leave. But the choice is yours. You will always be welcome here, whatever your decision."

Nux, this man had the most beautiful soul. I was so grateful I'd met him.

Chapter Twenty–Seven

I woke up to the sound and smell of rain. It took me several seconds to recognise my surroundings, remembering why I was here, and every memory came flooding back like a punch in the stomach.

Forcing myself out of bed, I discovered Truro had already left. Breakfast was waiting for me on the coffee table with a note saying, *Good morning, Beautiful*. I smiled at the gesture.

He'd been a gentleman last night, offering to sleep on the floor. But after a bickering discussion, we came to the agreement to share the bed. He'd cuddled me until I'd fallen asleep. If my heart hadn't felt quite so dead, it would be bursting with love for him right now.

With my mind wandering through endless quarries, I dressed and scurried to the Pasa. First, I checked on Yohan. I wasn't permitted to see him, but Nya informed me the medical team had been able to save his leg, although the functionality of it would take time to return.

I waved to Zamya as I passed by the busy corridor her patients waited in, then headed to the comms room. Kobe was sitting in front of the usual screens, typing commands into the obsolete keyboard. Aware he wasn't one for small talk, I approached with purpose.

"Kobe, I don't suppose you could rig up a drone with a camera or scanner?"

His face turned to me slowly, followed by his dispassionate eyes. An intrigued frown crinkled his forehead as he assessed me. His nose flared with an essence of disgust. "You do realise Rooke is out looking for you?"

Taken aback, I stared at him. "No, I didn't," I replied, in the same blunt tone he'd used on me. I gestured to the computer. "Can it be done? The drone?"

"Rooke's already requested it."

Has he? "Good."

Continuing to eye me questionably, he offered me the radio. "You'd better tell Rooke you're here."

Flicking my eyes briefly to his outstretched hand, I ignored the prompt and walked back through the open door. I heard the hiss of the radio, followed by Kobe's nonchalant voice, "Rooke. You there?"

With my back against the corridor wall, I discretely waited. A few seconds later, Rooke's voice crackled through the speaker, making my heart judder with nerves. "What is it?"

"Eden's here," Kobe replied. "She's in the village."

"Are you certain?"

"Yes. I've just spoken to her."

The radio fell silent, and I had no doubt Rooke was cursing my name to whoever he was with. I supposed it wouldn't affect the way he currently felt about me. The fact he was in the forest searching for me suggested he might feel an ounce of remorse towards his actions. But I couldn't understand why Truro hadn't informed anyone of my return. I pushed off the wall and headed to the east cliff.

Truro was observing the trainee archers from the back of the group. Arms crossed over his chest, he stood in his usual stoic, commanding manner. I marched up to him, stopping at his side. He peered down at me. "Hey. Did you enjoy your lay-in?"

Frowning, I turned face on to him. "I thought you sent word to Rooke last night, that I was home safe?"

In a strong, yet sheepish manner, his gaze shifted over my head to the archers.

"Did you not tell anyone on purpose?"

Dropping his stance he said, "Rooke's lucky his irresponsible actions yesterday didn't cause as much detriment as they could have. I chose not to inform him because I wanted to scare the crap out of him. He doesn't get to place my men in danger on an impulsive whim. He doesn't get to treat you like a piece of shit and get away with it. You could've died out there on your own because of *his* behaviour. I was hoping he would stew a little longer before he found out." He huffed, replacing his arms across his chest. I'd never seen Truro like this. He was tightly woven. He was angry.

"I told Jader," he said, in a far quieter tone. "We thought Zamya would be worried, so he informed her."

I smiled to myself. Zamya would've been overjoyed to keep that information from Rooke. No wonder she didn't seem concerned, or relieved, when I waved to her earlier.

"I'm going to collect my clothes from the crew house. Are you sure it's okay to stay with you?"

"Of course it is."

Rising on tip toes, I went to place a kiss against Truro's stubbled cheek. But he turned his head, meeting my lips with his own. Pulling me closer, he kissed me slow and masterfully. When I heard the gasps from some of the girls in the archers' line, I wondered if it was for show.

Suddenly full of concern, I broke contact. There was a glint of elation in his eyes. "Truro, if Rooke finds out, he…"

"You're sharing my bed. I'm sure he's going to find out one way or another. Why wait?"

I groaned. "I didn't think you were a conniving arsehole."

He flashed a devilish smile, returning to his commanding stance. "You can punish me later, if you like."

It took four days for one of the crew to approach me regarding the severity of the situation. Well, excluding Zamya. When she'd noticed I'd left the crew house, she'd sought me out and told me I was being a petulant coward and that I should stand up to Rooke. It turned out the main reason for her upset was she didn't want to be left alone with Kobe.

But the difference was, she hadn't been sent by Rooke. Today was different. I finished training and returned to Truro's treehouse, only to find Oz sitting on the steps by the bridge. Slowing as I approached, I was unsure of what to expect.

"I should've known he'd send somebody instead of coming to see me himself."

"He didn't send me," Oz mumbled, twirling his dagger on the wooden step between his legs. "I wanted to see you. You're just as much my friend as he is."

Giving him a sceptical, sideways glance, I sat down next to him, pulling off the leather bracer from my arm.

"I thought you should know," Oz said, "we found the Parvos."

"Behind the hologram?"

"Not exactly. Rooke and I came to the same assumption a couple of days ago. Yesterday we went back to the beach where we landed. It was there. Surrounded by a hologram."

My eyes widened. "Is it…can it be flown?"

He shook his head. "It's a complete wreck. The Igknamai have destroyed every surface. But what we can't figure out, is who obscured it from us. We're certain it wasn't the Akquarians. Highly probable it was the Hybrids, but potentially, it could've been the Redwoods."

"Why the Redwoods?"

"Think about it." Oz gestured to the village below. "By hiding our ship, we were forced to enter the forest, where the Redwoods could extract us from the Akquarians' clutches far easier than via their failing negotiations. The Redwoods have always craved our help."

"But…the hologram in the forest can't be the Redwood's doing. They didn't know about the river."

"I agree. But there's no denying they could have the same tech as the Hybrids."

I nodded, contemplating his words.

"That's why Rooke is so dubious of Truro."

My gaze shot to Oz. There was a glint of worry in the way he looked at me, worried about what the subject may trigger.

"Rooke's concerned Truro is using you."

I instantly shook my head. "He's not using me."

"Eden, come on…"

"I know he's not!" Deep down, I knew.

Oz sighed, straightening his posture. "You should come back to the crew house. This has gone on for long enough."

"That sounds like Kobe talking."

"I'm being serious. Rooke is in a raged state of despair. With you residing here, of all places, it has…has…"

"Has what?"

"Hasn't helped the situation."

Circling my temples with the tips of my fingers, I sighed. "Rooke thinks Truro is using me…he isn't. Rooke says Truro has changed me, well, he hasn't. It was me who decided to become more than the feeble woman Havav made me out to be. Me, not Truro.

Losing Cora ripped my soul apart. I couldn't save her, and I promised myself I would never let that happen again. I need to be strong to survive this world, stronger than I was. I'm by no means fearless, but I've become a warrior, able to fight for those who I love. Unfortunately, it seems I've lost Rooke in the process."

Oz gazed at the floor. His words were surprisingly gentle when he said, "If you love him, don't leave him out in the cold." He stood up, sheathing his dagger in his belt. He looked down at me, the scar across his cheek and neck prominent in the late morning sun. "Believe it or not, Rooke hasn't become the heartless, insensitive man you think he has. On the contrary, he feels everything. He struggles with the cold darkness of this world because he relishes in the warmth of the sun. And you are his sun."

Watching Oz walk away, my heart ached, processing his words. They were a contradiction to Rooke's own. Either way, I was left dwelling on them for hours.

Chapter Twenty—Eight

Over two weeks passed, and I hadn't seen or heard anything from Rooke. His actions spoke louder than words. Perhaps mine did too.

I distracted myself by spending my days training and hunting with Jader and Wrenn, my nights were spent with Truro. That's all I needed. I had convinced myself of that. Most days I tried to push thoughts of Rooke away. Sometimes it worked, other times, not so much. Those days felt as though a dark cloud loomed over me, forcing myself to withdraw into my thoughts and take shelter from the storm. Only to be thrown into the middle of an internal battle of wills and truths. It was exhausting.

A part of me had started to accept our fate. Rooke and I were never meant to be; as friends or lovers. Nevertheless, the thought left me tearful. I had loved him for so many years, it would be a long time before I let go of his memory.

Truro was helping with the adjustment. Just being in his presence grounded me. With him, I felt Rooke slip from the forefront of my mind.

As well as his genuine affection for me, I'd discovered Truro was impossibly witty and flirtatious. His home was impeccably tidy, which made me look like a domestic disaster. He was overly conscientious, always making sure my needs were put before his, and by no means was he modest. The number of times I found him strutting around the treehouse naked. His argument being, "It's my house, you'll just have to get used to it."

I usually huffed in response, trying to subdue my profuse blushing. It usually ended with him either laughing or trying to kiss me. More recently, he'd tackled me onto the bed, and we ended up making love. At first, I felt guilty, but after reminding myself that

Rooke had rejected me, then made me feel worthless, I embraced the fact Truro wanted to be with me.

I lay naked in bed one morning, wrapped in Truro's arms. It had now been three weeks since I last saw Rooke. The sun had started rising later and the air seemed cooler.

As I rested my head on Truro's chest, I listened to his steady heartbeat. Stroking the skin over my hip, he softly said, "Are you going to be alright while I'm gone?"

"I'll be fine." I smiled at how endearing he was, sensing his anxiety about leaving me.

He kissed my hair then returned to staring at the huge growth circles on the ceiling. I'd attempted to count them several times, always losing count around the three hundred mark. There were thousands of circular marks. This tree really was ancient.

"How long will you be gone?" I asked. He was riding to Kala that morning, approximately eighty miles away.

"A few days. I'm only overseeing a supply run. Ever since your team found the field of Mother's Promise, the council have more manpower extracting metal over at Kala."

I glanced up at him, intrigued. "What for?"

"Ready for when your people get here."

His comment gave me pause. "What exactly are the council expecting Solarfleet to do with it all?"

"Help us build bombs, so we can exterminate the bastards." Truro shifted beneath me, pushing himself up onto his elbow to peer down at my face. "Why do you not look convinced?"

"I…" I stumbled for words. A hint of defeat flashed across his eyes, jolting me awake. "There must be millions of Igknamai on this planet."

"Yes, but our locals are the only ones who have Hybrid manipulators. If we eradicate the Hybrids, we can deal with the Igknamai. Don't you see, if we've found acres of that flower, there must be more elsewhere. With Solarfleet's ships, we can access and harvest enough to lower the Igknamai numbers. It will make a significant difference between a struggle for survival and a balance of nature."

I nodded in understanding, but I was concerned Solarfleet may not see it that way. And persuading them wasn't in my hands, it was in Rooke's. "So, you want Solarfleet to help destroy the Hybrids, and assist in building and deploying bombs to deplete the Igknamai numbers?"

"Theoretically, yes."

"Are the Igknamai less violent elsewhere? Have your people ever tried to flee the danger net of the Hybrids?"

"Yes, people have tried. Centuries ago. With the Igknamai everywhere, they didn't get far. The village is, and always has been, the safest and most resourceful site. So no, we don't know how the Igknamai react without the Hybrids. They may be the same." He leant down and kissed my neck. "Now…I don't know…about you," he said in between kisses, "But I don't…want…to be talking about sadistic monsters," he moved over me, kneeing my thighs apart, "when I am due to leave in an hour." Lowering himself between my legs, excitement ripped through my body. Lining himself up, he ploughed into me, groaning his approval against my lips.

"I love the way you feel," he rasped as he picked up his pace.

Gasping as he filled me with each rhythmic thrust, my fingers trailed down the solid muscles of his abs. Nux, he was the most beautiful man I'd ever seen. I murmured through panted breaths, "I love the way you make me feel."

Truro had been away for three days. Wrenn and I offloaded our catch of the day with the butchers in the Pasa, while Jader went to find Elgin to offer his weekly report. Leaving Wrenn talking with some friends, I headed for Zamya's surgery. She'd asked me to meet her there.

The light above her door was green, so I knocked and pressed the button to enter. Stepping inside, the door slid shut behind me. The area was empty, with only the hum of the ventilation filling the clinical room. I was about to call Zamya's name when I heard a small groan, followed by an urgent whisper, "Was that the door?" It seemed to be coming from the closed cupboard to my right.

Another louder groan was dealt, followed by a whispered curse. I had a feeling Jader hadn't gone to see Elgin after all. He was in the cupboard with Zamya.

"I can come back, if you need more time?" I called, grimacing.

A sudden rush of movement ruptured from the cupboard and Zamya stepped out, closing the door behind her. Flattening her hair, she said, "Eden, um…I forgot I'd asked you to drop by."

"Uh-ha." I eyed the cupboard door. "I know who's in there. He can come out."

"He's, um, a little indecent." Zamya walked to the surgery door and gestured for me to follow. "I wanted to show you something, anyway." I noticed the rouge touching her warm brown cheeks. I'd never seen her look so flustered.

Out in the corridor, she led me through a set of double doors along another avenue of laboratories.

"Sorry, Zam. I didn't mean to intrude."

"It's fine. I didn't realise…no, that's a lie. I did realise the time. Jader…just makes everything else…less urgent. I forget myself. I should be the one apologising."

I smiled at her. "You like him."

Stopping beside a lab door, she mused to herself. "Yeah. I like him a lot." The wide smile on her face was more than enough confirmation.

She tapped the lab door, and as it opened, a wall of cold air hit my face. Following her into the dark, chilled room, Zamya said, "I came across this yesterday, and thought you'd be interested."

The lights flickered on, and I found myself staring at a long, thin room. Stretching down one side, stacked floor to ceiling, were rectangular tanks full of pink liquid. On the opposing side was the same, but blue. The vibrant colours were unnatural but familiar. I glanced at Zamya with intrigue. "Is this?"

"Yes." She nodded, eyeing the tanks. "Akquarian love juice. It turns out the Redwoods produce it here. Their mating season starts again in a couple of weeks. They offer a lot of high-end goods in exchange for this."

Walking further into the room, I looked up at the litres upon litres of glowing liquid, recalling what it did to my mind and body at the Sparzak ball. "Did you find out what's in it?"

"Oh, yeah. And you don't want to know."

I looked back at her, inquisitively. She flapped her hand. "The pink stuff contains a hormone enhancer which causes a sensory overdrive. The blue one is full of slow-release Viagra mixed with mild tranquilisers." She chuckled. "It's so inhumane. It's so Akquarian."

"Those poor females. Did you find out what caused the fainting?"

"I did. That's even worse."

"On second thought, maybe I don't want to know."

"To be fair, this initially had nothing to do with the Akquarians. Half a century ago, the Akquarians mentioned the sudden phenomena of the existence of soul mates, which came to light during the Sparzak ball. Several females had fainted after touching and kissing potential suitors. The Redwood scientists were baffled and started looking into what caused the fainting." Zamya pointed to one of the pink tanks. "It turns out a batch of pink juice was accidentally contaminated with a slow-release sedative. Nobody realised until it was too late. Of course, the Akquarians were overjoyed with the new discovery of the soul bond, and because of that, every mating season since, the Redwoods spike a small portion of the female drink."

"So it has nothing to do with kissing anyone?" I thought back to my own fainting episode after Rooke had kissed me. A part of me had always wondered if there was any truth in it. What an idiot I was!

"No. After drinking it, the sedative can take anywhere between five minutes to three hours to take effect. The more you drink, the more it takes hold."

I cursed under my breath. "That's barbaric."

"Apparently the Redwoods withheld the batch one season and there was uproar from the Akquarians. Nux, I'm so glad to be away from those morons."

It was a miracle I hadn't fainted when I was with Dybgo. I had drunk so much of that pink juice in the attempt to calm my nerves. Thank Nux I'd fainted when Rooke was nearby, even if it had been at the most demoralising moment.

"I think Oz was the most disgusted when I mentioned it. He's spoken about Oonla a couple of times over the past few weeks. I get the impression he still wants to kidnap her and take her back to Allura. Rooke seems to be softening to the idea."

I huffed a smile at the thought of Oz's romanticism. But at the mention of Rooke's name, images of him swamped my mind, pulling at my heart strings.

"How is he?" I asked for the first time since our argument. Not once had I mentioned him when Zamya and I met, and Zamya had purposely avoided the subject.

Zamya didn't answer immediately. She stared at me with a forlorn look of empathy, sending a prickle of nerves up and down my spine. "He's not great," she said, glancing up at the glowing tanks beside her. She sighed, choosing her words. "You should've seen his face when he realised you hadn't returned that evening. He was beside himself. I never told you this before, but I think you should know. He slept in your hammock all night, hoping you'd turn up. He went looking for you at first light. When he discovered you were in the village," she shrugged her shoulders, "he went apeshit." She looked at me. "He cares for you. He truly does. Please, *please* talk to him."

I shook my head.

"Eden, please." She stepped closer, her eyes pleading. "He's calmed down. I'm helping him…with meditation and ways of venting his anger in a methodical way."

My voice was barely a whisper, "I can't, Zam."

Zamya sighed. "You two are as bad as each other."

"You didn't hear what he said to me. It's been three weeks and I can still hear those words. I don't think I'll ever forget them. They were poison."

We both fell silent, and I squeezed my eyes together, trying to prize Rooke from my thoughts.

"How are things with Truro?" Zamya asked softly.

"Good, I guess." I sucked in a stabilising breath. "I'm thinking I might stay here, on Earth, when the rest of you return to Allura."

The look of shock froze her features. "Are you serious?"

I nodded. "I have nothing to go back to."

Zamya took a deep breath, replying on the outlet, "Okay, well, that's a surprise." Hands on her hips, she frowned at me. "We'll talk about it nearer the time. But for now, could you think about reaching out to Rooke…"

"Zam!"

"We all know he's the difficult one. He always has been, but…" She reached forward and squeezed my hand. "Nux, I can't believe you're thinking of staying." I watched her mind shift and she cursed. "Come on, I better make sure Jader isn't stuck in that medical cupboard."

I laughed and followed her towards the main corridor. Zamya returned to her surgery while I turned the corner, entering the old airlock. The area was busy, but, somehow, through the moving crowd, my eyes caught the glimpse of a familiar face. The face that had been disturbing my dreams every night for weeks—no, make that months.

The air was suddenly sucked from my lungs, the weight of my legs tripled, and I stopped walking, reluctantly locking eyes with Rooke.

I hadn't seen him for three weeks. He looked different. His dark hair was longer, he'd grown a short beard. Exhaustion dominated his features, and his skin was paler than usual. He was wearing the jacket he'd given me when we first arrived here. I'd chosen not to take it when I collected my clothes. Keeping it would've been a sore reminder of how caring I once thought he was.

The moment felt surreal. Time seemed to slow, and all I could hear were my laboured breaths. Only the pounding of my heart kept me from declaring it as one of my dreams.

Rooke continued to walk towards me, his dark eyes torturously assessing. Although there was a hardness lingering there, I saw no anger, no hatred. But there was something dwelling there, something unnerving.

For a split second, I thought he was going to stop and talk to me, but his eyes shifted, disregarding my presence completely. As he walked past, my eyes trailing his movements, the pounding of my heart juddered with an explosion of disappointment. The moment was excruciating. I didn't know how to process it.

Catching my breath, my legs thawed, and I found the strength to move. Without a glance backwards, I scurried to Truro's treehouse.

I drank too much while I sat alone that night, coming to the conclusion I was a lost cause. How had that brief encounter with Rooke left me feeling agonisingly confused? It was ridiculous. I couldn't live with him; I couldn't live without him. Loving Rooke Maddox was the definition of a losing game. I was destined to fail, whatever path I chose.

When I woke, the early morning light was filtering through the cracks in the wooden door. A sound on the decking outside roused me, although not enough to coerce me to move. The sound came again, and I realised someone was outside. The heavy footfalls were slow and precise, as if whoever it was, was trying not to disturb me.

At first, I thought it was Truro returning, but when the footsteps retreated to the stairs, my curiosity got the better of me.

Carefully, I sat up. Testing the extent of my hangover, my feet slowly found purchase and I walked steadily to the door. I peered through the gap as it creaked open. Nobody was outside, but something had been placed on the table.

Rubbing my arms against the morning chill, I glanced about. A fine mist restricted the view over the balcony edge. Anything further than thirty metres was no longer visible. But I could make out the figure of a man striding along the bridge below, hands in his pockets.

My heart stuttered, my stomach somersaulted. It was Rooke.

Full of roused intrigue, I scurried to the table. Lying there, delicately placed on the wood, was a bunch of white and pink wildflowers. The stems were tied together by a short length of string that affixed a torn piece of brown paper. My thundering heart intensified as I read the unexpected words.

Happy Birthday Eden.

Was it my birthday? I hadn't looked at the Alluran date for a while. But thinking about how long ago the anniversary of Jacob's death was, it could be right. Getting used to the difference between Alluran and Earth days and months didn't come naturally.

I turned the tag over, noticing more writing on the other side. And my heart stopped.

I miss you!
~Rooke x x

The simple sentence caused havoc in every sense. It was such a small declaration, yet a massive step. He missed me. He'd reached out and offered an olive branch.

The confusion made me feel dizzy. My head pounded in time with my heart, stabbing the statement into my brain. He *missed* me.

But there was an overshadowing question preventing me from running after him. Why had he said those horrible things? Why had he pushed me away? Maybe I was being petulant, but the thought of talking to him scared the shit out of me. He'd hurt me. And it was the most agonising thing I'd ever endured.

Chapter Twenty—Nine

Lost in my thoughts, I shot arrow after arrow at the training target. All morning my mind had been consumed by thoughts of Rooke, so much so that I'd forgotten about Truro's imminent return, until I felt hands circling my waist. Slacking my bow, he whispered gently in my ear, "Why didn't you tell me it was your birthday?"

He'd seen the flowers and Rooke's note. I'd left them visible on the table. I didn't want to lie to him.

"To be honest, I hadn't realised," I replied softly. "It also reminds me of my mum's death, so I don't tend to celebrate."

"Will you be mad at me if I told you I got us the day off?"

I turned to face him, my eyebrows knitting tightly together. "It's not necessary, Truro." Searching his face, I discovered he'd washed and dressed in casual clothes, not his usual leathers.

"If anything, let me steal you away for an early lunch." His smile was enlightening, those striking eyes enthralling. A few days away and I had almost forgotten how intoxicating I found him.

Leaning forward, he brushed his lips over mine. "I've missed you." But the words caused an emotional delay. He missed me, just as Rooke had. Yet Truro's words of sentiment held less value than those in Rooke's handwritten note. Nux, everything felt out of context. My mind was a spiralling mess.

I found Truro frowning at me, his cheerful expression replaced with one of concern. Gently pushing a loose strand of hair behind my ear, he said, "Are you alright?"

I nodded and dropped the arrow I was holding into the quiver on the floor. "I am hungry. An early lunch would be nice." Attempting a smile, I threw my bow across my back.

Truro took my hand, and we walked across the grazing field to the north edge. And there, laying in the long grass, overlooking the steep ravine below, was a picnic blanket adorning a basket full of food and a bottle of coral wine. A swell of warmth filled my chest and I glanced at Truro. A genuine smile thawed my frigid face and I squeezed his hand. *He'd done this for me.* "This is…this is lovely. Thank you."

Kissing my cheek, he said, "Anything for you, beautiful."

We sat down, unpacking the pastries and wicker punnets of fruit. Truro popped open the wine, offering me a glass. Holding my stomach, I declined. I was still feeling the effects of drinking too much last night.

As we ate, Truro spoke about the metal production in Kala. He may have even spoken about a new insight following the dispatchment of Kobe's drone through the hologram, but my mind kept drifting. I didn't feel well, and the image of Rooke silently walking onto Truro's balcony that morning sent my thoughts into overdrive. What would've happened if I'd been awake, if I'd approached him whilst he was there?

"You keep holding your stomach." Truro's words snapped me out my daydream. I found him frowning, glancing between my stomach and my face. "Is everything okay? You're not…" The concern transgressing his features had me following his train of thought. "Are you pregnant?"

"No…*no.*"

He sat up rigid. "Are you certain? You may not know yet…"

"I'm not pregnant. I take a tonic to ensure it doesn't happen." I caught the look of surprise in his eyes, followed by a glint of disappointment.

"I won't run away," he said softly. "I realise the events of my past don't bode well, but if you are, I'd never leave you."

I reached for his hand understanding his reasoning. "I know that, but I'm not pregnant. I can't let that happen. Not here. Not now."

Truro averted his gaze, his frown deepening. "You've decided not to stay, haven't you?"

I'd decided the moment I'd declared the opposite to Zamya. The words hadn't sat right, regardless of Rooke and his unexpected gestures.

"After Solarfleet have helped your people, I will be returning with them." I glanced at him, gauging his reaction. The growing mark of pain on his face squeezed my heart with a discomfort. "Truro, we always knew the amount of time we have together is limited."

"Is this because of the flowers?"

My paused response had Truro watching me intently. Gazing into the cloudy sky, I sighed. "I don't know."

"He's offered you a lifeline. That's why you want to return."

"Truro, this isn't my home."

"What if I told you I love you. Would that change your mind?"

I stared at him, studying the severity of his frown, his piercing eyes and the look of desperation held within. He didn't want me to leave because he thought he loved me. Nux, I didn't deserve him.

He cupped my face, the warmth of his palm burned against the chill of my skin. "I'm broken inside, I know that. I have been for years, yet somehow…somehow, you fix me."

"We fix each other, Truro. I'm not denying that." And I meant every word. My grandma had always told me people come into your life when you need them the most, and some have a tendency to disappear when that need is no longer required. Perhaps she was right. I'd needed Truro during the months of strain and trauma here, I still did. Even though a part of me wondered if it was possible to take him back home with me, I doubted he'd feel content there. Allura wasn't his home and Earth wasn't mine. We were like a fish and a bird, with nowhere to live happily together.

"I love being with you," I whispered. "Solarfleet aren't due to arrive for another week or so. This doesn't have to end now."

Leaning forward, his lips met mine, lingering there for several seconds. His hand moved, scaling from my hip up over my breast, halting at the clasps fastening my leather jacket together. As the material slackened around my shoulders, I reached forward, intensifying the power within our kiss.

Our time together *was* limited, and even though Rooke's actions confused me, Truro's were written in stone. And I loved him for that.

Tugging the jacket from my arms, the wonted sense of urgency grew between us. But Truro unexpectedly pulled his mouth from mine, placing a vertical finger over his lips, hushing me. Through panting breaths, I discovered his eyes had rounded, flicking in all directions.

An unusual sound fluttered on the breeze. It could've been an owl or a strange bird, but before I could ask him what was going on, he placed his hand over my mouth, forcing me onto my front. Lying half on top of me, he peered through the tall grass towards the grazing field. All the horses had scarpered. Jader and the trainees were no longer practicing. The only thing I could make out was a dark form near the archery trees. Then, another one appeared, scuttling across the grass.

Unsure of what I was seeing, I looked to Truro. His hand reached under the edge of the picnic blanket, pulling his swords free from where he'd hidden them. Placing a dagger in my hand, he caught the question on my face. He pushed me further into the ground and the faintest whisper fell from his lips, "Stay here. Do not make a sound."

With a stealth-like grace, Truro scampered through the long grass, around the perimeter of the field, taking shelter behind a cluster of trees. I glanced at the dark forms. There were three of them now. Holding my breath, I watched Truro emerge from the treeline. Swinging his swords in a flash of movement, he looked every part the courageous warrior. The only issue, he wasn't dressed in his leather armour. He wore a pair of leather trousers, but his top only consisted of his grey hoody.

The imposters noted his presence. All three of them rose on hind legs, revealing their true forms. As they straightened, sheer horror struck me. They were all dressed in dark clothing, but their bodies were horrendous, like something from a twisted nightmare. One was standing on robust human legs with a human face, but its multiple spindly arms were sharp points—no hands. Another had four, thin, gangly legs with pointed tips. Its body was shaped like an Igknamai, but the arms holding two vicious looking swords were human. The third, had a deformed human body with Igknamai arms and skeletal fingers. Half its human face was encased in scales, hooding four black eyes. All three of them were a horrifying merger of Igknamai and Hybrids.

Through the tall grass, I could see Truro's hardened features as the imposters hissed at him. They slowly hobbled and scuttled in his direction, and my heart pulsated with alarm.

Truro moved gracefully, meeting the brunt of their weapons with his swords. Cutting one of them down, it scuttled away before falling lifeless into the grass. But Truro seemed to find difficulty in outwitting the one holding the two swords. It was far larger than he was, using its pointed feet to attack Truro's legs.

Truro's groan of pain rippled through the air, provoking me to lift my head. I gripped the dagger, readying myself to charge out of my hiding place to help. Then, I saw movement on the far side of the field, and arrows were flying towards the monsters, hitting the scaled faced one several times.

Truro was still in close combat with the larger, sword bearing one, and he seemed to be struggling. Forced backwards, he fell to his knees, growling his disapproval. I saw the beast snarl down at him, bearing pointed teeth, sharp enough to rip a man's throat out with.

On the far side, Redwood warriors were charging across the field, preparing to aid their general, so I jumped to my feet, readying myself to help. But a heavy object collided with my back, sending me to my knees. Ignoring the pain, I flipped over to see what had hit me, only to be faced with another terrifying sight. Dark eyes, disfigured, scarred skin, and a snarling mouth encased in a human face. My breath left my lungs abruptly as it leant down and growled, "Hello Queenie. Someone wants to see you."

What the...

Who were these monsters?

Still clutching Truro's dagger, I thrust it forward into the monster's human-like body, but its teeth sank into my wrist before the dagger found purchase. Dropping the weapon, my scream echoed across the ravine.

Barely able to breathe, more pain entered my body through my leg, where the monster plunged its pointed-tipped arm deep into the fleshy part of my thigh. I screamed again. The pain was paralysing. Every movement was too agonising to endure. I was trapped.

The blanket crumpled beneath me, and involuntary, I began to move. Using its arm punctured inside my leg as leverage, the monster tugged, ripping at the flesh, hauling me feet first. Tears stung in my eyes as I tried to flip over, sending the bottle of coral wine spilling over the blanket. At the top of my lungs, I screeched

Truro's name, praying he was still alive. With no sword nor arrows, and with so much pain invading my body, I was useless. I couldn't fight. "Truro!"

With an abrupt jolt, the dragging stopped. A disconcerted spluttering filled the space behind me. Pain flooded my leg as I felt the monster's sharp arm pulled free.

Glancing in its direction, I discovered Truro holding the monster's long, scraggly hair, with an arrowhead pierced into its blooded throat. The primal rage in Truro's eyes was frightening. But when he looked at me, it faded, replaced with compassion and concern.

He threw my attacker to the ground and stepped forward. Crouching over me, he assessed my leg, my wrist, my face. Holding the latter between his blood-soaked hands, he said, "I need to get you to Nya, quickly."

He pulled me to my feet but the pain in my leg was too unbearable to ignore. After a few failing steps, Truro swept me up into his arms and he carried me to the Pasa.

I watched Nya as she tied the large bandage around my thigh. To stop the bleeding, she'd cauterized the wound. The bite on my wrist had left deep incisions. They had been stitched and bandaged.

Straightening her posture, Nya looked at me, then Truro, who stood by the wall still covered in blood. The scratches on his legs had been treated, a slash on his arm cleaned and stitched.

"I'd like to keep an eye on both wounds," Nya said to me. "You need to take some anti-biotics. It's a precautionary measure in case the Hybrid who attacked you was carrying any of the Igknamai bacterium."

"It was a Hybrid?" I looked to Truro.

"A lesser Hybrid," he replied. "They're the result of unnatural procreation gone wrong."

I grimaced at the thought, sending my mind into a chasm of anguish for those unfortunate women who were snatched to grow and birth those monsters.

"They're sent when the Igknamai are of no use," Truro continued. "They rarely show up in broad daylight, especially on Redwood soil. This attack was unusual."

"They must've been after something," Nya mused.

"Or someone." Truro's gaze met mine. I hadn't told him about the monster calling me Queenie. It would only cause more paranoia, but I had a feeling he'd worked it out already.

"Do I need to stay here overnight?" I asked Nya.

"You'll be more comfortable at Truro's." She smiled at me, glancing at Truro for approval, which he gave through a swift nod. "I'll give you some strong painkillers. They will make you sleep, but once the sedative wears off, you'll be in a lot of pain. My advice is to take them beforehand."

I nodded.

"I'll have someone stop over tomorrow to redress the wounds and check for anything sinister, but I think you'll be alright."

"Thanks, Nya."

She gave Truro a glass tub of tablets, then left the room.

Truro walked over to me. "It wasn't the birthday I wanted to give you."

I squeezed my lips together. "The unexpected excitement stopped me thinking about mum. That's a good thing."

"Let's get you home," he shook the tub of tablets, "so the real party can start."

I chuckled and he scooped me up into his arms. He carried me out the Pasa as if I weighed no more than a feather.

Back at the treehouse, he gently laid me on the comfortable bed. Carefully climbing on top, he straddled me, leaning over so we were face to face. His stunning blue eyes, full of concern, searched my own. "I love you," he whispered.

Holding his gaze, I stroked his beautiful face. I wanted to say it back, I did, but a part of me was convinced I still felt too much for Rooke to be truly in love with Truro. And Truro was the most incredible man I'd ever met. He'd been my idol, my teacher, my lover. I couldn't have asked for anything more. But all I could say was, "I know."

Dropping his gaze, he swiftly leant forward and kissed my forehead. "Sleep. I'll be here when you wake up."

After swallowing a couple of tablets, sleep came easily. It was deep and dark full of empty shadows. The only thing that briefly pulled me from my slumber was the sound of Rooke's voice. At first, I thought I was dreaming, but then I heard Truro's say, "Didn't expect a visit from you."

"Can I see her?" *Rooke.*

"She's asleep."

There was a pause, and I opened my eyes. I was facing away from the balcony, where I presumed they were standing. I could feel the tension building.

"How is she?" Rooke asked gently.

"Her leg and wrist were a mess, but Nya fixed her up. Mentally, she's…she's shaken. She was trembling when I got to her."

"Thank you," Rooke's voice transformed into a deep rumble, "for saving her."

There was another awkward silence, and I heard a couple of footsteps. I assumed it was Truro, because suddenly his voice quietened. "I think the lesser Hybrids were sent specifically to extract her. I have no idea why, but I'm pretty sure they knew exactly what they were doing and who they were sacrificing to get access to her."

I knew Truro had worked it out. He was too cunning, too observant.

"Then it's about time we both pull rank. She must remain in the village."

Rooke, No!

"I agree."

What?

"I'm glad we can finally agree on something."

"You're mistaken. We've always agreed on one thing. She's worth fighting for."

"True." I felt Rooke's eyes on the back of my head. I could feel him subconsciously reaching out, attempting to soothe me; protect me. "Can you let her know I came to see her."

"Sure."

Rooke's footsteps retreated to the stairs and silence fell over me again. As I drifted into that dark, dreamless slumber, the only thought circulating was that he'd offered olive branch number two.

Chapter Thirty

"Hey, sleepyhead."

I forced my heavy eyelids open, finding Zamya standing over me with an inquisitive pout scrunching her lips. Blinking to defog the sleep from my eyes, I groaned, and the bed dipped as Zamya sat down on the edge.

"How are you feeling?"

I ached all over. The pain in my wrist stung, the wound in my thigh unhappily pulsed. "I'll let you know," I mumbled, rubbing my eyes.

"Well, you've been asleep nearly sixteen hours. I assumed you'd be hungry, so I brought some food."

My stomach rumbled and Zamya laughed. She walked to the coffee table and picked up a tray of food and a glass of water. Placing it on the bedside table, she handed me the drink. I downed the whole thing, staring pensively at the bottom in my hands.

"I thought I was a goner, Zam."

She sat down again, placing her hand on mine. "You're a fighter. You're still here."

I swallowed back the bile rising in my gullet, remembering the facts. "I think the Hybrids are working with the Akquarians."

Zamya's frown confirmed how crazy I knew the statement sounded.

"I saw Llexzus near the hologram a few weeks ago. And the...the Hybrid monster, yesterday...it called me Queenie. The only person who's ever called me that is Llexzus. I have no idea why, but...but don't you think it's too much of a coincidence?"

Her expression changed to one of disconcerted puzzlement. "Does Rooke know about this?" I shook my head. "Does Truro?"

"I don't think so."

"I think one or both need to be informed."

Introspectively, I nodded. "Where is Truro?"

"He's at the garrison platform. After you've eaten and I've redressed your wounds, I'll take you over there. We can test that leg of yours."

An hour later, I was hobbling over the bridges towards the tree lift on the southern side. I was slow. The pain in my leg was tolerable but, even with Zamya's help, I kept losing stability.

"It'll take time," Zamya said, noticing my frustration. "A little walk each day will help the muscle reform."

The tree lift jolted to a halt, providing access onto the garrison platform, and a couple of the patrolling warriors dipped their heads in curtesy as we stepped off. Glancing along the expanse, I couldn't see Truro. Sounds of horses pulled my attention over the wooden rails to the forest floor below. At the sight of Rooke talking to Oz and Guz, I couldn't breathe.

Time slowed, and my skin prickled as I watched him speak, and nod, and frown. It was only when Zamya softly said, "Go, see him," that I snapped out of my trance.

Glancing back at her, I saw the hope in her eyes, a silent plea to take that first icebreaking step. With hesitancy, I agreed. I could do this.

Zamya helped me across the platform into the ground lift. My anxiety surged as the shaft lowered. I hadn't planned for this to happen today. I wasn't sure what to say to him. It had been three, long, gruelling weeks since we last spoke—argued.

The dusty red ground came into view, rippling like waves when the shaft hit the bottom. Hobbling non-gracefully, I walked towards Rooke's horse—towards him. He suddenly looked in my direction and his face froze. So much so, Oz turned to see what he was staring at. I caught the look Oz threw Zamya, the hint of relief passing between them.

Oz stepped towards me, encasing me in his huge, tattooed arms. "Good to see you, trouble."

Laughing, I pushed him back. He stepped away, taking Zamya with him. Guz and Ayelle, too, purposely moved behind the horses. It was if they'd been expecting me.

My eyes locked with Rooke's. Those dark green orbs I'd lost myself in so many times were looking at me, concealing a whirlpool of emotion. He slowly approached, awkwardly tapping his horse's neck as he left her side. Stopping a metre in front of me, I studied his face, his beard, his lean, strong physique under the leather armour. Nux, he made my heart race.

"Thank you for my flowers."

He continued to stare, making the encounter agonising. I felt sick.

"How are you?" I asked tentatively. "How is your mum?"

As if he snapped himself out of his stupor, he shifted on his feet. "She's, um, she's doing well. I…I received a message from her a few days ago. It was, um, addressed to you as well. I think she misses you more than she does me."

I smiled at that; at the memory of how warm and kind his mum was. For a brief moment the memory took me back years, to when everything was simple and easy. When mine and Rooke's relationship was solid.

"I miss her t…"

Rooke's arms snapped around my body before I could finish, his face burying into my neck. If it hadn't been for his unwavering hold, I think I would've staggered backwards with shock. But his smell overwhelmed my senses, loosening my tense muscles, stabilising me. Holy souls, he smelt like home, he *felt* like home.

Pulling my arms tight around his shoulders, my fingers trailed upwards through his hair, savouring the feel.

"I've lost count the number of times I've nearly lost you," he mumbled against my neck. I squeezed him harder, finding the sentiment overwhelming. But I remained silent, trying to keep myself grounded.

He pulled back, and a barrage of words fell from his lips, his eyes emphasising the gravity of them. "I'm sorry. I'm sorry, I'm sorry about everything. I didn't mean it. I didn't mean what I said. You aren't a burden or an unwanted obligation. Yes, as Jacob was dying, I promised him I'd look after you, but I would've done it anyway. My love for you, it's…it's unconditional. I'd rather die than see you hurt, and I know, I know it's me who has hurt you. I don't know why I did it. I can't cope without you, Eden. You are good for me. Too good for me. And since we've been in this hideous world, everything has got in our way. I hate the distance, this wall that's appeared between us. It's killing me." He placed his forehead against mine, cupping my neck with his warm hands. "Please come back to me," he whispered. "I need you. I need you more than you can ever possibly imagine."

Holding onto his wrists, trying to process it all, I opened and closed my mouth several times, but I couldn't find the words.

"Say something?" he said. "I may not deserve your forgiveness…"

"I forgive you." I angled my head so I could focus on his face. "As long as you forgive me."

He chuckled, relief shimmering across his features. "What for?"

"Telling you something you may not want to hear." Averting my eyes to his chest, I felt the flood of nerves tingle through my limbs. I had to say this, otherwise it was going to eat away at me from the inside. "I don't think things can go back to the way they were."

Stepping back, his hands slipped from my neck. I glanced up. The sorrow on his face was heart wrenching. "Eden, I said I'm sorry…"

"I want more." The words fell from my lips on a soft, whimsical breath. But he stared at me. An unreadable, traumatising stare. My stomach dropped, and I suddenly felt mortified. Why had I told him? I'd always known it wasn't something he'd wanted to hear.

"I shouldn't have said anything." I turned to move, only to hiss at the pain resonating down my leg. Rooke's hand caught my arm.

"Don't run away again." He appeared in front of me, placing his hands on my waist, drilling those dark eyes into my soul. "What are you saying?"

My confidence was failing me. Where was Zamya? I wanted to head back.

"Eden." Rooke gently shook me, forcing me to look at him. The unreadable stare had transformed into an incredulous gaze, one on the brink of impatience. "What do you mean?" The green of his eyes sank into mine, a sense of desperation filling the air between us.

He had been my best friend for years, I could tell him everything, so why was this so hard? Closing my eyes, I calmed myself. "You've…you've tried to control every aspect of my life here, and I have, I've despised you for it. But…if I've exasperated or angered you with the decisions I've made, believe me, I only did it to…to try and get over you. You've upset me and pushed me away more times than I think you're aware. But…what I don't think you understand is…I…I choose you, Rooke. I always have."

A deep frown lined his brow, his eyes intense. I watched, trying to distinguish his reaction as the words steadily sunk in. It was his turn to find difficulty in choosing words. But the words never came. Rooke's gaze shot past my head, his eyes widening with terror. The next thing I knew, he'd pushed me to the ground, throwing himself over me, and chaos erupted around us.

Zamya's voice penetrated the air, screaming Oz's name. Horses' hooves pounded the earth and the word, "Hybrid," was barked several times from the platform above. I tried to look up, but Rooke's body blocked my view. More shouting, followed by the familiar sound of arrows hissing through the air panicked me. We were under attack.

Rooke swiftly rose, dragging me along with him. As pain inflamed my leg, he pulled me abruptly behind the closest tree. Forcing me back against the rough bark, his body protectively engulfed mine. I watched his eyes assessing whatever carnage was playing out. I couldn't see anything. I could only hear the yells and groans, the swords clashing, the horses squealing.

I tried to adjust my position to peer around the tree, but Rooke stopped me.

"Stay hidden," he whispered, followed by a curse as he looked back at the scene. He stepped out of our hiding place and yelled, "Truro! Get Zamya!"

Truro was here? Where was he? Where was Zamya?

Rooke cursed again, reaching for the sword sheathed down his back. It hissed free as he stepped out of our hiding place. My hands flailed, trying to keep hold of him, only finding air and a sense of desperation. In horror, I watched as Rooke leapt into the path of an approaching Hybrid. By no means was this Hybrid like the raggedly clothed one, who had tried to snatch me along with Dawna. And he certainly wasn't a hideous lesser Hybrid. He was the embodiment of a trained warrior, encased in tarnished red-gold armour, agilely swinging a lethal-looking, steel sword. His eyes were dark and wide beneath a steel helmet, fashioned in the shape of a winged beast. The whole look, along with the sneer across his lips, was terrifying.

I was petrified. Rooke was physically strong, I knew he was, but he'd only been wielding a sword for four months. His opponent was far larger, fiercer, and it looked as though he was built to bring down mountains.

Their swords clashed, creating a flash of sparks. Rooke grunted, gritting his teeth with determination. He was standing his ground, but this was a matter of life and death. And there was no way I was allowing the latter.

Using the tree as an aid, I hobbled out of my hiding spot, snatching my dagger from my belt.

The Hybrid pushed Rooke backwards. I watched him stumble, righting himself at the last moment before the Hybrid attacked again. The Hybrid's sword came down on him, meeting Rooke's wavering strength.

Kicking up some loose soil, creating a plume of red smoke, the Hybrid snapped his eyes to me, allowing Rooke time to slash him across his calves. The armoured beast roared, driving his sword forward. But Rooke had nimbly moved, now able to plunge his sword into the Hybrid's exposed armpit. The growl emanating from Rooke was animalistic. It did something to my primeval self, exciting me.

The Hybrid jerked and spluttered, slumping to the ground under Rooke's booted joust.

Rooke lunged at me. "Stay behind the damn tree!" He glanced back at the mayhem. "Now!"

Still clutching my dagger, his primal command made me obey, and I hobbled back. Rooke didn't follow. It sounded as though he had charged into another threatening imposter.

Listening to the onslaught of agonising cries and screaming horses, I felt useless. I peered around the tree again, unable to see Rooke. My heart raced with fear for him. I couldn't stand here doing nothing. Hobbling around the enormous tree, it took me half a minute to navigate the perimeter. Peering out in the opposite direction, I could see bodies lying in the dust. Horses were rushing in every direction, and it was then I realised how the Hybrids had gotten so close to the village without being detected. They were on horseback, wearing grey hooded cloaks, similar to the ones the scouts wore. I doubted any of these circumstances were usual. I'd never heard Truro mention attacks like this before. He always made out we were safe inside the palisade.

I caught sight of Zamya huddled behind a fallen horse. Ayelle was beside her, shooting the odd arrow. I could've sworn I saw Truro wrestling a Hybrid a few metres in front of them. There was movement and dust everywhere, it was hard to distinguish friend from foe.

A body dropped from the garrison platform above, landing barely two metres from me. I flinched, jumping back, discovering a young Redwood warrior with multiple arrows in his chest. He was clearly dead, still holding onto his bow, with a quiver of arrows strapped to his back.

Ignoring the pounding of my heart, I lunged forward, my leg nearly giving way under the pressure. Yanking the bow free from the dead man, I grabbed as many arrows as possible. Crouching low, I set up a shot, aiming for the Hybrid attacking Truro. The arrow struck him on the back, but his metallic armour reflected the arrowhead.

Setting up another shot, more horses trampled across the scene. The red and black leather indicated they were Redwoods, their voices alerting me. The riders were Jader and Wrenn, along with two other hunters. The silver gleam of their swords shone through the red dust as they took down a couple of Hybrids. The next few seconds seemed to playout so fast, it felt like a rush of the wind whipping through a fleeting nightmare.

Zamya screamed Jader's name, alerting two Hybrids strategically hidden among the trees behind her. With a brutish swiftness, they ran from the shadows, one snatching Ayelle. Zamya jumped to her feet, fleeing towards me. I watched in horror as the second Hybrid ensnared her petite body with his long, muscular arms, pulling her towards a horse that had appeared through the dust. Zamya's legs flailed, her arms thrashing, unable to dislodge herself from the huge human-like monster. Her eyes met mine, reaching for me in despair. "Eden! Help me!"

Stumbling a few paces, I straightened, aiming my arrow at the awaiting horse and rider. But I hesitated. The Hybrid who had snatched Ayelle, threw her to the ground, then sprinted towards me. Adjusting my bow, I aimed for him instead. The arrow flew true, hitting him in the forehead, but it bounced off his gleaming helmet, landing on the ground with a pathetic tap.

Shifting my eyes between Zamya's kidnappers throwing her over the horse, and the Hybrid fully focused on seizing me, I had frozen to the spot.

From behind, strong arms grabbed my waist hauling me backwards. With my eyes still trained on the Hybrid, I watched Oz charge at him, both landing on the ground in a plume of dust. I didn't see what happened between them, I was swung around and pushed in the opposite direction.

"Get her off the ground!" The commanding voice directly behind me was Rooke's. I peered back at him, his face covered in sweat and dust. He stepped forward, placing a warm, sweet kiss on my forehead. "I'm sorry, but I have to do this."

Do what?

He launched me backwards, and I collided with something solid. As I was thrown over Truro's shoulder, I caught a glimpse of Rooke running into the rising dust towards Oz. My stomach griped and burned as Truro sprinted for the tree lift. Everything was a blur of haze coated colours and chaos.

"No!" I cried as the lift began to rise, swamping me in darkness. Huddling on the floor, with Truro's boots either side of me, I looked up at his towering form as daylight flittered through the opening onto the garrison platform. Light haloed his hair and shoulders as we rose to safety, and my heart wept at the realisation I'd left Rooke out there, Oz too. And Zamya...Zamya had been taken.

Chapter Thirty-One

I cried out, forcing myself to my feet, only to stumble when the lift shaft halted. Nux, with my injured leg, I felt *useless!*

"Eden, calm down." Truro's strong hand landed on my waist.

"Let me out," I screamed at him. "Let me out!"

The iron gate swung open and one of the garrison warriors called to Truro. "The Hybrids are retreating. What are your orders?"

"Let them go."

Ripping myself from Truro's grasp, I cast a mortified look at the man I'd come to admire; a look full of disapproval. Pushing past the warrior panting and sweating on the threshold, I staggered along the platform, grabbing the wooden rail to see what was happening below.

Oz was mounting a horse, Guz and the others were assessing the wounded or rounding up the frightened horses, Rooke was helping an injured Ayelle up from the floor.

"I'm going after her," Oz said, loud enough for me to hear.

Jader, still on horseback, appeared next to him. "So am I."

Rooke looked over to them, contemplating their words.

"We know where they're heading," Oz said. "We can outride them."

Rooke glanced up at me, holding my gaze for a reflective moment. So much had been left unsaid between us. And, as if he wrenched a dagger from my heart, he dropped my gaze and mounted a horse. The unwounded scouts followed suit, some jumping onto the back of others. There were ten of them as they rode away.

Pushing away from the railing, I stalked back to the lift, but Truro caught my arm. "What are you doing?"

"I need to go with them."

"Out of the question."

"It's not a question."

"That means no!" His eyes pierced into mine, so demanding and powerful.

"Truro please. Zamya is one of my crew. She's my friend. I can't leave her to…"

"Rooke and the others have gone after her."

"And I should be with them!" My head felt as if it was about to explode. Zamya had been snatched. Rooke and Oz could die trying to rescue her before she disappeared forever. This couldn't be happening. If they were all going to die, I wanted to die with them. I didn't want to be the one left holding the flag. I didn't want to be the survivor telling stories of what happened here. "Let me go."

"No!" He walked away.

As he directed his warriors to retrieve the bodies from the ground, I headed for the lift, but he grabbed my elbow again. "*I said no!* What is wrong with you? You can barely walk, for god's sake. You're not gonna get far!"

"Truro, please."

"If I let you go, you will be captured by the Hybrids. Don't you see what they came for? If that attack was simply to snatch women, they would've taken Ayelle and Wrenn and any other woman down there. But they didn't. They were looking for Zamya. And they were looking for you. That's what they were attempting to accomplish yesterday, but they failed. So, they sent their elite. Those Hybrids are never seen. Their existence is a legend. I've never seen one before and I've been fighting this war my whole damn life. If I let you go down to the ground or up to the clifftops, I might as well be offering you to them on a silver platter."

"Why do they want…" I froze, remembering my thoughts from yesterday and this morning. "They're working with the Akquarians."

"No, they're not."

"They are!"

"I can assure you, they're not."

I stared at Truro. His stoic adamance unfaltering.

"Please let me go. I can't sit here waiting. I'm an Alluran. Half of my crew is out there. I need to be with them. I need to be with him, protecting him…I can't, I can't lose him." Every bone in my body felt as though it was crumbling. Every instinct was screaming at me that something bad was going to happen. Air ripped through my throat, resembling a sound between a sob and a gasp. I couldn't lose Rooke!

Truro's softened words startled me. "You…you love him."

Holding the wooden rail for support, I looked up. His expression was tender, fashioning a forlorn frown. I forcefully placed my hand over my pounding heart. "I never intended to use you. I never wanted to hurt you…I desperately wanted to love you."

He licked his lips and glanced towards the floor. "I always knew. Even from the beginning. You murmur his name enough times when you're asleep. You've even said his name during…well, you know." He noted my mortified expression. "It's true. I'm the fool who chose to ignore it, hoping you may change your mind."

"Oh, Truro," I whispered, failing to hold the trembling at bay.

"I promised him I'd keep you safe. And I will hold true to that promise, for me as well as him." The command returned to his tone; the slight hunch of his shoulders uncoiled. "You're not leaving this village. So don't attempt it."

I watched him march away, my heart breaking into a thousand shards. They were splintering through my veins, bleeding me out. I didn't know what to do. Nervous energy ran through my body like a swarm of electric eels. I couldn't just sit here, pondering.

With a difficulty that frustrated me, I found myself walking back to Truro's treehouse. After dressing in my full leathers, with my bow over one shoulder, my sword behind the other, I walked towards the east cliff, only to be met by a barricade of warriors denying me access to the grazing fields.

Sulking back to the garrison platform, I attempted to hobble over to the tree lift, but Truro's authoritative eyes were on me. There was no point. He wasn't going to allow me to leave. And even though I tried to ignore it, the pain in my leg was excruciating.

Admitting defeat, I slumped onto the platform floor and waited.

It was mid-afternoon when I heard another pack of horses returning. Still slumped by the garrison railings, I glanced through the slats. I could make out Jader and Wrenn, both covered head to toe in dust.

Through the pain, I forced myself to stand, eager for answers. There was no sign of Zamya, but when my eyes locked with Oz, his solemn frown afflicted every pore in my body. Flicking my eyes to the horse he was guiding, my breath wavered, and my heart literally stopped...

Sagging over the horse's shoulders was Rooke. He appeared unconscious, tied to his horse to prevent him from falling. Then I saw the blood soaked into the mare's coat. At the realisation it wasn't hers, my thoughts almost crippled me; thoughts fuelled by dread and agony and distress.

Oz didn't stop at the lift, he continued under the village to the lift near the Pasa. Hobbling as fast as I could, I walked the entire breadth of the village to the north side. By the time I found where Rooke had been taken, he was lying on a solitary bed in a small medical room aboard the Pasa. He was conscious, writhing in pain—screaming. Oz was holding him down as Nya cut the leather from his left side.

I raced over, snatching Rooke's right hand into mine, hoping it would calm him, calm me. But it didn't have any effect on either of us. The leaking slash across the left side of his abdomen was gruesome. There was more than flesh and blood filling that wound.

I swallowed back vomit, squeezing Rooke's hand tighter.

His harrowing grunts and cries were beyond traumatising. I wanted to cry. Calling his name, Rooke eventually turned his head to me, meeting my glassy gaze. The plea in his eyes was soul destroying. The pain was ripping him in two.

Cupping his face with my free hand, my voice took on a tender tone of command, "Rooke. Rooke, focus on me, focus. You are strong. You can fight this." *Nux, please fight this.*

His eyes lingered on my face, stilling his body for the briefest moment before Nya's injected sedative took hold, and he closed his eyes.

I stared at his motionless face; at the face I'd come to love beyond measure. And my entire universe shattered around me.

Part Three

Hybrid

Chapter Thirty-Two

For days, I remained at Rooke's bedside, trying not to suffocate under the shadows engulfing me.

The Hybrid's blade had punctured a small part of Rooke's colon, fractured a couple of his ribs, and severed his spleen. The colon had been repaired, his spleen removed, but due to the extent of the trauma, he hadn't woken. And by no means, was he out of the woods.

The shadows whispered to me; *he could die.*

Those same shadows wandered to thoughts of Zamya every several minutes. Oz had told me they'd caught up with the Hybrids who'd taken her, but they hadn't got close enough to snatch her back. With so many Hybrids to get past, she was gone before they had time to engage in the assault.

What was she going through? If Truro was right in his adamance the Akquarians weren't working with the Hybrids, that meant she was…I didn't want to think about it.

I swallowed the sour taste in my mouth, returning my gaze to Rooke's pale face. His beard had been shaven to allow access to a couple of cuts across his chin. They'd been stitched and dressed. I had no doubt they'd leave a scar on his handsome face.

The sounds of the Pasa opening up roused my attention. Voices and footsteps echoed through the medical corridors. The day staff had arrived, probing my anguish further; Zamya should've been among them.

Heavy footfalls entered the small room, followed by Oz's compassionate rumble, "Eden, you've been here days. You need to get some rest."

I glanced over my shoulder at him. "I have slept."

"Okay, but you need to shower. Truro has brought some of your clothes over. Go and freshen up. It may make you feel better."

"I doubt it." I looked back to Rooke. Then felt a gentle hand on my shoulder.

"Come on, Eden. Do it for Rooke. He wouldn't want you wasting away in here." Oz eyed the untouched plate of food on the bedside table. "You need to eat."

A heavy sigh left me, and I reluctantly stood up. I didn't want to leave Rooke's side, but Oz was right.

I walked as fast as I could to the showers. My leg was still painful, my wrist was encased with a stinging tightness, but neither came anywhere close to the ache in my chest.

I could lose him.

Showering, then dressing in the clothes Truro had sent over, I rushed back to Rooke's bedside. I hadn't seen or spoken to Truro for three days. Apparently, he was heavily involved in reinforcing the perimeter to ensure attacks, like the one Zamya was taken in, did not reoccur.

When I arrived back at the small medical room, I found Oz speaking with Valina. Her grey eyes landed on me, and I saw a genuine compassion swimming there; one full of sympathy and grief.

"I hate to be the bearer of trying news," she said, twisting my stomach with an irritation, "but you have visitors."

I kept my face hard. "Solarfleet have arrived?"

"I'm afraid not." She flicked her eyes briefly to Oz. "The Akquarians are here. Asking for an audience with Rooke."

Could things get any worse?

"You can see Rooke is in no position to see them," I bit back.

"I informed them of the situation. They wish to speak with one of you. An Alluran. They refuse to speak with me or Truro."

I glanced at Oz. He looked concerned. "You are Rooke's second," he said.

Staring at Oz momentarily, I wanted to cry. I didn't want to deal with the Akquarians, not today. Havav was the master of mind manipulation and currently, my brain was mush. But what choice did I have? I was Rooke's second in command. It was my duty to do this for him.

Casting a doting glance towards my unconscious commander—my beautiful Rooke—I turned, heading out the door. Valina fell in step with me, Oz a step behind.

"How many Akquarians are here?" I asked Valina as we exited the Pasa.

"A small platoon. For travel protection, mainly." She sent smiles and waves to some of the villagers as we passed them along the bridges. "I've only allowed their ambassador and two others into the council chamber to meet with you."

"Who's the ambassador?"

"Havav's heir."

Trying to dredge through my memory, I couldn't remember the details of Havav's heir. Did I even know who he was?

Valina noted my confusion and said, "Do you not know? Havav's heir is Dybgo."

Dybgo? A part of me wanted to laugh. How had I missed that? I always thought of Dybgo as Havav's bodyguard, or the general of the fortress guards. But it made sense. Of course, Dybgo was his heir. The golden encased warrior with the gigantic, golden tattoo. Elegant and regal, oozing majestic power. I shook my head at how naïve I'd been.

"I'm guessing you also didn't know he is half-human."

"What the..." This time, the surprise sent iron weights down to my feet and I stopped walking altogether. "How is that possible? I mean, I know how it's possible, but I thought...I thought they didn't breed with humans anymore."

"Yes and no." Valina started to walk again. I kept pace, hobbling a step behind. "Our two races signed a treaty nearly two hundred years ago to put an end to that struggle. The common Akquarian is no longer permitted to breed with any human. However, every generation, up to three of the male royal offspring have the right to choose a Redwood woman to marry and procreate with. Those women must consent, of course. They aren't just taken. Dybgo still has to decide his choice."

I thought back to Havav's tale of his deceased wife, and how he was the only Akquarian expected to marry. I understood why, now.

"Human-Akquarian children tend to be female," Valina went on. "That's why they like breeding with humans so much. Occasionally a male is sired, but never before has the heir been half human. There have been whispers that some of the Akquarians are not happy about the situation. They want a full bred Akquarian on the throne when Havav renounces it."

"I can imagine, but aren't all of Havav's sons half human? I'm sure he had several."

"The younger ones were born after Havav's queen died. But nevertheless, even with a human queen, the royals are allowed to procreate with other Akquarians to guarantee sons. However, fortunate for Havav, his queen gave him both male and female offspring."

Of course. His wife had been his queen. That's what Havav had called her.

My eyes widened. *No, no, it can't be...*

Dybgo had tried to claim me. He'd tried convincing me to return to the fortress with him when we'd ventured into the forest, practically declaring his love for me. The day after the Sparzak ball, his warriors and sailors alike, all bowed to me with respect as if I was royalty. *Nux!* Had Dybgo wanted me as his queen, his human queen? Was that why Llexzus had called me Queenie?

I was finding it hard to focus. The thought of having to engage in civil conversation with him sent nails clawing down my spine. Had Rooke known any of this?

Walking over the sturdy bridge towards the council chamber, an ounce of relief hit me when I spotted Truro standing at the entrance. After our last words, I was unsure how our relationship had been left. But knowing he was here, ahead of a fraught encounter with Dybgo, it eased my anxiety.

His blue gaze landed on me. Behind the stoic, hard exterior, I saw concern brimming. Stopping mere inches from him, I spoke, quietly, "Do not leave my side."

He dipped his head. "You have my word."

Leaving Valina at the door, and with my head held high, I walked into the vast circular chamber, passing two Akquarian warriors standing just inside. Dybgo was gazing up at the names inscribed on the walls. I'd forgotten how much taller and broader he was compared to us humans. All six-foot-nine of solid muscle, currently accentuated beneath the dark, fish scaled leather armour. His long white-blonde hair was tied back into a tight knot, with a curving sword and an array of daggers adorning his hips.

He turned as soon as he heard our footsteps, immediately resting his gaze on me. Those crystal blue eyes appeared almost transparent in the gentle light, and I swore I caught his eyes flashing with surprise, just before a gentle smile tugged at his lips. "Eden. I heard Rooke is indisposed. I was wondering who they'd send. You look…well." He frowned at his last comment, roving his eyes over my body. "Akquarian attire suits you far better than…whatever this is you're wearing."

Rolling my eyes, I tried not to groan. Wearing a hooded jumper and a pair of leggings, I felt comfortable. He wanted me draped in chiffon and pearls, with no underwear on. The thought made my stomach gripe.

"Why are you here, Dybgo?" The coldness in my tone hardened his gaze.

"If you want to bypass chivalry, then fine. I'll get straight to it." He stepped closer, clearly irritated. "Rooke's time is up. He knows the consequences."

"What are you talking about?"

"We've had no communication from anyone for a month. I've waited long enough. It seems Llexzus is missing, so I've come to retrieve what was agreed upon."

Before I had time to throw more questions, Oz stepped in front of me, creating a barrier with a protective arm.

"I can assure you, Llexzus is not missing," Oz said. "Our ship has tried to contact you several times, but it seems your people still do not know how to operate a radio."

Dybgo gave Oz a pointed stare, then glanced at Truro, who had appeared in my peripheral. "He doesn't need to be here," Dybgo said, indicating to Truro.

"He does," I replied firmly. "You have two warriors. I have two warriors. I think that's fair."

Dybgo's eyes assessed me. "We can dismiss them all. This can solely continue between you and I."

"Over my dead body," Truro growled.

The smirk Dybgo offered was sinister, showing a side to him I had never witnessed before. "That can be arranged."

I could sense the agitation building under Truro's calm exterior. His posture was rigid, ready to snap.

Dybgo waved his hand. "Come. Let us not quarrel. I am not your enemy."

"Then why are you here making demands?" I asked.

"I've come to claim what is rightfully mine!" His powerful voice echoed around the room. And I saw it then, the prestigious leader he was destined to become. How had I never noticed this before? "Rooke assured us Llexzus would be safe. But he is missing, and we are presuming he may be dead. The plan didn't work!"

"What plan?" I noted Oz glancing back at me. A look full of knowing drowning inside an ocean of worry.

Dybgo smiled gently to himself, before addressing Oz directly. "Your commander didn't tell her about any of this, did he?"

Stepping around Oz, I asked him in an undertone, "What is he talking about?"

Oz's stance was formidable, but the uncomfortable expression on his face had my mind jumping in and out of turmoil and confusion. What had I not been told? Was this to do with why Rooke and Oz visited the Akquarians a couple of months ago?

Oz glanced at me, then back to Dybgo. "I can assure you Llexzus is not missing. His tracking device has a powerful signal which is easily traceable, even behind enemy lines."

"How do you know he's not dead?"

"He has a heart rate tracker on him, which is also transmitting. The last time I checked, that demon heart of his was just fine."

"And when, exactly, was that?"

"Two days ago. Kobe knows more about this than I do."

"Then where is Mr. Kobe?"

Oz huffed, his irritation showing. He was out of his comfort zone. He was a soldier, not a diplomat, but it seemed he was the only one who knew why Dybgo was here, other than Rooke, of course. It didn't surprise me Rooke had kept me in the dark about whatever this was. I was starting to question how often that happened, here, and back home.

"I can retrieve Rooke's tablet," Oz said, "to show you the evidence, if you wish?"

Dybgo nodded. "Please, do."

Oz turned, resting his eyes on me. "I'll tell you everything later," he whispered.

I watched him leave and my heart juddered against my rib cage with an anxiety fuelled by confusion. Thankfully, Dybgo's gaze had returned to the walls, seemingly fascinated by the thousands upon thousands of names inscribed upon them.

"I've often wondered," he said wistfully, "which entry is my mother's."

A sense of surprise, then empathy fell over me. "How old were you when she died?"

"Twelve."

"Why didn't you tell me you were half-human?"

He slowly lowered his gaze, resting his eyes on me. That look of sorrow and wanting I had often seen him give me had returned. "Havav forbade it. I hinted enough times. I'm certain you noted my hands were warm instead of cold. My feet not webbed."

Yes, I had noticed, but I never questioned it. To be fair, I hadn't known humans existed here back then.

"Would it have made any difference?" Dybgo asked.

I stared at him, at the attractive Akquarian who had previously danced in and out of my affection. Even if his devotion had been genuine, he'd lied. He'd tried to trick me into becoming his queen. If he'd told me the whole truth, would I have felt differently?

The answer was no. I'd always felt flattered by his attention, but he was no Truro. I shook my head. "No. No, it wouldn't have made the slightest bit of difference." I glanced at Truro, poised beside me. "I'm going to wait outside. I need some air."

Hobbling through the huge opening, I eyed Dybgo's two Akquarian warriors standing as rigid as statues. I felt Truro's presence behind me as I stopped on the bridge outside. Viewing the village below, I clasped the railings tightly. "Do you know what this is all about?"

To my surprise, he said, "Yes." He was surveying the trees when I looked at him. His expression was just as uncomfortable as Oz's had been. He turned to me. "Blake came up with a plan to utilise Llexzus in helping us to find the Hybrid lair. One of our scouting parties had seen him conversing with Hybrids a few months back. Laughing, joking, no animosity. Blake believed he could be accepted as one of them."

"They put a tracking device on him and released him into the forest," I mused, answering my own question,

Truro nodded. "I had my doubts at first, but it worked. We believe he's found the location. We are waiting for Solarfleet to arrive so we can gain access without being blown to pieces by the landmines."

"So, the lair is behind the hologram?"

"Yes."

Again, it seemed everything relied on Solarfleet's cooperation. Another blow to the plan if they refused to participate. My head could be on a spike before the month was out.

I took a deep breath. "What if Llexzus has changed allegiance?"

Truro frowned at me. "He's loyal to the Akquarians."

"Is he?"

"Why do you keep suggesting such things?"

"I think Llexzus was behind the recent attacks. The lesser Hybrid who tried to take me, he…he called me by a name only Llexzus has used."

"What name?"

I gazed at him, aware what I was about to say may spark a deeper realisation towards the larger picture. "He called me Queenie."

The penny dropped instantly, and Truro glanced back to the council chamber, a frown dominating his face. Before he could say anything more on the subject, Oz reappeared with Rooke's tablet.

"Let's get this over and done with," Oz grumbled, "so the fishmen can be on their way."

We re-entered the chamber. Dybgo was perched on one of the stools, still browsing the walls.

"Here." Oz produced the evidence, pointing out additional information Dybgo requested. I waited, watching the interaction, wondering if it was enough to convince Dybgo to leave.

Standing beside me as my wanton support, Truro lightly touched my hand. He could sense my nerves, my reluctance to be here. I needed to get back to Rooke.

Dybgo eventually stood up, heaving a deep sigh. "I will give you another month," he said to Oz. "But if he has not returned or gets injured or killed in whatever battle you are planning, I will come back for what was promised to me." His eyes rested on me, and a shiver ran down my spine.

He went to leave but turned back to Oz. "Oonla sends her regards."

Oz's face paled before stuttering, "How…how is she?"

"Blooming."

Oz nodded. "Let her know I think of her often."

Dybgo clicked his tongue. "I don't think that would be appropriate, given the circumstances." Disregarding Oz's reaction, Dybgo turned to me, flaring his nostrils. "Until next time, Eden. I'm hoping by then you won't be covered in this man's stench." His eyes narrowed towards Truro, then left.

Truro blew out a long, frustrated sigh before following Dybgo and his warriors out the doorway.

Now alone, I twisted to find Oz staring pensively at the ground behind me.

"What was that all about? About Oonla?"

Oz swallowed, then sat down on one of the council stools. "She's um, she's pregnant…with my child."

Blinking rapidly, I processed his words. "Holy souls, Oz." I plopped down on the stool closest to his. "Does Rooke know?"

"Yes. Don't worry, he's reprimanded me, several times." He rubbed his face vigorously before releasing a troubled breath. "It happened at that mating ball we were invited to. She snuck me away from the party, offering me a strange drink when we reached a private room. I was a little infatuated with her at the time, and, well, with Rooke and Zamya's words hammered into me, I wasn't going to…do anything. There must've been something in that drink. I can't even remember the act. But I remember waking up in her bed with a sore head and an overly sore cock. I must've lost control." He stared into his thoughts, regret seeping from every pore. "I didn't realise she had plotted to bed me purely for the purpose of getting pregnant. It turns out she wanted a human child. She's half human herself."

Of course, Oonla was Havav's only daughter, Havav and his queen's daughter. She was Dybgo's sister.

"When we arrived at the Akquarian fortress, ready to present Blake's plan to Havav, as soon as I stepped into the throne room, he ordered his men to seize me. That's when I discovered the truth. Havav refused to cooperate in any negotiations until I was punished. Rooke protested, and after persuading Havav he would punish me sufficiently himself, he broached Havav with the plan to use Llexzus." Oz shook his head, squeezing his eyes together. "Other than spouting out that the Redwoods had not paid their dues for the exchange of our custody, and that the human civilisation was the downfall of this world, he eventually agreed, but on two conditions. One being that every Akquarian male who had given Oonla their claiming token the night of the ball, was entitled to five minutes of non-retaliated assault."

"Meaning what exactly?"

"They had the right to beat the shit out of me, for claiming their princess without anyone else's knowledge."

"But it was Oonla who instigated it."

"No one saw it that way. I hadn't given her my claiming token, which meant I had broken their rules."

Typical Akquarians.

"Rooke refused the terms, ready to walk away. He was desperate to get the Parvos back, and at the time, we believed the ship was in the Hybrids' hands. I wasn't going to allow the plan to fail because of my actions. So, I told him I'd take the punishment."

"How many…how many claimers were there?"

Oz fell silent, clearly reliving the events. "Forty-seven."

I cursed, suddenly remembering Rooke's statement that Oz had gone above and beyond his duty to protect us. He'd accepted a brutal punishment to help guarantee an advancement in this relentless war against the Hybrids—a chance at getting our ship back.

"Two days of being a punching bag," Oz mumbled. "They were told not to touch my face or neck. It didn't look like I had a single bruise when we left a few days later. The amount of times I got punched in my package." He grimaced remembering the pain. "I'm surprised it all still works." He chuckled at that. "The only good thing was Oonla attended to my wounds. That's when she told me her ploy. It turned out Havav commended her for it. The bastard."

Why didn't that surprise me?

"How bad was it?" I asked, remembering he'd winced when I touched his shoulder, the day he and Rooke returned from that journey.

"Lots of bruising. A few fractured ribs, broken collarbone. My stomach ached for weeks. I'm alright now."

I shook my head with disgust. I could imagine Rooke dwelling behind a curtain of shame for putting Oz through that. I didn't envy him.

"You said there were two conditions. What was the other one?"

The look Oz shot me drained the blood from my body. I went cold.

"Oz?"

He shifted in his seat unable to look at me. "The second one was thrown at Rooke after I'd endured the first. Rooke, he, um, he had to…he had to promise that if Llexzus went missing, or was fatally harmed in any way, he'd…he'd have to… hand you over to Dybgo."

"What?!" I wasn't sure if I heard him correctly. "What?!" I couldn't breathe.

The condition was not as brutal as the one Oz had to endure, but regardless, this agreement would be permanent. So, Dybgo did still want me. He'd never let me go if he rightfully got his hands on me.

"Rooke knows how petrified I am of Dybgo. Why would he do that? Why?" I was on my feet, raking my fingers through my damp hair.

"It's not how it seems." Oz was now standing, trying to calm me. He grabbed my arms, halting my frantic, hobbled pacing. "He would never let him take you."

"This is the Akquarians! They impose and abide by rules. They live by deals and terms and treaties. Rooke would never be able to defy them."

"He made me promise that I'd get you off this planet before that happened."

"How? I don't want to state the obvious, but we have no ship!"

"Rooke knew Dybgo would be coming for you at some point, but until Solarfleet are here, we can hold him off until we can retrieve Llexzus from the Hybrid net. Once Solarfleet arrive, if needs be, I can get you off the ground."

"And then what?" I glared at him. I knew it wasn't his plan, but I needed to find a semblance of reason within this absurdity. "What happens then? When the Akquarians realise they've been fooled?"

"I don't know."

"Shit! How could he be such an idiot?"

Oz fell silent as I held my head with so much despair. Why would he agree to that? I didn't want to think about the consequences if Rooke's plan had gone wrong. "What if the Hybrids killed Llexzus? Dybgo could've rightfully taken me today." Nux, I felt sick. "Did Rooke really hate me that much at the time?"

"No! Eden, no! Rooke...he loves you!"

The words stunned me, and I stared at Oz, full of confusion. He looked as though he had confessed a dark secret, one he'd promised not to tell at all costs.

"He always has."

"Don't. Just don't, Oz. Don't make it sound like he loves me as I do him."

"He does! Ask anyone. We can all see it. Why do you think he's been so anti Truro? Not because he's wary of him. Because he's jealous of him. He regretted something that happened between the two of you at the Akquarian fortress and I convinced him to tell you. He psyched himself up to confess the night of the new moon celebration. The one where you wore that sexy orange dress. But you disappeared with Truro. When he realised what had happened, he was, well, I've never seen him so distraught. Turns out he's an angry jealous type."

I thought back to that night, to when Rooke had suggested we sneak away at some point during the party. I presumed he'd needed to talk about work.

Oz noted my frown and chuckled. "You are both as blind as each other."

It was a joke, but I wanted to cry. A part of me didn't want to fall victim to his words. I'd been hurt enough times. But what if his words were true? What if Rooke loved me as I did him? Had we really wasted so much precious time fighting and bickering when all we needed was each other?

Nux, hadn't Zamya told me that enough times?

I heard Oz call to me as I hobbled through the doorway. I needed to get back to the Pasa. The past hour had offered a minefield of information and my head wanted to explode. But the part I kept musing over was that Rooke loved me. Did he? Did he really? I'd convinced myself otherwise so many times, it was hard to believe.

Opening the sliding door to Rooke's medical room, I was met by a hubbub of activity. Two nurses rushed past me, holding dirty sheets and bandages. I glanced over to Rooke, to where Nya was injecting medication into his arm.

"Is something wrong?" I asked breathlessly.

Nya placed the needle back on a metal tray before looking up at me. Her light green eyes were sorrowful and tender. "He has an infection. Without his spleen, he will struggle to fight it." She walked over to me, placing a gentle hand on my arm. "I'm sorry, Eden. I suggest you prepare for the worst."

Everything went cold, my thoughts spiralled out of control, and I didn't realise Nya had left the room until the haunting silence became deafening.

I stared at Rooke's lifeless body, tucked underneath the red blanket, vulnerable yet peaceful. A shadow of intense grief began to suffocate me, causing my legs to buckle under the weight. Clutching at my chest, I sobbed. I was losing him.

Finding a semblance of strength, I staggered over to the bed, reaching for his hand. His skin felt unusually cold. I stared down at the rakishly handsome face, the black eyebrows and long lashes, the perfectly symmetrical nose, his heavy bottom lip. He was my Rooke. The man I had loved for so many years.

"I love you," I whispered, tears streaming down both cheeks. "I'm sorry I've never told you. But I do, I love you. I love you more than anything and anyone. You are the centre of my universe…you are my everything."

Please don't die.

Chapter Thirty—Three

Two days later, I watched Nya assess Rooke's stats. With a heaviness in her eyes, she looked at me. "His pulse has weakened and his temperature is dangerously high. There isn't anything else I can do. He must fight this himself."

With sore, puffy eyes, I peered down at Rooke, noticing his skin was clammy and tinged with a translucent grey. He was dying and I couldn't do a single thing about it.

I barely noticed the door sliding open. It was only when Kobe's voice twanged in a tone far from nonchalant, that I registered what he said.

"Solarfleet are here."

I glanced at him. His almond shaped eyes were wide, full of a relieved excitement.

"General Murai is aware of the situation. She wishes to speak with you and the council."

"Has she landed already?" I asked.

"Imminently."

Nya flicked her eyes to me. "I best get some inoculations ready."

Nodding, I glanced down at Rooke. I didn't want to leave him. What if he died while I was gone? The thought prickled my eyes with more tears; tears I wouldn't allow to fall. I'd cried enough.

Stroking his hair, I leant down and kissed his forehead. "Keep fighting."

Grabbing my jacket on the way out, I absentmindedly walked behind Kobe towards the east cliff. At the top of the ladder, a huge gust of wind hit my face, my eyes landing on the streamline, metallic ship hovering above the grazing field. All the horses and animals had vacated the area, only the trees and grasses danced vividly against the battering air.

The whirling sound of engines and thrusters deafened my ears, coming to a halt only when the ship settled on the ground and the landing ramp had extended. It felt like an age since I last saw a spaceship, something that was so alien to this world.

Three figures dressed in Solarfleet blue emerged at the top of the landing ramp. As we neared, they descended. I recognised General Murai. She was a stern looking woman, tall with broad shoulders. Her short brown hair was neatly slicked back. The two soldiers either side of her were shorter and far younger, both displaying active comms clipped to their left ear. I'd forgotten how normal that was.

Murai's eyes locked with mine. Both Kobe and I stopped walking, stood to attention, and saluted her.

"At ease, at ease," she said, raising her hands in gesture. Glancing across the expanse of green, towards the trees and the mountains in the distance, I could feel the pause in her actions, struck with an overbearing sense of amazement.

"I'm not sure what I was expecting," she said, "but this wasn't it." Flicking her eyes to me, then Kobe, she subtly examined our clothes. "I hear the past week has not fared well."

"No, sir."

"What condition is Commander Maddox currently in?"

"He's dying." I swallowed back the warble in my voice. "An infection has taken hold. The doctors have done all they can."

"We shall take him up to The Hector." Murai nodded to the soldier on her right, who scurried back up the landing ramp. "Our medical team may have alternative treatment. And if not, he'll be in the right place to be escorted back home for a formal burial. I'm told they burn their dead here." She eyed a burnt pyre in the distance with distaste.

Again, I swallowed back the rising anguish. "They do. They endure too many deaths to bury them all."

Her brown eyes surveyed me, then she said, "Lead the way, Lieutenant. The sooner I meet with these people, the sooner we can end this debacle."

Unsure of what debacle she was referring to, I accompanied her down the ladder and across the bridges to the council chamber. I noticed her observing the villagers, the huts, the bridges, the nets below. The villagers, in turn, stopped and watched as we walked by, resorting to frantic whispers when they considered us out of earshot.

As we neared the widest tree in the village, I noticed Oz standing with Truro and Blake. Valina, too, appeared from inside the doorway. Her usual calm exterior resonating a tense anticipation.

Oz saluted the general. She inclined her head. "Masters. Glad to see you are well."

"And you, sir." Oz dipped his head.

I introduced the three present council members. Valina shot Murai her standard charming smile. "Thank you so much for coming. I would shake your hand, but until you and your crew are immunised against our common diseases, it is best we remain at arm's length."

"I completely understand the precaution," Murai said, following Valina into the council chamber.

Truro's gaze caught mine. The empathy pouring from his eyes confirmed he knew about Rooke. Ignoring it, I sucked in a breath and followed the others inside.

A circular table had been placed in the middle of the ring of stools. A map, similar to the one Rooke always had on his desk, dominated the centre. Small wooden pieces, in different shapes and colours, were scattered across it. Murai lifted her eyebrows with intrigue, raising my scepticism Solarfleet were likely to help.

Valina gestured for Murai to take a seat. She did so, glancing at the Solarfleet soldier positioning himself behind her.

"And regarding the immunisations," Valina went on, "thank you for testing and sending over confirmation of your crew's medical status. Although, we have only received a few dozen."

"That's because I only have forty men with me."

Valina's immaculate face distorted before glancing at me, then offered Murai a sweet smile. "Forty? I assumed you were bringing far more."

Seating myself next to the general, I noticed she ignored Valina's passive-aggressive question and gestured to the map. "What is this?"

"It's our battle plan," Valina confirmed. "We thought it would be easier for you to envisage it this way…"

Murai held her palm up, silencing Valina. "Don't get hasty, young lady."

To Murai, these council members must've appeared as political amateurs. She was well into her forties, perhaps older. Anyone from Allura would assume experience came with age, as I had once done. I wasn't sure where Elgin or Ferrol were. Their presence could've eased the discrimination.

Valina looked put out, but her expression changed to one etched with frustration as Murai continued her speech.

"Following the communication Solarfleet has had with Commander Maddox, we are aware of the extreme circumstances that occur here. My corporation heads have spoken to the Alluran government, and they have agreed to offer you sanctuary."

"Sanctuary?" Valina's eyes found mine. I mentally avoided the daggers she was failing to suppress.

"Yes, a piece of land more than adequate for the amount of people you have residing here. The soil is fertile. I have no doubt you will thrive there."

"And what happens," Blake grumbled from across the table, "when the Alluran people become unhappy that we've freely acquired this land?"

"You will be treated as rightful citizens."

I glanced at Truro sitting adjacent to Blake. His eyes were trained to the map before us, his face hard and unreadable. There was no way of telling what he thought on the subject. I knew he had been set on eradicating the horrors of this world, but had he just realised he could live in a world without those terrors; live in my world with an opportunity to expand and grow.

"We do not want sanctuary," Valina ground out.

Murai sighed. "For some reason Commander Maddox knew you would say that."

With a look of confusion, Valina glanced at Blake. His eyes boring into Murai's head. I could feel the walls of their fortress already rising. This wasn't going well.

"And for that reason," Murai said, "I appointed Lieutenant MacIntosh to scan the entirety of the world from The Orka, while he waited patiently for my ship to arrive. He has found several areas where the beasts do not inhabit. After a thorough examination of these areas, which I will oblige in helping you with, we can relocate your whole village…"

"No!" Valina rasped. "This is our home. We will *not* be moved!"

"Perhaps you should speak with the members of your village before stating that conclusion."

"I can guarantee," Blake said sternly, "that the majority of the village would agree with Valina. As do I."

I glanced at Kobe sitting beside Truro, Oz standing behind. They both looked uncomfortable. We'd always known what the Redwoods wanted, but was it really too much to ask for?

Murai's face hardened. "There is a saying we use on Allura. It goes along the lines of, beggars cannot be choosers."

"We are not begging," Valina snarled.

"I believe you have done, several times in fact."

"This is not what we want!" Valina snapped her eyes to me. I'd never seen her so volatile. "You promised us they'd help."

Shit! "I promised we'd relay the severity of your situation, which Rooke has done. I believe General Murai has delivered two suitable solutions."

"You promised, Eden!" I could see tears lining her eyes.

Damn it! Deep down I always knew Rooke was right about this outcome. I felt like a fraud. Flicking my eyes over to Blake and Truro, I noticed the despair riding their stances. Truro looked at me. There was a prod of disappointment in his vivid gaze; a gentle plea.

"Is that your final statement?" Murai asked, coldly. "You wish to decline our help?"

"We do not want your charity."

"Whatever you ask of us is charity. Nothing we are offering is given without consequence. What exactly do you think we are gaining from helping you?"

"We have fed, clothed, and sheltered your stranded people."

Murai clicked her tongue. "And what of their safety? Half those Allurans are either dead, dying, or have been abducted." Murai rose to her feet, straightening her blue-grey jacket. "If this is how you see our generosity, I regret we could not agree on a way forward for…"

"General," I stood up, preventing her from ending her sentence.

The burden of responsibility had taken hold, and it suddenly dawned on me why it had been me who agreed to help these people, why it had been me who had initially arrived on this world, and the reason why I was standing here now, instead of Rooke. Regardless of my reluctance to admit it, this was my destiny—to help these people. And a part of me had always, somehow, known it.

Murai's brown eyes assessed me, and I swallowed back the nerves.

"Perhaps...perhaps you could listen to the Redwood's battle plan," I said, "before disregarding it altogether. If there's one thing I've learnt in residing here, it's...it's that these people are remarkable, and there really is no place like home. This world could be a paradise. It once was. Do we not owe it to our Alluran forefathers to try and save the world the ancients recklessly destroyed?"

Murai's shoulders straightened, her eyes discovering the names imprinted into the bark wall surrounding us. I watched her mind tick over, the moral principles weaving their way in and out of her conscience. Slowly, she lowered her eyes, resting them on me, before flicking them to the table.

"Very well," she said, retaking her seat. "Let's see what you've got. Then I can voice my opinion on whether your plan is plausible or not."

A charged contentment fell about the room as I lowered myself onto my stool. I listened as Truro explained the attack strategy. Then Blake and Kobe went into detail regarding the bombs they wanted help building, and Truro caught my eye. He was gazing at me with a look of awe. His lips twitched into a brief smile before he winked. I smiled at the gesture, at how much I admired that man. But the weight in my heart suddenly returned, forcing my eyes to the map. Rooke was dying, and I knew if he did, my heart would never recover.

"If we could utilise a small ship, we could scan the area with far more precision than we have already done." Blake was pointing to an expanse of water near where we had found the hologram. "We have recently discovered that the Hybrids potentially reside within an ancient damn, which would make sense. They can use the continual flow of water to generate electricity. That's how they're able to maintain their power sources and technologies."

"And once you know the layout," Murai asked, "you intend to invade?"

"Yes. Flush them out. All of them. With an army waiting to intercept."

Murai sat back, contemplative. "What you're proposing is genocide."

"We are aware of that," Truro said. "But they are unnatural, intelligent beasts disguised as humans. I'm certain even your people would exterminate ravenous beasts who rape and slaughter."

"Indeed."

"We did assume you'd be bringing more ships and soldiers," Valina chimed in, flicking her disappointment my way again. "In order for this plan to succeed, we need more men."

"In all fairness," Murai sighed heavily, "I do not intend on losing any of my men in this fight. However, I do have another ship due to arrive in orbit in the next few hours. As well as another three over the next couple of weeks. Each carrying one hundred and twenty Solarfleet personnel, half of which are soldiers."

Valina nodded, keeping her expression flat, but she could not retain the spark of hope in her eyes as she did the math.

"There is one issue, though." Murai glanced at Valina. "Placing my interstellar ship into orbit was hazardous. There are far too many satellites floating about. With another four larger ships needing space, this will prove impossible."

"We can move the satellites," Valina said. "Not a problem." Her eyes suddenly flashed; her cheeks rouged. I don't think I would've noticed it if she hadn't glanced at me, darting her eyes awkwardly to Blake. I frowned. What had I just missed?

"Well then," Murai stood up. "I will have to relay this information to my commanding committee. I will let you know our decision in the next few days."

A hum of gratitude fluttered between the others. Leaving them to converse, I followed Murai and the Solarfleet soldier out of the room. Oz fell in step behind me. I glanced over my shoulder at him, and he raised his eyebrows as if to say, *that went better than expected.*

Murai remained silent, pensively deliberating with herself. It was only when we stepped onto the walkway along the east cliff rockface, she spoke, asking Oz to leave us. Oz saluted and retraced his steps. The Solarfleet soldier, too, made himself scarce.

Murai's eyes surveyed the hubbub of the activity among the trees. "I get the impression you have warmed to these people."

"Yes, I have. I apologise for my interruption earlier. I forget my place."

"Riley." She turned to me, a gentleness appeared in her mannerisms. "You have been through hell. A situation no Alluran should ever have encountered. Forgetting your place is the least of my concerns." She stepped closer, lowering her voice. "To be honest with you, I am relieved the Redwoods did not agree on my first option. Solarfleet only approached a couple of the Alluran governors, the ones they deem reliable. The non-corrupt type. We are weary of what the news of Earth will spark back home, especially among those who would jump at reclaiming this world as their own. This way, Earth can remain a secret."

To be fair, I hadn't even considered that. Even though Allura was a humble world, there were plenty of opportunists and organisations that would jump at breaking the Alluran net and claim a part of Earth as their own.

"Every Solarfleet personnel who has joined this mission has had to sign a disclaimer to never speak of this place. The pilots, additionally, to never uncover its location. Unfortunately, plausible deniability is not an option when you require so much manpower."

"So, you were always going to opt for the Redwood's plan?"

"I would've preferred the relocation option, but I can understand their objections. Liberation is far more appealing. My only reservation is the complexity of the task at hand. And it is a major task. Solarfleet are not a charity. They will want something in return for this."

"What do you suppose that will be?"

"I don't know. I only hope it doesn't make them the corrupt ones."

She took in another eyeful of the sight surrounding us. "Dr Chang has advised that a case of inoculations is ready, so my crew can be immunised this afternoon. Following which, we will need a few days in quarantine. I will be in touch. In the meantime, continue to meet with the council. If this alliance is going to be successful, I need to know every last detail."

"Of course."

Prompting my salute, she nodded, and strode away towards the east cliff ladder.

Glancing back at the village, a sense of worry hovered over me. Why did everything have to involve politics? This could get extremely messy. Rooke was so much better at this than I was.

I needed to get back to him, but movement on the bridge towards the Pasa caught my eye. Valina and Blake were talking to one another, radiating a sense of hushed urgency. My mind flicked back to Valina's flustered reaction earlier. Whatever it was, it didn't sit right with me.

I did need to get back to Rooke, but first, there was something I wanted to check out.

Chapter Thirty-Four

Remaining a good distance from Valina and Blake, I scurried to the Pasa. As usual, the main entrance was busy, but through the crowd I could make out Valina's blonde hair glistening in the unnatural white light.

Their pace was fast, prompting my suspicion. Walking as quickly as my injured leg would allow, I kept my eyes trained on Valina. Continuing straight for several minutes, they turned left, into a corridor I'd never seen before. Here, it seemed quieter. Only a couple of Redwoods, wearing engineering overalls, loitered. I stopped walking, glancing about, noting Valina and Blake had passed through a set of double doors at the far end. Not wanting to lose sight of them, I followed.

On the other side of the double doors, the corridor split into a T-intersection. To the right, was another long, empty corridor. To the left, were metallic, slatted stairs. They must've gone up there.

Cautiously, I climbed the steps, grimacing at the pressure it was putting on my leg. At the top, and twenty metres along a dimly lit corridor, I caught a glimpse of Valina standing in a bright room, just before a door slid shut, obscuring her from view. The door was guarded, but I recognised both guards.

With his leg strapped into a leather brace, Yohan stood chatting with Guz. Taking a deep breath, I casually approached them. "Hey, you two. Didn't expect to see you here."

They both eyed me. Yohan looked a little taken aback, while Guz's face froze with an unsoundly awkwardness.

"Eden," Guz cleared his throat, "how are you?"

Rubbing my lips together, I nodded, glancing about the otherwise deserted area. "Good, thanks. Um, I need to speak to Valina."

Guz's stance stiffened, puffing his large chest out a little. "She'll…she'll be out soon."

"Could you, um, let me through? Saves me standing about." I gestured to my injured leg.

"I can't do that, Eden."

"Really?"

"Yes, sorry."

"Why?"

"Authorised personnel only."

The door button beside him had a keypad and digital scanner. That was no normal access button. I searched his perturbed face, then Yohan's. I admired their loyalty, but the more they denied me access, the more I needed to find out what was hidden behind that door.

"You need to let me through."

"I can't. I'm sorry."

Flicking my eyes back to Guz, I remained calm. "If you don't let me through this door, you'll leave me no choice. I'll be forced to contact the Solarfleet ship; the one that arrived not so long ago. And tell them not to cooperate with your people, as it appears you are keeping vital information from me. Do you really want to be the one who stands in the way of your people's liberation?"

I watched Guz's face fall. "You wouldn't," he questioned, but he already could tell by my defiant expression I wasn't lying. I could easily do it. I could collect my things and leave, along with the remaining Orka crew. We could be heading back to Allura within the next hour. The thought was tempting.

Shuffling on his feet, he exchanged a panicked look with Yohan.

"Let me through, Guz!" My glare shot firebolts at him, and he gulped back his words of rejection. He continued to throw me a strong, yet wavering glare. In the next breath, he flinched, reaching for Yohan's hand. But it was too late. Yohan had activated the keypad, and the door was slowly hissing open.

"I'm not risking it," Yohan mumbled.

Shielding my eyes from the blinding light streaming through the opening door, I heard Guz swear under his breath. Yohan slumped against the wall, whilst I nodded my thanks.

A rush of cold air hit my face as I entered the enormous room, and I clenched my teeth at the sight that met me.

The high-ceilinged room was lined with computer command desks. Each wall was coated with rectangular, digital screens stacked four high, six wide. But it was the non-static images being displayed on those screens that rooted my anger. To the left and directly in front, multiple screens were filled with images of Earth from different locations in orbit. I saw parts of The Orka fill a couple of them, as well as live footage of General Murai's atmospheric ship redocking with The Hector.

To my right, were moving images of deep space. These images must've been transmitted from probes moving ridiculously fast somewhere out in the abyss.

When my eyes fell upon the two screens in the top right corner, hesitation struck. As I took in the images being displayed, I felt my jaw tighten even further. They were images of a gold and orange world, one in which was more than familiar. I'd viewed it numerous times from space myself—Allura.

My eyes flicked to Valina and Blake standing over the only operative in the room. With their faces turned to the screens before them, they hadn't noticed my presence. I watched Blake point to several screens, telling the operative which satellites to move, and my fists clenched, painfully embedding my nails into my skin.

They'd lied to us. From the moment Rooke and I had first met with them, they'd lied. They'd told us the Hybrids had stolen their satellite module, that the Hybrids had sent the probe that lured the scouting ship here. Judging by what I was seeing, that was utter bullshit. Had they been spying on Allura this whole time?

Peering up at the images of my home world, I questioned if they were static photos or delayed live footage. And that's when I heard Valina's gasp from the corner. I snapped my eyes towards her, fixing my glare on her paling features.

"How…" she stammered, glancing at the closed door behind me, "how did you…."

Ignoring her half question, I continued to shoot daggers. Perfect Valina, the embodiment of a young, genteel oracle. She was no better than the majority of mankind; selfish, deceptive, fake.

"It was you who sent the probe." My voice was calm, yet full of bite.

Valina's face paled even further, and Blake shot his head round, taking in the unexpected sight of me.

"It's not what it looks like." Valina took a step closer, her hands gesturing with grave caution.

"And what does it look like?" I growled, flicking my eyes between the two of them as they exchanged a troubled glance. "How long have you been watching Allura? How many times have you attempted to ensnare one of our ships? It was you who sent the probe that lured The Challenger here, not the Hybrids. It was you who forced the ship down to the ground, destroying it, leaving the crew to die!"

"We didn't intend for that to happen. It was an accident."

"What else have you lied to us about?" I searched their faces. They were pissing themselves with fear. "Did you...was the jamming signal you?" They remained silent, confirming my suspicion. "What about the hologram surrounding the Parvos?"

"Please, Eden..."

"Was that you, as well?"

"We were desperate for your help."

"And all this time, I've defended your integrity."

Valina looked as though she was on the brink of tears, her eyes pleading with mine. "It was the only way we could get your attention."

"You lied! You outright lied! Rooke was right not to trust you."

I turned to leave, but Valina's hurried footsteps sounded behind me. I felt her fingers pull on mine. Repulsed by her touch, I snatched my hand back. Glaring at her, all I could see was red. Every sense, every feeling was coloured by anger; I was ready to explode.

As if Valina could sense it, she took a step back. The look in her eyes a mixture of despair and defeat. "Please." Her eyes watered. "Please don't withdraw your people's help. We need you. Yes...yes, we withheld information, but we never intended to deceive you."

"Deception is one thing." I pointed to the images of Allura. "A master plan put into play is another."

"What choice did we have?" Valina quickly wiped a tear from her cheek. "We were abandoned, left here to die. This civilisation has barely survived by the skin of its teeth. If we had confessed everything to you, would you really have cooperated?"

"How fickle do you think we are?"

She remained silent. Her eyes wide, expecting me to sever the already fragile bonds of our coalition. "Please, we can't do this alone."

"And you won't," I snarled, glancing between her and Blake. He was still frozen by the computer panels. The operative beside him was watching the conversation unfold with as much despair as his leaders. "Luckily for you, I have formed attachments here. People who I have come to love. For them, I will not walk away. For them, I will ensure Solarfleet fight for your people's justice. But don't. *Ever.* Think I am doing this for you."

Leaving them in stunned silence, I left the room with an abruptness that could've shattered worlds. So much so, Guz and Yohan cowered as I passed them in the corridor.

I couldn't think straight. I felt like a naive idiot. How many times had they smirked and schemed behind our backs? Yes, they needed our help, but what breadcrumbs had they strategically placed, waiting for us to discover them, manipulating our decisions for their benefit? What else had I not realised?

As I neared the bottom of the stairs, the double doors to the right opened. Stunting my descent, Truro appeared before me. His eyes widened, taking me in, then the direction in which I'd appeared from.

My heart sank as I read the regret and worry in his eyes. There was no disguising it. No matter how remorseful he looked, it didn't erase the fact he'd lied to me as well. Of course, he'd lied. He was one of them. But I never thought it was possible. I thought I knew him; I trusted him. It was another example of how gullible I'd been.

With his eyes caught in my hardened glare, I descended the final steps. His worry amplified and he went to block my path.

"Don't!" I felt so angry, I wanted to lash out at him. "I have nothing to say to you." I slipped through the gap between his body and the doorjamb, my heart and soul ripping to shreds as I hobbled away. I struggled to breathe. It felt like someone was standing on my chest.

It didn't overly surprise me that Valina and Blake had lied. There'd always been something suspicious about them. But

Truro…Truro had become more than a friend. I trusted him. I had trusted him with my life.

I could feel the anger being replaced with anguish as a well of tears threatened to burst. He'd sworn he'd never lie to me. He promised everything between us had been real. I was starting to doubt it all now.

Nux, I needed Rooke. I needed Zamya. The painstaking thoughts fractured the well and a cascade of tears silently flowed down my cheeks. With my head down, I scurried to Rooke's medical room.

I couldn't suppress the sob when I found the door open, Rooke's room empty, his bed stripped and bare. My mind erratically jumped to the conclusion he was dead. He'd died and I hadn't been here with him. The thought made my chest pulsate and spasm. I couldn't breathe.

Through the sounds of my sobs, Oz's voice echoed behind, "Oh Eden." His footfalls stepped closer, then arms were pulling me into a solid chest. "They took him up to The Hector. He'll get better treatment there. He'll be alright. I'm sure he'll be alright."

For several minutes Oz held me as I wept.

Chapter Thirty—Five

I sat at Rooke's desk, twiddling his mini Nux figurine between my fingers. I'd found it on his bedside table attached to a neck chain. For some reason, I presumed he'd left it on The Orka's bridge. He must've carried it with him the whole time we'd been on Earth.

It had been three days since Solarfleet arrived, and I'd received no further communication with General Murai. Troy, too, had become noncontactable. Not knowing if Rooke's condition had worsened or improved was killing me. For all I knew, he was dead.

Unable to remove Rooke's unconscious face from my mind, I envisaged the grey tinge to his skin, the balmy feel against my hand. A part of me couldn't accept he was dying. I'd always imagined I'd see him grow old and grey. I would witness him turning into a cranky old man who I could poke fun at.

I smiled at the thought, my mind skipping to the ways he used to inappropriately banter with me, and that devilish smile of his. I didn't think I could ever forget that smile and the way his eyes sparkled down at me. Those dark green eyes full of mesmerising wonder. Had he looked at everyone the way he looked at me?

The question of whether he loved me struck a wavering chord deep within. Oz was adamant he did, Zamya had always suggested it without confirming as such. Had I been so absorbed in shielding my love from him, I'd deflected his?

My mind flicked to memories of the Akquarian ball, to his lips brushing mine as if asking permission to kiss me. I thought of his hesitation when I'd asked him to the lake, then how he'd seemed uncertain when he'd suggested we sneak away at the new moon celebration so many months ago. That wasn't Rooke. He was confident, nothing fazed him. Had I made him nervous? Because of the way he felt about me—about us?

I'd hurt him by sleeping with Truro. But I'd thought he was playing around with Valina and, then, Ayelle. I'd always assumed I was less than second best, that I wasn't what he wanted. I'd tried to convince myself of that so many times, in the hope I could move on. Had I been completely and utterly wrong?

Glancing at the wall next to the open doorway, I recalled him kissing my neck while I stood there a few weeks back, blubbering uncontrollably. I could've sworn he'd wanted to kiss my lips. I was certain he was going to if it hadn't been for Valina's interruption. Nux, things could've been so different. And now I was afraid I was too late, that I'd lost him forever.

Looking down at the Nux figurine again, I wondered what Rooke would've done if he'd discovered the Redwood's master plan; that Allura had always been a part of it? I wasn't sure if I should tell General Murai. What good would it do?

A knock on the open door had my eyes flicking in its direction. A reluctant breath caught in my throat, registering the brown armour.

"Can I come in?" Truro's voice was a gentle rumble, his blue eyes full of uncertainty.

I hadn't seen him since I found the satellite control centre. I'd sent Oz to the council meeting yesterday. Everything still felt too raw for me to endure being in the same room as the Redwood leaders.

Truro remained in the doorway, waiting patiently. Eventually, I nodded, and he stepped inside, coming to a halt on the opposite side of the desk. Still fixated on the Nux figurine, I noticed Truro bob down, placing his arms flush along the desktop.

"You're mad at me," he said. I remained silent, still not meeting his eye. "I understand. I would be too." He exhaled, deeply. "There's been unrest within the council for a while. Well, since the ship before you arrived. From the start, Valina and Blake were adamant to keep the bigger picture away from your knowledge. In case it altered your opinion of us and our situation."

"Because it makes you out to be the antagonists in this damn horror story?"

I felt Truro's eyes on me. I could sense the frown forming. "Is that how you see us now?" he asked.

"A lot of my people are dead because of your people's indirect actions." I shook my head. "All the lies make me feel like an idiot."

"You're not an idiot." He reached for my hand, catching it awkwardly. I stared at our connection, at his warm, calloused touch that I still felt uncontrollably drawn towards. I *was* an idiot, for believing them, for always defending them. Did I really know Truro at all?

Still clutching my hand, he stood up and walked around the desk. Squatting down beside me, he said, "For some reason, Ferrol and Elgin follow Blake's lead these days. Quinn sits on the fence. Nya and I wanted to be up front with Rooke. We wanted to tell him everything. Unfortunately, the majority voted against that."

"You could've told me in confidence."

"I couldn't. It goes against everything the council stands for. I've sworn an oath to protect this village. It doesn't mean I always agree with what is implemented. If I am unhappy with the decisions made, I voice my opinion, but the majority vote always wins."

"Politics," I mumbled.

"I hate it too." He looked down at our entwined fingers. "You underestimate how grateful we are to you. For your sacrifice." His voice softened further. "How's Rooke?"

"I haven't heard anything."

"I'm sorry. I know how much he means to you. Eden, I…I want you to know, I won't stand in your way…"

"He's dying, Truro. I doubt I'll ever see him again." The thought unleashed a single teardrop. I wiped it away quickly.

"I'm just saying…"

"I don't want to talk about it."

"Okay." He released my hand and stood up. "A council meeting has been called. It starts in an hour. I believe General Murai will be attending. Your presence is desired."

I nodded. "I'll be there."

His gaze lingered a little too long, and my shoulders finally relaxed when he left, prompting another wave of sorrow. I never thought I'd feel that way about Truro. He had become my comfort zone, my safety net. Now…I was confused about how I felt about him.

Voices outside caught my attention, and I glanced at the doorway as a large, familiar figure emerged. The smile across Oz's face was wide and infectious.

"Guess who I found loitering about?" he said.

Another figure stepped into the hut behind him, and my eyes lit up.

"Troy!" I rushed around the desk, literally jumping into his arms. Squeezing him tightly, he tapped me on the shoulder. Sensing his awkwardness, I laughed and stepped back. "Sorry, it's just…it's so nice to see you. Nux, you look pale."

He laughed, but his young face looked hauntingly tired. Even his smile didn't brighten the gaunt planes. "Eleven months in space tends to do that to you. I must look like a ghost compared to Oz. Look at him, all sun kissed and glowing."

I frowned at Troy. He was skin and bone, his clothes hung off his shoulders like they were on a coat hanger. I couldn't imagine the trauma he'd been through, coping with Cora's death alone. "Are you okay? I've tried to contact you over the past couple of days…"

"The Orka's been commandeered by Solarfleet. Hence why I opted to come down to get some fresh air. I swear the gravity here is heavier than that on Allura."

"It's not noticeable." I eyed him, concerned his smile was forced.

"Eden, stop looking at me like that. I know I look a state, but I promise, I'm fine."

I glanced down at myself. I hadn't washed for three days. Oz, too, didn't smell inviting. His leathers had probably moulded into a second skin. "We don't exactly look great, either."

Oz chuckled. "Speak for yourself."

Rolling my eyes, I stepped forward and hugged Troy again. I'd missed him. Nux, I'd missed them all.

"If you need a decent shower," Troy said, "Solarfleet have a huge atmospheric ship which arrived on the second interstellar called The Indigos. I'm told it will remain on the clifftop. There are showers onboard, and plenty of sleeping quarters, if you'd prefer to sleep there."

"Good to know," Oz said, sniffing himself.

I laughed at him. "I think I'll stay here for now, but thanks for the heads up. Actually, I'm glad you're both here. I need to ask your advice."

They both looked at me eagerly. I took a deep breath and told them about discovering the Redwood satellite command centre, plus Valina's reaction. "It seems the jamming signal and the hologram surrounding the Parvos were also their doing."

Oz stared at me. Troy's nostrils flared, his arms crossing over his body defensively. I frowned, glancing between them. "I get the impression neither of you find this a shock."

They exchanged a cautious look, sending my mind into a spiral of thoughts.

"We already knew," Troy said gingerly.

Surprise struck me with pause. "Rooke knew?"

"About the signals, yeah. When the interstellar signal stopped, it blipped and lingered in one area for several seconds before disappearing. That area was here. To be exact, it was where the Pasa is embedded under the mountain."

"It's one of the reasons Rooke was so wary of the Redwoods," Oz said. "It was why he was adamant we find the Parvos, in the hope it would be repairable. His objective was to get us off this planet as soon as possible."

In amongst Rooke's irrational anger, there had been a logical reason behind his actions. He never stopped protecting us. Never ceased to find a way off this planet to get us home. I closed my eyes trying to blot out the pain in my head. "Why didn't he tell me?"

"Rooke was concerned you may confront Truro about it, which could've rocked the boat." Troy shrugged. "Besides, you, Zamya, and Kobe were happy here. He wasn't going to admit anything to the Redwoods. You were all safe, and leaving the village wasn't an option."

"And we certainly weren't going to return to the Akquarians," Oz mumbled, pensively staring at the floor.

It was evident Rooke had become drained from the pressures of his responsibility. And I hadn't helped at all. I'd been a selfish bitch. Shit, I hated myself.

"Do I tell Murai?" I asked.

"That depends on whether you want to help these people or not," Troy said. "Murai will leave at the slightest notion."

I looked to Oz. He shrugged. "Other than Valina, I like most of the people here. I wouldn't be at peace with myself if we left without helping their cause in some way."

I nodded.

"There is," Oz cleared his throat, suddenly appearing uncomfortable in the way he stood against the hut wall, "there is the matter of Zamya. She could be alive."

Even though Zamya flashed through my mind several times a day, twisting my stomach into sickening knots of grief, I'd been so absorbed with Rooke, the Akquarians' demands, the council, and the arrival of Solarfleet, I hadn't considered what Oz was suggesting. "You want to try and rescue her?"

"The Redwoods know where the Hybrid lair is now. They have a plan to flush it out. To me, that means someone will have to go in."

Both Troy and I stared at him, unravelling his reasoning.

"I don't think I could live with myself if I didn't attempt to get her out. Jader, too, has voiced the same thoughts."

Freeing Zamya had never been an option, but perhaps it was possible. It had been over a week since she was snatched. It was going to take at least another three for the plan to be finalised and to wait for the Solarfleet reinforcements. Depending on what the Hybrids wanted from her, she could be dead by then.

"Let's see what battle plan is drawn up and take it from there." I looked down at the Nux figurine in my hand, asking it for an essence of courage and strength. "I have no intention of leaving Zamya behind, either."

Chapter Thirty—Six

Oz and I attended the council meeting. General Murai introduced me to the three Solarfleet commanders who accompanied her. Their names went over my head.

I listened as much as I could as they discussed strategies with the council. All seven council members were in attendance today. Truro and Elgin took centre stage, Valina avoided any eye contact with me, and Blake continued to be the demanding ass he'd always been.

Dozens of meetings followed over the next three weeks. Each one inching closer to finalising the invasion plan.

One of Solarfleet's smaller atmospheric ships had flown over the dam where the Hybrids resided, scanning the layout of the huge concrete structure, estimating their numbers. Photos and 3D images had been relayed and were displayed upon the circular table in the council chamber. I caught Oz's eye several times during that specific meeting, both understanding what we needed to do to achieve our own mission's objective.

The three additional interstellar ships, delivering over three hundred and fifty Solarfleet personnel, finally arrived. All aboard were inoculated and left in quarantine for three days. The numbers began to trickle down into the village during the week that followed.

As I walked through the village with Jader, I easily spotted the clusters of blue-grey uniforms milling about. Today, I was wearing a fresh uniform myself, with Rooke's Solarfleet jacket over the top. A stark contrast to Jader's black leathers.

"Are you certain you want to go ahead with the plan?" Jader asked in an undertone. "Especially when both our leaders have specified rescue attempts are not permitted. There could be dozens of women still alive. I don't understand why they can't see the necessity to try."

"I know. And yes, I'm certain."

"This is going to be highly dangerous."

I stopped at the bridge leading to the food hall and looked up at Jader. His towering form appeared weakened since Zamya's abduction. He was crumbling without her, drowning in the thought of her torment. Too involved with the communication between our two peoples, I'd neglected to see his suffering. I was barely coping with my own.

Word of Rooke had still failed to reach me. Whenever I asked Murai about him, she brushed the question off, claiming she did not have time to check in on injured individuals. To her, Rooke was a mere commander of a small scientific crew. He was just another name on a disclaimer list; another number floating in a sea of faceless employees.

She'd denied me permission to leave the ground to visit him; Troy, and Oz too. I was starting to get the impression she valued my opinion on the Redwood matters more than she let on. And keeping me away from any distressing news would benefit her.

With those thoughts creeping their way around my head, I'd come to the conclusion Rooke had died. Why else would I have not heard a single update? That, alone, gave me ammunition to continue with Zamya's rescue attempt. It was a worthy distraction.

But nevertheless, like Jader, I was crumbling beneath my visage. Without Rooke I was suffocating.

"The risks don't outweigh our reasoning," I said to Jader. "Besides, someone has to set the bombs."

"Let's hope we're not still inside when they go off."

Yeah, okay. It was risky.

A raucous of voices carried over to us from the Pasa's food hall. From where we stood, it looked as though shades of black, brown, and red were being engulfed by shades of grey and blue. The chorus of voices didn't sound joyous, they sounded more like a war cry.

Jader and I glanced at each other before rushing over the bridge. Fighting our way through a jeering mob of Solarfleet soldiers and Redwood warriors, I scarcely avoided a fist to my face. Jader pulled a Redwood off a Solarfleet member snarling on the floor, while another pair threw punches at each other.

Pushing a handful of onlookers out of the way, Jader tried to pull the pair apart. A Solarfleet soldier pounced on him, sending him flying into the mob. For a moment, I became engulfed by people. I felt small; incapable of resolving anything.

I could hear Pepa shouting over the voices, telling them to stop. For some reason, I felt responsible. I'd brought the Solarfleet soldiers here and it was inevitable they would clash with the Redwoods at some point.

Using my elbows and shoulders, I nudged bodies apart. I reached forward, grabbing the blue jacket of the man hitting Jader. With all my might, I pulled him back. The man staggered, ready to lash out at me, but hesitated when he took in my face. The crowd quietened and I registered Truro pulling the other pair apart.

"What the hell do you think you're doing?" I eyed the man before me, his comrades behind him. "You're supposed to be representing the Alluran people. I don't remember Allurans being complete dicks, or have things massively changed over the past year?"

I noted the sheepish looks around us as the man screwed his mouth up, averting his gaze. "My apologies, sir."

Sir? He was calling me sir? I wanted to laugh. I doubted I was any higher ranked than he was. Looking over the Alluran, I said, "If you don't like being around the Redwoods, don't come down here. Stay up on the frigging clifftop. You have everything you need up there."

"But the food down here tastes amazing."

I stepped closer. "These people go through hell assuring they have enough food to feed their village each day, let alone you. Show a little respect!"

He lowered his gaze again and nodded. "Yes, sir."

"Just…just go back to your food. And in future ignore or walk away from whatever this was." I didn't want to know. I'm sure it was nothing more than a petty misunderstanding.

I walked to Jader. He was on his feet next to Truro, rotating his jaw cautiously. The Redwoods had dispersed, the hum of gentle conversation returning to the hall.

"Are you okay?" I asked him.

"Yeah, I've been hit by larger men." He looked at Truro. The jape in his tone made my lips twitch, but my smile vanished immediately when Valina appeared, speaking with a hushed aggression. "This is why we could not accept Solarfleet's offer of sanctuary. The Allurans would never accept us."

"You don't have to be so disrespectful, Valina," Truro said.

"But still. This," she gestured around us, "does not work."

My skin crawled with rage. My tolerance for her was dwindling by the day. It didn't matter that I agreed with her, it was the way in which she voiced it that pissed me off.

I huffed loudly. "It's a good job you've got what you wanted then, isn't it?" I still felt as though she didn't appreciate what Solarfleet were offering. It was as if she expected it, as if it was our duty. Did she not know we could leave at any moment?

I stalked off, making my way to the large atmospheric ship on the clifftop. Lunch could wait. I wanted a shower and some peace.

Even though I still slept at the crew hut, I showered on The Indigos every day. The crew's locker room held twenty shower cubicles, all tiled, with sturdy, lockable doors. The water was hot, and the pressure was good. If I closed my eyes, I could envisage being back at home.

The hot water flowed over my body, easing my tender muscles. The wound on my wrist had healed, leaving a hideous bite mark. My leg was scarred and occasionally the muscle weakened when I caught my balance wrong. But that was the least of my concerns.

Valina concerned me. Blake too. Was there anything else they were hiding? I prayed Truro would inform me of any other misgivings or surprises, but could I truly trust him?

Whatever the Redwoods end goal was, the objective of the battle plan was to exterminate the Hybrids, then cull the Igknamai numbers. But anxiety fizzled through my veins at the thought of what I was tasked to do during that battle. One of us needed to find Zamya, but the more I thought about it, the more I realised how hazardous the mission was. Swaying from the details of the actual plan could jeopardise others. But if the shoe was on the other foot, I knew Zamya would try for me. I knew Rooke would, for both of us. He'd sacrifice anything for each and every one of his crew.

The thought sent a surge of pain through my chest. Was he alive? Could no news mean good news? Or was Murai keeping his death from me to ensure I kept my mind on the task at hand?

Staring at the water droplets racing down the tiled wall, I recalled Rooke's smiling face. Remembering how he always drove me home after we returned from work assignments, always invited me out to hang with his friends, always turned up at my front door on Saturday mornings, regardless of if he had a girlfriend or not. He always stayed with me until early afternoon, just chatting, being the friend I needed. He sensed my struggle with being alone. It allowed me too much time to think about my mum, and he knew I blamed myself for her death.

Rooke had always been my protector. I don't think I fully realised the extent of that protection until now. Now that he wasn't here.

Voices in the locker room startled me and I turned the water off. After pulling my hair up into a tight bun, I wrapped myself in a large towel. A faint citrusy smell wafted around me, bringing forward so many memories. I opened the shower door and for a surreal moment, I thought I was dreaming.

The white lights along the long, slim room created a tranquil aura, a dreamlike state of mind. And there, sitting on the bench before me, dressed in Solarfleet uniform, with his head hung to the floor, was Rooke.

Frozen to the spot, I couldn't breathe, dubious as to whether what I was seeing was real. But he looked up. His face pale, but there was no grey tinge. The stubble around his jaw had returned, his hair cut shorter—smarter. And his smell…I could smell his citrusy scent.

His dark eyes flashed as they glimpsed my towel exposing my bare legs and feet. Slowly, he stood, trapping me in his gaze.

I swallowed back a sob of relief, blinking rapidly in the attempt to prove I wasn't hallucinating. But he just stood there, with his hands in his pockets, looking at me as if his mind was ticking over a lifetime of questions.

"Rooke?" I took one cautious step forward, and in a blur of movement, Rooke walked over, cupped my face, and placed his lips assertively on mine.

I whimpered as he pulled me tenderly close. His soft kiss was slow, deep, full of meaning, sending my body and mind into a vortex of emotions. I was like putty in his hands, moulding against him, responding to his touch, focusing on his kiss. It remained soft; sensual. He made me feel treasured and respected. He made me feel loved.

My feet were moving, being guided by his, and I felt the coldness of the lockers against my bare shoulders. I tried to break our kiss, wanting to see his face, hear his voice, but he pinned me with his mouth, his tongue, his body. I smiled, pushing at his chest. "Woah, tiger. Talk to me."

"I am talking to you," he rasped, tracing his lips along mine. "We should've been talking like this years ago."

Stunned by his words, I allowed him to reclaim my mouth, enticing my body with his. It was me who intensified the kiss now, swimming in the realisation he actually wanted me.

The exchange of heavy breaths and pleasurable groans were the only sounds I could hear above the pounding of my heart. I almost growled as Rooke stepped back, leaving me panting with lust-filled eyes.

A rakish gleam expelled from his gaze, a hint of a smirk to match. Fixing me in place with those mesmerising eyes, he reached forward and gave my towel a tug. To my despair it fell away far too easily. I grabbed for it, but Rooke whipped it away, throwing it behind him. My mind screamed with worry. I was standing there, butt naked. Anyone could walk in. But with his eyes raking my body, I felt my breath hitch. He was drinking in the sight of me with approval.

He stepped closer, placing his hands against the lockers either side of my head. "Turn around," his voice rumbled.

Taken aback, I gave him a quizzical look. "I haven't seen you in weeks. I thought you were dead, and the first thing you ask me to do is turn around?"

He smiled. "Turn around."

"Rooke, I'm naked."

His eyes lowered. "Yeah, you are." He flicked them back up to my face. The smirk across his lips was devilish, flooding my body with desire.

Placing one hand on my hip, he directed me round to face the wall of lockers behind me. He met no resistance. Intrigue and arousal had gotten the better of me.

The fabric of his clothes felt warm as he placed his body flush against my back. His arms slid around my waist, across my stomach, over my hips. He kissed the side of my neck, flicking his tongue in that sensitive spot below my earlobe. He was driving me wild.

"I've had a lot of time to think," his voice was a deep rumble, "lying in bed, circling this world over and over again. And those thoughts have been consumed with you." His thumb brushed the underside of my breast. Stifling a groan, my back arched in response. "I've been a complete bastard to you…"

"No." The word was barely a whisper, too aware of his hands roaming my abdomen, his body pushed against my back.

Placing another kiss on my neck, he said, "I have. I've denied you so much. Too much, for reasons I don't understand myself." His mouth hovered directly over my ear as he whispered, "I owe you."

His hand moved lower, and I gasped as his finger trailed through the curls at the apex of my legs, pushing down on the spot buried beneath. I grabbed his wrist, but I didn't pull his hand away. The pleasure was already building as his fingers delicately curled and circled.

"Your actions at the Akquarian ball baffled me." His soft rumble was against my ear, his breath flowing across my bare chest as his fingers teased. "I thought you were drunk. I pushed you away because of that. And I've regretted it ever since. If I'd known you felt the same as I do, I would've taken you on that balcony ledge. I would've pleasured you with my fingers, my tongue, my cock. I would've made love to you all night."

I whimpered at the thought, at his hot, delectable touch currently turning me to jelly.

"You looked exquisite that night. I couldn't take my eyes off you. I couldn't contain myself when you started flirting with me, and once we were alone, once I'd gotten you away from the rest of those arseholes, I needed to feel you against me. And for a moment, I didn't care about the consequences. And you…you kissed me back. Shit, Eden, you did things to me with that kiss. You drove me crazy. You had always played on my mind, but since that night, since I pushed you away, I've wanted you more."

His strokes between my legs became longer, fiercer, and I melted into him, aware his own arousal was pressing against the groove of my buttocks. I couldn't stifle the moan building in my throat. His fingers, his words…they were…*Oh Nux.*

"The number of times I'd been tempted to test the boundaries with you. But I didn't. Instead, I've watched you date guys I hated…holding my tongue. I wanted to tell them to fuck off, that you were mine." His fingers deepened, nearing my entrance, and I felt myself grinding against their rhythm, enticing them closer to where I wanted them. "I've hated seeing you with other men. It's been easier over the past couple of years. You haven't dated anyone, and I've wondered, I've always wondered why. Wondering if I had a chance. But I kept you away, placing a barrier between us using all the women I dated."

"I hated all of them," I whispered.

He chuckled. "They never came close to how I feel for you. Not one." He nibbled my earlobe before deepening his voice further, sending an avalanche of desire through my core, down to where his fingers were now pushing inside of me. "After the words you last said to me, about wanting more, I realised how blind I've been. I guess, a tiny part of me has always known, yet I was too scared to break down those final barriers. But believe me when I say, I want you to be mine. I want to be the one you come home to everyday. I want to be the one you think of when you're dripping wet with excitement, just like you are now." He cursed, nuzzling at my ear. "You feel amazing. Nux. I want this. I want more, and you're right. We can't go back to how it was, 'cos, Nux, my darling, Eden, I can't live without you. And I'm sorry I've never told you, but I was…I've been petrified to admit it. But not now. No longer will I be the one who keeps us apart."

My body tingled as I turned my face to his. Through the torturous pleasure heightening below, his words reached my soul, making me finally believe every word. I understood every action he'd previously made, from seeking me out to be his pilot, to his reaction towards Truro.

I reached behind his neck, pulling his face closer, and his lips met mine. His tongue flicked in sync with his fingers, sending me so close to the obliterating edge. But he stopped, swiftly turning me to face him.

"Please. Don't stop." But before I could regain my breath, he reclaimed my mouth, driving his fingers deep inside of me again. My groans were loud, uncontrollable.

"I'm sorry I've made you wait."

I wanted to laugh, he sure as hell was making up for it.

Arching into him, I threw my head back against the metal lockers. Then, I felt him move. His breath was now against my wetness below, the warmth of his tongue flicking the swollen, sensitive nub between my legs. My hand instinctively found his hair, dragging my fingers through the short, thick strands. His fingers groped the flesh of my buttocks pulling me closer, and I felt his own moan of desire.

Glancing down at him, our eyes locked. His dark eyes; those eyes that had driven me crazy for years, were now speaking to me with a depth full of lust and love and passion, touching parts of my soul only his name was imprinted on.

He moaned again, and my whole body shattered, rupturing the seams of reality.

My legs began to buckle as I swam the sea of ecstasy, my prolonged pleasure bouncing off the walls around us. I would've slumped to the ground if it wasn't for Rooke's sturdy hands holding me upright.

He straightened us both, that rakish smile still dancing across his face. Nux, he was so devilishly handsome. He was pure temptation.

My cheeks flamed as he leaned in and said, "Well, that was hot." He kissed the tip of my nose and I reached for his belt, wanting to pleasure him, to feel him closer. Catching my hand, he clicked his tongue. "No, no, not now, my little nymph."

"Why," my voice was a gruff pant, "why not?"

"Because," he kissed my nose again, "you need to get dressed."

I watched him turn and pick up the towel. Handing it to me, his eyes sparkled with triumph. Clutching it to my chest, Rooke chuckled again, glancing at my poor attempt at covering my body.

"An urgent meeting has been called." He began to saunter to the door. "Everyone is waiting for you."

"What?" I glared at him as he turned. "They're waiting, like, now?"

"Yep."

"Why did you…why didn't you…"

"I couldn't pass up such a perfect opportunity." His smile both annoyed and teased me.

"Rooke Maddox! If I had more than a towel in my hands right now, I would throw something at you. Preferably something hard."

He laughed before reaching for the door panel. "Chop, chop."

Chapter Thirty—Seven

My legs were still tingling as I hurried to the council chamber. Holy souls, Rooke knew how to tease and pleasure. I hadn't cared I was naked in a public locker room. I'd lost myself under his tantalising touch. The thought of him filled my body and mind with more desire. Nux, I was in a lot of trouble if this was how our relationship was going to continue…and that brought a smile to my face. Rooke wanted me. He wanted me as his friend, his lover, his someone special. I was walking on air.

Entering the council chamber, I froze. The usual culprits were there, but a quarter of the benches circling the room were also occupied by, what appeared to be, Redwood and Solarfleet team leaders. All eyes turned to me, and I gulped.

"Riley," General Murai's voice echoed about the room, "nice of you to join us." I did not miss the scornful tone.

"My apologies, sir." I cleared my throat. "I got a little," my eyes flicked to Rooke seated in the front row of benches behind Valina. He smirked, and my cheeks coloured, "…held up."

Murai hummed her disapproval, and I quickly took my usual spot around the centre table. My eyes shot to Rooke again. He was smiling at me, but no longer with tease. His expression was full of admiration and pride.

A light from the centre table drew my attention back to the meeting. An enormous 3D image of a curving dam, with a square, concrete building at the far end, and a smaller one at the base, illuminated the area. It was Blake who spoke loud enough to address the whole congregation. "Due to unexpected Hybrid activity, we have brought the attack forward. We advance tomorrow."

There was an avalanche of whispers around the auditorium, questioning the sudden change.

"What Hybrid activity?" Oz asked from beside me.

Blake flicked his eyes to him. "Over the past couple of days, the surveillance ship picked up an area of the dam that's being modified. We believe they are building some kind of anti-aircraft weapon."

"With the number of aircrafts flying overhead recently," Murai said, "it's not a shock. It means, however, there's been a change to the plan, as well as the change of date. We can't risk any aircraft flying within a mile of the perimeter. It interferes specifically with the drop off point of the bomb team." She looked at me.

Landing my eyes on Kobe, he said, "Eden, your team will no longer advance from the base of the dam. You will be dropped here instead." He pointed to the illuminated image as it was zoomed out, indicating to an opening of trees two miles from the dam.

I nodded in understanding.

"The only issue is your route towards the dam is now lined with Igknamai nests." He pointed to a long cluster of mounds in the earth. "You will have enough MP bombs to prevent the Igknamai from effectively attacking."

"How many are there?"

He held my gaze before tentatively saying, "Just this stretch. At least a hundred, maybe two."

I swallowed back the incertitude nagging at me.

"We are going in at noon," Blake cut in, "in the hope they will be inactive. The weather is forecasted to be fairly warm for this time of year. It should deter them."

"I doubt that," Truro snapped, exchanging a strenuous glance with Blake. "They were active in thirty-six-degree heat during the summer. Twenty-four is not going to deter them."

"The main army," Murai said, "will be causing a distraction around the lake and the upper side of the dam. This should draw away any lingering Igknamai in your path. The Hybrids, too, should be preoccupied with the main attack to notice your advance."

"Do we have any accurate idea of Hybrid numbers?" I asked.

"No." Blake pointed to the square building on the far side of the dam. "The fortress only has a small garrison. But we believe the majority reside underneath and within the dam. We are still uncertain if our scans have offered a reliable account."

"So, we're still walking in blind?"

"We do, however, estimate, from the size of the structure, there cannot be any more than four thousand."

I smiled down at the table, amused by his delusional naivety. "Thirty-six of us against four thousand."

"Don't think about the odds," Murai said. "You get in, you get out."

A voice called from the benches behind us, "Why haven't we just dropped bombs on the dam and been done with it all?"

Blake lifted his gaze to the man and said, "If it was that simple, we would've done it. The dam structure is too thick. The bombs need to be detonated from the inside to cause the detrimental effect we desire."

"Maybe I should take more men in." Truro's eyes were flicking between Murai and the image before us. I shook my head, aligning my thoughts with Murai's. "No," she said. "You and your men are needed on the battlefield. You'll need as many as possible."

"And where exactly will your men be?" Valina's voice pierced through the professional tone of the room. She'd been so quiet; I'd almost forgotten she was present. I glanced at her. Her eyes were wide, resting on Murai with an intense speculation.

Murai puffed out her chest with irritation. "My men are flying the ships, giving your men access. Two are entering the dam itself. The majority will be waiting at the rear, preventing any counterattack."

"If your ships have deployed enough MP bombs over the past week, there should not be a counterattack."

"Rule number one in combat; always cover your back!"

Valina tsked. "We need men on the field. I wouldn't be surprised if you're strategically placing your men at the rear so you can easily retreat at any moment."

"Is it not enough that my men have been surveying the whole area for you? Detonated and removed landmines to allow your men access to this unpermitted location. We've provided your people with the ammunition you have designed to defeat these monsters, provided you with gasmasks and guns. Dropped thousands of bombs to eradicate the imminent threat around this area. Is it not enough?"

"We *need* more men on the field!"

"And where exactly are *you* going to be when this battle takes place?"

Valina sucked in a breath, quieting her voice. "I will be here, in the village, attending to the children and those who are too weak to fight."

"So, you are not joining the attack?"

The plea in Valina's eye, aimed at Blake, was ignored. She lifted her chin an inch higher and said, "I'm not a physical fighter. I'm a diplomat."

Murai mumbled her response, loud enough for Valina to hear, "And a bad one at that."

I tried not to smirk, aware of the tension building within the room. Valina looked denounced, and I shifted my eyes to Rooke behind her, intending to exchange a roll of the eyes. But his gaze was not light. There was a hard heaviness behind his eyes accompanying a frown, openly displaying his concern. He'd realised what part I was playing in this battle. And he no longer had any power to do anything about it.

My eyes dropped to the table before me. A sense of guilt and apprehension flooded my body. I'd only just got him back, and I could die tomorrow.

Chapter Thirty-Eight

Once the extent of the battle plan was delivered, the meeting concluded. After a final word with Murai, I exited the council chamber, nerves holding my mind prisoner as I contemplated tomorrow's outcome. But I saw Rooke standing on the platform outside, hands in his pockets. He tried to smile as I approached, but it was distorted by the frown.

"Please don't look at me like that?" I said.

"Why? Why bomb squad? You're a pilot for Nux sake."

I shook my head, and he reached for me, placing one hand on the small of my back, the other cupping my face.

"Eden, it's suicide."

"I know." I closed my eyes, taking in a lungful of his comforting scent. "I offered when…when I didn't have anything left to live for." I felt his thumb stroke my cheek. "They wouldn't tell me anything about your condition. I assumed…I thought you were dead." Looking up into his dark eyes, I glimpsed a slither of silver.

"I understand," he whispered. "I would've done the same."

I stared at him, looking through the green into the depths of his soul. It could've easily been a reflection of my own. We were two sides of the same coin, completely useless without the other. We were a team, a duo. We always had been.

Glancing down at his T-shirt, I gestured to his hidden wound. "How is it?"

Rooke placed his palm over the area. "It's healed, to a point. The infection took its toll. I'm not as strong as I used to be."

My eyes lingered on his hand. Sensing my worry, he took mine and placed it over his chest. "I will get better. And for now, this," I felt his heart steadily beat below my palm, "this is strong. I'm not giving up."

I smiled at that, at the hope resounding in his tone, the love pooling in his eyes.

"Commander." It was Truro's voice that startled us both.

Pulling his eyes away from me, Rooke looked towards the chamber opening.

"Blake and Murai would like a word."

Rooke peered down at me. "We'll talk later."

He walked away, and I suddenly felt cold in the absence of his touch. He disappeared inside and, to my surprise, Truro didn't follow. He ambled towards me, surveying the village around us, before his eyes landed on my face. His smile was forced, yet his voice was genuinely warm. "Good to see Rooke's better."

"Yeah."

Truro loosed a deep breath and leant against the wooden railing. "If I'd been given the choice, I think I would've taken the sanctuary."

Somehow, I'd always thought that of him. "You're not happy with the battle plan."

Subtly, he shook his head. "Too many chiefs, or whatever the expression is. It doesn't matter how many times we go through it, I just...I can't see how it'll work. We don't know numbers. And if the Hybrids have guns, what else do they have?" He sighed again. "I get the impression General Murai wants to go home. And I don't blame her."

Reaching for his hand, I squeezed it. He was tired. Tired of this world, tired of listening to Valina and Blake, tired of fighting. How many times had I toyed with the idea of taking him back to Allura. Perhaps that was before I knew there was a future for Rooke and I, but still...I'd always wondered if he'd fit in.

"Whatever happens," I said, watching his eyes scan the village below us, "you will always be welcome in Torla."

He looked up at me, shock lining his brow. "You sure Rooke would be alright with that?"

"He'd have to be. You're my friend, Truro. You've helped me through a lot."

He smiled. "You were worth helping, among other things."

I chuckled, noticing Valina scurrying across the bridge behind Truro. "If the plan does succeed, your people will need you."

Following my gaze, he huffed. "Yeah, I don't doubt that." He glanced back at me. "Otherwise, I may have taken you up on your offer."

I spent the afternoon with Oz, Jader, and our bomb team. Over the past couple of weeks, Oz had taught the Redwoods how to shoot a laser gun. Today, we were trying to perfect their aim. Following that, we all had figured out how to carry multiple weapons, from bows, swords, and daggers, to guns, structural bombs, and bombs laced with Mother Promise poison. The uncertainty of how many enemies we would face was terrifying. We needed to be prepared.

Exiting the Pasa, the sun was low in the sky, blinding us with a strong orange light. A dark, ominous cloud was threatening to swallow the brightness, and a cool breeze circled.

"Do you think that's a good or bad omen?" Oz asked, nodding towards the conflicting sky.

"Didn't think you were the superstitious type," I said, eyeing Oz's large form next to me. It amazed me how he still opted to wear his leathers within the village, regardless of the offer of freshly cleaned Solarfleet uniform.

"After being stranded here for so long, I'm not sure what I believe. I'm worried when we get home, I won't be able to adjust to normality again. I don't think I know what normality is anymore."

He had a point. Allura was a completely different world to Earth, and Redwood life had become our constant. But after such a traumatic mission, would any of us cope with returning to the life we'd left?

The sound of Rooke's voice pulled me from my thoughts. He and Troy were striding towards us on the opposite side of the bridge. Both were dressed in black leather armour, and Rooke had his sword sheathed across his back.

My frown matched his as I crossed the bridge, closing the distance between us.

"Where have you been?" he asked, his voice slightly clipped.

Before I replied, I took in what he was wearing, worry suddenly consuming me. "Where are you going?"

"I'm going to get help."

"Help? You mean…you mean the Akquarians?"

He nodded. "Valina's right. They need more men, and I appear to be the only one available who has a chance of getting an audience with Havav." Stepping forward, he swallowed nervously. "With tomorrow looming, I wanted," he cupped my face, "I'd wanted to spend tonight with you." Shaking his head, a groan escaped him. "I promised myself if I ever told you how I feel, I'd take things slow. I didn't want to rush things with you. I wanted to…to do things properly. But I fear we've run out of time." He squeezed his eyes together. "Shit, Eden, you need to get off the bomb squad. I need you to…"

"It's too late, Rooke. The plan is set. And this…this is what I'm destined to do." I touched his face, aware his eyes were glistening with despair. "I now believe I'm the reason we're here, why Solarfleet are helping these people."

His face brightened, a smirk forming on his lips. "Starting to believe in yourself, are you?"

"I don't know about that. I still think all the prophecies are nonsense, but this is my calling. I have to do this. I have to lead this team."

"I can't lose you, Eden." His voice cracked on my name, tugging at my heart strings. "I know you're special. Perhaps that's why I never thought I was good enough for you, but…Shit, I can't…this can't be...I'm sorry I never told you before..."

"Hey, this is on me, too. Our friendship's been my rock, and I was afraid if I messed with the foundations, you'd back away. Because, what we…"

"What we have works."

I almost sobbed. "Yes. Exactly."

"But it didn't work, did it?" He chuckled softly, then shook his head. "Not really. Especially since we arrived here. Something…something inside of me snapped, it nearly broke me seeing you with Truro. I hate myself for making such a scene when I found out you'd slept with him, and I knew…I knew he made you happy. You needed him. And with Valina monopolising my time, we were drifting apart. That's why I got you pulled off the hunting team. It was selfish, but I needed you beside me again."

"I thought you liked Ayelle."

He chuckled again. "I did, kinda. She reminded me of you. But how many times did I tell you I prefer Alluran women. No one could ever replace you."

Shaking my head, I wanted to scream at my blindness. "I had no idea. I never imagined you'd return my affection."

He huffed a smile, gazing down at me with a doting warmth. "I loved you before you even saw me." The expression on my face made him smile widely. "Can you remember the night you went to that acid-rock concert in the Mossas Valley? You were underage. It was a couple of weeks after your seventeenth birthday."

I frowned at the memory. It had been one of my rebellious stunts, testing the boundaries with my mum, trying to fit in with a new set of friends.

"You'd lost contact with your friends, and you'd missed the last transport home. You called me because the alternative was to call your mum, and you knew she'd be angry." He smiled tenderly. "I'm pretty certain I fell for you the moment I saw you staggering across that field, drunk as a fart, dressed in fishnet tights, builder's boots, and a cute denim dress. And you had this luminous gel in your hair. I'll never forget the way you smiled at me, how you were overly thankful for the rescue. You didn't stop talking all the way home, and from that day, I no longer looked at you as Jacob's little sister. You were Eden. I was no longer protecting you as a promise to my dear friend. I was protecting you because you meant everything to me."

"But…that was…"

"Nine years ago." He smiled. "And I've fallen more and more in love with you as the years have gone by."

His words caused my heart to swell, my eyes to dampen. Nux, how was that possible? I'd been an awkward teenager with a strained relationship with my mum, trying to fit into my adult body and act cool. And he'd noticed me. Even back then when I felt so lost.

"I love you, Eden Riley."

I grabbed his neck and pulled his face to mine. Through sobering breaths, I whispered, "I love you, Rooke. Nux, I love you beyond the fabrics of this universe and the next."

His lips took mine and he kissed me with such an intensity, I thought I might implode. Pulling him closer, I could feel his heart speaking to mine, my soul touching his. Regardless of what tomorrow would bring, I finally understood that I was his and he was mine, and nothing, *nothing*, in this whole, entire universe could break us apart. He was my forever.

There were tears in my eyes when he pulled a fraction away and whispered, "Come back to me. Follow your orders and don't do anything stupid. Do you hear me?" His eyes were pleading. "You set the bombs; you get out. No looking for Zamya."

Guilt froze my breaths. He didn't know the extra risk we were intending to run, but he'd guessed, because he would've done the same.

He grabbed my face, forcing my eyes to meet his. "Promise me."

I nodded, wanting to hold true to that promise, but how could I?

Movement from behind Rooke caught my eye. The look on Troy's face was apologetic. "Rooke, we need to get going."

Rooke nodded reluctantly. Still holding my face, he whispered, "Come back to me." He took in my features, as if it may be the last time he ever saw them. After placing another kiss on my lips, he strolled over the bridge towards the east cliff. I watched him go, my heart in a conflicting process of bursting and breaking.

It wasn't until the heavens opened that I realised the dark clouds had devoured the setting sun. Rain pelted my face, soaking my clothes, but I still watched the man I loved stride away.

His steps faltered, taking one last glance over his shoulder. My heart jerked as he assertively turned, running back, meeting me halfway across the long, swinging bridge. Our lips collided; our bodies moulded together. I savoured everything about him, his smell, his warmth, his fingers threading into my hair. I mentally retained the taste of him, the feel of him. Nux, I loved this man beyond physicality, beyond reason.

This couldn't be the end. Tomorrow, I needed to walk out of the Hybrid dam alive. I needed more time with Rooke. I wanted to see him grow old and cranky. I had to make it out in one piece.

I will return to you.

I promise.

Chapter Thirty-Nine

The squad was hauntingly quiet as the small Solarfleet ship jolted upon landing. Daylight slowly seeped in as the landing ramp was lowered, and the only thing visible outside was a haze of purple smoke.

Securing my gasmask, I nodded at Jader opposite me. Armed to the teeth with both Redwood and Alluran weapons, we swiftly, yet cautiously, led the team out the back of the ship.

My heart hammered inside my chest; adrenaline fizzled down every limb. I felt sick to the stomach. So much was riding on us completing our mission, regardless of finding Zamya or getting out alive. The future of Earth's human world was resting in our hands.

Stepping onto the barren soil, we moved into formation—Oz and I to the right, Jader and Wrenn to the left. The rest of the squad followed behind, including Guz, who confirmed we were heading in the right direction. "No Igknamai presence detected," his voice came through the earpiece attached to my left ear.

Still blinded by the purple haze, we were unnerved by any rustle or scrape nearby. The sound of bombs exploding in the distance didn't help the eerie sensation.

As the haze thinned, I gripped my bow and arrow tighter. My peripheral vision was restricted by the gasmask visor, but they were compulsory. Purple-fumed Mother Promise bombs had been dropped prior to our arrival. They were lethal to the Igknamai and potentially the Hybrids. To us, the gas would cause a nasty headache, at worst a fever. Something we could do without given the situation.

My focus sharpened as soon as the haze cleared. Scaling down a small incline, I spotted the mounds in the earth Kobe had warned us about.

"The sensor says they're empty," Guz said, holding a palm-sized digital device Kobe had constructed.

"Let's remain vigilant," I raised my bow slightly. "We don't want any nasty surprises."

Our footsteps were muffled by the powdered floor as we swiftly travelled through the trees. Openings to the earth mounds lay in clusters on either side. Peering in as we passed, nothing seemed to be inside. The chambers were shallow, only large enough to shelter three, maybe four Igknamai. My only thought was, *if they're not here, where are they?*

Ten minutes into the daunting walk, we still hadn't encountered any Igknamai.

"This doesn't feel right," Wrenn's voice echoed in my ear.

"Maybe the main battle has drawn them away," Oz responded.

"I doubt the main battle has even started," Jader said. "Those bombs are just an announcement, letting the Hybrids know they have visitors."

"I hate waiting," grumbled Wrenn, "I need to do something."

"We'll be there soon," Guz said, flicking his eyes between the small device in his hands and the route we were treading. I kept catching a glimpse of the enormous concrete structure through the trees. Doubt and fear were playing their part in willing me to turn back.

"Do you think Rooke convinced the Akquarians to help?" Oz's words startled me. I had tried not to think about Rooke, about if he was welcomed by Havav, and what terms he had to shake on to ensure their allegiance. I was trying to avoid the question of whether yesterday was the last time I'd see him.

"Time will tell."

"Eden," Oz pressed gently, "we need to find Llexzus. Get him out alive. Kobe confirmed he's still residing here this morning. And if the Akquarians have joined the battle, that puts you…"

Snapping my eyes to him, my tone was short, "I know, Oz!" It was another predicament I didn't want to think about. Setting the bombs was my first priority, finding Zamya my second. Llexzus was just another obstacle blocking the road to my happily ever after.

To my relief, Oz fell silent, and we rounded a slight bend in the treescape. A flat terrain appeared before us, where a small river flowed away from the dam. Trees towered either side, and peering through the leaves, I could clearly see the top of the huge, concrete structure. It must've been over one-hundred and fifty metres tall.

A distant pitter of what sounded like gun shots stunted our steps. Each team member instinctively froze, surveying the perimeter. Squinting through the tree canopies, I could make out a mechanical structure moving—swivelling. It was the anti-aircraft gun Blake had mentioned at the meeting yesterday. But it wasn't pointing up into the sky. The sky was clear of aircraft. It was aimed away from us, at the outskirts of the lake, towards the Redwood, Alluran, and potentially newly joined Akquarian warriors, lining the perimeter. The battle had begun.

I looked at Oz as he cursed. "If the others have the slightest chance of surviving that, we need to get to the dam, quickly."

"Move, move, move!"

Our pace increased. The number of Igknamai nests lining our path was disconcerting, but, still, they appeared empty.

As the full extent of the dam came into view, we moved to the right of the river, remaining undercover by the towering trees. The flowing water was coming from the base of the dam, and next to it was a brick building. That was our entry point.

There was still quarter of a mile to the wall, but I could make out two large guns positioned on the curving ridgetop of the dam. Not one, but two. Inwardly I cursed, raising my hand to halt the rest of the team.

"Oz, are those guns manned?"

He pulled his rifle from his shoulder, balanced it on a fallen tree, and peered through the scope. "Looks like each gun has two operatives."

"How easy a target are they for you?"

Oz squinted, adjusting his gun for a better view. He looked up at me. "As long as they're aiming towards the lake, pretty easy."

I nodded, my mind ticking with strategy. "Stay here. Wait for my signal." Flicking my eyes to two Redwoods standing behind him. "You two stay with him. Protect him. The rest of us, we make for the dam. Stay under the trees. We don't want those guns turned towards us at any cost."

"Um, Eden." Wrenn's voice was tentative, sceptical. I turned to her. "Have you seen this?" She pointed at the mounds of earth on the opposite side of the river.

Taking a few steps closer, I peered through my mask visor. Puzzlement took over, utterly baffled by what I was seeing. The openings to these nests appeared to be blocked...by bars.

"Are there any beasts in there?" I asked Guz. He glanced at his device, confirming there were.

Jader called from several metres behind. "It's the same this side."

I walked over to him, viewing a pair of sleeping Igknamai imprisoned behind vertical, iron bars. One opened an eye, taking in our presence, but seemed too sluggish to react.

"It makes sense," Jader said, "how they've recently been appearing at odd times."

"You think..." I stumbled with my words, trying to process this discovery. "You think the Hybrids keep them imprisoned?"

"We always knew the Hybrids could control them. Maybe this is the only way they can ensure their compliance."

"Perhaps we're not the only victims in this war," Wrenn mumbled.

Her words hit a compassionate part of my soul, but they were quickly scraped away by the reality of the situation. "They still need to be disposed of."

Wrenn didn't hesitate. She swiftly took half the team through the shallow river to release MP bombs into each caged nest. The rest of us did the same our side.

Several Igknamai were awake behind the bars. They growled and snapped at us, slumping to the ground almost instantaneously after inhaling the smoke. Similar to gas bombs, the MP bombs weren't audible. Only a simple hiss indicated they had been activated. Then the purple smoke followed.

It felt barbaric. It *was* barbaric. I had to keep reminding myself it was for our survival, and more importantly, for the survival of this entire region.

We were only a couple of hundred metres from the dam now. Gassing the last of the nests, we kept to the shadows under the trees, remaining hidden from the potentially prying eyes at the top of the towering wall.

"There seems to be movement." Guz's voice shattered my optimism.

"Where?" I snapped.

Everyone our side of the river halted, waiting for his confirmation. Guz's eyes flicked from the screen to where Wrenn and seven warriors were distributing their bombs. He didn't need to say anymore; two Igknamai came charging over a huddle of mounds, taking out one of Wrenn's warriors in a blur of yellow scales and blood.

Wrenn's team ran. The rest of us took aim. Our arrows flew, but Wrenn had the gumption to throw a MP bomb backwards, landing inches from where the beasts ripped the man apart. His screams filled the air, only silencing when the Igknamai became sluggish, falling to the floor beside him.

I poised to go to him, but Jader held me back. Glancing at him, he placed his finger vertically across his lips, then pointed to the top of the dam beyond the canopy, where voices carried down from above.

Everything seemed to fall silent. With eyes wide with fear, I glanced across the river at Wrenn and her team. They were cautiously stepping backwards to get out of eye shot. But the whirling sound of the mechanical gun rotating confirmed we were too late. My orders ripped from my throat, "To the dam! Now!"

The squad sprinted towards the wall as I screeched more orders, "Now, Oz! Now!"

I launched myself after Jader and the others, fully aware of Oz's laser shots flashing overhead. There were only four in total, which heightened, then silenced the voices above. But the whirling sound continued.

The squad was now out in the open, the sun beating down on us with the dam in touching distance. I glanced up at the towering structure, flinching when the barrel of a long black gun came into view, poking over the edge. It wasn't pointed at us, there was no way it could. It was pointing in the direction of…Oz.

As the sound of the automatic fire echoed off the wall, my stomach dropped. I couldn't see Oz or the two warriors with him, but I could see fragments of bark flying in the air around the fallen tree where we'd left them. I could make out leaves vigorously swaying, battered by the assault of bullets.

The barrage lasted several, long seconds. Only when the gunfire silenced did I find the ability to breathe.

"Oz?" I said, hoping he'd respond through my earpiece. "Oz, are you there?"

Silence.

"Oz!" I took a desperate step forward, but Jader pulled me back.

"We need to keep moving," he said.

"What if they're injured? What if they're unconscious? When the dam comes down, they will be swept away…"

"We've lost the element of surprise. We need to move. Now!" The emphasis in his eyes reminded me of our role in this battle.

Sucking in a breath, I acceded, and the team burst into action. Each one of us attached a structural bomb along the base of the wide, curving dam wall. My hands shook, trying to blot out the fact Oz could be dead.

"Set charges on my mark," Jader's voice came through my earpiece. We had forty minutes to distribute and set the bombs inside the lair, find Zamya, and get out. The pessimistic part of me had resurfaced. Without Oz, I no longer thought the task was possible.

Before I had time to ponder any further, I was running to the concrete building at the base of the dam. It was integrated into the mountainous rockface to the left. The single door, obscuring our access, was swiftly wired up to Guz's handheld device. A pop of electricity sparked along the locks and hinges, and within seconds, two burly Redwoods had dislodged the thick metal door, encouraging it to tip forward. It flumped to the ground creating a plume of dust.

We cautiously entered the previously secured building. It was a contrast to the heat and brightness outside. There were no windows, no lights. The sound of churning water filled the air, and tiny water particles sprayed onto my visor making it hard to see. I vigorously wiped at it with my leather sleeves, half clearing it, half smearing it. It made the climb up the set of uneven steps difficult. Our boots sounded too loud in my ears as we went, my heart pounding in time with them.

In front of me, Jader stopped at the top, peering round the opening into a wide, dimly lit corridor. Two warriors stepped through, low and armed, both confirming the area was clear.

I stepped out, wiping at my visor again. Out here, the sound of the water was deafening. A metallic mezzanine stretched into the gloom to the right. Concrete pillars lined the walkway on either side. In between stood metallic railings—the only prevention from the steep drop to the roaring water below.

It was here we'd split up. I watched Jader's team scurry away along the mezzanine, attaching structural bombs to the concrete pillars as they went. My team's task was different. We needed to climb before we got to work.

We found the lift shaft we'd been instructed to find. Blake had been adamant it was derelict and unused. Glancing up inside the dark, cylindrical tower, it seemed to stretch for an eternity. What would meet us at the top was another concern, but first we needed to climb.

From his backpack, Guz pulled out a Solarfleet mining ladder. Unfolding it, he placed it against one side of the circular wall. Two warriors held it in place, as Guz typed a code into the keypad on the top of the two-foot contraption. It immediately widened, then began to elongate upwards, speeding up after it reached about five metres. The ladder grew taller and taller, disappearing into the dark abyss above us.

A green light flashed on the keypad, confirming the ladder had reached optimal height and was locked into position. Guz nodded at me, and Wrenn instantly started climbing. I followed, thankful for this Alluran piece of machinery. Once everyone was securely on separate slats, Guz tapped the keypad, and the ladder began to recoil. Only this time, the top remained in place and the bottom lifted off the ground. I could hear the slats at the top slapping into place as all ten of us travelled up the lift shaft, much faster than if we'd climbed.

The sound of a distant gun shots startled me. Glancing down at the floor below, I could see only darkness. Jader and the others must've encountered Hybrids. It was miraculous we hadn't met any resistance thus far. Perhaps the battle outside had drawn their attention away. But the nerves still prickled through me, making me feel restless and impatient.

The top of the ladder appeared, the slats clicking and

disappearing inside the mechanism as we rose effortlessly. The ends were locked onto the ridge of a shaft exit point. As predicted, the metallic doors were shut.

Wrenn hopped onto the ridge, offering me a hand when I reached the summit. Pulling one of Kobe's digital devices from my pocket, I hooked it onto the door, typing a set of revised commands into it. We waited, expecting the door to pop, in the same way the outside door had, but nothing happened.

Aware more of the team were joining us on the narrow ledge, I tried again, but to no avail. With time ticking away, we attempted to leverage the doors apart. They began to reluctantly open, revealing a small crack in between. Peering through, I could only see a dimly lit corridor with metallic walls and floors.

"It looks clear," I said.

Wrenn and the others tried to haul it open further but the mechanism was resistant. This was taking too long. We only had twenty-nine minutes left on the clock.

A squawk—the sound of something powering up—echoed down the lift shaft. Trying to keep calm, I looked at the warrior hanging off the ridge beside me. Guz had stopped the ladder from recoiling, giving us time and room to open the doors. There were still five warriors holding on.

The young man's eyes lifted, growing wider with fear. The sound had turned into movement from above. Something solid, filling the width of the cylinder, was lowering. It was…it looked like an elevator.

"I thought Blake said it wasn't operational!" Wrenn grunted.

"He must've made a mistake." Sheer horror prompted me to act faster. "Get those frigging doors open!"

My knees hit the floor, finding the only space available to place my fingers along the door edge. We heaved in unison, groaning and growling through tiresome effort. The doors inched apart and Wrenn managed to wedge a shoulder and leg in between. She pushed and shoved, steaming her visor with exertion.

The lift was still moving, the sound getting closer. The warrior hanging off the edge was sweating, watching the lift lower. Wrenn was making progress, but it wasn't enough.

I reached for the warrior's hand. "Get on," I commanded him.

"Guz, the doors are jammed and there's not enough room for us all. You need to lower the ladder. Get to another shaft exit below."

He cursed through my earpiece before saying, "I'm not sure we'll outrun it."

"Just try!"

The warrior squeezed onto the slim platform. The one behind him followed. She was a slight woman, but still, space had become more than a little scarce. I could barely move without toppling over the edge.

The sound of Wrenn's grunts overshadowed the clicking of the lowering ladder. As the contained elevator rumbled past, all seven of us wedged into the tiny space, held our breath. I felt the air whip around my head, the suction pulling us towards the vessel. All the while, the elevator slid past, only a fraction away from touching the three of us balancing on the very edge.

On first contact with the top of the ladder, the lift wailed and screeched. Sparks flew just before the ladder was dislodged, falling out of sight.

My heart juddered inside my chest. There were three Redwoods still on that ladder.

"Guz! Guz! Can you hear me?"

There was no verbal response. But a sudden electromagnetic squeal ripped through my earpiece, attempting to rupture my eardrum, and I suddenly fell backwards.

It was only when I found myself staring up at Wrenn in the corridor outside, I realised I had been balancing myself up against the warriors behind me. The access doors were now wide open and my team stood around me.

I sat up, wrenching the mask from my face, then the earpiece from my ear. The others had already done the same.

"I guess that means our comms are down," Wrenn said, helping me to my feet.

"They clearly know we're here." I glanced down at my watch. "We have twenty-four minutes." I discretely counted our team. There were seven of us. Nearly half of the amount there should've been. My mind flashed to Oz, then Guz. *Shit.* We were dropping like flies.

"We still need to split up," I said, "to fully cover the area."

Dividing ourselves into three groups, I held Wrenn's gaze as we parted. She knew the additional objective, the others didn't. And I had no intention of risking their lives further than they already were.

There was a strange, rancid smell as I scurried down a long corridor with two warriors. Attaching bombs as we went, we climbed several sets of concrete stairs. Every turn was empty, every corridor abandoned. The lack of Hybrid presence was disconcerting.

Passing an intersection at the top of a stairwell, the sound of voices halted our steps. Pressing our bodies up against the wall either side of the open doorway, we waited. I clutched my gun tightly as the male voices moved closer, their words piquing my interest.

"You can't be serious?" rumbled one. "We need to evacuate before we are fully surrounded."

"Manta's orders still stand!" snarled the other.

"If we are to survive…"

"Survival is to protect the foetuses."

"Only four of the foetuses have any chance of survival, if at all. You are being irrational!"

"Irrationality is to give up. The humans will never outsmart us."

"It's not just the humans. More have arrived from the sky."

"Good. Perhaps they'll bring more women."

"They're better equipped!"

"I highly doubt that."

"You are delusional. I am not staying to protect a morgue!"

"Go then! Your actions will be seen as cowardice. I doubt you'll be welcomed back."

"There will be nothing to be welcomed back to!"

The sound of angry steps grew fainter. I glanced across the corridor and pointed at my two comrades, then to the stairs. They needed to get out of here. I, however, wanted to check this out.

The two warriors tiptoed away, out of sight, and I peered around the wall, replacing my gasmask. The gloomy corridor was empty. A cool air filtered from grates along the top of the metallic walls. Small blue ceiling lights reflected on the floor as I treaded carefully towards where the voices had come from.

I heard movement from the doorway up ahead, to my right. Gripping my gun in one hand, I brushed the fingers of my other hand over the top of a small MP bomb hanging around my waist.

As I approached, I could see bright lights streaming through the open doorway onto the corridor floor. The movement and footsteps had stopped, so I paused, waiting another few seconds before finding the courage to enter.

With my gun raised, I quietly stepped around the wall, not prepared to see the sight I was met with.

Chapter Forty

I froze, quickly shooting my eyes around the large, square room. It was empty, apart from a dozen hospital style beds spaced out along all four walls. Each one was occupied by an unconscious person— all women. All wearing nothing more than a thin cotton smock. Wires and tubes were attached to their arms and chests, infiltrating their bodies with Nux knows what. A tall, metallic machine stood beside each bed, displaying several monitors on the centre panel. Some bleeped sporadically. Most were silent.

Horror filled me as I scoured the motionless faces. I recognised half of them. They were all women I'd seen at the Redwood village. All had been snatched over the past few months. Young, healthy women, once full of laughter and life.

I hesitated. My eyes finding the face that had haunted my dreams for several weeks—Dawna.

I walked to her bedside, noticing the trails of dried blood below her nose. The ghostly quiet of her face shone traces of despair and terror beneath. What the hell had she been through?

More blood drenched the sheets beneath her pelvis and legs, and I glanced at the monitor beside her. There was no heartbeat, no line of rhythmic life. The screen beneath was an image of what looked like a tiny foetus. It, too, laid silently still.

I flicked my head around the grey, chilling room. So much blood littered the sheets on every bed. I could sense the anguish, the distress, the fear each one of them had endured.

Where was Zamya?

My legs found a new lease of life, and I hurried along, checking each woman. From the colour of their skin and the lack of sounds coming from their monitors, most were dead, or dying. But Zamya's face didn't lay among them. Hope and despair ripped at my heart. Where was she?

Heavy footsteps alerted me, and I turned to a doorway at the back of the room, one I hadn't noticed. A tall, scraggly-haired Hybrid stood with his back to me, closing the door behind him. He slowly turned, locking his two, monstrously black eyes with mine. There was no ounce of concern on his face as he examined the gun I aimed at his head. Instead, he smirked.

The long grey coat he wore indicated he was some kind of doctor or scientist, and I felt my blood boil. He had done this. He had exposed these women to suffering and death. My muscles tightened, and my mind filled with a rage strong enough to shred him apart with my bare hands.

With a swagger full of arrogance, the monster stepped forward.

"Don't move!" I commanded.

"What are you going to do, woman? If you kill me, they all die." His hands motioned to the beds surrounding us.

"What have you done to them?"

"They're vessels. Female sacrifices to honour my kin. They would tell you how privileged they are, if they could."

"You sadistic bastard!" My body trembled, the aim of my gun wavering. The shock of finding these young women in such a state was crushing my composure. I was emotionally entrapped in their horror, disgusted by the thought of how these unnatural monsters had used them against their will.

His smirk widened to an evil grin and his eyes raked the entire length of my body. "Take the mask off!" The demand in his voice shocked me.

I reaccentuated my aim, snarling my refusal.

He stepped closer. "Take it off, woman. Let me see your face." His black gawk intensified, causing more waves of panic to dampen my initiative. I wanted answers but his formidable presence frightened me. He was getting too close. "You're one of the sky people, aren't you?" He seemed to relish in the discovery. "Have you come to offer yourself to me?"

"Where's the other woman?" I barked. "Petite. Brown skin. Black hair!"

"They're all the same to me."

"Where is she?"

A deep, wicked laugh exuberated from his chest. "Wouldn't you like to know."

Then he pounced.

The blur of unnaturally fast movement stunned me, causing my finger to flinch over the gun trigger. I screamed, and he dropped to the floor, now with a smoking laser hole in his forehead.

A relieved sob ripped from my throat, and I glanced at the lifeless bodies suffocating me. I doubted they could be revived from whatever stasis they were in. If by a miracle they could, they'd never recover from the emotional and physical trauma.

I felt too disturbed to cry as I hurried around the room, switching the machines off one by one. Most had died already. Now, all of them were gone. It was the lesser evil. Wasn't it?

Glimpsing at my watch, I rushed to the door. I needed to find Zamya, but time was trickling away. Was she even alive?

My mind flew to thoughts of Rooke. I'd promised him I'd get out of here. At this rate, it was a farfetched hope. That's when the tears started to prod at the corner of my eyes, but a muffled sound halted my steps, sending another bout of shivers down my spine. It came again, leaving me sceptical, yet hopeful.

The sound was emanating from behind the door at the back of the room. Cautiously, I approached, gripping my gun tighter. As I neared, a muffled voice called, desperate and urgent, coinciding with a vigorous thrashing.

Holding my breath, I tested the door handle and my adrenaline spiked. The muffled voice intensified. Without hesitation, I whipped the door open and, to my utter relief, I found Zamya lying awkwardly on a simple bed. She was wearing the same styled smock as the others, however hers was torn and dirty, but no blood. Bruises lined her arms and legs. Her hands and feet were shackled. Those on her hands were linked to a long chain attached to the wall. A gag was preventing her from speaking, and the tears in her eyes proved how desperate she had been to get my attention.

Tearing my mask from my face, I reached for her gag, pulling it away.

"Eden, you need to get out of here!" Her words were frantic, displaying an irrational panic, one I'd never seen in Zamya before.

"It's okay. I just killed that bastard."

"There are more. Many more. You need to…"

"Zam," I placed a comforting hand on her shoulder, "I'm getting you out."

She began to sob. "Eden, you need to go. They know you're here."

"We're getting you out. Jader's here…"

"No, no, they'll kill him! They're monsters! Eden, please. This place is a different kind of hell." She flicked her gaze over my shoulder, and I heard a whimper behind me. Turning, I discovered another woman on the bed opposite. She, too, was shackled and gagged, but what caught my attention was the bulge of her belly.

She murmured again prompting me to approach her. I removed her gag and hesitation struck me. She looked familiar, but I couldn't place her from the Redwood village. Her skin was tanned, her hair dark with matching eyes. But it was the small tattoo on her collar bone that suddenly made me realise—she was Alluran.

"This is Louisa." Zamya's voice wavered. "Lieutenant Louisa Chorla."

"The missing crew member from The Challenger." I reminded myself. We'd never found her body. "What happened to you?" I asked her gently.

"The beetle beasts took me from the beach outside the ship. I must've passed out from the pain because the next thing I knew, I was dangling from someone's shoulder, walking along a gloomy corridor. They chained me to this bed and…" She looked down at her stomach, tears streaking down her face.

Reaching for her hand, I squeezed it tenderly. "I'm getting you both out."

Pressing my laser gun to the chain in between the cuffs around Louisa's ankles, I noticed the healed puncture marks on her legs. This could've been my fate if it hadn't been for Truro. Nux, I felt sick. "Hold still."

Using a steady laser, the chains burnt and crumbled away in seconds. I did the same with the restraints binding her hands together, then the long chain holding her to the wall.

Turning to Zamya, I bent down to cut the chain between her ankles. But Louisa's shriek of warning came milliseconds before I was engulfed in darkness.

Before I knew what was happening, heavy hands squeezed at my arms, and I was being hauled across the room. Zamya's screaming echoed in my ears, followed by a slap of skin and a whimper.

More hands were on me now, and the harsh coldness of metal touching my wrists intensified my sense of panic. I thrashed and squirmed, still unable to see anything. The evident sound of chains being heaved stifled my attempts as my hands were forcefully hauled above my head.

My chest rose and fell strenuously. Now standing haphazardly on my tiptoes, with my restricted hands in the air, confusion and fear charged my emotions. Zamya's whimpering was all I could hear until a pair of footsteps drew closer. Holding my breath, I sensed a dark figure emerge in front of me. The bag over my head was plucked away and I stifled a bleat of despair, discovering a strange, scarred face examining me. His eyes were black and lifeless, his hair long and dark, thinning on one side.

Licking his lips, he drawled. "Well, what a treat we have here." He flicked his head over his shoulder. "You've done well. I was starting to believe she'd never show up."

"I told you she'd come."

A taller, broader Hybrid appeared to his left, and my eyes widened with recognition. He smiled at me, the turquoise pulse within the blackness of his eyes confirmed my suspicion. "Hello Queenie, meet Manta."

Chapter Forty-One

"You fucking bastard!" I wrestled against the shackles restricting my arms, tearing the skin around my wrists. "You deceitful wretch."

"Now, now, my precious piece of heaven," chuckled the other one—Manta. "That's not how you should address your new masters."

I winced at the scolding touch under my chin, dragging my eyes from Llexzus to his scarred faced accomplice. Manta's gaze was cruel, swimming in an abyss of possessiveness. I was bathing in repugnance as he licked his lips, roving his eyes over my face. I had to look away, but his fingers on my chin tightened their grip, forcing my head back to him.

"You are mine," he snarled, his breath hot and putrid. "You and I will reinstate the superiority of my race. The Redwood and Akquarian scum will bow to us." He groped my neck, his hand trailing downwards over my breasts. "My Eden. My delight." When his hand paused, groping the area between my legs, a sob of despair ripped from my throat. He pressed his face hard against my cheek. "You will give me sons and daughters. You will strengthen the blood line of my kin, setting a new precedence for a solid future for Hymen. With you as my mate, we will be unstoppable."

I grimaced at his words, his touch, the smell of this sadist invading my personal space. And as the last strand of my courage finally diminished, my mind fell to Rooke. I no longer believed I would return from this mission. I had been a fool to believe otherwise. Never would I see his face again, feel the warmth of his touch, smell his heavenly scent. Never again would I hear his laugh, or blush at his harmless banter. I'd sacrificed my happily ever after. The only consolation was the conceited bastard, who was inappropriately touching me, seemed oblivious to his fate. He considered the Redwoods and Akquarians inferior. Never would he believe his impenetrable fortress was about to light up in a spectacle of fireworks.

But confusion dawned on me. I flicked my eyes to Llexzus. He had known the Redwoods were using him for this purpose. He knew they had a plan. Why had he not told his new family? Why hadn't...

My eyes followed Llexzus' hand as it reached for the set of Akquarian daggers sheathed at his hip. Realisation struck me. The snarl on his face wasn't a symbol of triumph, it was a sneer of aversion.

In a blur of dark fabric and a flash of gold, he spun, sending two daggers towards the Hybrid guards detaining Zamya and Louisa. Before their dying gargles had reached my ears, Llexzus drove another dagger into the back of Manta's neck.

The shock on Manta's face was an image I could've framed. His pure arrogance and gloating pride was his downfall. I couldn't help but smirk as he spluttered on a mouthful of blood, desperate to voice his final words. But as Llexzus pulled Manta's slumping body off me, throwing it to the ground with distaste, the life in Manta's eyes flickered out.

"Could you not have done that weeks ago!" Zamya screeched.

"Keep your voice down," snarled Llexzus through gritted teeth. "There could be more of them close by."

"Don't pulse your freaky eyes at me, fish-beetle."

Grinding his jaw, Llexzus ignored her. He reached for my wrists, twisting a tiny key to unlock the shackles. "How long do we have?" he grumbled, his mannerisms full of urgency.

Pulling my arm free, I checked my watch. *Shit.* "We have nine minutes."

A string of Akquarian profanities fell from his mouth as he marched to Zamya, unshackling her bonds. "What weapons do you have?"

"Two guns, arrows, a few bombs."

"Nine minutes for what?" Zamya asked.

I helped Louisa to her feet. "Nine minutes until this place becomes a pile of rock submerged in a shit load of water."

Zamya's eyes widened. "What the hell are we waiting for?"

Llexzus was the first to burst from the room, a dagger in each hand. Zamya launched herself off the bed, picking up the laser gun I'd left there. She hobbled behind Llexzus, but she was still fast, as if a pack of wolves were hot on her heels.

Holding her round stomach, Louisa ran as swiftly as she could. I kept to her back, pulling my other gun from my belt.

With Llexzus as our guide, we navigated the fortress with ease. The lower areas were deserted, but as daylight began to trickle into corridors from adjoining rooms, evidence of fighting laid before us. Most of the dead were Hybrids with laser marks burnt into various areas of skin. A handful were Redwoods—my bomb team.

As I stumbled across the two warriors I'd sent on without me, my breath caught in my throat. I had sent them to their deaths. I'd wanted them to escape this place.

Haggard coughing wrenched my eyes from the dead. Llexzus was staggering to one side of the corridor, suddenly falling to his knees. Wafts of purple smoke fluttered in from the open doorway up ahead.

For a split second, panic paralysed me. I hadn't picked up my gasmask from Zamya's bed. The MP bombs were potentially lethal to Hybrids, and I needed to keep Llexzus alive.

Looking down at my fallen comrade, I dislodged the gasmask from his face. Pushing past Louisa and Zamya, I sprinted towards Llexzus. He was holding his throat, hacking up phlegm. Bending down, I placed the mask over his head. "Breathe deeply."

Sucking in several lungsful of sterile air, his breathing began to stabilise. After a tenuous minute, he produced a thumbs up, and as I helped him to his feet, the floor shuddered beneath us. An explosion, big enough to rupture the whole fortress rumbled through the corridor.

"Are we too late?" Zamya shrieked. She was holding Louisa, who's cheeks were streaking with tears.

I looked down at my watch. "We should still have five minutes."

Another rumble shook the foundations surrounding us. Grey dust seeped from the ceiling and walls, merging with the slowly increasing purple haze.

"Are you sure?"

Coughing, I checked my watch again. "Yes! It must be

something else causing the explosions."

"Let's hope your watch is correct."

I could barely see Llexzus through the smoke. His deep breathing through the gasmask's vent was the only indication of where he was. Keeping Louisa and Zamya close, I trod carefully over several mounds of bodies.

A hand grabbed my arm, and Llexzus pulled us over to a side door, where a steep set of metal stairs stood. Pushing the others in front of me, we climbed, sunlight spilling through cracks in a door at the very top.

At the summit, Llexzus wrenched the door open, and I suddenly felt blinded. The sun was high, bright, and hot. An intense contrast to the cold hell we'd just travelled through.

But the hell didn't stop there...

As I rounded the top of the stairs, stepping through the door onto the crest of the dam, I stared across the huge expanse of water before us. On the banks of the lake and within the trees beyond, chaos had erupted. Igknamai, Hybrids, humans—Redwood and Alluran—were engaged in a raucous battle. Bodies lay everywhere with casualties on both sides.

On the horizon, a wave of blonde-haired warriors caught my attention. The Akquarians had joined. Rooke had succeeded.

Shit, where was Rooke in amongst the chaos?

Reality sunk in. We had less than three minutes to clear the dam before this huge, concrete structure was obliterated.

The plan was to head to the mountainous rock to the left, but currently a garrison of Elite Hybrids, encased in rose-gold armour, barricaded the exit point. Smoke billowed between them and us, coming from where one of the mechanical guns had once stood. It was now a flattened mass of molten metal. The fumes, thankfully, obscured our presence.

I turned in the opposite direction. The other gun had been subjected to the same fate. My eyes flicked to movement in the sky. Small, Alluran fighters circled the area. They must've achieved this. That was what the explosions had been.

"We need to move!" I said, glancing at my watch again. *Two minutes.* With the Elites blocking our easiest exit route, we had the whole expanse of the dam to clear. I grabbed Louisa's arm and ran.

Llexzus was faster than the rest of us. His agile, long legs accelerated along the crest of the curving dam. But I saw him hesitate, then drop to the floor, hiding behind the ruins of the smoking gun. My heart lurched inside my chest at what lay ahead. A team of Redwoods—Jader's team—were engaging in combat with a handful of Hybrids. Two had turned, shooting arrows at Llexzus.

"No!" I shouted at them. "He's with us!"

Jader must've heard my voice. He turned, shouting commands at the two warriors. In that moment, the strength Zamya found in her legs surprised me. She ran straight into Jader's arms. Cocooning her, he kissed her with desperation. Lifting his eyes to me, I shouted. "I don't know where Wrenn is."

"She's up ahead." He looked at his watch. "We're nearly out of time."

Grabbing Llexzus from his hiding place, we launched into another sprint. We'd only made it halfway across when, from our exit point, a hoard of large Igknamai thundered along the dam towards us. The warriors up ahead slowed, pulling their bows into place.

"NO! DON'T!" Llexzus took flight. He was unnaturally fast, throwing himself in front of the warriors to halt their attack.

I continued to run towards them. At first it looked as though Llexzus was arguing with the Redwood warriors, but then he turned, somehow addressing the five beasts approaching. Their snarling aggression softened and the savage deadness in their eyes dissipated. But when their pace quickened, my body stiffened with dread. I was expecting to witness a massacre. But the Igknamai halted, barely a few feet from the Redwoods, turning and lowering their bodies. Full of sceptical hesitation, the Redwoods began to climb the yellow scales of the beasts' backs, seating themselves as if they would a horse. Once loaded with four riders each, three of the Igknamai scuttled along the dam ridge at an alarming pace.

With a tone full of impatience, Llexzus barked to the rest of us, "Come on!"

"I'm not getting on one of those things," Zamya meekly protested.

Jader turned to her, cupping her cheeks. "Sweetheart, you have to. There's no other way."

"I can run."

The dam rumbled beneath our feet, followed by the distinctive sound of structural crumbling.

"There's no time!"

Zamya whimpered as Jader forced her onto an awaiting beast. Holding her small stomach bump, Louisa climbed on behind them, closely followed by Wrenn. In a blur of movement, they were away.

Rumbles of internal explosions cracked the concrete beneath my feet, and arrows flew past my head. I flinched and ducked, almost falling to my knees. Several Elite Hybrids were behind, charging towards us on horseback. Llexzus grabbed my arm, forcefully pulling me onto the remaining Igknamai's back. Its putrid smell stung at my nose as I sat down behind Llexzus, clamping my hands around his waist.

We began to move. More arrows whipped past our bodies, too close for comfort. Up ahead, Jader and the others had cleared the dam crest. We were so close to the edge ourselves, so close to where the dam met the grassed verge and the threshold of trees. So damn close.

I clenched my eyes together as I heard the final eruption—the one to end it all. The thunderous explosion penetrated every sense. My ears rang, deafened by the roar. The air pressure thickened, my skin tingled with heat, and the ground became the sky. We were launched upwards, and my breath ripped from my lungs in the attempt to hold onto Llexzus.

It felt like an eternity as the Igknamai ploughed through the air. We landed on the grass verge with a dislocating thud, rolling uncontrollably off the beast. I curled into a ball as hazardous debris rained down on us, stabbing and burning as it collided with the skin of my hands covering my head.

The smell of chemicals polluted my panting breaths, and I remained paralysed, waiting for the shower of debris to end.

The sound of roaring water began to overpower the settling destruction. Lifting my head, I slowly sat up, taking in the spectacular sight. The full expanse of the dam was missing. Even the concrete fortress on the far side was now a pile of smoking rubble. The garrison of Elite Hybrids were gone. Only a few stragglers climbed the rockface towards an awaiting platoon of Redwoods at the top.

Taking in a sobering breath, I watched the water pour down the valley. Trees were swallowed by the tremendous volume of water, and my mind flicked to Oz. I prayed he wasn't hurt, that he'd cleared the area in time.

Tears would've made an appearance if it hadn't been for the sound of Llexzus chuckling beside me. I snapped my head to him. He grinned, exposing his wickedly sharp canines. "I'm alive," he said. "I'm alive!"

"Good job you chose the right side," I groaned, noticing the dead Igknamai strewn on the ground beside us.

"Lucky for you." He licked his teeth and mused to himself. "Dybgo will be pleased I saved you. Well, I'm sure the jealously will supersede his thanks." Llexzus stood up, dusting down his dark clothes. I looked between him and the dead Igknamai. He was right. He had saved me. He'd saved us all.

"Thank you," I said. "That was an unexpected take on controlling the beasts."

"They're not as bad as you all think," he scorned.

"I suppose it depends on how malicious their masters are." I stood abruptly, remembering how Cora died and the part in which Llexzus played. Yes, he'd saved me today, but it didn't erase the fact he was a Hybrid. Just as malicious and malignant as the rest. "I need to deliver you to the Akquarians."

"I can find my own way back."

"I don't think so," said a male voice behind us. The gleam of a sword appeared at Llexzus' throat before Truro came into view. Dust and mud coated his armour. Splatters of various shades of blood trailed down his arms, coagulating on his hands. "You need to give me some answers."

Llexzus spat. "I don't answer to you!"

"On your knees!"

"I accomplished what you shitheads wanted!"

"*On your knees!*" Truro's voice was powerful, intimidating.

Suddenly concerned for his safety, Llexzus followed Truro's command. Cautiously lowering himself, he remained rigid, his eyes trained on the dirty blade at his throat.

"You informed the Hybrids of ways through our defences," Truro grumbled through gritted teeth. "You showed them how to access the village."

"What choice did I have? Your people wanted me to make friends with them. What better way of ensuring their trust than providing them with an insight to their enemies secrets."

"Your actions killed dozens of my men."

Llexzus rolled his eyes. "And?"

Rage rippled off Truro's usually stoic calmness. I knew him well enough to anticipate his next move. I snatched his hand before he could strike. Truro's blue eyes found mine, a questionable frown forming across his brow.

"You can't kill him," I said.

"He's a Hybrid. They all need to die."

"Not this one. My fate is bound to his."

The puzzlement on Truro's face doubled. He glanced down at Llexzus as the Hybrid chuckled sardonically. Returning his gaze to me, I explained, "If any harm comes to him, I am given to Dybgo."

"Given?"

"I thought you knew. It was part of the deal."

"No." The edge of Truro's sword slowly lowered. "Did you agree to it?"

"Not exactly."

"Then who the hell did?" My silence caused an unexpected outburst. "It was Rooke? Wasn't it?"

"Yes, but…"

"How can you possibly love that man? How could he play with your freedom so carelessly?"

"He had no choice. He had to agree to it to guarantee the Akquarians' aid. So your people could utilise *him*." I pointed to Llexzus. When we both looked down at him, he was no longer cowering on his knees. Only an indentation in the soil indicated he'd been there.

Frantically searching the trees beyond, we spotted him, sprinting for an opening to a grassed field. Truro reacted quicker than I did. He was up the grass verge before I'd forced my aching and battered bones to move.

By the time I had rounded the top, Llexzus was halfway across the field. He was a dark contrast to the bleached-out grass and trees.

Still with a sword in his hand, Truro impersonated a radiant god charging after him. But his steps suddenly slowed. As I caught up, rushing past, he grabbed my arm halting my steps. Glancing between Truro and Llexzus, I discovered why Truro had hesitated. Through the trees, on the far side of the huge field, were platoons of Alluran soldiers. All armed, aiming their guns at Llexzus.

"No!" I wrenched my arm free from Truro's grasp, sprinting after the Akquarian-Hybrid, who had somehow become the key to my destiny.

Both the Allurans and Llexzus ignored my pleas as the first gun shots were fired. My steps faltered for a split second when Llexzus bellowed in pain, dropping to the ground, holding his leg.

I kept running, shouting at Llexzus to keep down. He looked up at me with pure repugnance in his eyes, before forcing himself up. Speeding away, he changed course, trying to avoid the Alluran soldiers, and me.

As laser shots continually fired, a hissing sailed through the air overhead, and Llexzus was suddenly engulfed in a plume of purple smoke. His vigorous coughing signified he no longer had the gas mask, but I could no longer see him. The smoke was too thick.

The sound of swift footsteps behind me indicated Truro had caught up, all the while more laser shots pulsed around us. I was so desperate to get to Llexzus, I disregarded the danger I was putting myself in, even when I felt a pelt of fire hit my shoulder. It was only when the burning resonated down my arm, stalling my steps, that I realised I'd been shot.

Stumbling back, I half fell into Truro. He wrapped his arm around me, pulling me away from the onslaught, back towards the trees.

Sweating and panting, the coolness from the shaded canopy was a welcomed relief. Our breaths were laboured as we slumped to the ground. I closed my eyes trying to blot out the pain in my shoulder, but the thought of Llexzus overwhelmed me. I couldn't let Dybgo win. I had to return Llexzus to him, alive.

Groaning with effort, I sat up, finding the strength to go after him. The guns had quietened. It was now or never.

I poised my body, readying to stand, when Truro grabbed my

wrist.

"No," he said, through a breathless groan. "Don't leave me." The pain in his voice forced me to look back at him…and my stomach dropped. He was lying on his back. A freshly blood-soaked hand gripped his brown leathers over his chest. His breaths were short and sharp, the colour in his face draining.

Throwing myself at him, I pulled his hand away to apply pressure to the wound.

What had I done? Truro had followed me after Llexzus. I'd led him into danger, and now…now, he had a laser wound in his chest.

Holding back the tears, I glanced at his face. He was squeezing his eyes together, the honey glow of his skin paling by the second.

"I'm going to get help."

"No." He grasped my hand. "There's no time." He swallowed, flashing a grimace of teeth laced with blood. "Stay with me…please."

Ignoring the intensifying pain in my shoulder, I leant in closer, still attempting to clot the deadly wound on his chest with my weight. He gulped down a wavering lungful of air and I felt his eyes on me. With tears filling mine, I met them. "I'm sorry," I whimpered.

"Don't apologise." His laboured fingers found my hair, brushing them through the dishevelled strands. "You saved me."

"How can you say that?" I sobbed. "My selfish actions have gotten you shot. By my own people!" *How could this be happening?*

He attempted a smile, his blue eyes sparkling up at me. "You revived my heart months ago."

"Truro please, let me get help."

His fingers shook as they delicately touched my face. "I never thought it would beat again, but it did…for you. I was so drawn to you, your essence."

"Truro…"

"I wanted you to be the one…who…replaced her." *Her*, his first love. I didn't even know her name.

"I know." The guilt seeped through every pore in my body. I knew he loved me, but I'd rejected him. I'd chosen Rooke over him. I'd always known I didn't deserve Truro. He deserved someone better, someone pure and noncomplicated. But it didn't matter anymore, he was dying. He was dying before my very eyes.

"I'm glad…you're here with me…at the end."

His breathing became erratic. I could barely feel his heartbeat beneath my palm. "Truro, please. You can't die. Your people need you."

"Not anymore," he said on a whisper, still fighting the urge to close his eyes. "It's true what they say." He sluggishly brushed my cheek, and I grabbed his hand, holding it close to my chest. "The prophecy…it's true…*When Eden Falls, another…will arrive…to replace it.* And you did."

"It wasn't just me," I wept. His skin had turned a deadly shade of grey.

"It couldn't have…happened without you. An…and I'm honoured…to have served be…beside you…you truly are a miracle…my…" He gasped, and I felt his hand weaken in my grasp, his arm becoming a heavy weight pulling on my fingers. I looked into his eyes. The stunning blue gazed up into the sky beyond me. The twinkling sparkle of his light diminished.

Gone. He was gone. And my soul screamed.

The cry unleashed from my lungs sounded like an animalistic roar. He was gone. This selfless, courageous man, who had sacrificed his young life for duty. He wouldn't see the dawn of his people's liberation. He'd never live in freedom. He'd never find his happy, peaceful life.

I looked down at his marbled face, taking in one last glimpse of the colour of those stunning eyes; that beautiful soul, who had spoken to me in ways none other ever could. Brushing my fingers across his forehead, down his nose, his eyelids finally closed.

I wasn't sure if I believed in an afterlife, but in that moment, I prayed to all the ancient Nux lords there was one.

"Go be with her," I whispered to him, kissing his forehead, my tears soaking the skin as his earthy scent filled my senses. "Find Fheo. Be the family you were always meant to be. Go. Find your peace." I rested my head against his cheek, in the same way I had done so many times those few weeks we spent every night together. "I'll never forget you."

Closing my eyes, a wave of vertigo struck as the burning pain in my shoulder took hold. I shivered, trying to stabilise my sobbing breaths, but I succumbed to the dizziness, slumping to the floor beside Truro. With my watery eyes, I traced the profile of his sculpted face. My vision began to blur, and I slowly fell into darkness.

Chapter Forty—Two

The crackling of a hearth roused me from an exhausted slumber. Opening my eyes, I was met with a semi dark room. The embers of a fire illuminated the circular ceiling above me, creating ripples of light against the swirling texture. Transfixed by the dancing shadows, a familiar smell of earth and bark hit my nose, and a whimpered cry built in my throat at the realisation of where I was.

Movement beside me averted my gaze, and a dark figure leapt onto the bed beside me.

"Hey." Rooke cupped my face. The firelight twinkled in his concerned eyes as he searched my own. "Hey. You're okay."

I whimpered again as the memories came flooding back, tearing and ripping at my heart. My body felt battered and bruised, a weak comparison to the pain in my chest.

"It's okay." Rooke's face came closer, kissing my forehead. "You're safe."

"Why…why am I here?" Being in Truro's home, lying on his bed was too much to bear. I could smell him all around me.

"The Pasa and Indigos are overridden with casualties. Your hammock wasn't practical, and Oz is taking up my room."

"Oz? He's alive?"

"Yes. A minor head injury, but he's fine. We brought you here because we knew Truro would want it."

At the mention of his name my heart constricted, creating a deep incision of pain I had become all too familiar with. Tears pooled in my eyes and my words were a mumbling sob as I said, "Please tell me it isn't true. Please tell me he's alive."

Dropping his soothing gaze for an agonising moment, Rooke swallowed, shaking his head. "We found him dead beside you."

I knew it hadn't been a dream, but I had clung to the faintest hope that it could have been. Truro, the most selfless and attentive person I'd ever known. He'd saved me from drowning in the first months after I'd arrived here. He'd taught me to fight, to survive, to live.

"Why does everyone I care for have to die?"

The flash of hurt in Rooke's eyes pained me further and I reached for him. "I didn't mean…"

"It's okay." He took my hand and kissed it.

"I'm so scared, Rooke. I'm so scared I'm going to lose you. Everyone I love leaves me. Everyone."

"I'm not going anywhere, baby. I promise." He laid down beside me as more tears streamed down my face. Gently pulling me in close, he kissed my hair. "I'm not going anywhere."

My sobs filled the room, overpowering the crackle of the dying fire. Rooke held me. He held me as he'd always done in times of grief and despair. And I clung to his warmth, his soothing presence, and as the exhaustion took over, I drifted into a dark void of memories and pain.

It was light outside when I woke. Curled up in a ball under layers of blankets, my eyes felt tight and sore.

Rolling onto my back, I winced at the pain shooting through my shoulder. Rooke was no longer next to me. He wasn't in the armchair beside the bed, either. The room was empty.

I struggled to sit up, blinking away the nostalgia from not so long ago. Truro had always kept his home neat and tidy. Several times he'd picked up my clothes strewn across the floor and frowned at me, teasing me that I wasn't an ancient princess, that he wasn't my servant, and I needed to tidy up after myself. A smile at the memory tingled at my lips, replaced, resentfully, by a lone tear.

Wiping it away, I sucked in a deep breath and got up, heading to the toilet. As I washed my hands, the sound of footsteps roused me from another trance. Walking into the main room, I whimpered again. This time at the sight of Zamya standing by the bed. She was dressed in a clean black tunic and leather trousers. It didn't conceal the excessive bruising around her wrists and neck. Was her whole body in the same state?

She hurried over, throwing her arms around me, squeezing me tightly. "Thank you." She pulled back, looking at me with ardent respect. "Thank you for bringing me back from that hell. I never thought I'd see daylight again. I never thought I'd see any of you again."

The smile I offered her was laboured but genuine. Studying the healing bruises across her cheek, I asked, "What happened, Zam? Why weren't you hooked up to the machines like the others?"

She pulled me across the room, and we perched on the edge of the bed. "At first, I wasn't sure, but...there was one Hybrid, a scientist. Not the one you killed, another. He liked to talk. And you know me, I got him to divulge information about what they were doing. It turns out, for the past few centuries, procreation had become difficult for them. At first, it was simple. They created offspring like we do. Although, their method was non-consensual." I felt her hand tremble beside me. I snatched it up in mine and she continued. "Most were born in the image of a black-eyed man, the Hy-men, they call themselves. Others were born deformed."

"The Lesser Hybrids."

She nodded. "Apparently, centuries ago, a small percentage of women miscarried. But it didn't just kill the foetus, the miscarriage killed the woman also. It got worse, to the point where only a small percentage of purebred Hy-men were being born. That's when they introduced the machines. Forcing the human body to become a vessel with no physical awareness. A baby making machine that could be monitored and flushed with hormones and chemicals as and when needed. Once the baby reached full gestation, the vessel could no longer be sustained, so the child was extracted and the machine switched off, killing the host."

I thought back to my fingers switching off the machines at the Hybrids lair, wondering if it was the moral thing to do. Now, I believed it was.

"But over time, the number of births declined, even whilst using that barbaric procedure. It's as if nature was acting against them, trying to eradicate them from this world. And it was working. Over the past four decades, only ten Hy-men have been born. Ten."

"So, you're telling me they were dying out?"

"Slowly, yes. But then they discovered Louisa. And their hope was reignited. Not only did she conceive easily, but she also made it past the first trimester without complication. And to exceed all their expectations, somehow, she was carrying a female."

Blinking several times, I wondered if I'd heard correctly. "Female? I thought the Hybrids only sired males."

"They do. Or they did." She shook her head. "There must be something different about Alluran genetics, or perhaps the radiation from space travel alters the PH levels in the womb. Just because the Hybrids have never sired a female before, doesn't necessarily mean they can't."

"Is Louisa okay? How far gone is she?"

"Six months. Poor girl. She'd been trapped there on her own, living in a cold hell for over half a year. She still hasn't decided what to do about the child. If it's born, it'll be an outcast, labelled a monster."

"Nux, that can't be an easy decision." I eyed Zamya's flat stomach. "Are you…were you…"

Her petite features froze, her eyes staring into a void of terrifying memories. She took a deep breath and said, "Several bastards forced themselves on me, but they didn't break me. And they didn't succeed. Which, in turn, pissed them off…see, when I started Solarfleet, I took the standard pre-space radiation fertility test. Turns out I…I can't have children."

"Oh, Zam."

"It's fine. I've come to terms with it. It acted in my favour, though, didn't it? There was no possible way the Hybrids could get me pregnant." She chuckled. "And they were furious."

"So, they purely sought us out to breed with."

"Yep. Although, they were far more interested in you."

"Me? Why?"

"Something about your name. Apparently, there's a prophecy that suggests a new Eden will arrive…"

I groaned. "The Redwoods have something similar."

"The Hybrid leader was obsessed with the idea that you would provide him with the next generation of Hy-men and Hy-women."

"I don't understand why my name caused such a stir. It's just a name. Nothing more."

"In a time of desperation, the smallest of coincidences can forge hope. The Hybrids were dying out. You were their spark of light, their miracle." Just as I had been for the Redwoods. Hope was the fuel to survival. We all fell victim to that.

"I'm sorry about Truro." Zamya's sombre words jolted my aching bones. My only response a meek smile full of sadness. She tenderly refitted her hands around mine. "How are things with Rooke?"

I nodded, still too saddened to fully smile. "We're good. Better than good, actually. We just haven't had the chance to embrace it yet."

Zamya hummed. "You will. You're going home soon, together. I always knew he loved you."

"Yeah, yeah. As I recall quite vividly, your recurrent words about him were, *he's a dick*."

She laughed. "Well, he is! Although, my opinion of him has risen considerably since he nearly got himself gutted trying to rescue me. But only by a bit."

A figure appeared on the balcony outside, preventing Zamya's titters from escalating. With gauze stuck to one side of his bald head, Oz stood in the doorway wearing Solarfleet military attire. But it was the prominent line of worry wrinkling his brow that caught my attention.

With traces of sarcasm in her tone, Zamya said. "Hey Ozmun, how's the head?"

It was unlike him not to banter back. Instead, he looked at me. The intensity of his frown grew by the second. "Eden, I…I need you to come with me."

I paused, questioning his strange behaviour.

"Ooh, that sounds ominous," Zamya chimed. Both Oz and I ignored her.

"Please, Eden. We need to go…now."

"Go where?" Drenched with uncertainty, I slowly stood.

Oz swallowed nervously, doing nothing to ease the panic prickling down my spine. "Rooke, he, um…he…"

"Where is Rooke?" I prayed this wasn't what I thought it was. There could only be one reason why Rooke would send Oz in this mysterious manner. And after yesterday's battle… "The Akquarians have arrived, haven't they?"

"Eden…"

"Where's Rooke? Oz!"

"If you don't come with me now, I will have to throw you over my shoulder and carry you."

"Stop avoiding the question!"

Oz stepped forward.

"Oz!"

"What's going on?" Zamya looked between us.

"Okay, yes! The Akquarians are here!" Oz's voice was gruff and unusually tight. "Will you now, please, come with me?"

"No!" I pushed his solid body away. "If Llexzus is dead, I'm not leaving Rooke to pay the consequences for my disappearance."

"Eden…"

"No, Oz. The Akquarians could kill him. I'm not losing him. Not now." I began to walk to the stairs, but Oz blocked my exit.

"I promised Rooke I'd get you off this planet."

"And Rooke promised me he'd never leave me. I do not intend to encourage the opposite."

Oz searched my face as I glared at him. I saw his defiance falter, and he stepped aside, allowing me to pass. It wasn't long afterwards, I heard his heavy footfalls behind me, accompanied by Zamya's dainty ones. My body ached, my head throbbed, my heart pounded uncontrollably inside my chest, but I marched on with purpose. As long as my heart was beating, it belonged to Rooke. And there was no way in hell I was giving up on him now.

Chapter Forty—Three

As we approached the council chamber, General Murai exited. Aiming straight for us, her glare was spilling with disapproval. "Commander Maddox has gone too far," she spat. "This is a political detriment of his own making, and I will not intervene. I did not come here to end one war and start another. He is on his own."

She began to walk away but called back, "Riley." I looked back at her. "My ship is leaving tomorrow. My intention is to escort The Orka and all her surviving crew back to Allura. I'm hoping you will be among them."

Her words haunted me as I watched her march out of view. I could feel my happy future slipping through my fingers. If I walked into that council chamber, I would be taken. If I turned away and headed to a space shuttle with Oz, Rooke would be condemned. There was no alternative…or was there?

Without hesitation, I marched along the bridge through a huddle of Redwoods loitering outside the arched entrance. Noticing my presence, they stepped aside, allowing me to enter the huge circular chamber. Inside, passing through a throng of towering Akquarian warriors, the thick tension hanging in the air hit me. It was suffocating.

Standing alongside Blake and Nya, Valina noticed my unexpected arrival, darting her gaze between myself and the spectacle occurring near the centre of the room.

Havav sat on one of the council stools behind the temporary strategy table. Immaculately dressed and oozing with regal grace, his coral cape pooled on the floor behind him. Rooke stood a few paces before him, wedged between a leather cladded Akquarian warrior and the infamous Dybgo. He was suited in his golden armour with the symbolic blue cape draped behind. Standing offensively close to Rooke, he towered over him, baring his teeth, snarling his displeasure.

"Ah, look what we have here." Havav stood up, glancing my way. A wide, charming smile graced his lips sending shivers down my spine. "Eden, my dear. It's so lovely to see you."

Rooke snapped his head towards the crowd, searching their faces. When his eyes found me, they widened as if pleading with me to leave.

"Your commander was just informing us how you perished in the battle. He must've got his information wrong."

I glanced from Havav to Dybgo, aware Dybgo's crystal eyes were raking every inch of my body. The hunger held within them was an unwelcomed sight. I quickly looked away.

"You are looking a little worse for wear, my dear," Havav drawled, stepping closer.

"I guess that's what happens when you come back from the dead."

He chuckled. "Come, now. We all know that was a tangible lie."

"One your commander will be punished for," Dybgo mentioned.

"I am here, aren't I? There's no need for punishment." My gaze was transfixed on Havav, although my words were aimed at Dybgo. He hadn't taken his eyes off me, but I refused to give him the satisfaction of acknowledging him.

I sensed Dybgo leaving Rooke's side, coming to stand directly in front of me. His hand sat firmly on the hilt of his curving sword, the other clenched by his side, resonating an aura of impatience. "Now that you are here, we can take our leave."

"I am not leaving with you," I said, still not meeting his gaze.

"I'm afraid there will be no negotiation. Your commander made the decision for you months ago. Llexzus is dead. You are now rightfully mine."

Glancing at Rooke, his furrowed frown was brimming with shame and regret. Would I have done the same if our roles had been reversed? I wasn't sure. But it wouldn't have surprised me to discover Havav had manipulated the situation, tricking Rooke into agreeing to these terms.

"Is it not enough," I looked at Havav, standing a couple of metres to the right of Dybgo, "that we helped liberate your people? I found

Llexzus in the Hybrid's lair and helped him escape before the dam blew up."

"From where I was standing," Dybgo's tone was taunting, "Llexzus rescued *you*."

Of course he'd seen that. I swallowed back my frustration. "He would've been returned to you unharmed, but he chose to run into an army of soldiers who had no idea who he was."

Dybgo turned and walked over to his father, seeming unfazed by the subject.

"I tried to save him," I pointed out.

"Regardless of Llexzus' fate," Havav drawled, "there is another matter which needs addressing."

I stared at him, waiting for him to enlighten me. He studied my attire. Not in the same way Dybgo did, but as if he was disgusted by my bedraggled appearance. I was still in my leather trousers, wearing a burgundy-coloured shirt I usually wore under my armour. It was stained with circular patches of blood from the wound on my shoulder.

"Dybgo made a claim to you the night of the Sparzak ball," he said. "It is law that any female who attends the ball must choose a mate if she is claimed."

"Not a law I was aware of."

"I'm sure I relayed the premise of your attendance beforehand."

"I assure you, you did not!"

"You told me we were guests," Rooke said, still being detained by the Akquarian warrior at his side.

"That you were, but the law still stands. And as Dybgo was the only one to claim her…"

"He wasn't the only one." I glanced at Rooke, noting a hint of surprise, quickly replaced by understanding and a flash of relief. "I was claimed by another that night. I still have the bracelet, somewhere, if you wish to see it."

"Claimed by who?" Dybgo snarled.

With a wickedness, I found the courage to lock eyes with the golden warrior. "By my commander."

The room stirred, and Dybgo flicked his eyes to Rooke. A fountain of jealousy was visibly spilling overboard, conflicting with his regal demeanour.

Havav chuckled. "That doesn't surprise me."

"It means nothing," Dybgo growled.

"If I am forced to choose a claimant," I said boldly, lifting my chin a fraction higher, "then, I choose Rooke."

Dybgo smiled down at his feet. "It doesn't work that way."

"I believe the rule states I have to choose someone who's claimed me."

"Eden, my dear." Havav stepped forward. "Dybgo is my heir. He supersedes any other claimant. He is your only option."

Really? Shit, I vaguely remember someone telling me that. "I...I don't see why I am obliged to abide by your rules. I was told the bracelet was for decoration. *And* I am now under the care of the Redwoods."

"Even the Redwoods abide by my laws when they are under my roof. And your current carers have stalled the appointment of Dybgo's claim several times. My son has a right to a human mate, and he has chosen you. You should show a little honour and respect and come willingly."

I glanced at Valina. She looked flustered, an aspect of shame filling her eyes. She had known this would happen yet failed to warn me, even when Dybgo arrived a few weeks ago. But why hadn't Truro said anything? Was it his demands that had kept Dybgo away?

Movement had my gaze snapping back to Havav. I didn't miss the subtle smirk of triumph crossing Dybgo's lips. He'd won.

"Come," Havav gestured for me to approach him, "it is time we took our leave."

When my feet remained planted to the spot, Dybgo began to close the distance between us.

"No!" Rooke's words echoed around the vast room. "You can't take her!" He strived to free himself from the large Akquarian detaining him, but with every attempt, he was hauled back into place.

I met his gaze. A distraught desperation was crumpling his handsome face. He looked as though he was about to cry, aware there was nothing he could do.

I tried to bat away the relentless wave of panic flushing through my body. This couldn't end so abruptly. My intention was to live my life with Rooke, back home, back where the golden hills filled the horizon through my kitchen window. Where we could snuggle up, listening to music and playing boardgames on wintery Sunday afternoons while the snow fell outside, blanketing the world in white and silver. I wanted to resume our Saturday morning coffee and pastries, and our spontaneous hikes through the golden forests. I wanted to savour the sense of safety I'd never truly appreciated.

I had no intention of becoming Dybgo's mate. There wasn't a chance in hell I would allow him the right to use me in whatever primal manner he chose. I wanted to live my life, not be hidden away, where I'd slowly wither into a dark, demoralising solitude.

A silent suspense gripped the air. I glanced at the Redwoods standing around me. Most were warriors, covered in wounds and bruises from the recent battle. Jader and Wrenn stood amongst them, their expressions of uncertainty shattered every ounce of hope I had left. Oz and Zamya stood behind me. Oz staring at Rooke, as if awaiting orders, and Zamya's eyes glistened with outrage more than despair. But looking at her, a thought bounced into my head, one that could shut this whole political debacle down.

"Wait," I said, holding my hand up, halting Dybgo's steps. Ignoring his looming presence, I spoke to Havav. "What about the soul bond? Does that not supersede any claim regardless of rank?"

Havav's pale brows knitted together. "It does," he replied sceptically.

"Rooke and I are soul bonded."

I had to force myself not to look at Dybgo as he snorted his opinion. Havav sighed. "Please. No more lies."

"I'm not lying. It happened at the Sparzak ball. Rooke kissed me and I fainted. Is that not what generally happens in such cases?"

This time, I couldn't help but rest my gaze on Dybgo as he threw Rooke a threatening glare. His fists clenched into balls, whitening the knuckles of his already pale skin.

"That is one serious claim, my dear," Havav said.

"And one that cannot be proven," Dybgo put in.

"I believe it can." I glanced at Zamya. "The Redwoods must still have samples of the drinks you acquired from them, from your recent mating season."

"That we do," Nya's voice pierced through my doubt. Meeting her gaze, I gave her a subtle smile full of gratitude.

"Well then," Havav flipped his cape back, retaking a seat, "if you are adamant this is not another ruse, please, proceed. But if there is no obvious reaction within ten minutes, you will be leaving with us. No more objections."

"And if there is? You will leave without me?"

"You have my word."

A disapproving grumble emanated from Dybgo's chest as flutters of hushed conversation began to circulate the room. Zamya and I exchanged a look just before she and Nya scurried away. She knew this could work. I only hoped she didn't lace the pink juice with too much sedative, so that it could kill me.

Rooke watched them leave, his face full of puzzlement. I tried to catch his eye, but I was suddenly engulfed by gleaming gold. Stifling my wavering breath, I slowly raised my eyes to meet Dybgo's half-human leer.

"It won't work," he said, low enough for only the two of us to hear. He walked around me, his breath now hot in my ear. "It's never worked twice."

Inwardly I smiled. The Akquarians were oblivious to how their soul bond occurred. For once, I had the upper hand.

I caught Rooke's gaze. He was watching Dybgo with contempt. His eyes flashed as I felt Dybgo's fingers tugging on my shirt over my shoulder wound. I flinched, pulling away, but he snatched my arm in his burning hand.

"All those months ago, you should've come back to the fortress with me." He was stooping, his face uncomfortably close. "It would've prevented you from being subject to all these injuries. A female shouldn't be put in a position where they need to fight. It's a male's duty to protect her."

"I like fighting," I sneered, attempting to dislodge my arm from his hold.

A smile twisted at the corner of his mouth. "Once I get you back to my quarters, you can fight with me for as long as you wish."

"I will never come back with you."

He pulled me hard against him. "You belong with me. I will treat you far better than anyone else can. I will give you everything you desire."

"If you think being draped in pearls and luxurious clothing with your baby in my belly is what I desire, then you are greatly mistaken."

Leaning closer, he growled in my ear, "You will desire me by the time I am done with you."

Keeping my jaw set and my chin high, I attempted to shut out his disturbing words. If this plan didn't succeed, his quarters would become my home, and my freedom would be the dregs of a distant memory.

Pushing us apart, an object was wedged between us. Looking down, I discovered Oz's large laser gun.

"Give her some space, big boy," Oz said standing beside us. "She's not yours yet."

Dybgo glared at Oz, thankfully stepping back before swaggering over to his father. I squeezed Oz's arm as a sign of thanks.

Oz stayed at my side as we waited for Nya and Zamya to return. I remained quiet, staring at the thousands of names inscribed on the walls around us. A sudden yearning to find Truro's consumed me. What would he have done if he was here today? He'd probably be standing right beside me instead of Oz. He'd never let Dybgo take me. But I knew Rooke wouldn't either.

I glanced across the space at Rooke. He was staring at the floor, no doubt trying to work out a solution. I needed this plan to work. Nux, it had to work.

Before my scepticism took over, Zamya and Nya returned, each holding a glass bottle and a clay cup. The bottle Zamya held was full of pink Akquarian love-juice. She walked over to me while Nya headed to Rooke with the blue one.

Pouring the liquid into the cup, Zamya offered it to me. "Drink all of it."

Everyone's eyes were on me as I downed the full contents. The zing of flavour was unusual, but the aftertaste left me yearning for more, in the same way it had done at the ball so many months ago.

Nya moved away from Rooke, confirming he had consumed the blue juice.

"How long do we need to wait?" I asked.

"Ten minutes," Nya said.

"Oh, I'm not sure about that," Havav chimed. "I would've thought the effects would be instantaneous."

"I don't think it works like…"

"Just get on with it," Dybgo snapped.

Nya's concerned glance worried me, but I nodded, accepting the prompt. I walked slowly across the dusty, wooden floor, taking my time to reach the cleared space a couple of metres in front of Havav. As I stopped, Rooke was shoved towards me by his detainer. He still looked baffled, nervously glancing at Havav when he reached me. "I don't understand what's going on," he whispered to me.

"I know." I took his hand. "Just trust me."

Without hesitation, he gave three tiny nods. "What do you need me to do?"

A vulnerability flittered about in his dark green eyes. He was petrified. I smiled up at him, trying to make this moment count. "Kiss me," I whispered. "Kiss me like you did the night of the Akquarian ball. Kiss me like there is no one else here. Just you and me."

His frown remained prominent on his brow, his eyes were trained on me. "I can do that."

We searched each other's faces, waiting for the other to make the first move. Nerves tingled down my limbs, aware too many eyes were watching. I knew this was just for show. Theoretically, it only needed to be a short, sweet kiss. But if the plan didn't work, if the sedative didn't affect me in time, this would be my last chance to be with the man I loved.

I sucked in a breath, blotting everyone else's existence from my mind, and I reached up. His lips immediately found mine.

Sensing his uncertainty, I kissed him slowly. I pushed my body against his, raking my fingers up through his hair, and an intensity began to build. The kiss deepened. His tongue ploughed into my mouth, and I couldn't contain the groans of delight trickling down into my core. He tasted as he had that night of our first kiss. The night I revealed my true intentions to him. The night he'd pushed me away because he was scared I was drunk. Well, I was drunk now. Drunk on him. Drunk on freedom and hope.

Released from a new wave of confidence, I felt a rush of excitement. The juice was taking effect. Everything had drowned out, and the only thing I could think of was Rooke's hands on my waist, his lips caressing mine.

Rooke's hand moved lower, gripping my thigh. He bent slightly, raising my knee, pulling me in closer. The arousal within me escalated tenfold when I physically felt his. His breaths had become ragged, his movements emanating with an urgency I responded to; drinking in the feel and taste of him again and again.

We lost ourselves in each other, our actions becoming more sensual as the seconds ticked by. Awareness of where we were only hit me when Dybgo's voice penetrated the air, "I said, that's enough!"

Heavy hands locked around my waist, ripping me from Rooke's embrace. My feet barely had time to find purchase before I was pushed down and forced to sit on one of the stools.

With his lust filled eyes still fixed on me, Rooke was ushered back to his previous spot by the Akquarian warrior and his curving sword. A sadness swam within the desire. He knew, the same as I did, that could've been the last time we were together. We'd wasted so many years questioning our feelings, avoiding the risk to confess our hidden desires.

A well of agitation bubbled inside me, and I realised Dybgo was pacing, intermittently obscuring Rooke from my view. His cape flapped in the breeze he was aggressively producing. His golden armour twinkled in the light flooding in through the open doorway, where more faces had appeared, eager to witness what was occurring.

"How much longer?" Dybgo snapped at Havav, who sighed in response, gesturing to Nya for answers.

"It's only been five minutes," she said.

"It's obvious nothing is happening." Dybgo pointed to me.

"Give it the full ten minutes," Havav replied, seemingly unfazed by whatever the outcome would be. In comparison, Dybgo was becoming agitated. There was something strange in his unusually abrupt mannerisms. It made me wonder if he was nearing an episode of Tektrasc. Was that why he was so adamant to have me? The thought was terrifying.

Other than Dybgo's impatient footfalls, the room was so quiet, you could've heard a pin drop. The suspense charging the air was stifling. I knew the sedative was working. The pain in my shoulder had completely subsided and my fingertips were tingling. But there was no nausea, no dizziness.

I wriggled my toes whilst rolling my shoulders back, hoping it would pump the sedative around my body faster, but still, nothing indicated I would pass out anytime soon.

Glancing at Zamya, I could see she was watching with anticipation. The flash of encouragement in her eyes gave me hope, but Dybgo's pacing was starting to infuriate me, and I was beginning to lose my nerve.

"Ten minutes must've passed by now!" he growled.

Nya slowly raised her watch, pretentiously reading it even slower. She lowered her arm and looked at me. "Ten minutes is up."

My eyes dropped to the worn bark floor below my feet. There was nothing else I could do. This was it. This was my fate. I'd become Dybgo's human mate, his queen, his prisoner. I suddenly felt sick to the stomach.

Black boots appeared in my view. I didn't need to look up, I knew who it was.

"It's time," Dybgo said, offering me his hand.

I looked up at his towering form, meeting his eyes with a disdain aimed to haunt him. How had I once seen him as an honourable person? How was it possible that I felt a bond of friendship with him over the first weeks after we'd met? He was cold and self-righteous. I doubted I'd ever warm to him again.

I stared at his hand, fighting the urge to scream my refusal, but there was no point. No one could save me. I had gambled with the Akquarians and lost.

"Now!" The aggression in Dybgo's voice compelled me to stand. He grabbed my upper arm and forcefully escorted me into the crowd. A raucous of urgent conversation escalated around the room. Oz reached for me as I passed, only to be pushed away by another Akquarian.

Rooke's voice shattered in my ears, shouting my name several times. Attempting to look back, I saw him wrestling several Akquarian warriors.

"Don't even think about it," Dybgo snarled, tightening his grip. "I assure you, you won't be seeing him again."

With a sneer of repugnance, I poised myself to lash out at him. But I suddenly felt an intense pounding in my head. My vision became impaired; my legs weakened. At first, I suspected it was the stress of the situation, but as I was hauled into the bright sunshine outside, through the throng of spectators, a relentless dizziness riled at my stomach.

Dybgo caught me when my footsteps stumbled. Leaning into his chest, I looked up at him. I couldn't see the full extent of his expression through the fog forming in my eyes, but I gave him a cruel smile and said, "You lose."

And the world turned dark and silent.

Chapter Forty-Four

Dybgo's angry eyes were all I could envisage. Choking and gasping for air, I could feel his hand clenching around my neck…

I gasped, opening my eyes abruptly, expecting to see the large, golden Akquarian before me. Instead, I was met with an empty room. It was small, enclosed, familiar. Wooden slats lined the walls with a high-pitched thatched ceiling. The faintest hint of citrus soothed my senses, and…

My stomach roiled. I launched myself out of bed, towards the sanitary room on the opposite side of the room. Expelling the contents of my stomach into the toilet pan, my head pounded with such intensity, I thought I had a brain haemorrhage.

"Oh, thank the holy souls!" Zamya's voice came through the doorway behind me. "I was worried I'd put you in a coma."

Retching again, I groaned my discomfort. "How much sedative did you use?"

"A lot." I heard the squeak in her tone. "Perhaps a little too much. But in my defence, I had to make sure it worked."

I sat back on my heels and laughed. "So, it worked?"

"Yes." Zamya squatted on the floor beside me, offering me two painkillers and a cup of water. "Although, Dybgo insisted you were faking it. It caused quite a stir. He tried to kidnap you in full view of everyone. Oz, Wrenn, and Jader were on him in seconds, and with Havav barking his disapproval at his irrational actions, Dybgo had no alternative but to leave without you."

Holding my aching head, I swallowed down the tablets. "Do we think that's the end of their demands?"

"I believe so. Havav even commended Rooke on his triumph, insisting the bond was sacred and how he should never forsake it."

I chuckled. "Havav, the born romantic."

"I would call him stupidly naive." She smiled. "Rooke was so confused. He just frowned and nodded at Havav. You should've seen the look on his face when he realised they'd left without you. Just…just tell me one thing? Did you and Rooke actually kiss the night of the Akquarian ball?"

My answer lingered on my tongue, remembering the time I found the confidence to flirt and seduce him. "Yeah. We did."

"Wow." She tittered to herself. "That explains a lot."

Hurried footsteps hammered on the floorboards, juddering my already throbbing head. "Zam, where is she? Is she awake?

I peered over my shoulder. The sight of Rooke standing in the doorway, dressed in Solarfleet uniform, with his hair dishevelled, and a brooding frown lining his forehead, had my heart pounding with delight.

"You didn't kill her then?" he said to Zamya, his smile transforming his face.

She stood up and tutted. "Of course I didn't." She walked to the door, slapping him on the chest. "She's all yours, commander."

I stood up, wiping my mouth with my shirt sleeve, and Rooke's warm hands were cupping my face in a heartbeat. He went to kiss me, but I turned my head away. "No. I've just been sick."

"I don't care." He wrapped his arms around me, but I wriggled away, turning towards the sink, where a wooden toothbrush and a bar of tooth-soap sat on the edge. I quickly applied the soap to the brush, attempting to scrub my mouth clean. It became more than a little difficult with Rooke's hands sliding over my hips and thighs, nibbling at my neck and earlobe. "That's my toothbrush," he said.

Laughing, I spat the bubbles out into the sink, and whipped my body round to face him. He grabbed my neck and waist, pulling me into his chest, his lips instantly colliding with mine.

I melted into him as he took control, exciting every morsel part of me. My head whirled. I wasn't sure if it was my reaction to his divine kiss or the lingering effects of the sedative, but nevertheless, I surrendered to it, savouring every moment.

He pulled away a fraction and I opened my eyes. His gaze sparkled, casting me into another mesmerising trance. "How?" he asked. "How did you know about the pink and blue drinks?"

I smiled, wiping a splodge of toothpaste from his lips. "Zamya is a very knowledgeable woman. Don't underestimate the limitation of her inquisitiveness."

He chuckled, before resting his forehead against mine, his expression becoming solemn. "I thought I'd lost you again. Too many times that's happened recently. I couldn't breathe when I saw you standing in the council chamber. Oz was under my orders to get you up into orbit."

"An order I overrode."

"Eden." He sighed.

"I wasn't going to leave you, Rooke. You really don't understand how much you mean to me, do you?"

"And you me." Searching my eyes, he stroked my cheeks with the pads of his thumbs. "I would suffer an eternity of damnation to keep you safe. I would've accepted whatever punishment the Akquarians threw at me."

"They could've killed y…"

"I would die for you."

His words silenced me. Studying the truth in his eyes, I swallowed back the shock. Only in my wildest dreams had I ever imagined anyone would say that so convincingly.

"I love you," I whispered, cherishing the freedom in those words.

His lips found mine again. Lifting me onto the edge of the sink behind me, I felt him smile. "Do you love me enough to allow me to have you up against this sink, right here, right now? Even when I know you haven't washed for three days."

Throwing my head back, I chuckled. "Trust you to know that piece of information."

He ran hot kisses down my neck. "Don't underestimate *my* abilities, Miss Riley. I find you extremely attractive in whatever washable state you're in. Perhaps more so when you're filthy."

His hand gently cupped my breast as the passion poured through another insatiable kiss. Now that I knew he was mine, I couldn't get enough of him. I pulled him closer, reaching for the bottom of his T-shirt. My fingers stroked his abdomen and his breath wavered—not in an excitable way, but rather in pain.

Frowning, I leant back. He lifted his shirt, revealing the newly healed, pink wound spreading from his naval, around his back, to the edge of his ribcage. It was the horrifying wound from where the Hybrid had nearly gutted him weeks back. But it looked as though it had reopened.

"I thought it had healed."

"I ripped it open battling the Akquarian warriors yesterday."

"Oh, Rooke."

He sighed heavily. "I fear I'm not in a fit enough shape to make love to you."

I smiled gently. "I thought you wanted to take it slow, anyway."

"Yes. No. I guess. But…what if you get bored of me? I know how much of a nympho you are." I gasped in horror, making him laugh. "When we get home…"

"Home? Do we really have to wait five months? You weren't taking it slow last week in the locker room."

"That was a one off."

"Don't you think we've waited long enough?"

"Look, you. For years, I've been wanting to romance you. I want to buy you flowers and take you for long, romantic walks at dusk. I want to take you to that posh restaurant in Torlan City. You know, the one where the tables are laid out on separate tiers along the riverbank, where you can watch the sunset. I'm gonna take you there. Wine and dine the pants off you."

"You'll have to take me shopping first. I don't own anything exquisite enough to wear to that place."

"Maybe I should've asked Dybgo if he could lend you that dress. You know the one with the really plunging neckline…"

"Stop it!"

"What?" He chuckled. "We should give the Akquarians some credit. They do know how to dress."

"You mean inappropriately expose the female body."

"I don't think you show it off enough."

"Rooke." I could feel myself blushing under his teasing stare.

"You should. Your breasts are amazing. And…I really like your legs." He eyed them as he trailed a hand down my thigh. "I can imagine they'll look even better wrapped around me."

Smirking, I said, "There's no way you're lasting five months."

He sighed. "Yeah, you're probably right. But I need to heal first.

So do you." He gently stroked my injured shoulder, then kissed my forehead. Looking deeply into my eyes, he said, "Shall we go home?"

I nodded, relishing in the fact we finally could.

"The village is so quiet," I said, as Rooke and I walked along the bridges towards the east cliff. After washing and dressing in a Solarfleet jumpsuit, it only took me five minutes to pack the small number of possessions I had.

"They lost a lot of people," Rooke said. "The village is still in mourning."

"How many died?"

"Hundreds." Rooke shook his head. "It equates to nearly ten percent of their community."

I cursed.

"Once the pyres have died out, they *will* celebrate."

A child's voice called my name. Glancing about, I found Saff. Her long auburn ponytail swishing and swaying as she ran towards me. My heart constricted, noticing how sore her eyes were. I bobbed down as she approached, opening my arms to her. She ran straight into them, squeezing my shoulders so tightly I had to stifle my wince.

"Before you go," she said, pulling away, "there's something I'd like to show you."

I looked up at Rooke. He nodded and offered to take my bag. "We leave in half an hour."

Handing him the backpack, I took Saff's hand. "I won't be long."

She remained silent as she led me into the centre of the village. As we travelled down a tree lift, I realised we were heading for the council chamber.

The circular room was empty when we entered. Light flooded through the open doorway, illuminating the wall on the far side. Hand in hand, Saff guided me through the circle of stools, past the strategy table, towards a section of inscribed wall.

"Look." She pointed to a section of wall that was lit up by the sun, to where a six-pointed star had been freshly carved into the bark among the sea of names. And on each tip, sat the names of the remaining Orka crew. Mine was at the top, with Rooke, Zamya, Oz, and Kobe on the middle points. Troy sat at the bottom, encased in a drawing that symbolised a childlike spaceship. "You are now officially a Redwood."

Grinning, I squeezed her small hand, truly humbled by the gesture.

"We thought it was fitting," Valina's voice echoed behind me. I turned and found her draped in a black chiffon gown—the embodiment of an illustrious leader deep in morning. "Although the six of you are Alluran, you have proven your loyalty and your worthiness of the Redwood title several times over."

My gaze was soft as I studied the sincerity on her flawless face.

"Eden," she cleared her throat, a flutter of nerves sailing through her expression, "I'm aware we haven't always seen eye to eye…and, at times our partnership has felt strained, maybe forced. But you have to admit, it was a partnership that worked."

I nodded my agreement.

"I am overly grateful to you, especially," she said, raising her chin an inch higher, "for giving us a second chance."

"It was the right thing to do. Hopefully your people can now live in peace."

She offered a gentle smile. "I believe we can. The majority of the Hybrids were killed in the explosion. We are hunting the few survivors. As for the Igknamai, Solarfleet have been so efficient at dropping the MP bombs, we haven't seen any in days. According to Kobe's reports from the orbiting ships, the whole region is rid of them. So, yes. I truly believe we can." Her smile grew, shining brightly with an elation doused in gratitude.

My own smile did not match hers. It felt forlorn, feigned. "I wish you well, Valina."

"And you." She reached for my hand, squeezing it as in goodbye, before smiling down at Saff and leaving.

Taking one last glance at the thousands of names lining the barked wall surrounding me, I followed Saff outside. My heart stuttered, noticing a figure on the bridge before us. Haloed in the morning sun, strands of auburn hair whipped about a female figure in the breeze. The woman approached, offering me a smile that was unbearably familiar.

I looked down at Saff and she peered up at me. "Mum wanted to meet you."

My eyes were tingling with tears when I found the courage to look up at Truro's mother. She smiled again, but I didn't miss the sorrow dwelling in her stunning blue gaze.

"I am ashamed," she said, "I never got to know you." Her voice was a soft hum full of warmth and compassion.

"That is on me, also."

"Still," she said, glancing at Saff, "my son adored you. My daughter still does."

Her words pierced my overwhelmed heart. Fighting the temptation to break down in front of her, I replied truthfully, "And I always will adore them."

Her smile tightened and she pulled an archer's bow from her shoulder. Stepping closer, she offered it to me. "I'd like you to have this. It was Truro's."

Eyeing the wooden bow, I was utterly speechless. I looked to Saff, then back to Truro's mother. "But…but wouldn't you or Saff want…"

"Saff has her father's, and Truro would want you to have it."

I looked deep into her eyes. She wasn't old, but the grief of time had taken its toll on her features. She'd lost her husband, her two sons, and her grandchild, all from fighting the war she was able to witness the end of. My heart wept for her.

Reaching for the bow, I took it, settling my hands into the grooves Truro's fingers had worn and moulded over time. I swallowed back the swell of remorse, the overwhelming burst of pride. I would cherish this until my dying breath. "Thank you. I am truly honoured."

I felt Saff's hand retake mine. Her voice was full of tenacity. "I'll walk you to your ship."

After bidding her mother farewell, we took our time walking through the village. I could sense Saff's reluctance, but she continued, fighting the urge to stall me any further. I was so proud of her. She had grown so much in the short amount of time I'd known her. A part of me wished I could stay to see her transform into the wonderful woman I was certain she'd become.

Her blue eyes sparkled up at me as we approached the east cliff ladder. They reminded me so much of her brother's—warm, attentive, full of awe. Nux, I was going to miss them both so much.

Rounding the top of the steep ladder, we discovered the grazing fields were flooded with Redwoods and Allurans. Most were carrying supplies to and from the Indigos. Others were milling about, talking. In the distance, I could make out General Murai standing on the landing ramp speaking with Blake and Kobe.

My stomach twisted in knots. This was really happening. I was going home. Whether I was excited, relieved, or disappointed, I wasn't sure, but everything felt surreal and out of context. With an uncertainty dragging at my heels, I clenched Saff's hand tighter, and we walked towards the large ship.

Through the crowd, Wrenn appeared ahead, holding her arms out, swaggering towards me with raised eyebrows and a taunting pout.

"So, you are actually leaving me?" she said.

I stopped in front of her, peering at her unamused face. "What, you gonna miss me?"

A wide smile slowly spread across her lips, and I found myself swamped by red leather armour and red hair. With a fierce intensity, she hugged me. "I'm gonna miss you so god damn much." Holding me at arm's length, she locked eyes with me. "Don't tell him, but you're a better hunting partner than Jader ever was. It's true." She eyed the bow in my hands. "Make sure you keep it up."

"Hunting is illegal on Allura."

Wrenn screwed her face up with distaste. "Your planet sounds awful."

I laughed, embracing her again, before spotting Jader standing behind her. He stepped forward and I hugged his towering form.

"Thank you, Jader. For everything."

He shrugged and I saw the flash of sadness in his brown eyes. "It wasn't just me."

"I would be saying it to Truro if he were here. I'm…I'm so sorry. He would've been a great leader."

"He was a better friend."

"That he was." I glanced about the field, searching for the horses, but none were visible, only crowds of people. "I haven't had the chance to say goodbye to Io. Will you give her a rub behind her ears for me?"

"I will. She's been gallivanting with Titan. I think they're going to be just fine without you both."

I huffed a smile, noticing Zamya. She was still dressed in her Redwood attire. "You're cutting it a bit fine," I called to her. "I doubt Murai will allow you to fly wearing that."

Stopping at Jader's side, she sniggered, but her smile didn't reach her eyes like it usually did. In fact, her mannerisms were sheepish. And like a slap in the face, it suddenly dawned on me…

"You're not coming, are you?"

She shook her head. "I have nothing to go back to." Glancing at Jader, she said, "Here, I have everything I need. Don't look at me like that, Eden. It was you who planted the idea in my head."

For an agonising moment I couldn't breathe. The selfish part of me took over and I felt the tears surface.

"Eden. I've already made Oz cry. Don't you start."

"Oh, Zam." I reached forward, heaving her petite body close. Against her silky hair, I murmured, "We've been through so much together."

"I know. I know." She took my face in her delicate hands and said in earnest, "You are a friend for life. And even though we won't be residing on the same planet, we can keep in touch. Solarfleet will have a presence here for a while, if not indefinitely. We can still talk."

I chuckled. "With a two-week delay."

"Ah, it'll give me a better chance to say what I really think."

"As if that's ever held you back before."

We laughed, and I looked up at Jader. "Make sure you look after her."

Gazing down at her devotedly, he snaked his arm around Zamya's shoulders. "Of course I will."

"And you," Zamya pointed at me, then over my shoulder, "make sure you don't take any shit from him."

Rooke appeared next to me. "Hey. I'll treat her just fine."

"You better," Zamya snarled, "Otherwise…"

"Hey, Zam." Rooke raised his palms in surrender. "Can we not be friends? Just this once?"

Reluctantly, Zamya smirked. "I suppose. Come here." They embraced and she slapped him on the back. "But only because this is the last damn time I have to put up with your shit."

Rooke rolled his eyes. "It's been a pleasure, Doctor Hirani.

Thank the Nux you are no longer one of my crew."

Zamya stuck her tongue out at him, before positioning herself protectively next to Jader. Watching them smile at each other, I knew she was making the right decision.

Turning to Rooke, I asked, "We're not leaving anyone else, are we?"

"Oz, Kobe, and Troy are all waiting on board. Louisa is also joining us. And we best get going."

I felt a gentle hand brush my palm, reminding me of Saff's presence. Peering down at her, I noted the glistening moisture lining her eyes.

"Goodbye, Eden." Her voice was a shaky whisper. She was still holding onto the courage not to cry.

I squatted beside her, looking at her brother's bow. "I'll never forget you, Saff. Maybe one day I'll come back to visit. I'm sure by then you'll be a far better archer than even Truro."

She gave me another hug and said, "I'd like that very much."

Our embrace lingered, prolonging the sentimental, yet torturous moment. Giving her one final, reassuring smile, I rose and walked away from the friends I'd come to love so dearly.

A pang of hesitation struck as I neared the landing ramp, and I turned, taking in the remarkable view around me. The towering treetops swaying in line with the edge of the grazing fields, the sparkling sea on the horizon far in the distance, the shades of greens and reds, the endless blue sky. This world was a paradise of colour; one I would hold dear to my heart. Even in a time of fear and uncertainty, this place had called to me, welcomed me, as if it truly was where I belonged. A piece of my heart would always remain here, for the friends I was leaving behind; for those who I'd lost.

The cool breeze picked up, whipping around my hair, sending shivers down my neck, and the faintest hint of an earthy scent tingled at my nose. I took a deep breath, savouring the memory it incurred. I would never forget him. I'd never forget Truro.

With a haunting pain in my chest, I continued up the ramp to where Rooke stood waiting at the top. I mentally pinched myself. *He was waiting for me.*

We had scaled physical mountains and fought through emotional tempests to get to this point. I thanked all the Nux lords and the holy souls that we'd come out the other side together. I was finally leaving with him. He was all I truly needed. And nothing, *nothing*, could keep us apart.

I took his hand, sinking into the warmth of his gaze. "Let's go home."

T h e   E n d

Thank you so much for reading this story. It has been a huge part of my life for so long. I hope you have fallen in love with the characters and their world as much as I have.

If you want more from Eden and Rooke, there is an additional chapter waiting for you.
Join my mailing list to find out more.
You can sign up here:
https://www.alanafayewilson.com/sign-up

Reviews are a huge deal to Indie Authors. If you have enjoyed this book, please leave a review on Amazon and/or Goodreads.
Your support is most appreciated.
#supportindieauthors

Website:
www.alanafayewilson.com

Instagram:
https://instagram.com/alanafayewilsonauthor

Acknowledgements

I can't really believe I've finally got here. It has been a long journey for sure. One I couldn't have completed without the wonderful support of my husband, daughter, family and friends. Your encouragement has kept me going; your love is irreplaceable.

Big thanks to my editor, Jess, who has helped me cull this beast of a book. And a huge thank you to the Bookstagram community, who have given me inspiration and advice many times. I'm so glad I found you all.

About The Author

Alana is a Sci-Fi Fantasy writer who has a massive fascination with the universe. When she's not writing, she is trying to be a corporate administrator, although the dream is to become a full-time writer. She loves spending time with her family, going for long walks with the dog, and can usually be found in a coffee lounge. Reading and writing are her escape from the stresses of life. Her other creative passions include music, art, and photography.

Printed in Great Britain
by Amazon